I0671230

# GRAB

# BAG

# 7

A Gay Erotica Anthology

# BarbarianSpy

## FOR LITERARY HEAT

BarbarainSpy
Toronto, Australia

# Grab Bag 7

by

# habu

# TABLE OF CONTENTS

# INTRODUCTION

Habu's *Grab Bag 7*, representing standalone short stories habu wrote in the winter of 2014–15, is the latest in a series of short story anthologies with eclectic gay male settings and plotlines presented in the order in which they were delivered to habu by his muse, within the period since the previous *Grab Bag* collection was assembled. In addition to random stories streaming down from habu's muse, this collection includes stories written for themed and seasonal contests. Variety and setting are always important in habu's stories, and, as usual, the settings of these stories span the globe, from such settings as the Carolina coasts; Mystic, Connecticut; the Mid-Atlantic states; Ohio; the Colorado Rockies; and Albuquerque in the United States to the United Kingdom, Australia, and China. The time periods also vary. Although most of these stories are set in the present, one moves to cowboy country in the early 1900s and others take the reader to Broadway in the 1960s and Allentown, Pennsylvania, in the 1970s. And, as always, there are unusual stories that take fresh approaches to men taking their pleasure with other men.

The overarching motivation for a habu story is that it try to be different in some way from ones he has written before, a tall order for a writer who has some 800 short stories published, but a goal we think has been achieved here. As with the previous Grab Bag series, we hope that readers will find stories to entertain, arouse, and evoke thought in this collection.

The collection kicks off with "The Invisible Missing" set at Halloween time, with young migrant workers going missing from a North Carolina gay-employee-friendly produce farm. "Snowbound" moves the action out to the Colorado Rockies in the early 1900s, where one bottom and two randy tops are trapped up in the mountains together in the snow. "Make Me a Star," set in New York City in the 1960s and an excerpt from habu's novella *Danny's Choice*, provides a cynical look at the price paid for a place on the Broadway stage. "Baby, It's Cold Outside" moves on to the mid 1970s, where a young man on the make in Allentown, Pennsylvania, is served up at a snowbound Christmas Eve party for three. The theme of "party from hell and heaven" continues with "The Blind Date."

"Rain Check," set in any U.S. southern beach town in the present shows that hookups are even possible in the paint section of a hardware store. "Blue Dragon" moves the action to the Midwest, to a small, dying town in Ohio, where a café waiter dreams of adventure—and finds it. Turning from gay BDSM to romance, "Simpatico" tells of a perfect lover's loving Valentine's Day present. In "Noah Flip Flop," an excerpt from habu's novella *Tramp Steaming*, an American college student on winter break wraps up a South Sea adventure by hooking up with an Australian street musician in Sydney. A young Smithsonian Museum curator in Washington, D.C., uses an online threesome dating service in "Three on a Date" to find something more than vanilla sex—and certainly finds it.

A young guy down on his luck is picked up off the streets of Albuquerque by a man with a secret in "Sarge." The American protagonist of "Unexpected Inheritance"

8

discovers that what he had thought were fantasy UK pen pals in a threesome turn out to be a real couple who believe he actually had done what he'd only written as a fantasy. The experience of being initiated in China, bound by red silk, leads to Chad's building of a South Carolina porn empire in "Shanghai Silk." In "Confessions," a young Englishman acquires a farm, a new wife, and a baby that's not his in an unsuccessful bid to escape his past. The collection ends with a romance in which a young man returning to Mystic, Connecticut, for the funeral of his mother learns that you can, in fact, go home and again take up what you once enjoyed.

# THE INVISIBLE MISSING

I didn't know if it was the unseasonal heat or the heavy work we'd done that day or Chet's scary stories or Miguel's empty bed that kept me awake in the dormitory that night, but I had nervous energy to spare. I would doze, but I'd wake up with a start and look over at Miguel's bed, the emptiness of it now explained, and then I'd check all of the other beds to see if guys were there. And sometimes they weren't, and then I'd speculate. Did they get up to piss or get a smoke or just stand outside the Quonset hut dormitory that was like an oven in the October North Carolina heat? Or were they hunting or being hunted.

I had gravitated for the fall harvesting toward Lunsford Farm in Yanceyville, North Carolina, dead center in the east-west range of the state but just a few miles south of the Virginia border because of who I was and what I wanted and what Lunsford Farm tolerated. But it was because of what Lunsford Farm tolerated— encouraged even—as well as the danger for a man like me that I had discovered here that had me on edge and nervously watching the movements of those around me.

And maybe, just maybe, it was my own need that kept me awake. Miguel had been a relief valve for me. He and Raul. It was that college student—Frank Lunsford's young man—who I'd really like to get to. But thus far I had stayed with the other migrant workers—mostly with those from the south of the border, like me. In scratching my itch, I'd had to waltz around the big, black Cuban, Duardo, who was fucking the same young Mexicans I was, but thus far we'd managed to stay out of each other's way.

There also was the American black, Rufe, a tall, gangly, rangy long-time worker here, who was only half here mentally, but whose snake-like dong went with his height and thinness and either was an object of fear or desire for those he sniffed after. Whether it was fear or desire depended on how masochistic the day worker poor-white-trash types were who came to work here straight out of high school because their prospects weren't any greater and because Lunsford Farm was a haven for young guys wanting to be dicked. Rufe stuck mostly with screwing the white day worker twinks, like Matt and Shawn, because he had some sort of mad on about those of us coming up from south of the border for the farm work and, he said, taking work from real Americans. He'd go around muttering under his breath something about the only good "wetback" being a dead "wetback." And he refused to touch any of us for sex.

He didn't say that right to my face or Duardo's, and he was respectful enough to us—because if he wasn't either one of us was quite capable of kicking his ass up between his ears—but he steered clear of the Mexican boy pussy and, despite being black himself, strictly stuck to white meat. That was fine with Duardo and me; it meant more spicy meat for us. But with Miguel gone now, Duardo and I had to sift in some white meat from time to time ourselves. We both had to have it nearly daily. It wasn't all that hard, though. Although the white-trash day workers weren't bunked here in our dormitory, they wanted it so bad that they often were here at night.

Duardo usually kept to other Hispanics, but he was eyeing the young, white college student, Kyle, today, I had noticed. But Kyle was Frank Lunsford's. I didn't think either of us would get a piece of that plump, young tail. It was tantalizing, though—especially today, when we'd all been in the pumpkin patch pulling out pumpkins for the big sale at the farm's produce store out on Highway 158. The apples, raspberries, tomatoes, and corn also needed to be harvested, but this was the big push weekend for those buying pumpkins for the Halloween season they marked here in the States. So we were all in the pumpkin patch, working double time. Even Lunsford's young man, Kyle, had been there—all of us stripped down to the waist, muscles straining, sweat pouring off our bodies in the unseasonable heat.

It wasn't until today that I saw how tantalizingly arousing Kyle's body was. I could see that he had as much effect that way with Duardo as with me. Duardo moved around all day, eyes glued to Kyle, with a raging hard on—and Duardo's hard ons definitely were raging. The white boy, Kyle, could hardly miss Duardo's interest—or mine, for that matter. And he was being a little tease with us.

Kyle usually worked in the produce store and only on weekends, as he was in school at some North Carolina university. I had no idea how cut and perfectly muscled his body was until today—and what sultry, sulky dark-haired, "come-and-get-me" luscious looks he had. He had bedroom eyes and thick lips that looked at a man in a knowing, interested way. I thought, but couldn't be totally sure, that he was doing this purposely to make men lust after him—which both Duardo and I, and even the overseer, Chet, did that day—but I did know that Frank Lunsford was a lucky man to have Kyle in his bed, if only for the weekends.

But it was more than the presence of Kyle in the pumpkin patch that set the tension of the day for the migrant workers. Miguel had been missing for two days. Chet, who slept in the dormitory with the migrant workers and who had worked at Lunsford Farm for a good many years, dismissed this as a concern for those two days, telling us that it was a normal occurrence for migrant workers to pick up stakes and just leave.

"He's just another invisible wetback," Chet had said.

I normally would have agreed with him on migrant workers not being that married to sticking around, if not that Mexican migrant workers had little value, but today was payday for the past month's labor. No migrant worker I knew would take off two days before payday. They'd leave the night of the day they got paid if they were going to split.

And then, while we were out in the pumpkin patch, near the main house, a police cruiser had driven up. Two officers went into the house, and, after a while, Mr. Lunsford came out of the house with them and left with them in the cruiser. Chet had gone up to the house to see what was what, and when he came back, he told us that the police had found a body in the woods nearby and wanted to take Mr. Lunsford off to discuss the matter.

At dinner that night, eaten at picnic tables outside the dormitory building, and with several of the day workers hanging around for free food and maybe a roll in the hay later, Chet completely changed his tune. The body had been confirmed as that of Miguel. It had been found less than a mile away from the farm in woods that were part of a huge parcel owned by a logging firm but nowhere near being ready to be logged again.

Not only did Chet say it was Miguel, but he also told us stories of other young migrant workers who had been found dead near here during previous harvest seasons. He, though, again passed them off as just being throwaways from south of the border—not worth worrying too much about. Duardo chimed in to confirm there had been two in the previous season when he'd worked here, and the other long-term worker, Rufe, nodded his head in agreement.

Chet proceeded to tell us of the circumstances of the deaths, and it wasn't pretty, involving slashing with a large-blade knife. The victims were naked and had been sexually messed with—whether assaulted or not wasn't clear, as all had reputations for giving it easily. He went on to spin a horror tale from the past for us as he'd been doing almost nightly in the weeks coming up to Halloween.

"Way back, nearly two hundred years ago," he said, "the farm house here was once the mansion house for a plantation that covered nearly this whole county. Some say I'm related to this here family, which would be something, wouldn't it?—under other circumstances me owning this whole kit and caboodle rather than just herding you lot around for Frank Lunsford and sleeping in the bunk house with you rather than in my own mansion house. Wouldn't that be divine justice?"

After patting himself on the back with that claim, Chet continued. "Well, that didn't happen, because that there house over there was the scene of a mass murder of the entire family save my ancestor, who was off studying. Some dozen darky slaves—young men all—rose up and slaughtered the family one night—close to Halloween, they say hereabouts—in their beds. All of the family members had been defiled before being murdered. Since then, legend has it, that the house has been haunted by the ghosts of the family, who won't rest until a dozen young men are sacrificed to make up for the slaves' crimes."

"Sound to me like that's been happening around here," Duardo spoke up and said in a strong voice. We all were thinking of Miguel's death. I, for one, though, just thought Chet was trying to scare us. The younger, more impressionable workers—Raul, Shawn, Matt, and Francisco—drank Chet's stories in, eyes wide with fear and interest.

"Yep," Chet answered. "Miguel this season, but there have been others before. All wetbacks, though, and we all know how flighty they can be and risk takers, anxious to get in with a dangerous crowd even though Mr. Lunsford provides them a place here where they can get what they want without mixing with those rough homo bashers livin' hereabouts. Them wetbacks just want it rough and sometimes they sneak off from here and get it rougher than they were bargaining for."

All the young dick takers sitting around the picnic tables were squirming, the Mexicans—Raul and Francisco—more than the rest. Well I guessed they should be concerned, I thought, as they were ripe young bottoms like Miguel had been, and as had been all of the young migrant workers Chet had said had been used and murdered in previous seasons. I assumed that Chet was exaggerating both the body count and the circumstances of the deaths and the connection of all of this to the claims of haunting of the farm house because this was the Gringos' season for such stories. But I couldn't discount Raul's and Francisco's concerns. They were ripe young bottoms, used by Duardo and me just as Miguel had been. And, who knows, maybe they snuck out some nights to have it from strangers outside the farm family.

And then later that evening, as the men, groaning from the strain of the work of the day, were trying to settle in their beds, events became more ominous. The different-pitched contest of the snoring of Chet and of Duardo woke me after it seemed I had just gotten to sleep, and I instinctively looked over to Miguel's bed, still in shock about why it was empty. It was still empty. But so was Raul's bed, beyond Miguel's. Raul hadn't left the dormitory yet, although he was stealthily moving toward the door.

One of the day workers, the dirty-blond-headed scrawny boy pussy, Matt, was stretched out on Rufe's bed back in the corner of the dormitory. He was making purposely muffled moaning sounds as he grabbed the slats of the headboard and Rufe side-splitted him with the deep, snake-like exploration of that long shaft of his.

I already was hard, and listening to them fuck and watching the undulations of Rufe's hips, knowing how deep inside Matt's channel he was plumbing, wasn't helping. I hadn't had a fuck since the day Miguel had disappeared. I assumed Raul, who wasn't in his bed, was going to the port-o-john to take a leak. If I followed him and waylaid him on the way back to the dormitory, I knew he'd let me fuck him on a picnic table. And my need was great, so I quietly left my bed and followed him out into the night. I saw him stride right past the outhouse, though. He had a flashlight. And when I looked off toward the farmhouse, I saw another light moving away from the house and toward the pumpkin patch.

All sorts of weird ideas floated through my brain, fueled by the ghost stories Chet had told at dinner. I didn't believe this had anything to do with a ghost, though. And I was right.

The pumpkin patch was surrounded on two sides by a wooded area, and, once I ascertained that the two points of light were headed for and converging on the pumpkin patch, I skirted around to the wooded fringe of the patch and positioned myself to where I could see into that field. The moon was full, which made the outline of everything clear in an eerie sort of way. Wisps of ground fog were floating around near the surface of the earth and swirled around the pumpkins not quite ready to be harvested. I could think of no better setting for one of Chet's Halloween stories.

At first I thought what I saw was a large dog—a wolf even—but my eyes adjusted fully to the dark and I realized that it was Frank Lunsford. For the first time it occurred to me how much like a hairy wolf the man was. Or one of the satyrs Chet told us about in his stories. Chet always included strange and rough gay sex in his stories—his favorites being werewolves or satyrs—because he liked to see us all get hard and start touching each other and leave the dinner tables in twos and threes, headed for the bushes.

Lunsford was broad chested and narrow hipped and had a swarthy, fox-like countenance. It was only now, when I saw him naked, though, that I realized how dark and hairy his body was.

He was already fucking Raul when I had taken up my position in the fringe of trees. He fucked Raul like a dog in the pumpkin patch, with Raul on all fours and Lunsford crouched over his back and hips, a hairy arm wrapped around the younger, smaller Mexican's belly, and a thick, curved dick—prominently displayed in the light of the full moon—pumping in and out of Raul's ass—a very sweet and accommodating ass channel, as I well knew. Lunsford was pulling the dick almost all the way out with each stroke and then cruelly thrusting up deep inside Raul's channel in slow, deliberate lunges. Raul cried out with each thrust and Lunsford huffed and puffed and snorted like the wild animal he was appearing to be.

I couldn't help myself. I was only wearing sleeping shorts, and my hard shaft had pushed its way out of the open fly of that without my willing it. My hand went to my club, and I was pulling on my meat as I watched.

It wasn't long, though, before heavy breathing from nearby made me turn my head in shock. There off to my left, also behind some trees on the verge of the pumpkin patch, was the sweet young Kyle. He was lying on his back in a mossy patch, naked, his legs bent and

17

parted, and his hand encasing and stroking his dick. His bedroom eyes were on me, though. His smile was sensual, inviting. Entreating.

Without a second thought, I was on him, my knees pressing in between his, one of my hands clamping over his mouth, the fingers of the other entering him, brutally. He was moaning and whimpering through my thick, muffling fingers of the one hand and moving his pelvis in rhythmic thrusts against the invading fingers of my other hand. I removed my fingers and thrust my throbbing cock inside him, smothering his mouth tightly against his scream. He arched his back and counterthrust against my stroking club with his straining hips. There was no question that he would take me—that he wanted me.

When we had established a rhythm of the fuck, I felt the heels of his feet rubbing against the top curve of my buttocks. I released the hand covering his mouth and exchanged it with my own lips. He opened his mouth to me and sucked on my tongue as I thrust, again and again, deep inside him, releasing all of the sexual tension I'd built up in the last two days. He wanted me and was going with the fuck.

He broke away from the kiss and turned his head to the side, whispering, "Yes, yes" over and over again as I increased the pace of my pumping and worked hard to get as far up into him as I could, overwhelmed at my good fortune to have an angel under me, clutching my sides with his hands, rubbing my buttocks with the heels of his feet, and counterthrusting his hips up to meet my dives.

With a jerk he came up my heaving belly. I felt my own jism bunching and rising, I held in a withdrawal, only the bulb of my cock inside his entrance, ready for the killing thrust. Beyond the trees, from the pumpkin patch, a primeval wolf-like howl went up. Lunsford had climaxed.

Kyle dug his claws into my shoulder and cried out "Now, Now! Now, Javier!" I brutally dove down deep, releasing my load with a grunt. And then again . . . and again. I hadn't so much as taken the next breath when Kyle was pushing me off him, over on my side; scrambling up; and disappearing in the dark. He had wanted me, I was sure of that. But he'd just squirmed from underneath when it was done and racing off.

I took a moment to catch my breath. When I raised on my knees, I turned toward the opening through the trees to the pumpkin patch. Lunsford, loping along slowly, was already at the other end of the field, moving toward the dormitory. He had Raul slung at his side, draped over an enclosing arm, arms, legs, and head dangling at Lunsford's side. Their figures were caught squarely in the curve of the moon. I hadn't realized before, but part of the wolf-like aspect of Lunsford was that his arms were disproportionally long for his torso.

When I crept back into the dormitory, Raul already was there, belly down on his cot, his arms dangling on either side of the bed. His eyes were open and glazed. I had to look closely at him as I got back into my own bed to be sure that he was breathing. He was, although shallowly. The hint of a smile on his lips told me that he had enjoyed the encounter with his employer.

I woke in the middle of the night to the sounds of heavy breathing and groaning. Duardo doing the heavy breathing; Raul was doing the groaning. Raul hadn't changed position or expression, but now Duardo was stretched over and above the small Mexican's back, his fists stiff-armed into the mattress of the cot above Raul's head, his feet lifted on his toes, and his dick—the biggest and thickest of all the workers'—pumping up and down between Raul's butt cheeks, as the big, black Cuban put on a pushup display.

I looked around the dormitory, in the just-before-dawn hazy light, and saw that nearly all of the other men, including the overseer, Chet, had their eyes plastered to Duardo's morning calisthenics.

I went to sleep with the thought that, with Miguel gone now, Raul would be taking the brunt of giving the men's men, like me and Duardo, their needed release. I hoped he was up to the challenge—or that someone else like him was hired to join the migrant workers soon. I was hard again just from watching Duardo fuck him; I planned to have my own session with Raul the next day.

* * * *

Raul didn't look too good the next morning. He hadn't changed position or expression. He still lay belly down on his cot with his arms dangling over the edges. He was breathing, though, and mouthing words. When I put my ear near his mouth, I found he was mumbling about glorious fucks, so I decided that he at least was happy.

No pumpkin harvesting today, Saturday. We were going to be in the trees in the orchard, picking apples. Farmer Lunsford had decided he had enough pumpkins in the produce store for this weekend, so he was sending the migrant workers to the orchards. Kyle would be working in the produce store. I was finding I wanted to know where Kyle was all the time—and whether I could isolate him and fuck him again. He'd left me in a hurry the night before, but I had every reason to believe that he'd appreciated the servicing.

We were ready to go and Raul was still in bed—or at least he was until Chet stood over him and barked, "Raul. Up. Mr. Lunsford wants to see you up at the house."

20

With a groan, Raul rolled out of bed and stumbled off in Chet's wake.

It was the last time I saw Raul.

We were in the trees, picking apples, when I realized that not only hadn't Raul returned to the field—which didn't surprise me all that much; I assumed he was up at the house being humped again by Lunsford—but also that Duardo wasn't there anymore. He should have been down on the ground under the trees, taking filled bushel baskets that the rest of us were handing down. He was too big to go into the trees himself without breaking the branches. So, he and Chet were supposed to be on the ground, under the trees, Now neither one of them were down there.

I figured that left me as the next one in line to call the shots, since Rufe was only half here mentally, so I told the rest to take turns trading off being in the trees and on the ground, and I took off, looking for Chet and Duardo.

I found them both, over by the produce store—or rather behind it—but managed to maneuver to where I could see them. That took a bit of positioning, because Chet was positioned to see Duardo without being seen, just as I was doing. Chet was in the shadows of the building, behind some barrels, his dong out of his pants and in his hand. Duardo was leaning against the back of the produce sales building, his hips and legs jutting out from the wall, a look of sheer pleasure on his face, and his hands cupping Kyle's head. Kyle was kneeling in front of him, a hand wrapped around the base of Duardo' dick, and his mouth, jaw unhinged, working hard to get all of Duardo's shaft inside his mouth cavity. That wasn't going to be possible, but I had to admit that the young white guy was giving it a good try.

As both Chet and I watched, Kyle gave a low, guttural laugh, and suddenly stood, slapped Duardo's dick with this fingers, pulled away from him, and started to stride off. Duardo was too quick for him, though. He launched his large, supple, powerful body off the wall, lunged at Kyle, and caught him in his arms. He pulled Kyle into his body, turned him to the wall, and slammed his back against that. With one hand, he stripped down Kyle's shorts and briefs while holding the young man against the wall with the other.

Kyle was laughing—just like this was what he wanted. So, I didn't move to do anything. Chet was too engrossed in the entertainment to do anything but stroke his cock. It wasn't long before Duardo's cock was inside Kyle's channel, Kyle's knees were hooked on Duardo's hips, and the big, black Cuban was pushing Kyle's back up and down the wall with the strength of his dick.

Just when I thought Kyle was lost to the big black, though, I saw the young man's hands go to the Cuban's neck and his fingers apply pressure to strategic points of Duardo's throat, causing the Cuban's eyes to roll up into his head and his body to slowly sink to the ground.

With a laugh, Kyle pulled up his shorts and walked slowly around the side of the building toward the front. I looked over to where Chet had been hiding, but he was gone.

The big black isn't going to like this, I thought. There wasn't a bit of humor in the man. He was at least twice as big as Kyle and built like a brick wall. I feared that he'd beat the young man senseless the next time they met, no matter what Mr. Lunsford might think about it.

I couldn't have been more wrong about that, though.

When I woke in the middle of the night on Saturday, I found the dormitory nearly empty. Not only hadn't Raul come back from the farm house that day, but now Duardo was missing too. So was Rufe. But that wasn't a big surprise. Since he concentrated on the white boy local workers, he often was roaming away from the farm at night. Chet was on his back on this bed, mouth open, snoring up a storm. I rose from my bed and went to the door of the dormitory. Off across the field, beyond the pumpkin patch, I saw the glimmer of a light. There also, though, was an apparition in white.

One of Chet's ghosts, I wondered. It was only a week until Halloween, well into the time period that Chet had told the men the members of the murdered plantation family rose from their graves and roamed the property, looking for the murderers who had fled the plantation and never been caught.

Then I saw another light, moving from a closer location toward an intersection with the ghostly visage. I waited for a few minutes after both lights faded into the trees beyond the pumpkin patch, and then I moved toward where they intersected.

Kyle, naked, was spread-eagled, his wrists tied to the branch crotches of two trees that stretched his body out. Duardo, also naked, was crouched, facing Kyle, his hands fisting Kyle's ankles and raising and spreading wide Kyle's legs. Duardo already had his dick inside Kyle and was pumping him.

Kyle's head was flopped back, his face facing the full moon. He was crying out, "Yes, yes, Duardo. Harder. Deeper."

At his feet was the white sheeting he'd covered himself with to pad out to the grove to meet Duardo. He obviously was getting the punishment he wanted from Duardo, so I turned and walked away.

What a crazy kid, I thought. What a tease. I couldn't wait for my next chance at him.

But the next morning, in spite of Sunday supposedly being the migrant workers' rest day, I was told that I was needed to sell pumpkins and other harvested items at the produce store because Kyle apparently had gone back to college early.

That didn't worry me until I saw the police cruiser drive up to the front the farmhouse. Then it worried the hell out of me. Had Kyle suffered the same fate as Miguel had? And where was Raul?

It was Raul. The police had come because of Raul. His body had been found in the woods at the edge of the farm. He had been sliced up. He'd also been defiled, but who was to say that part didn't happen the night before, with me and others watching?

Once again, Frank Lunsford was being placed in a police cruiser and driven away.

It was Chet who told me they'd come about Raul. When I said the police needed to stop this killing, Chet just shrugged. I could tell he wasn't all that concerned because Raul was just a wetback Mexican—just another of the invisibles.

* * * *

I fretted through the week about Kyle. I asked Chet about him—I could not have gone to Frank Lunsford himself, who had been returned by police car some four hours after having been taken away on Sunday. Chet insisted the Kyle was back at his college and would appear again on the coming Friday evening. The next Saturday was Halloween. That afternoon would be a major sales day at the produce building. Kyle would surely be returning at the weekend to help with that.

On Wednesday a new worker appeared. His name was Hosea, and, like Raul and Miguel, he was young, good-looking, small of stature, and accommodating, ready to lie down and open his legs on request. Duardo fucked him, standing over the jackknifed figure of the Mexican and pile driving down into him, on Wednesday afternoon between two rows of tomato plants while the rest of us split our time between picking tomatoes and watching the

24

action. Chet made clear that Hosea had been hired to keep the tops among us happy and productive in the waning days of the harvest. Another hand wouldn't have been hired otherwise. As an aside Chet had said Frank Lunsford wanted another like Raul and Miguel here as well for something planned on Halloween. I almost thought of warning Hosea of that, but I didn't. Chet said my turn with the little piece would be Thursday.

Indeed, on Thursday afternoon, it was so hot out that we went back to the dormitory at the height of the day for a siesta—and Hosea rode my dick cowboy style while I lay on my back and the others watched. He seemed to be well versed in the extra services he rendered. I still wondered if anyone told him what had been the fate of some of those who had preceded him. I didn't see it as my duty to tell him, however.

On Friday afternoon, my concerns for Kyle were relieved. I was in the field of raspberry bushes when I looked up and there he was, smiling at me—and looking oh so sexy.

"Miss me?" he asked.

"I was worried about you," I answered. "You heard about Raul?"

"Sure, I heard about Raul. That's so touching that you worried about me. Chet said you asked for me every half hour or so."

"Yes, I did," I answered. "You take too many chances, I think."

"Like this? Here, now. With you?" he asked as he stripped off his shorts, briefs, and T.

"Oh, god," I whispered, feeling myself go hard at the beauty of his body.

"Lay on your back," he commanded.

I did so, and he pulled my shorts off my legs. I wasn't wearing a shirt.

"Oh, god; oh, god," I whimpered with a groan, as he took my shaft in his mouth, gripped my balls in his hand, and tugged on them while he sucked.

"I hear the new punch rode you cowboy style yesterday," he said when he had come up for air. And when I could do no more than groan at the way he was rolling my balls in his hand, he continued. "I wonder if you think he can do that better than I can."

He straddled my hips, facing me, and moved his channel down my shaft. I was breathing heavily and moaning as he raised and lowered himself on the shaft. "You do it," he whispered, and as he lowered his face to mine for a kiss, I gripped his waist on both sides and raised and lowered him on my hard, throbbing dick.

"Oh shit, oh fuck," I murmured as he turned around on the dick, gripped the knees of my bent and raised legs and pumped himself vigorously on my shaft until I shot off my load—and then relaxed, prone, with a sigh.

Turning on the still-hard cock, he lowered his torso on mine, his cheek against a breast, and played with one of my nipples with his hand. "Was I as good as the new guy?" He asked. "Frank bought him from a male whore house. He apparently is meant for Frank's Halloween ritual."

Ritual? I asked myself. Too shocked by the possibilities to say anything out loud—especially as Kyle was talking about it so casually.

"Why do you ask? Are you jealous?" I asked.

"I don't like the competition, no. First Miguel and Raul this year—and now this professional male whore."

Shock again. A new possibility was entering my mind. What could Kyle's jealousy have led him to do? Was he involved in the deaths of Miguel and Raul? And what was this ritual he spoke of?

He was just a little bit crazy. I couldn't discount any erratic behavior on his part.

* * * *

I found out about the ritual the next night, Saturday, Halloween night.

It started after we were all supposed to have retired for the night. My bed was located so that, when I was turned toward the entry door, open because of the unseasonable heat, I could see out over the field—the pumpkin patch. I was only half awake when the dancing of the flames caught my attention. A bonfire was blazing just beyond the pumpkin patch.

I sat up in my bed. The new man, Hosea, who had been sleeping in Miguel's bed when he was sleeping in the dormitory at all, was gone. So were Duardo and Chet. Rufe wasn't there either. I got out of bed and padded over to the door.

I could see figures—covered in white—supposedly the ghosts of Chet's stories?—moving around the bonfire in the field beyond the pumpkin patch.

Of course I went to investigate. As I crept through the pumpkin patch, crawling so that I would not be detected, I soon discerned that there were four figures moving around the bonfire in a slow dance. They were covered in white cloaks—their heads hooded as well. Next to the fire stocks had been set up—a platform with a low wall of wood at one end, with a hole for the head and smaller ones set off to the side for the wrists. The stocks were occupied—by the new worker, Hosea. Another one of the young migrant workers, the thin young redhead day worker named Shawn, was lying on his side, naked, wrists and ankles bound just inside the circle of fire. His mouth was encumbered by a ball gag.

As I watched, one of the figures tossed off his cloak. The wolf-like Frank Lunsford was accounted for. He loped over to the edge of the circle, pulled Shawn up on his hands and knees, crouched over the young man's hips, mounted him, and began fucking him like a dog. This must have been some sort of signal, because now the cloak came off Duardo, who saddled up behind the pilloried Hosea, grabbed the young man's hips with his hands, and thrust inside him. A third figure, not removing the cloak, moved to in front of Hosea, parted his robe to reveal a plump, hard cock, and presented it to Hosea for servicing with his mouth. Hosea complied, willingly, it seemed, although something about his expression gave me the impression he had been drugged. Looking over at Shawn, I saw that he had the same drugged expression on his face.

Chills ran down my spine. These were two willing bottoms. What might be in store for them that had meant that they should be drugged to take it?

The fourth figure was crouching at the edge of the circle of light, watching the ritualistic fucking. But not for long. Duardo pulled out Hosea's ass, only to be supplanted by the still-cloaked figure whose cock Hosea had been sucking. Duardo walked over to the fourth figure and pulled Kyle's cloak off him. Duardo pulled a naked Kyle up off the ground and slid the young man's belly up his black, powerfully built torso until he could position the bulb of his cock at Kyle's asshole. He then lowered Kyle on his shaft, while Kyle wrapped his legs around Duardo's waist and his arms around Duardo's neck. The big Cuban proceeded to walk around the circle of light, bouncing Kyle up and down on his cock. Kyle was groaning, but not objecting.

When Duardo was finished with Kyle, he let the young man slide down his legs and into a heap on the ground. By then Frank had moved to behind Hosea and was fucking him, and Duardo went over and took a crack as the trembling and moaning Shawn.

Sometime while I was watching these two with their changing conquests Kyle had picked himself up and left the circle. I probably wouldn't have noticed that anything was wrong if I hadn't seen the fourth, still-cloaked figure walking deliberately out of the circle as well—with a long-bladed knife in his hand.

I looked at both Frank Lunsford and Duardo and saw that they didn't seem to notice that two of their rank had left.

The sight of the knife sent off fireworks in my brain and a chill up my spine. I had asked around about the deaths of Miguel and Raul. Both men had been fucked, but what had killed them were multiple slashes of a long-bladed knife.

Instinctively, I frog-marched my way to the edge of the pumpkin patch and went after the cloaked figure with the knife.

\* \* \* \*

"How did you know it was Chet who had murdered those young men, Javier?" Kyle asked. We were laying, limbs entwined, fresh from sex, on Kyle's bed in the farmhouse.

"I didn't," I answered. "Not until I saw him with that knife—and even then I couldn't be sure it was Chet. He was still covered with the cloak. I should have considered in from that ghost story he told his. In hindsight, it was clear that he saw himself as responsible to fulfill the legend of who he believed was his family—to off a dozen young men to appease the ghosts of his past. I'll admit that I thought at one time that it was Rufe. I'd been suspicious of him all along, knowing what he felt about Hispanic workers coming in the States to work. But, really, I mostly thought that the murderer was your lover, Frank."

"Frank? Frank's not my lover. He's my uncle. We both like sex—but not with each other. I just work for him on and off to help with my college expenses. What made you think he killed those men?"

"You mean other than how kinky he is and how much he looks like a wolf?"

"Yes, besides that," Kyle answered, with a low laugh, obviously conceding both points.

"He hired those men—and said it was natural that they had disappeared; that they had just drifted on—and the police kept coming to pick him up for questioning."

Kyle laughed again. "He left the hiring to Chet, and it was Chet who was saying they probably just drifted on."

I let that sink in. I, of course, hadn't heard Frank Lunsford say any of that himself. I'd relied on Chet's word. Mistake. I had reached Chet on Halloween night before Chet had reached Kyle. When Kyle saw me struggling with Chet and that Chet had a nasty knife, he came back to help me. But he wasn't much help. He'd been drugged. Chet was drugged up too, or he surely wouldn't have been so bold as to try to make Kyle his next victim and to snatch him from the pumpkin patch right under the noses of Lunsford and Duardo. I had wanted Kyle to put Chet to sleep using the throat pressure points as he done with Duardo, but he couldn't manage it. I had to club the man senseless with a heavy branch I'd picked up from the ground.

I still hadn't accounted fully for my belief Lunsford was the murderer. I'd even considered Duardo and Rufe and, for a few brief moments, Kyle himself. "But the police cars showing up?" I asked.

"Frank isn't just a farmer—and a man willing to hire men who fuck men because he fucks men himself—he's also the county coroner. He reported those men

30

missing promptly. And when their bodies were found, the police came and got him to examine the bodies. I don't think he ever was under suspicion as the murderer, although the police around here certainly don't like his willingness to let our kind work here."

"Oh." I chomped on that a bit as Kyle's hand moved back to my dick and he started to bring it to life once again. "So, Frank's not your lover. He doesn't have any sexual hold over you?"

"You should know by now that I fuck whoever I want, Javier. And right now I want you to fuck me again."

I complied—but on my terms. If the little piece was going to sleep around and tease his fuck partners, when he was with me I was going to be in charge as strongly as I'd seen Duardo handle him once he'd manhandled him. We struggled a bit on the bed, with him trying to maintain control, but when I'd gotten his wrists tied off on the rungs of the brass headboard with the leather ties Frank had used on Shawn and had him on his belly, and had mounted and skewered him and begun to pump, he settled down with a moan and a laugh and gave me a first-class ride.

Yes he was just a little bit crazy. But a little bit crazy turned me on.

# SNOWBOUND

"I'll go with him."

"Of course you will," the Lazy S foreman said, turning and giving me a leer and a snicker. I thought that was a bit mean because Sam wasn't getting anything the foreman hadn't gotten before him. Who was he to be showing judgmental?

The foreman told Sam that someone needed to go up to the Culbertson farm up the valley half way to the top of Hahn's peak to check on the fences there before the snows came. Old man Peyton was a cattleman himself, but he'd bought the Culbertson farm up the valley with his brother over at the Circle K ranch. The Peytons saw the end of King Cattle coming and decided to dabble in farming themselves a bit, especially since growing your own feed for livestock was a whole hell of a lot cheaper than buying it off some other farmer. But a man couldn't maintain his claim on farming land out here on the edge of civilization without maintaining the fences. Homesteaders were drifting in, and the law let them grab anything thought to have been abandoned.

I turned to Sam Saunders and gave him what I thought was a secret smile but what probably wasn't a bit of a secret in the Lazy S bunkhouse. I was kind of a screamer—couldn't help it—and there wasn't much privacy attached to sudden hard on sex in a bunk house. Sam smiled back, clearly pleased I'd agreed to go with him. He looked good enough to eat. A good six years older than me, but in a lot better shape than I'd managed yet. I presented a more boyish figure. I was getting there, though. It's a big reason I'd come here.

I had only recently arrived from back East to try my hand at being a cowboy. It was such a romantic thought and was being played up in the adventure literature for young men. Especially mentioned among my friends in Pennsylvania was how hard bodied and randy cowboys could be. I liked both the idea of hard-bodied men and me being hard bodied too. In the meantime, I didn't mind a man being hard bodied with me.

It certainly had been one big adventure for me so far. Although only of average height and pretty slim, Sam had been at it long enough to have really muscled and toughened up. Back East he could have traveled with a troupe as the muscle man, I thought—and a handsome one at that. Curly reddish hair, a dandy's handsome face, and an "aw shucks" demeanor that turned into something else when he was fucking me.

"Remember to camp out at Dayton's mill on Slater Creek until you meet up with the man Peyton's brother is sending from the Circle K," Chuck told Sam. "His name's Jake."

We did just that, stopping at Dayton's mill to camp before riding our horses up the valley and into the mountains, where the air was crisp and nature was both beautiful and wild. Exhilarating was the word I thought of for it.

"Smells like snow," Sam said, as we were unloading the horses and setting up camp next to Slater Creek. "And the water's already icing up."

"Good thing you brought all that liquor, then," I said, with a laugh.

"Ain't that the truth? It might snow a blizzard up at Culbertson's while we're there and we'll be stuck up there all winter with nothing to do but to keep our insides warm with liquor."

"Nothing to do?" I asked as I heaved my saddle off my horse and set it down not far from where Sam was getting an open fire going. "Is that the only thing we could do up there to keep warm?"

"Not at all, not at all," Sam muttered in a hoarse voice as he reached out and drew me into him and into a deep kiss. "We ain't had a go of it for a week, and I've been hard for your sweet tail since ten minutes after the last throw."

Our bodies were rocking against each other. Our hands had gone straight for each other's crotches. We were both hard. I'd been hard thinking about him for the past five miles as we climbed to the camping area, and I had been anticipating what would happen there. I got the top four buttons of his rough cotton shirt open and latched my mouth onto a nipple. I knew that nipple play turned him into a wild man. And it was working here.

He was scrabbling at my belt and then the buttons of my fly, and I felt my jeans gliding down my legs. I stepped out of them, and he unbuttoned the flap of the union suit I was wearing underneath. He pushed that down between my legs to where he could lodge a leather-gloved finger in the entrance to my hole, wiggling it there as I opened to him. Satisfied I was opening to him, his gloved hand took possession of my cock and started stroking.

"Don't make me wait," I whimpered in a low voice.

"Not a chance of that," he growled back.

I was on my belly over my saddle, my arms flung out above my head gripping the base of two saplings at the edge of the stream, my butt pointed to the sky. The flap of the union suit had been pulled through my legs and up my back so that my puckering hole was exposed. Sam was on his haunches behind me, between my spread legs, one gloved hand spreading my buttocks to expose and stretch my hole, his tongue driving me crazy inside my crack, and his other hand having pulled my cock through and stroking it. I was doing a lot of egging-on screaming . . . until I came. He milked my cock for everything he could get out of it, and being young and in pretty good shape for an Easterner, I kept giving him cum for a few seconds.

"Now you. You. Fuck me! Give it to me now."

Sam complied, moving over my back, latching onto my pecs with his gloved hands. Entering, entering, entering me, and pumping, pumping, pumping. I writhed under him. Never before had he given it to me so hard and deep. Never before had we had such privacy to be able to let it all out. Never before had I felt free enough to scream for more of it, deeper. At the ranch, we'd never been far enough from the ears of others to engage in the wild fuck Sam now was giving me.

I felt him tense, hold for several seconds, and then, in a heavy release of breath, give me his load deep up inside me. Once, twice . . . four times in all. I was swimming in cum.

It was only while we were cooling down that we both looked around and saw him—over to the side at the edge of the clearing, down on his haunches, elbows on knees, a long blade of grass extending from his mouth as he chewed on the end of it, an enigmatic smile on his face, one hand holding the reins of the horse grazing beside him and the other open and dangling between his legs.

Who knew what he'd been doing with it before we saw him, but the bulge in his crotch was huge. Everything about the man was huge—not as in fat—but as in tall, bulky, muscle bound. He made Sam look scrawny. Dark, curly hair, swarthy complexion—he must have had some Mexican in him—hair in profusion. Five-o'clock shadow on his face, but the promise of hair everywhere else— spilling out of the neckline of his shirt, on the backs of his hands and on his knuckles. A face that was so ugly that it was mesmerizing and arousing; a body that was powerfully built, a real muscle man. A man my friends in Pennsylvania had said was out West, just waiting for me.

"You must be Jake, then," Sam said, trying for a calm voice conveying that we weren't doing anything out of the ordinary at all.

And, indeed, we weren't—really. The reality was that there were so few women out on the frontier as yet that the men mostly had to do with just their right hand or other men. Still, there was no way of knowing how one man would react to coming upon that as opposed to another man.

"Don't let me interrupt anything," the man who didn't deny he was Jake said. "Mighty entertaining, I must say."

But he, of course, had broken the mood.

\* \* \* \*

It had been a rough ride from the campsite up to Culbertson's farm, and Sam had said we should start checking the fences right away. It looked even more like snow was coming up here than it did down at the Lazy S. I stuck to Sam, and Jake went his own way. Something in the way he eyed me as we rode along gave me chills of both fear and arousing anticipation.

Sam and I would be staying in the same cabin with this man for a week or more. I hadn't thought about that before. I assumed I'd have Sam all to myself. We'd have to be more careful and observant than we were at the campsite. But now it wouldn't be any different from being in the bunkhouse with other men, and I'd been looking forward to it just being the two of us. As wide open as the spaces out West were, it seemed that there was little privacy to be had.

I may have been apprehensive of the man as we rode along, but he and Sam were having a good old time jawing and talking of shared experiences, which included, again to both my apprehension and arousal, their visits to the same male brothel in Hayden. They discovered they both were fond of the same male whore and what they said about what they liked in how he looked and what they could do with him, sounded awfully familiar to me.

I wasn't shocked, though, because, again, I didn't find this as unusual as most publicly claimed to think, considering the needs of men and the male-to-female ratio on the frontier. There were a whole load more fit and randy men on the frontier than there were women—lots of healthy men needing release. It wasn't uncommon for the men to turn to each other. Most, indeed, could enjoy both women and men as long as they regularly could get off. Without someone else, they had to take the matter into their own hands, and it's not hard to get tired of that.

It was because of the virile, muscular, and randy men that I'd come West. I wanted the knees of a strong man between my thighs. The men in Pennsylvania were OK, but I'd heard arousing stories about the doings of the men on the frontier. I had tried several men out at the Lazy S before settling on Sam, and none of the men before him had thrown me out on my tail. I had learned that size mattered too. Sam was the biggest of all who had fucked me. Within three weeks of my arrival at the Lazy S, half the cowboys in the bunkhouse—and the foreman as well—had fucked the "sweet little piece coming in from the East." There was even talk of not needing to make the run to the brothels of Hayden this fall. I was just shopping, though, and when I settled in for Sam, I kept my legs closed to the rest of the men in the bunkhouse—when I could. Some men got into such a state of need that they just took what they wanted. Sam stood up for me when it didn't look like it would lead to a fight, but peace in the bunkhouse took priority over my wants even with Sam.

That night, after Sam had tended to the horses and I had cooked our meal—and Jake had gotten started on the drinking—we celebrated our arrival by dipping into the large supply of liquor Sam had brought up—the clinking of the saddlebags on the horses reminding us of good times to come all the time we were riding up into the mountains.

As was the custom in the bunk house, we were down to our union suits, all three of us. I melted at the look of Jake in his. It barely contained the muscle mass of his body. He'd unbuttoned the top of his suit down to his waist. I could see why. His chest was so muscular that it strained at the suit, the rough material of which must chafe his big nipples. The effect was a magnificent hairy chest spreading the top, exposing his powerful torso.

The bulge at his crotch strained the buttoned flap to hold him in too. As it was, the flap was pushed forward by his equipment and curly hair and glimpses of a cock were visible in side looks at him around the edges of the flap. It was all I could do to contain myself while watching him strut around the single room of the cabin. It grew more maddening when he got more comfortable and left his flap hang open and his cock and balls hang and swing free. I have to admit that, in our time in the cabin, I saw the cock more in erection than hanging and swinging, though.

To put it succinctly, Jake was one hairy muscle stud. I was wishing that he'd been on offer in the Lazy S bunkhouse when I'd arrived from the East. I was with Sam now, though.

The two of them were passing the bottle—and then another one and another—between them and laughing and jawing. Occasionally, I got a swig or two—or three—too. I wouldn't say I was drunk on my tail, but I was gone enough to easily give into what happened as the evening wore on. So was Sam.

Sam had pulled me down into his lap. I was naked except for my boots and had no idea how I'd gotten in that condition, other than I might have done that myself. I know I was swaying in front of him and finishing off a bottle that the two had passed to me. The two men were sitting in straight chairs against the wall, side by side, and watching me do the dance I thought I was doing.

Sam pulled me right down on his cock—both cocks were now out of their union suit flaps while I was swaying in front of them. Jakes' cock made me moan. It was twice the size of Sam's in both girth and length. Jake was twice the man that Sam was in every way. Twice as cruel too, I was to find out.

I slid down Sam's cock as I was pulled into his lap, facing him. I unbuttoned the top of his union suit, spread the sides wide, and played with his nipples while I bounced up and down on his cock until Sam came. I'd already come, but I was gone enough that I hadn't been aware enough of it to enjoy it.

"You gonna share some of that with me?" The question was spoken in a growly voice. I looked over at Jake. He was looking straight into Sam's eyes. He was asking Sam, not me.

"Sure, have at it. We like the same thing, the same whore at the brothel. So, you'll like this little piece too," Sam said in a slurred voice, as he started handing me over and Jake got his strong, beefy arms around me. The bulging slabs of his chest were busting out of the top of his unbuttoned union suit and showed nearly all of it. His chest was as hairy as a bears.

I protested, not too effectively or forcibly, I'll admit, considering that I had drunk more than I should have and the dancing display I'd already put on. Much of the protesting centered around the size of the man's cock. I didn't think I could take it. I protested I couldn't take it. I was here with Sam, not Jake. Both men were laughing and drunkenly chanting. "Take it, take it, take it," I heard Jake belt out in a deep bass voice.

I gave one last plaintive look at Sam. His voice heavily slurred, he was chanting "Take it, take it" too—and pushing me over onto Jake.

Jake pulled me down into his lap, facing him, just like Sam had done. I wouldn't have put it past him to have schemed that if he did just as Sam had done, Sam would be better with it that way. Just a friendly sharing of what Sam had. Just like sharing his liquor. A generous man, Sam was, and he was really getting along with this cowboy from the Circle K. Sam was sitting there, watching us, with a sloppy grin on his face, and fisting his cock. Obviously Sam was good with it.

The big, hairy cowboy got the bulb of the monster in me, but just that, showing I couldn't take it. I screamed of not being able to take it. He pulled me down farther on it. I couldn't take it. My walls were stretched to the limit. But they began to give way as he pulled me down farther on the cock, relentlessly. And then I could take it. And then I wanted it. I always wanted a cock inside me. The bigger the better. This was the biggest.

"Arch back to the floor," he growled. "Grab my ankles."

I did as he commanded and screamed my fear and taking to the sparse furniture—the two beds—across the room in an upside-down view. With beefy, hairy hands on my waist, he slid me on and off of his club, the cum Sam had deposited there already aiding in both the friction and the lubrication. My screams turned from ones of pain and splitting to "Yes, yes. Fuck me hard. Deep. Split me! Pound me! Give it to me! Just like that. Just like that! Oh, shit, I've never had it this big."

I heard him snort and mutter, "Just bet you haven't, you sweet little honeypot. Tight as a virgin."

We both knew I wasn't, though.

He came in one heavy flooding, followed by several weaker afterbursts. I lay there, spent, tears running down my cheeks, cum burbling up my channel and down my inner thighs. My belly wet from the cum of my own spouting. Panting, panting, panting.

Wanting nothing now so much as the bed I could see in my upside-down view across the room.

"Shit, oh holy shit," I weakly murmured as he started to pull me on and off the cock again. He was still hard. He hadn't finished fucking me.

Sometime later I was looking, at first plaintively and later warily, over at Sam slumped over in the chair against the wall, his head hanging down, snoring. At first I thought I wanted him to wake up and come to my rescue. Increasingly, though, I wanted him to stay comatose, not to see what Jake was doing to me on his bed. Sam had been good, but Jake was twice the man Sam was.

Jake was on his back on his bed, and I was on my back as well, on top of Jake. He was gripping my pecs with his hands, pinching my nipples, and his bent legs encased mine and had them spread wide and raised. His dick was pumping up into me deep. Thick and reaching deeper than Sam had ever reached. The bed was creaking and bucking as hard as Jake and I were. I didn't want it to stop—and it didn't for a long time into the night. He was twice the man that Sam was.

* * * *

41

It had already started snowing when we stumbled out of the cabin in the early morning, on our way to checking the fences. Before braving the fence inspection, I was preparing the breakfast and Sam went out first thing before that to take a leak and to feed the horses in the barn. I was walking gingerly and sighing and giving Sam hard looks while avoiding looking at or talking to Jake at all. I don't know what I wanted Sam to do—or Jake to do or say for that matter. I don't know what I would have done if Jake had apologized, blamed it on the liquor, and told me he wouldn't touch me again. My feelings were mixed. Sam should be my man and act like it. He should know what Jake did and do something about it. But if he knew—or showed he knew—maybe Jake wouldn't give me another roll in the hay. And what Jake did with me the previous night was the best fucking I'd ever had.

And Jake was a whole lot bigger than Sam. There were men in the bunkhouse who weren't as big as Jake who Sam didn't fight to keep away from me when they were drunk and in high need.

Something inside me told me that Sam should be asserting his rights. But he didn't even seem to notice that I had a burr in my saddle or how tense the atmosphere in the cabin was. When he went out to take care of the horses, he was gone long enough that Jake pulled me over to the wall beside the door, pushing me against the rough log surface with his hairy chest, bursting out of the top of his union suit, which was still unbuttoned down to his navel, with the flap at the crotch open.

"No, we can't," I murmured. But we obviously could. His dick was so hard he couldn't have stuffed it back in his suit if he'd wanted to, and I could tell that it was going to get what it wanted. He scared me, but he sent my heart racing too. He was so much bigger than Sam, and I had taken it all. My channel was twitching. I couldn't help it. I wanted him inside me again.

"Then be quick about it," I whimpered. I was Sam's, not his.

He laughed. He reached around and unbuttoned the flap in my union suit, jerking it between my legs to expose my hole as well as my cock and balls. He lifted one of my legs, pushing my knee into the curve of the log wall. Crouching down, he came back up under my buttocks, got his cockhead positioned, and slowly pushed up into me. I moaned and groaned, turning my face toward his, my eyes locked on his, seeing a determined, cruel, sneery look on his face. He moved his beefy, hairy forearm to under my chin and pressed me hard to the wall. I fought for breath, my eyes watering. I opened my mouth to cry out at the deep, thick invasion of him.

"I'll be quick about it if you're quiet about it," he growled. "You don't want Sam to hear, do you?" I clamped my mouth shut, my silence aided by the pressure of his forearm pressing into my throat. I didn't know if I wanted Sam to know what he was doing with me or not, but I knew that if my cries summoned Sam, there would be no option of pretending or hiding anything.

I counted the stuffing, cruel, glorious strokes. One, two . . . eighteen, nineteen, twenty. He jerked and creamed my intestines.

When Sam returned from feeding and watering the horses, Jake was sitting at the oak table, drinking coffee and looking very pleased with himself, and I was hobbling around the kitchen counter, finishing up breakfast preparations, and not able to look Sam in the eyes.

We weren't out, Sam and I, on the fence line much beyond noon. The snow was piling up and it was accumulating deep. When we'd managed to trudge back to the cabin's porch, it nearly was over our boot tops.

"We're gonna be snowed in real good in another hour or so," Sam said. "I'll go look to the horses and you go on in. Don't know where Jake's got off to."

43

It was just about the first thing Sam had said to me that day, He was moving slow, after having passed out the previous night. We said nothing about the previous night. I didn't think he even remembered that he'd handed me over to Jake. That Jake had fucked me—fucked me better than he had. Fucked me longer, deeper, than he ever had, flooded me with more cum than he ever had—while he was passed out in a drunken stupor.

Snowbound. With Sam and Jake. With Jake. I shuddered, feeling frozen. But I waited on the porch for Sam to return. I didn't want to go into the cabin alone. I didn't trust myself with Jake. I was here with Sam; I'd be going back to the Lazy S with Sam—although I'd already thought about how it would be going back to the Circle K with Jake instead. If Jake was showing me the least bit of affection—as seeing me as more than a hole he wanted to fill—I'd maybe broach him with the possibility of going with him rather than Sam when we got back to the bottom of the mountain. But so far, I was just a hole to him.

Jake was in the cabin, sitting at the oak table and swigging coffee. There was no evidence he'd gone out that day at all, and when Sam mentioned it, Jake changed the subject. And Sam let him. Sam was taken with Jake, I could tell. Wanted to be buddies. Liked jawing away with the man. And drinking with him. Didn't mind sharing me with him when Jake asked half nicely. He obviously thought that Jake was more a man than he was, someone to follow rather than lead. In that I agreed with Sam completely. He was less a man in my eyes now compared to how he had been before we'd come up to Culbertson's farm.

It would be hard for Jake to think he didn't have clear sailing with me as far as Sam was concerned. And the looks Jake was giving me made me scared he might not ask half nicely the next time.

The two put away a lot of the booze that night. I tried to limit myself. From time to time one or more of us went to the cabin window, looked out, and announced how far up the window pane the snow was piled. "Yep, snowbound for sure," was an overworked phrase in the cabin that night.

Sam was lying on the end of our bed, his booted feet on the floor, in his union suit, but with the chest open to give my hands and mouth access to his nipples, while, facing him, I knelt over his pelvis and rode the cock jutting out of the open flap of his union suit. I sensed I was losing him—that he was so drunk that he was drifting away from me before ejaculating. He was going softer rather than harder.

I had purposely not looked around to see what Jake was doing. I couldn't bear to watch him stroking that gigantic club of his while I was riding Sam—Sam, who I previously had thought of as hung, as the cock of the walk in the bunkhouse. Maybe in the Lazy S bunkhouse, but what about in the Circle K bunkhouse? I hadn't really known what hung was until I'd had that cock of Jake's inside me. I was riding Sam's cock but I was thinking of Jake's cock.

And then I knew where Jake was. He was behind me, standing between Sam's spread thighs. Breathing hard in my ear. Pushing me down on Sam's chest, my mouth going to Sam's nipples. Causing me to roll my buttocks up to his searching fingers, entering me with those fingers on either side of Sam's buried cock. Expanding inside me and working to stretch my channel wider.

Sam snorted, but his head rocked to the side. He just about was gone. His cock inside me was withering, but he was long enough to stay inside me. Now the giant bulb of another cock was at my hole, caressing not just my hole but the top of Sam's increasingly flaccid cock as well. I moaned, feeling my opening and channel walls

45

loosening. They wanted him. They wanted Jake's cock. They didn't give a fuck that Sam already was in there.

"Got tired of waitin'," Jake growled softly.

"Yes, yes, fuck me," I mumbled.

And then he was inside me, above Sam's cock and doing just that. I bit Sam's nipple at the first cruel thrust up into me, and Sam groaned and stirred, but didn't fully awake. He was aware of something arousing going on, though, as his cock was engorging again.

Jake wrapped his arms around my chest and pulled me back up to him. I luxuriated in the scratching of his curly chest hair on my back. He palmed one of my pecs and slapped his other hand over my mouth and nose, making me fight for air but also cutting off any loud vocalization I would do otherwise.

Jake pounded away at my ass, and Sam, hard again now, the two dicks stretching me to the limit, was slow-pumping his cock too, even though he remained semiconscious. Sam gave me a weak ejaculation, but Jake gave me another heavy, prolonged one.

I woke up in the night, lying on my side, looking out toward the other bed. Sam was stretched behind me, snoring and dead to the world. I found I was looking at Jake in his nearby bed. Although night, it was nearly bright as day in the cabin from the reflection off the snow bank of the full moon streaming through the cabin window. I could see that Jake was looking back at me. He was on his side, facing me and staring at me. His hand was on the erect cock sticking out of the open flap of his union suit. I felt my hand go to my cock as well, to find that I also was hard.

Our eyes moved between the eyes and the cock of the other. I found I was matching my strokes to his. We were engaged in sex even while being a few feet from each other.

"Jake, please," I murmured across the space separating our beds.

He didn't answer, just continued staring at me and pulling at his cock. But I saw the corners of his mouth pull up in a cruel sneer.

"Fuck me again, Jake," I whispered. "I want it so bad."

He had me bent over the oak table, hunched over my back, my legs spread as far apart as I could, and was pounding my ass hard, when Sam came alive across the room and bounded out of the bed. No doubt it was my screams of passion that had brought Sam fully back into the land of the living.

"What in the fuck are you doing to him," Sam cried out as he moved, fast, across the room. It was as if he hadn't been conscious when he'd been willing to share me—and no doubt he hadn't been conscious of that, or any of the rest of it.

Jake pulled out of me, leaving me there, clutching the sides of the table in white-knuckled hands, panting heavily, and regretting his withdrawal. He turned deftly as Sam roared up and punched Sam in the chin, following up with a gut shot, and then an uppercut to the chin again. Sam folded down to the floor beside me. Jake pulled him off the floor by the scruff of his union suit, hauled back and punched him yet again in the face, and let him drop back down into a puddle.

I know I should have been in shock and feared for Sam, but Jake had brought me so close to an ejaculation that all I could think of was him getting back inside me and pumping me to a big finish. He turned back to me and thrust inside for a few more strokes, but didn't come. I whined in the loss of the load.

"That's it; no more pussyfooting around him. He was getting on my nerves anyway," Jake muttered, as he withdrew, picked me up and slung me over his shoulder, stepped over Sam's prone body, walked back to the bed—Sam's and my bed—commanded "On all fours," and doggy fucked me to an ejaculation as I held onto the bars of the headboard for all dear life. It was a great, exhausting fuck. I collapsed, rolled out from underneath him when he'd creamed me, and went instantly to sleep.

"Where's Sam?" I asked the next morning when I woke. Jake was sitting at the oak table, drinking coffee, still in his union, his hairy chest still bulging out of the unbuttoned top of the union suit, his cock, still half erect, standing proudly up from his open crotch flap.

"He decided three were too much to be snowbound in this cabin. He left an hour ago. Back down the mountain to the ranches."

"In this snow? The drifts must be almost as tall as he is now."

"Let's not talk about Sam. Come here. Suck me." He was fisting his cock and leering at me.

I struggled out of bed, padded to him. When I got there, he reached up, grabbed a fistful of hair on my head, and pulled me down on my knees between his thighs. I gagged as the bulb of his cock hit the back of my throat.

\* \* \* \*

After I've served him breakfast, Jake went over to his bed, laid down, and soon was lightly snoring. If Sam was gone now, I guessed it was up to me to feed and water the horses. Jake hadn't shown signs of doing anything but drink Sam's liquor, swill coffee, and fuck me since he'd been here. I didn't think he'd even been out to check any of the fence lines, which was why we were up here.

The blizzard had blown over in the night and the temperatures were high enough to start melting the snow. There were still three-foot drifts around, but there was no difficulty in moving around in the yard, so I pumped water into a bucket in the kitchen area and left the cabin. Jake was still sleeping.

I was back almost before I'd left, standing in the doorway, the bucket empty because I'd spilled it in the barn. I was trembling from fear.

Jake's eyes opened as soon as the cabin door banged against the wall.

"Where have you been?" he growled.

"I . . . I . . . the horses needed fed and watered." And then it tumbled out. "The horses are there. All of them. Even Sam's horse. Where's Sam? What have you done with Sam?"

Jake leisurely unfolded himself from the bed and walked toward me. I shrank from him in confusion and fear.

One pop to the chin and I was out like a light.

When I came to, I was naked, on my back, and spread-eagled on Sam's and my bed, tied off at the four corners of the head and foot boards. The pillows from both beds had been shoved under the small of my back, elevating my pelvis and hips, and Jake was kneeling between my spread legs. His knees were pushed in well under my buttocks. He had his hard dick deep inside me, was grasping my waist with his hands, and was pistoning me hard.

I merely looked up at him with dull eyes. My jaw hurt. It felt unhinged. And, being disoriented, all I could think of was how I was going to take a cock his size in my mouth with a painful jaw.

I should have been thinking how I was going to survive this.

He moved his hands to my throat. His thumbs were on major arteries, through which blood was trying to pound through to my head. He had a sneer on his lips, and his brown eyes were flashing. The throbbing in the arteries in my neck was increasing, as he applied pressure to them with his thumbs. I shot my load and then he did as well inside me. I blacked out.

I woke up still bound and spread-eagled. Jake was sitting at the oak table, swigging liquor from a bottle and loading bullets into a revolver.

A knock at the door caused us both to look up as it opened. A young cowboy was standing there, his saddle hung off his back. His eyes first went to Jake.

"You must be Sam. I'm Jake. Jake from the Circle K. Missed you at the Dayton's Mill rendezvous so I came on up when the snow let up."

The eyes of the Jake I knew turned to me, which made the new Jake look over to me too and exclaim, "What the hell? What the fuck's going on here?"

# MAKE ME A STAR

"Just settle down and stop pushing at me, Danny. I'm in now."

He wasn't in as far as he was going to get, I was soon to learn. The pain was excruciating, not least because it was so strange compared to anything I'd experienced before. But I'd been assured that it would lessen and that, eventually, I usually wouldn't notice it much at all—not compared with the pleasure it would be giving me. And there was some of that already. The expectation of it; the "it's finally happening" of it.

"Stop pushing on me. I'm in. You're fucked already. Got your cherry. No reason to fight it. Open to me and enjoy it. You're a dancer. Dance on the cock."

I was on all fours on the studio couch in his office—the proverbial casting couch—and he was standing behind me, between my calves that jutted out over the end of the couch. I had twisted around and swung an arm behind me, the palm of my hand extending through his open and separated dress shirt and pushing at his muscular, hairy chest. I was bearing the weight of my twisted torso on a fist buried in the surface of the couch. He was crouched behind me, his hands gripping my hips, his dick inside me. Only a few inches, it turned out. He was going to be much deeper than that soon.

I know I was giving him a wild look. The look in his eyes was one of determination and of being a bit perturbed. I know I was crying out something, but I was trying my best that it not be a demand for him to stop. He wasn't raping me. I'd agreed to it—I'd agreed to it months earlier, in fact. I'd signed a contract. It's just that now it was happening, it was overwhelming.

"Oh, for Christ sake," he growled. And I felt the hands leave my hips and he was twisting around to the nearby chair that he'd hung his coat over. The hands came back with a long, cashmere neck scarf, which he whipped over my head; pulled my wrists together, causing me to collapse my chest on the surface of the couch—my tail still in the air, still skewered by his dick—and tied my wrists together with it.

"That'll keep them out of the way," he muttered. The hands went back to my hips, grabbing, pinching. And that's when I discovered he'd lied about already being in—and already having been fucked, for that matter. All of my sensations went to my ass channel, which his dick was penetrating more deeply. God, it was big.

"You're going to split me!" I hadn't meant to cry out, but I hadn't been able to keep it in.

Soothing shushing. "It will take it; I won't split you. Relax, push it out. Open to me; you'll be fine."

"There, in to the root," I heard him whisper in my ear through heavy breathing. "When you learn to open to it faster, there won't be this pain." And indeed, now that he was all in and had stopped pushing at me—and I began to relax, knowing that I wasn't resisting anything that hadn't already happened—the pain was a bit less. "Turn your head, look into the mirror over there. Here, I'll turn your ass a bit. Look at what's inside you. You can take it. You have taken it."

I moaned at the sight of how thick the root of his dick looked to be as reflected in the mirror, where just the base of it was visible in my hole. And my hole. Who would have known it would open that wide? I didn't find his "help" in showing that to me in the mirror reassuring. Well, not immediately, but there was a little thrill of having taken all of that. And that's as big as his dick would get—surely. But maybe it would get bigger while he fucked? I moaned again.

And the pain. When the hell does the pain lessen, I wondered as I moaned and groaned and voiced every variation of "ouch" and "oh, shit" that bubbled up to my lips. "Ouch" didn't express a fourth of the pain, though.

"So sweet, and fresh. I've wanted to do this for months. And so tight. I'm the first one, right? Tell me I'm the first one. I paid to be first."

"Yes," I answered through shallow pants and clinched teeth. "You're the first one."

He was. Would I be doing this if he didn't have something I wanted badly? I wanted a speaking part in the Broadway play he was producing to go on stage in 1964.

"Good boy." His hands were off my hips and gliding over my torso, patting and pinching. "Sleek young body—if I hadn't seen your birth certificate myself, I'd—"

My groan covered what he was saying. Not only had a hand found and encased my dick, but I also felt movement in the throbbing dick inside me—or at least I thought the dick was throbbing; I knew my channel walls were throbbing from the alien invasion. He was beginning to move the dick inside me. Drawing back, pushing in, drawing back, pushing in farther than he'd reached before.

"Take it, take it, take it." Each thrust punctuated with a command.

"Oh, shit, Oh, fuck! That hurts like hell!" All senses returning to my ass channel. What he'd done before tying my wrists together wasn't being fucked. *This* was being fucked! Pumping me as I writhed under him. His grip on one of my pecs and on my dick vice-like now.

The grip eased and he was stroking me with his hand to the rhythm of his dick stroking my channel.

I shot out onto the nice red vinyl of his studio couch. "Good, good, come for me. Good," he growled. He let loose of my dick and lifted his hairy chest off my back. He had been holding me close and covering me.

Standing behind me now gave him more thrust leverage. He was pumping me hard and deep. I felt a hand running into the curls on my head, gripping my hair, jerking my head back toward him, arching my torso back in a tight bow.

And fucking, fucking, fucking. I was groaning and moaning to match his grunts and crying out who knows what. At that stage it must have been variations of "too much" and "please stop." But he didn't stop right away; he was too taken up with enjoying the ass of a young dancer-would-be-actor being fucked for the first time.

He did start to calm down and slow down after a short while, and he lowered his chest on my back again, tickling my shoulder blades with the coarse, salt-and-pepper hair swirling on his chest, and whispered, "Sorry, you're just so sweet. Have trouble remembering it's your first time—and that you're eighteen. But I paid for this and you want even more from me. Say that I paid for this."

"You paid for this," I said, with a gasp. "But It hurts, it hurts," I whined softly. The reminder helped me focus. He'd paid for this and hadn't taken the privilege until I wanted more. He wasn't raping me.

"It's going to hurt the first couple of times. But it will get good for you. Just bear with me—and work on relaxing, opening. I know, maybe this would be better."

He was pulling out of me—such a relief—and carrying me over to an overstuffed chair in a dimly lit corner of his office half way up the Empire State Building. He sat in the chair and pulled me down into his lap. He started to pull my shirt up and off my back, encountered my bound wrists and took the time to unbind them and then rebind them with the scarf once I'd been stripped of the shirt. I was naked except for my socks, and he was still fully dressed except for his shirt gaping wide open and his dick jutting up out of his open fly. Somehow the discrepancy made me feel doubly vulnerable and this whole situation seem sordid.

I'm not being raped; I'm not being raped, I chanted in my mind. I want something he can give me badly enough to do this.

His fumbling with my shirt and the binding was a pause I probably didn't need. The fear of the first taking and what might yet to be coming flowed back in.

Once my wrists were rebound, my arms went over his head, my wrists lodged behind his neck. "Run your legs up the back of the chair on either side of me," he commanded. "You're a dancer; you can do it."

When I'd done that, he lifted and spread my buttocks and speared my now-more-open ass entrance with the bulb of his dick. I panted hard as he pulled me down on the shaft, whispering all the time, "Breathe, breathe, relax, open to me, baby. You're doing fine. Oh sweet Jesus you are so nice. And I fucked you first."

I fought hard to relax, to open to him, discovering how I could do more of that, how I could relax my channel muscles and start letting the tension flow out of me. He was right. I had nothing to protect. I was fucked now. I had agreed to it.

He began to lift my torso and pull it back down, his shaft moving up and down inside me again. It was better than before. Still painful, but I was becoming more resigned to it, more aroused by what it was we were doing. Now even that I was naked and he was clothed was making me feel sexy.

"There, good. Better for you?"

"Yes," I answered in a small, labored voice. He continued for a while and I could hear his breathing becoming more ragged. If he'd just blow. There must be relief from this if he'd just fire his wad.

"Kiss my nips," I heard him say, and I pulled my face into his hairy chest and kissed one of his nipples after brushing the hair aside with my tongue. "Yes, lick them. The other one too." His shirt front was wide open, his muscular, hairy chest pushing out at me. "Bite them lightly. Oh, fuck. Yes, yes." They were engorged, hard. I felt him shudder. And maybe ejaculate? No, maybe not. Would I be able to tell when he had?

I lost contact with the nipples and was arching my back and crying out to the ceiling because he was slamming me up and down on his dick with the hands gripping my waist in response to my having followed his command and fired up his arousal.

This didn't last for long, though. He slowed down and dipped his face to my chest and did the same with my nipples that he had commanded me to do to his. "Perfection," he murmured. "Young, sleek body. Dancer's body. Just the right hard muscling. Nips are hard too. You like this."

And I did like it. For the first time, I was whispering, "Yes, yes, like that," and moaning a moan of pleasure. And I felt my ass muscles relax even more. He no longer was too taxing for me down there. He moved his face up to mine and took my mouth in a deep kiss. I sighed behind the possession and, involuntarily, my channel was coming to a life of its own, caressing the shaft inside it, my pelvis beginning to move, almost imperceptibly. Rising and falling on the dick, sliding up and down on it, caressing it. So this is what those I'd asked about sex said on how glorious it could be to be fucked.

He broke from the kiss and gave a low laugh. "Yes, you want it now, don't you?"

"Yes, yes," I whispered. And I did want it.

"Fuck yourself. Move your feet down to where the arms of the chair meet the back. Use those feet for leverage. Fuck yourself on the cock."

I did so, and unless my sensations were deceiving me, he was going harder inside me, and throbbing harder too. So, he *could* get bigger during the fuck. And with my controlling the stroking, the pain was less, the pleasure more. More throbbing slide along undulating walls, as the fear and tension drained from the core of my body and I opened more to fit the shaft better.

We were both calling out variations of "Yes, yes, fuck me." I gave him my load again up his belly and heard him laugh and mutter something like "Oh to be young again." I kept sliding up and down on the shaft, pumping my knees and pushing off on the crease where the chair arms met its back, getting better at it and being more in tune with it with each stroke. He growled a "Got you interested now, don't I?" in a strangled voice, went rigid, and cried out a final, "Oh, Fuck!" I felt the entirely new, and not unpleasant, sensation of being creamed by his cum high up inside me.

Yes, I would know when he dropped his load inside me. And when I thought the spurt had ended, another one came. And then another one. He resumed the stroking, and the slide was looser, aided by the added lubricant. I experienced a flash of arousal. "Yes! Fuck me, fuck me. Harder, deeper."

But as if I now was too much into the coupling, he was slowing down, his dick losing its hardness—just when I could have been lifted to a new level of want. "No, no," I whined.

He laughed. "There will be more."

We held there, forehead to forehead, our eyes locked, while, panting shallowly, we cooled down. At length, he asked in a low voice, "So, it was good for you in the end, wasn't it? You can take it now? You want it, right? Because we're going to do this again."

"Now?" I asked in mixed fear and anticipation.

"In a bit. But soon. I promise. You get over these first couple of fucks and you'll want it bad and will have it good, very good."

"Yes, I want it again," I answered in a small voice. I wanted what I'd come for and been prepared to take this for, but I wasn't lying. I wanted him to fuck me again. I'd gotten over a barrier I'd worried about for months. I wanted it again, until I was comfortable with it—and then I wanted it again and again. He'd creamed me. Now I could really say I'd been fucked by a man.

"Your choice, Danny. You want the part in the play or not? This, whenever I want it, if you do."

"Yes, I want the part."

His hands pulled my arms above my head, and he untied my wrists and let my arms fall to my sides. I became aware that I was near exhaustion. Letting my arms dangle at my sides, I arched my torso back, away from his chest, and let my head drop back. I could feel him going flaccid inside me. I no longer feared this dick of his. I wanted to feel it hard inside me again.

"Beautiful dancer's body," he murmured, and I felt his mouth return to one of my nipples. And then the other. Sucking.

"Fuck me. Please fuck me again," I whimpered. It's not so much that I wanted him to fuck me again as that I wanted him to want me. I wanted that part in his play— and in the play he produced after that.

"We'll get back to that. Now, go down on your knees between my thighs. Clean my cock with your mouth. Then start showing me how fast you can learn to give a great blow job."

# Baby, It's Cold Outside

1974 was Rick's first Christmas away from home, and he was feeling a bit down. He'd stayed home, in Baltimore, Maryland, for his first year in college, but his mother hadn't been able to hack the expenses of even a junior college, although she could afford to go gambling in Las Vegas for Christmas this year, and reality set in that he needed more money to get through college than he now had access to. Reality also was that he'd have to earn the money on his own. If he had a dad, although, of course, there'd been a sperm provider somewhere, his mother had never spoken of him. Rick was an "almost" for a soccer scholarship to the state university in College Park. What he'd managed in the year at junior college was to bring his grades up enough to get into the University of Maryland "sometime in the future."

What he needed now, the university coaches had said, was to toughen up more. More muscle mass. College soccer had become a very physical sport. There wouldn't be a spot on the team or a scholarship for him this year, but if he muscled up and trimmed down a little, maybe next year.

And the point remained that he had to get all of this done on his own—with only whatever assets and abilities he himself possessed.

He'd done a good start on the "muscled up and trimmed down" part, so things were looking up for him—if he could get ahead of the ball financially. And where he'd done the muscled-up part was here in Allentown. A buddy of his—a gay buddy; a gay buddy who had tagged Rick out as gay too and had convinced him he was gay, and a gay bottom—had a lead on a gym in Allentown, Pennsylvania, that, yes, catered to gay clients, but that also was looking for a towel boy, especially a good-looking, not too effeminate gay bottom. The job paid pretty well, if you took side work into account, and it provided free use of the gym whenever the towel boy could work it in.

The friend declared that Rick looked like a winner for the job, which flattered Rick. So, he applied for—and got—the job.

Because of his need to quick quick toughen up even more, Rick made the gym his entire life in Allentown. He had a room and bath in the basement of a middle-aged widow's house who gave him a cut rate in exchange for a fuck once a week. Other than the few hours he spent there, he was at the gym the entire time.

The work conditions were fine, and the clientele was friendly—increasingly friendly as he hardened up and trimmed down more—and learned from the other guys working in the gym how to dress right, cut his hair right, and how to shave his chest and legs and trim his pubes stylishly. Increasingly, the side work offers came, but he was pretty busy most of the time, and they weren't coming from the men he was most attracted to. He needed the extra money, though, so there was a blow job here and a quick fuck in the shower or the private rooms they offered at the gym there, and he was able to put aside an extra $150 or so a week.

All very impersonal so far; something he could handle and not get emotionally involved in. Just using his assets to move along the plan.

What attracted him were the thirty-something, self-confident, handsome and cut businessmen who came in and Leon, a black farm team football player with a magnificent physique, who was always working to make his body even more perfect.

The businessmen seemed to be out of Rick's league, though, and the arousal factor and massiveness of Leon scared Rick shitless, so he kept to the older businessmen who had money. Both Leon's musculature and dangerous look—not to mention how Rick saw the man hanging in the showers—provided a mix of arousal and fear. Feeding that were the whispers Rick overheard between the attendants. "Have you done the big black bull, Leon, yet? Ooolala, you haven't been fucked until you've been fucked by Leon."

The younger guys working out at the gym who were closer to Rick's age mostly didn't have money and wanted it for free. When Rick was really horny—like when he'd watched Leon work out—he'd sometimes give it to the young guys for free, but not often—and never twice, without a big tip. He didn't have the time or energy to get involved with anyone who wasn't going to pay for it.

It was getting around the gym that Rick would sometimes suck a man's cock or take his cock for a price. And one of the masseurs was teaching Rick to give sports massages—which, at this gym, could easily include a blow job, a quick ride, and a big tip. The longer Rick worked there, the better he looked to the clients—and the higher the price he could demand. It also meant the more he was drifting into being a genuine rent boy. Athletic, trim, blond, young men were in high demand. Guys at the gym were telling him he could make more with a pimp, and he was considering it.

Rick had only recently turned twenty. He could have passed for eighteen.

* * * *

"Hi, Rick. It *is* Rick, isn't it?"

Rick looked up from where he was working at the gym's reception desk.

"Um, yes, I'm Rick. Hello, umm, Mr. . . . ?"

It was one of the thirty-something businessmen types. One of the better-looking ones—by far. Dark haired, the hair cut so that a lock drooped fetchingly over his forehead in a studied effort at "ah shucks." There was nothing else ah shucks about him, though. He'd come off the exercise floor and was just in running shorts and sneakers. Those looked first class expensive, and the running shorts fit him like a glove, showing a distinct bulge. Great musculature and a deep tan. Almost swarthy looking. Italian, maybe. Fetching perpetual five-o'clock shadow on his cheeks and chin. Not an ounce of fat on him. Black curly hair swirling around huge aureoles, plump nipples that really stuck out, and the curly hair running down his sternum and flat belly and into his pubes, the top edge of which showed above the dipped waistline of his shorts.

Rick went hard just looking at him. He fancied the man was hard himself. Definitely out of Rick's league. But the guy knew his name.

"I'm Winston," the man said, flashing a million-dollar smile.

Of course you are, Rick thought. You probably even own the cigarette company. Definitely out of his league.

"Hi, Mr. Winston."

"No, Winston's my first name. I'm new here. Live over in Bethlehem."

Ah, the better part of the area, east of Allentown, the two cities having grown together. A bit far to come for a gym. But then this wasn't just any gym. This was a gay clientele gym. And a cruising gym at that. So Winston was probably gay—and cruising. That didn't make Rick's cock go down any.

"I'm told you haven't been here for long either," Winston was saying. "Don't come from Allentown, then?"

"No, my family's in Baltimore." No reason to tell him that his mother was the only family he had and that she said she was going to Las Vegas to gamble for Christmas.

"So," as if Winston had been reading his thoughts, "you got anything going for Christmas Eve? It's just a couple of days away."

"No, other than coming here and working out."

"You look like you've worked out real well already."

Rick's T-shirt and short shorts, the uniform of the gym staff, let Winston know that he was in really good shape.

"The gym here did that for me. And you have to be in good shape to work here."

"I've noticed that," he answered. "It's good incentive for sluggards like me to get in shape. You have to be other things to work here too, I understand."

Rick let the final remark pass for now, but he didn't question it. They both knew what Winston meant. "You look like you're in great shape to me, Mr. . . . ah . . . Winston." Rick wasn't buttering the man up. He looked like he could do an International Male layout with pride. Rick had seen hot models in this guy's age bracket in the International Male mail-order catalog. Clearing his throat, Rick continued. "I'm trying to get on a university soccer team. Coaches told me I had to toughen up more. That's why I took this job."

"Ah, soccer. Just now entering college?"

"No sir, I'm just twenty. Had a year of junior college and now trying to get into the university on a soccer scholarship."

"Ah, twenty. I would have guessed eighteen. And money's tight, I'll bet."

"You bet right. But glad to have met you." The attendants weren't paid to do a lot of chitchat with the clients, although Rick was reluctant to let this one go. Maybe he'd meet him in one of the private rooms someday. Maybe the guy would like to buy a sports massage—a full body massage. But, again, the man definitely was out of his league.

"Say, if you don't have anything better going for you, I'm having a small party for a few of the guys here at the gym at my house on Christmas Eve. You might drop in. We'll have a lot of fun."

"Thanks for the invite. Can't drop in much of anywhere, though—and not as far away as Bethlehem. No wheels." It wasn't uncommon that he didn't have a car. He'd rarely been in one. It was the mid seventies. His usual wheels were a city or a Greyhound bus.

"Well, of course you haven't. Leon—you know, the big black bruiser football player—is coming. I'm sure he'd be happy to give you a ride."

Yeah, Rick knew Leon all right. His dick gave another lurch at the very mention of Leon giving him a ride. But his scare meter went up a notch too. Rick's dick won out, though. "Yeah, well, if Leon can give me a ride, then maybe."

\* \* \* \*

"But, baby, it's cold outside." Winston was singing the line.

"Eh, what?" Rick asked.

65

He felt trapped in the corner of the long sofa, facing a frenetically flashing Christmas tree that was bigger than Rick's room that he paid for largely with a weekly fuck. Winston was sitting close to him, his arm on the back of the sofa behind Rick. Leon was sitting across from them, next to the Christmas tree, hunched down in a club chair, looking intense and a bit mean, but probably with no intent to. He just looked the part of a brooding hulk.

Winston was shirtless and in some sort of loose lounging pants just for Christmas, all green and red and white in some abstract Christmas tree design. He'd met them at the door that way. Barefoot too. He had a gold medallion on a gold chain around his neck—something he didn't wear in the gym. His nipples were standing out hard, long, and thick in the center of his large aureoles and peeking out of the swirling black curls on his chest. The trim and pattern of the chest hair swirl was so perfect that Rick thought the guy must groom it. Again, Rick's thought went back to "International Male model."

From looking at the erect nipples, Rick knew the man must be hard elsewhere too. Rick hadn't really been fooled what this party was about, but he'd expected several more men, which he'd thought—probably foolishly—would be some sort of protection.

"You keep saying you should leave or you have to go. But Leon doesn't seem ready to go. And look outside. There's a blizzard out there. You really don't want to go out in that. You can stay for one more drink. Maybe it'll let up."

One more drink is going to dissolve a blizzard? Rick wondered. He didn't really have a choice, but he was going to find that one or more drinks could cover a multitude of sins.

It had been snowing when Leon picked him up at the gym in his truck. Rick had said that maybe it wasn't a good night to try to go to a party over in Bethlehem, but Leon had been insistent. Leon could be insistent with just a look in his eyes.

Rick had already felt he hadn't dressed warm enough. Just a leather jacket over tight jeans and a T, with sockless sandals. Not even any underwear. He'd known from the beginning what sort of party this was going to be. But it was Christmas Eve and he was lonely. And thinking of Leon and Winston and any number of other guys from the gym who would be at the party had made him horny. And scared. He was thinking gangbang, yes, but probably not of him. He was just a towel boy. Some old, ugly guy would probably just do him against the wall in a hallway, while Leon and Winston were in on a gangbang of someone more desirable and experienced in the other room.

But when he got to Winston's house and three drinks later, it still was just Winston, Leon, and him.

Leon hadn't said much on the way over from Allentown. He'd established Rick's age, of course, and made the usual remark Rick had come to expect about looking younger than that. He had asked about relatives and about Rick's Christmas and New Years plans—and he'd made clear to Rick that he was gay, no surprise to Rick, and an exclusive top, no surprise to Rick either—but after a while the snow had required his full attention in navigating the increasingly slick streets. He'd done no more than grunted at Rick's several suggestions that they turn back.

As sort of a hint, Rick asked Leon if he lived alone, but Leon hadn't answered that. It certainly wouldn't do for Rick to bring anyone home with him in a snowstorm.

Rick's mind had wandered, though, to thoughts of them getting stuck in a snow bank and Leon doing him here in the truck cab, with the radio playing cheery Christmas carols. That thought had held over until they reached Winston's place, a large ground-floor apartment in an imposing old town house in the old part of Bethlehem, the area all lit up and decorated for Christmas as would be expected in a town named what it was and inhabited by rich, competitive people.

The thought of Leon doing him in the truck cab held until they arrived, so, of course, Rick was hard inside his tight jeans—and of course Winston had seen that right off and, no doubt, decided from the get go that Rick was going to let Winston lay him.

Everything Winston was doing was operating from that premise.

"You don't want to go yet," Winston said. "Not sure you and Leon can even go now until morning. Does that upset you?"

"Probably means the other guys won't make it here for the party either," Rick answered, evasively. "You said you were having some of the guys from the gym over for the party."

"I said a few. There are three of us. Leon, you, and me. That's a few of the guys from the gym."

He didn't actually say he hadn't invited anyone else, but Rick got the message that they weren't expecting anyone else. "Well, if Leon thinks we can still—"

"You know, you have a perfectly shaped mouth," Winston said, interrupting. He moved a finger to Rick's lips and rubbed across them. Instinctively, Rick let his lips open, and Winston pressed a thumb inside. They held there for a few seconds.

"Are you going to let me kiss you?"

"Yes," Rick answered in a low, trembly voice. Not in his best diction, though, with a man's plump thumb in his mouth. What could he say? Winston was a god compared to what Rick usually dealt in. And who was he kidding? He knew he'd come here to be fucked. He knew from the way Winston had been acting since they'd arrived that the man was going to do more than just kiss him. And there was Leon sitting over there in that club chair next to the blinking Christmas tree too. Unless he was just a watcher, Rick knew Leon was going to more than kiss him too. Rick had actually dreamed about it in the truck on the way over.

Coming out of the long, sensual kiss, Winston resumed tracing the curve of Rick's lips with the thumb that had already been inside. "Such beautiful lips. You know what else those beautiful lips would be great for?"

"What?"

Winston's free hand pulled a thick wallet out from somewhere in his loose lounge pants. He slapped it down on the coffee table in front of them. The snap almost made Rick waken from the lethargy the strong drinks had floated him into, but not quite.

The wallet was thick with bills. Winston obviously wanted Rick to see that it was. He opened it with his fingers and took two fifties out, laying them side by side on the coffee table.

"I'll bet those beautiful lips of yours give divine blow jobs. The guys at the gym tell me you give good blow jobs. First me and then Leon over there."

Winston's hands went to the back of Rick's head and guided him down as Rick turned in the sofa and sank to his knees between Winston's spread legs. Somehow the man's fly had gotten open already, and a long, long, long—not terribly thick—but really long and erect cock was curving up from a trimmed, curly haired black bush.

When Rick was done with Leon's cock too—with Leon sitting mostly impassive but grunting his pleasure— Rick moved his jaw around to make sure he still could do it. Leon was hung like a horse—or something larger, although Rick couldn't think what had a bigger cock than a horse. Hung like an elephant didn't sound quite right. Rick had known Leon was hung from the peeking he'd done in the shower room at the gym. He looked over to Winston who was busy laying out several lines of white powder on a sheet of paper on the coffee table.

When Winston looked up, he motioned Rick back to the corner of the sofa. "A jaw-breaking giant, isn't he?" he asked with a smile. He didn't wait for a reply, though. He was crowding Rick into the corner of the sofa again, pulling Rick's T-shirt over his head and, after a deep kiss on the mouth, moving his mouth down Rick's smooth chest, while he unsnapped and unzipped Rick's jeans and flared the fly open.

"Um, came for more than giving blow jobs, didn't we?" he murmured as he discovered that Rick wasn't wearing briefs. Rick threw he head back over the arm of the sofa, gasped for breath, and moaned, as Winston sucked hard on his bulb and then glided his lips down the shaft and started to suck Rick off. Rick drifted off into wonderland, moving his hips slowly against Winston's face. The blow job was maybe the most expert one he'd ever had. He was absorbing pointers left and right.

When Winston was done, he sat up on the sofa and looked over at Leon. "Want a snort?" he asked.

Leon demurred with a shake of his head, not changing expression at all. He was trouserless now, though, his huge dong arching out between his spread legs, drooping toward the floor from the heaviness of the bulb.

"You?" Winston asked Rick, turning to him. "It's Christmas. A snowy Christmas present for you?"

Rick, his head already in a muddle, sank to his knees at the table and took the paper straw Winston was handing him. He'd never done anything hard, but he'd always been curious. And it was Christmas.

* * * *

Winston was leaning over Rick's torso in the corner of the sofa. Rick was naked. There hadn't been anything for him to lose except the jeans off his legs and his sandals when he'd taken his first snort, but he had no idea when he'd lost those. Winston was still wearing his lounge pants, but his cock, throbbingly erect, was jutting out of them. Rick had only snorted one line, but even that was making it hard for him to concentrate. Thus far Winston had snorted two, with negligible effect. Rick hadn't done anything but pot before, and rarely that. It was out of his price range and had always been supplied by someone who was going to lay him.

That was exactly what was happening now. Winston was getting ready to lay Rick. He'd just pulled four hundred-dollar bills out of his fat wallet and stuffed the money in the pocket of Rick's jeans, now puddled on the floor between the front of the sofa and the coffee table. The money for the blow jobs had already been stuffed in a jeans pocket. Winston went out of his way to show that he was paying for this.

"Two hundred for me; the other two hundred for Leon when I'm done. Anything we want."

Rick just lolled his head, a half smile on his face. He didn't see any need to answer. Winston didn't seem to need an answer.

Winston started slow, lifting Rick's long, finely muscled right leg that had been trapped between Winston's side and the back of the sofa and kissing and licking up Rick's leg, whispering to him how nice and long the leg was. Rick watched him with a glazed smile on his face while Winston kissed and sucked his toes.

Rick thought they'd reached the main event when Winston turned him over sideways in the sofa, his knees pushing into the cushions under the sheet Winston had covered the end of the sofa with to keep the sofa clean. Rick's chest rested on the cool leather of the sofa arm. He let his head and arms hang down over the side. He was so mellowed out, despite what he anticipated was going to happen now, that he could have dozed off.

He might have dozed off, if Leon hadn't appeared at the side of the couch, lifting Rick's head by the hair, and presented his cock for sucking while Winston ran his hands over Rick's buttocks, spread the butt cheeks, and blew on Rick's hole.

Winston wasn't ready to mount him yet. His lips and tongue went to Rick's asshole and Winston started to open the young blond up. Rick moaned, a moan that segued into a deep groan, muffled by Leon's thick staff moving in and out of his open mouth, as Winston grabbed and squeezed, rolled, and distended Rick's balls while he rimmed his asshole.

Rick came for the second time that night. He seemed to be losing all control of that and would be coming easily again and again throughout the night, until his balls were aching a dull ache of being milked dry and then milked again.

Rick gagged as Leon creamed his tonsils. The black bull withdrew, and Winston turned Rick on his back against the sofa arm again, stuffing a pillow under the small of Rick's back so that his ass was elevated. Winston twisted to hover over Rick's torso. Rick's left leg was bent and reached his jeans on the floor in front of the sofa. His right leg was raised and trapped between Winston's left side and the back of the sofa. Winston's right leg was also bent, his foot buried in Rick's jeans. He'd use that foot for leverage in his thrusting.

Winston placed his forehead on Rick's and looked into Rick's glazy eyes. "It's Christmas. I'm Santa. And I'm coming down your chimney now." His little laugh at his own joke preceded the long, long journey of his cock up into Rick's channel. It was a slow sinking, with Winston glaring into Rick's eyes, watching for every expression

Rick showed. He was fisting the back of Rick's head with his left hand and had the fist of the right hand pressed into the side of the sofa arm, keeping Rick in place. The cock slowly came out to where only the bulb was encased and then a long glide in. Again and again. Long, slow glides, with Rick quivering and sighing with each withdrawal, arching his back and moaning with each long sinking in. Winston took his time, savoring the fuck of the beautiful, young two-hundred-dollar blond man. If only the honeypot realized what some men would pay for his ass.

Rick savored it too. He wasn't being passive. He got his right heel buried in the sofa cushion and his left heel in the carpeting in front of the sofa and used the leverage of these to lift his pelvis up to meet the slide of the cock deep inside him and then lower his pelvis as the cock withdrew, using every inch of the long cock to caress his passage walls. There was nothing quick or furtive or insistent about this fuck. Rick had never been fucked as sensually as this before. By such a hot man with such control. "Yes, yes," he murmured. "Like that, deep. Yes, fuck me like that."

"You want it, don't you?" Winston murmured.

"Oh, shit yes, give me more," Rick whispered.

The palms of his hands went to Winston's butt cheeks and he helped, with slight pressure on the buttocks, the slow, deep fuck. Winston had the best-looking, most perfectly formed body of a man who had ever fucked him. And the long cock was taking him slow and easy. It was reaching deeper than Rick could remember before, but was thin enough that it didn't tax his channel walls. They were shimmering from the attention, undulating over the long shaft as it glided in and out, in and out.

This went on for a good ten minutes, Rick reluctant to do anything to turn what Winston was doing

73

in his channel into anything else. But he felt Winston trembling and picking up the pace. Rick moved one hand to his own cock and stroked it. The other hand moved farther up Winston's back, to his shoulder blade. Winston was throwing his head back, using the leverage of his foot to make the thrusting stronger.

Winston's heaving chest was in Rick's face, the gold medallion knocking against Rick's chin and cheek. Those long, plump nipples in the wide aureoles were swimming before Rick's face and he lifted his head to one of them, nipped it with his teeth, which elicited a shudder and a deeper than usual thrust of the cock, and he began sucking on it. And then the other. Winston was breathing heavily, muttering under his breath, stroking harder, deeper, faster.

Rick took the nuisance gold medallion in his mouth and sucked on it, if only to keep it from knocking against his face. His pelvis was moving fast too, keeping up with the rhythm of the fuck. His head snapped back, the medallion falling out of his mouth and he cried out to the ceiling as he ejaculated up Winston's sternum.

Ten more fast, deep strokes, and Winston too tightened, held, and then creamed Rick deep with three strong spurts of cum.

"That was nice. You take fuck good," Winston said, as he straightened up, sank to his knees at the coffee table, and snorted another line of white powder.

All this time Leon had been sitting, crouched and overflowing the club chair at the other end of the room next to the Christmas tree. He was fully naked now, a magnificent gorilla dwarfing the piece of furniture. His eyes slitted, keeping his huge cock erect with his hand, while he watched Winston fuck Rick. The tension in him was palpable. He seemed ready to spring at any second.

He wasn't forced to wait.

Winston stood up. "Gotta take a piss. Snort another hit, Rick. You earned it. You did good. Give me a rest and I'll do you again."

Rick moaned. He could sure use a rest after a fuck like that himself.

Winston was heading for a corridor that evidently led back to bedrooms when he turned around and spoke to Leon. "He's all yours now, Leon. It'll take me some time to recharge. Fuck him good."

Rick had already sunk down to the coffee table and had the straw to his nose. He only had time for a quarter of a line when Leon was there, pulling him up, taking him back to the club chair. Who would have known a man that big could move so fast? Of course he was a semipro football player, paid to run fast with the ball. Tonight he was running with two.

Rick did a good bit of screaming, not all of it in the nature of asking for more of what he was getting—but enough of that not to prompt Leon to stop—as Leon had him sitting in his lap, facing him, Rick's legs were hooked over the arms of the chair, Leon grasped Rick by the waist and pulled him on and off the monster cock, as Rick helplessly arched back, his head touching the floor and his elbows digging into the carpet, trying to hold himself as steady as he could.

Rick moaned and groaned at the brutal taking, Leon twice the man Winston was in cock girth, although not nearly as long. It didn't matter. Rick's channel walls didn't give a damn. They were getting the workout of their life in terms of trying to accommodate the rapidly churning thrusts of the cock.

Rick came again, weakly, with no aid of a hand, and endured several more gloriously taxing minutes of being pulled and pushed brutally on the big, black cock, Leon's massive, muscular chest glistening from the sweat of his efforts, until Leon's cum mingled with Winston's inside Rick's channel. Only two blasts of cum, but blasts they were that rumbled on for several seconds.

Rick lay there, still skewered, breathing heavily and moaning deeply, but smiling a big smile. Leon had worked up a bit of a sweat but his breathing was regular.

"Would you believe the Eagles are still playing tonight," Winston said from across the room. "Turns out the game is in New Orleans, not Philly, which has got to be under three feet of snow, just like us. Come on back to the den and we'll watch the second half, Leon. Grab a beer from the fridge on your way."

Rick was pushed off Leon's lap and onto the floor, where the young blond lay for the next hour and half, still panting, reliving the two fucks by the first-rate studs, huddled there next to the Christmas tree with the irritating flashing lights. Wondering if *he'd* ever be offered another beer.

\* \* \* \*

Leon was the first one back into the living room. He leaned down, scooped Rick up, threw him over his shoulder, and walked down the corridor Winston had disappeared down earlier. He was searching for, and found, a room with a bed, a king-sized one.

When Winston joined them, Leon had Rick on his cock again. Leon was sitting on the end of the bed, feet flat on the floor, thighs held tight together. Rick, facing away from him, was suspended in front of the black bull. Rick's torso was jutting out over the carpet at the end of the bed like a figurehead on the prow of a sailing vessel. His long legs were flared back on each side of Leon's hips, and his toes were pressed into the bedspread. Leon was holding Rick suspended in front of him by grasping the wrists of Ricks swept-back arms. Leon was using this grip to pull Rick on and off his cock.

Rick's cock was caught, tight, between Leon's thighs, and Leon was rubbing his thighs together and giving Rick's cock a good rub in the process.

In coming weeks, Rick was going to find that Leon had an inventive way to take him each time. Christmas Eve was only the beginning of Leon fucking Rick.

Winston watched for a while—until he saw Leon jerk and exclaim and Rick's eyes go wide at the flooding of his ass.

"Want another beer?"

"Sure," Leon answered, once again letting Rick's heaving body sink to the carpet below.

Rick wasn't offered one. They were gone for maybe fifteen minutes, time enough for Leon to recharge, as was evident from the state of his cock when they reentered the room.

Winston had three hundred-dollar bills in one hand, and Rick's jeans in the other. Rick watched in panting anticipation as Winston stuffed the bills in a pocket of the jeans.

"It's after midnight. Christmas morning. Time for presents. Leon and I discussed it, and we decided our present will be to share you."

Rick groaned a deep groan and threw an arm over his face as if to make the world go away. But the thought excited him too. He'd heard about doubling but never had done it. He'd always assumed he'd do it someday. It hadn't been a question. Merry Christmas.

Today was Rick's day.

They worked him together, standing, Rick wedged between them, his back pressing into Winston's chest, his head buried into the hollow of Winston's shoulder. He was facing the glistening, black, muscular chest of Leon. His legs were bent, hung on Leon's hips and bulbous buttocks. All three of them were straining. Leon and Winston to keep their cocks inside him and pumping;

Rick in not passing out. Winston was holding a small bottle of poppers under Rick's nose, encouraging him to inhale, keeping him conscious.

"You don't want to miss any of this, sweet pea," he mumbled.

Leon started flowing first, which triggered Winston's spurts. Rick had already come twice.

Late in the night, Rick woke up lying on the bed between the two snoring men. He worked his way out from a tangle of their arms, padded to the bathroom, and took a leak. He checked for damage as he walked, finding nothing unbearable. He thought about the experience, deciding that it might have been the best Christmas he'd ever had. The Christmas of 1974. He wondered how long he'd remember it. Probably for a good long time. Two hot studs who knew what they were doing—and even paid for it.

Two hunks, each with special talents. Both out of his league. Doing things to him he'd dreamed of experiencing but never had the balls to volunteer for. Except he'd volunteered for this. He'd come prepared to be fucked. He'd come prepared to be gangbanged. This had been better than that—and more profitable.

How profitable, he didn't know. Hundreds of dollars, though. Close to a thousand. More than he could put aside in a string of months. He tried to figure it out in his mind, but his brain felt like a handful of sparklers were going off inside.

His padding took him into the living room. The tree was flashing away. Somehow it didn't bother him now. It seemed to be in synch with the flashing going on inside his head. There was still half a line of powder on the coffee table. He bent over it, picked up the straw, and snorted up the white powder.

Returning to the bedroom, he couldn't walk a straight line—kept bouncing off the walls on each side.

In the bed, he rolled Winston over on his back. He stripped off those damned Christmas lounging pants. Winston swam into consciousness realizing he was being given a blow job. With a low laugh, he reached down, pulled Rick up his body and settled the young blond's channel on his cock. Rick slowly rode him, palming Winston's pecs and thumbing at the man's nipples. Winston propped his head up on his bent arms and looked up at Rick with slitted eyes and a somewhat bemused smile.

"I'm not paying for this, you know," Winston whispered.

"Right," Rick answered. "A Christmas present. Wanted you know that I appreciated the party."

Winston unwound the arm on the side where Leon was sleeping, stretched out on the bed, facing the fucking pair, and punched the big black in the bicep. "Hey, Leon, wake up. The sweet pea is going to give us a Christmas present."

Leon's eyes opened and he started hardening up immediately from what he saw.

This time Winston asked. "Hey, kid, OK with you? Both of us again?"

"Why the hell not?" Rick answered.

Leon came into position behind Rick; pushed Rick's torso over onto Winston's chest, causing Rick's buttocks to roll up; and started pushing his cock into the hole, gliding in on top of Winston's. Rick was so hopped up on the drug that he opened right up for it. Winston pushed the nozzle of a popper bottle up one of Rick's nostrils. Rick inhaled, which relaxed him and his channel further.

When Rick wandered back from the next time he got up to take a piss, he found the two of them going at it. Surprised, he dropped his butt into a chair and watched Leon languidly fucking Winston in a side split, Leon holding Winston close to his chest, with an arm around his torso, Winston's buttocks jutted back into Leon's groin, and Leon holding Winston's right leg up with his right hand. Leon's thick cock was buried to the root in Winston's ass, and then not, and then again.

Rick had wondered what the arrangement here was, Winston and Leon doing him together, that being the mix of this party, Winston being the one doling out all of the cash. Leon obviously was Alpha dog here. It figured.

Taking Rick home late in the morning, the streets still covered with snow, but not badly so, Leon pulled over into a deserted park parking lot and Rick got the fuck in the cab of the truck that he'd dreamed about what seemed to be eons ago. After Rick's face had been pushed down into Leon's lap in the driver's seat to suck the big black hard, Leon scooted over to the passenger seat, put Rick on his cock, facing the dashboard, bent Rick over to where the top of his head and both of his fists were pressed into the floor carpeting and slammed Rick's channel hard up and down and back and forth and around on the monster cock. With Leon it was always a different position—no doubt part of what the other gym attendants twittered about. And Leon never paid. He never had to.

Rick's only regret, when he got home to his room the next afternoon with just a scrawny fake tree on his desk, with no lights on it at all, flashing or otherwise, was that, try as he might, he couldn't half remember what he'd done on Christmas Eve and why it had been so special. He only knew it had been something special. And what in the hell had he done to earn all the money he found in his jeans pockets? The soreness of his body *did* tell him he'd earned it. The liquor and drugs may have taken away a big chunk of his memory, but they'd also made him relaxed enough to take two cocks together—twice.

He couldn't quite remember that had happened—although he clearly remembered Leon in the cab of his truck this morning. He thought much of the rest of it had been a fantasy. But a good one. He decided he wanted to try that double penetration position he had imagined them doing on him some day.

# THE BLIND DATE

"Whoa, is that a photo you're shredding on your dart board?"

"Yeah, what's it to you?" Lionel Nicks walked over to the board, took the five darts out, and went back to the other side of the bar in his apartment.

"Peace, big guy. I was just asking." Andre Sanders took a closer look at the photo. "Say, isn't that Devin? Your Devin? You guys no longer a couple?" He didn't bother not sounding hopeful.

"Devin, dear Devin, decided we should cool it. Should see other people. Said he wanted to date around. That we just weren't clicking right. Stand away, if you don't want to be needled."

Andre backed off from the board as Lionel scored a hit right between Devin's eyes.

"I'd like to see that Devin gets a date around or two he'd never forget." Zing went another dart.

Andre thought for a moment. "I might be able to help with that . . . if . . ."

"If what, Andre?"

"Seeing as how you two aren't an item anymore—that you're as free now as Devin is . . . well, you know I was after you to fuck me before you hooked up with Devin and claimed a one-and-only arrangement. I'm still interested. And, you know, I'm the equipment manager of the Triangle Nighthawks."

"Yeah, how does being a semipro football team's equipment manager have anything to do with this?"

Andre told him.

\* \* \* \*

Andre had told Devin the guy would meet him at the Tracks bar out on the edge of Benson, near the stadium where the North Carolina league semipro football team, the Triangle Nighthawks, played. A wide receiver for the rival East Carolina Rams who was a friend of Andre's was in town to scout the Nighthawks in a game and had asked Andre not only to get him tickets to the game on the sly—Andre shouldn't be helping a rival team—but also to line up a date to go to the game with him. Andre well knew the guy's preferences. Andre's ass still hurt from that knowing.

"I heard you were dating and open to a blind date," he said when he pitched Devin about going out on a blind date with one of his friends.

"Yeah, I might be interested. I'd just meet him at the game and sit with him?"

"He'd stand you a dinner too," Andre said. "He'd meet you at Tracks and take you to dinner before the game."

"OK, that sounds cool."

"He's black. I may have forgotten to mention that. You have any trouble having a blind date with a black guy?" Andre was black. What could Devin say, no matter what he felt, if he didn't want to insult Andre? Truth be told he hadn't thought about how he should feel about being seen with a black guy.

"No, I guess not. Haven't dated a black guy before. But a drink, dinner, and the game? No problem."

"Sure. That's it."

When Devin entered Tracks, he was wondering if he'd recognize the guy. The bar was pretty crowded—mostly with other guys going to the game—almost all guys. It was a gay bar. He shouldn't have worried about picking him out, though. A black guy was rising—and rising and rising—from a table and waving to him. Andre had said he'd give a photo of Devin to the guy—in fact, he had done so in arranging the blind date with the guy. Devin hadn't been shown a photo of his blind date, but he had no trouble picking him out of the crowd.

The football player, Marcus Black, was hard to miss and couldn't have been more different from Devin. Marcus was at least ten inches taller than Devin's five foot seven, and seemingly as wide across the chest as Devin was tall. And he was built like a Sherman tank, coming in at close to two-hundred pounds, at the top of the range for a wide receiver. He outweighed a willowy, twinky Devin, with his curly blond hair and face more pretty than handsome by fifty-five pounds. Devin felt like a dwarf in coming up beside him. His hand disappeared in Marcus' at the handshake, and he steeled himself for the grasp to be crushing. But it wasn't. It was firm enough, but it also was gentle—almost caressing.

"Devin?" The smile was broad, friendly. The face had been beaten about but had arrived into something that was ruggedly handsome and honest. The voice a smooth baritone, promising cultured diction. Devin had been told Marcus hailed from the tidewater of Virginia and had graduated from the posh College of William and Mary, in colonial Williamsburg, but he was still surprised at how smooth and sophisticated the man appeared to be.

He was elegantly dressed too. Yet another surprise. Devin hadn't been sure how to dress for a minor league football game in the summer. Devin went to concerts and plays. He watched pro football games on TV just like everyone else, but he did it mainly to watch the big bruisers' butts in their tight-fitting football pants. It's not that Devin was a pansy—not by any means. He worked out, he worked hard at looking clean cut. He just was a happy bottom in private. Not a promiscuous one, though—he'd been satisfied with Lionel at the start. He wasn't sure what had made him a little restless. It could have been the writing he'd been doing—and managing to sell through an erotic publisher.

So, when it came to dress, Devin had decided to wear khakis and a checked sports shirt and loafers without socks. He'd brought a sweater as he didn't know if it would turn cool in the stadium in the evening. He had this reversed on his back, with the sweater arms tied across his chest. For him, preppy was always in season. If it was preppy from the sixties, he didn't care. He knew he looked cool and twinky.

He'd half expected Marcus to come in cutoff jeans and a sweatshirt. But he was wearing pressed slacks, a fitted white shirt that obviously was expensive, and a camel-hair sports coat. He had on boots, but they were black shiny leather polished to a mirror sheen and rose just a bit higher than his ankles. Of course his feet were enormous—boats. As was everything else about him—his hands, his thighs in the tailored slacks, the bulges of his chest and biceps . . . and the bulge at his crotch. But he had the grace of a dancer at the same time, an attribute, Devin assumed, of having to dance down the football field and pull in a guided missile. One would think that his dreadlocks, the tips of which reached his shoulders and were capped with gold metal clips, would belie the rest of his appearance, but the whole package was so neat that they seemed a natural accompaniment.

They sat, chatting, over their drinks, at the table. Devin had expected beer, but Marcus ordered a vodka martini, so he felt comfortable enough to order a

Manhattan on the rocks. He normally would have been embarrassed to do so in the presence of someone he didn't know well, but he felt completely comfortable in ordering a cocktail in this situation. In fact, his whole expectation of what going on a blind date with a black football player would be like was being exploded.

"So, I hear you are a hairdresser."

"Yes," Devin answered, ready for the inevitable follow-on stereotyping comments. Maybe he'd been wrong to order a Manhattan.

"That must pay well, and is probably a pretty creative field," Marcus said without a hint of sarcasm or judgment in his voice. "I wouldn't have imagined you to be that if I just saw you on the street."

"Oh, what would you think I was?" Devin asked. No, he knew he didn't appear effeminate. No he didn't have the mannerisms and flamboyance everyone seemed to expect of a gay hairdresser. Still, here he was, drinking a Manhattan.

"Oh, a college student, or maybe a young stage actor or male model. Andre said you were twenty. I can hardly believe it, seeing you in person."

So, what was he saying, Devin wondered—that Devin looked too young to be in a bar and Marcus might be nabbed for buying liquor for a minor? Or was he saying he liked them young enough to seem illegal? From looking into Marcus' face, he couldn't get a hint that this wasn't more than just ice-breaking chit chat.

"Yes, all of twenty," he answered. "Twenty and a couple of weeks."

"I'm twenty-eight. Getting old for football. If I don't make it up to the pros this season, I might have to hang up that dream."

"And do what?"

"I have an architectural degree and my family has a construction firm in its portfolio. I have a financial

86

parachute. That makes pursuing the dream of football easier."

"Don't you have to go longer than normal for a degree like that? Isn't that like an advanced degree?"

"Yes, I went for six years."

"Wow." He wasn't anything like Devin had imagined. His speech had been as sophisticated as Devin first thought when he heard him speak. And his manners were impeccable. His hands might be massive, but his fingernails were clean and manicured. Devin worked in a beauty salon. He always looked at the fingernails. Lionel chewed his. And the hands were so expressive. Devin had visions of them stroking his forearm—he'd wondered whether the blind date would be all over him. This wasn't at all what he expected. He almost wished . . .

"Where were you thinking of eating dinner?" Marcus asked.

"I hadn't thought," Devin answered. "Andre said you'd pick someplace." A steak house, Devin now wondered. He'd originally thought it probably would be McDonalds or KFC.

"I know of a Japanese restaurant that serves the best tempura. Sushi too, if that's your interest."

"Tempera would be fine," Devin said. More than fine.

Devin had taken a taxi to Tracks because Andre said Marcus had a car. It turned out not to be the pickup truck Devin expected. It was a Pontiac Solstice, a sleek sports car that was out of production—the whole company was out of business. But the Solstice was a collector's item now.

"How do you keep this honey on the road?" Devin asked, as he entered the car. The inside was impeccably clean. Devin doubted that a take-out meal had ever seen the inside of this vehicle.

"My family owned a Pontiac dealership too," Marcus said. "Kept enough parts for a Solstice to keep this one going. I worked there for years and can maintain the car myself."

When they both were in the car, Marcus looked over at Devin. Would he or wouldn't he, Devin wondered. They were finally alone; if a blind date was interested in anything at the end of the date, this, Devin thought, would be a time to signal that.

Marcus would, in a much more understated way than Devin thought might be the case when they were alone.

"Would you mind?" Marcus asked, leaning a bit into the passenger side of the car and putting an arm on the top of the seat behind Devin's head. "You are just so much more than I expected."

Devin leaned a bit in acceptance toward Marcus, who cupped his chin lightly and came in for a gentle kiss on the lips. "Umm, that was nice, sweet," he murmured. He lingered for a moment looking into Devin's eyes, his thumb tracing the curve of Devin's lower lip. Devin fought the urge to open his mouth and pull the thumb in.

But before that naturally could happen Marcus twisted back to face the windshield, pulled on driving gloves, and turned to concentrating on his driving. He drove fast and unexpectedly aggressively, but expertly. In total control. Devin felt totally safe in the man's hands.

The perfect gentleman, Devin thought. The signal the Devin got was that Marcus would continue to be the perfect gentleman—that he wasn't really all that interested in anything beyond having company for the evening, with just a hint of sensuality so that Devin wouldn't feel rejected. This was just going to be a companionable evening.

The football game was mostly business with Marcus. It's what he had come here for. Marcus was there for a purpose, but he also paid attention to Devin, explaining the intricacies of this and that. He didn't treat Devin like an idiot, though. He even took time to ask about the concerts and plays Devin went to—and didn't give a sour look when Devin mentioned opera and ballet. Their conversation at dinner had centered on the arts, and Marcus seemed to know as much about many aspects of that as Devin did.

After the game, they went back to Tracks for another drink and some dancing. A lot of the guys on the dance floor tried to cut in for Marcus' attention, but he politely waved them off and concentrated on Devin.

At the entrance to Devin's apartment building, when Devin assumed it would be another brief, sweet kiss, and the end of a tame, but surprising and interesting blind date, he was proved right about the kiss, but not about the rest.

Pulling away from a sweet, short kiss, Marcus looked Devin directly in the eye and said, "May I come in for a few minutes? Maybe a drink?"

"A few minutes? A drink?"

"Or maybe something more? I think you're really cute. And I think we hit it off fine. You know I'd like to . . . with you . . . to you."

"And?" Devin whispered.

"On you . . . in you. Inside you. I could take good care of you, baby. Don't you want to feel me inside you?" He looked like a little hopeful puppy dog. His voice, the smooth baritone, was so soft spoken that the words themselves—the unmistakable sexual intent of them—were muted. He had an arm behind Devin again, the fingers of that hand pressing into Devin's shoulder. And he was tracing Devin's lower lip lightly with a thumb of the other hand, having taken his driving glove off first.

Devin sighed. He had originally thought it would come to this—or strongly suspected it would, although he had been beginning to question that. Question it enough to maybe be slightly disappointed it might not become a choice, a possibility.

He leaned forward and they kissed sweetly again, with Devin pulling away just as Marcus' lips were pressing his to open and Devin felt the flicker of a tongue between his lips.

"You can come in . . . for a bit. We'll see."

"Is that a yes? I want to fuck you."

"That's a we'll see how it goes," Devin said, as he opened the passenger door and rolled out of the sports car. He still didn't know himself. It was a blind date, a first meeting. He was attracted—hell, more like aching for him, while still being scared of the size of him. But he didn't want to seem to be a pushover. The guy was cultured and sensitive. Surprisingly so. And he was big and black. It was new, possibly dangerous ground for Devin.

Devin was returning from his kitchen with two glasses of white wine—what they'd settled on that Devin could supply—and almost dropped the glasses.

Marcus was sitting on the sofa—naked. His clothes were neatly folded on a nearby chair, his polished boots lined up perfectly under the chair. A bigger shock than that he was naked was that he didn't really look naked. In his clothes he had looked clean cut. His nakedness revealed that his body was a riot of tattoo patterning and coloring on nearly every square inch of skin that had been covered by his clothes. He had suddenly transformed from a southern gentlemen—albeit a black one—to a primeval native. And there was no hiding that he was enormously erect or that there was a thick silver Prince Albert ring in the bulb of his cock.

His demeanor made the extraordinary change to the wild side as well.

"Come here, baby," he commanded, a harder edge to his voice than Devin had heard before.

In a trance, Devin put the wine glasses down on the dining room table he was standing beside, spilling both, his hands were trembling so badly. He took one tentative step toward the sofa, confused and in shock.

"I said come here," Marcus growled. "How did you think this fucking date was going to end? Been thinking of getting inside your sweet little ass since Andre showed me that nude photo of you."

Nude photo? What nude photo? No one but Lionel had nude photos of him. Without thinking, Devin had moved close enough for Marcus to reach out, grab him by the wrist, and pull him down on his knees between the black footballer's spread thighs. His cock was enormous. It didn't look exceptionally thick only because it was so long. And hard. It was only because it nearly dislocated Devin's jaw that he realized it was thick too.

Devin was made to deep throat it and hold, again and again, gagging and fighting for breath, while Marcus chanted "Take it, take it, take all of it" in a raspy growl. The thick PA ring in the cock head clicked against Devin's teeth until the bulb got to the back of his throat. Marcus held Devin's head between his massive hands like a vice and pulled his face on and off the cock again and again. Then Marcus was forcing Devin to deep throat and hold until Devin was gagging. Release, and then again. Pulling out after more than ten minutes of this, he creamed Devin's cheek and eyelids, up into the blond curl that kept falling over Devin's forehead. He came in for a brutal kiss and licked the cum off the still-shocked young man's face.

Marcus came up off the sofa, pulled Devin off his knees and quickly stripped him of his clothes. Devin, working his jaw to ensure that it wasn't unhinged, remained numb to what was happening to him and docile as the items were shed and thrown haphazardly to the side. How does a small twink like Devin fight off two-hundred pounds of black bruiser anyway?

Having gotten Devin naked and done a bit of groping and fondling—enough to have Devin, aware of what came next, moaning and whimpering, "Oh, God, be good to me; don't split me," Marcus slung him, belly down over the back of the sofa. Devin's arms and head hung defenselessly, uselessly in the face of the size and weight difference between the two, toward the floor. He moaned and groaned as Marcus spread his butt cheeks apart and ate his ass out, muttering "Open it, open it, open to me." Other than Marcus' mutterings in that deep baritone of his, all Devin could hear was the clicking of the metal clips against each other at the ends of Marcus' swaying dreadlocks.

Devin grunted and groaned as Marcus reached through his legs and grabbed his balls, rolling and squeezing them, and then roughly milked the young blond's cock while slapping and biting his buttocks, thumping his hole with his fingers, digging his fingers into and tonguing his hole deeply, Marcus sharply commanding throughout that Devin "Relax, open to me, baby. We're gonna do this; you're gonna take me. You're gonna take it big. You're gonna love every inch of it." Devin writhed and moaned under the onslaught.

How could Devin relax to this assault on his privates? How could he take that monster cock? But then, miraculously, as Marcus tongued the hole deep and his milking of Devin's cock became rhythmic, less rough, and after Devin had released his cream with a jerk and a sigh, Devin did feel himself sighing, relaxing his passage, and moving his hips back rhythmically to meet the dig of the tongue.

This didn't last too long until Marcus was satisfied that Devin would take him—something Devin would never have imagined he could do, but that he did. Devin felt the weight of the two-hundred-pound muscular athlete crouch over him close as he was draped over the back of the sofa, and he let out a deep, rumbling cry as, preceded by the thick PA, Marcus' cock split the difference between the curves of Devin's butt cheeks and started its long journey up his passage. Marcus reached down, grabbed a handful of blond, curly hair on the back of Devin's head and pulled it hard toward him, arching Devin's back to him.

The fuck started off with a deep pounding, built up from there to the music of Marcus' thrashing dreadlock clips and Devin's plaintive cries of "Fuck me, fuck me, fuck me," involuntarily pulled from him by the intensity of the attack and the depth of the digging cock, and only settled down into a rhythm of long, deep slides, after Devin was reduced to a whimpering rag doll under the relentless power of the big, black muscleman.

Half way through the fuck, Marcus latched the broad palm of one hand on one of Devin's pecs and grasped Devin's chin with the other one and held Devin tight into his muscular torso, Devin's cheek next to his, as he thrust up into Devin's channel, resuming the chant of "Take it, take it, take all of it" in Devin's ear. Devin dug his fingernails in the top edge of the sofa and held on for dear life.

Marcus took him hard, deep, swiftly, and at great length, while Devin moaned and whimpered, his begging for mercy turning into declarations of how totally he was being taken until it all subsided into gurgles and soft whimpering.

When Marcus filled out the bulb of his condom— Devin had long since come a second time—he remained plastered on Devin's back, running his hands over Devin's body and whispering what a cute little trick he was. About the time Devin thought that was all there was going to be to the assault, though, Marcus pulled away from him, slung Devin over his shoulder, and headed for the bedroom.

He put Devin on all fours on the bed, mounted him, and fucked him hard and fast to the music of his gyrating dreadlock clips to another ejaculation. As he felt the hard curve of the PA at his hole, reamed now to fit Marcus' requirements, Devin lowered his chest and cheek to the bedspread, presented his tail for a straight shot, widened the spread of his legs, stretched one arm out to grab a fistful of material to steady himself, reached under his belly with his other hand to fist his own cock, and, with a whimper, surrendered all to his master. Gripping Devin's hips between strong hands, Marcus pounded, pounded, pounded away inside his young blond prey, rightfully claiming victory. Meeting no resistance; taking no prisoners.

"Ah, yeah, good, a perfect fit now," Marcus muttered as he pumped. "That gets it now, doesn't it?" He could—and no doubt did—take Devin's low, drawn-out moaning as agreement.

Devin was so worn out by the second fucking that he just collapsed on the bed, softly moaning. His head and an arm hung over one side of the bed where the thrustings of the black giant's cock had moved his battered body. As Marcus rose off him, the black bull slapped him hard on the rump and cheerily exclaimed, "That was a good workout. Good date. A sweet, tight ass. Great little body. Takes a little work, but the hole opens up enough. Andre told me you were a good lay; he sure was right about that." After that favorable and cheerful assessment of the evening's work, he sauntered off to the adjoining bathroom to help himself to a shower.

"Not tight anymore," Devin murmured, with a deep groan.

After he'd dressed, once more becoming the Virginia gentlemen, Marcus briefly visited the bedroom, leaning over Devin's prone and still-trembling body, ruffled Devin's curly blond locks affectionately, and gave him a tender, lingering kiss on the back of the neck. This time, when Marcus rubbed a thumb lightly over Devin's lower lip, Devin pulled the thumb into his mouth and sucked it for a few seconds. To the victor go the spoils.

Devin waited to hear the front door to the apartment click shut before he dragged his bruised body off the bed, struggled over to his desk, turned on the computer, and started to work the keys.

* * * *

"It's you," Devin said, as, rubbing the sleep out of his eyes the next morning, he answered the door. "I thought you still had a key."

"I do," Lionel said. "But I didn't think we were on that ground of familiarity anymore."

There was something in his voice, something smug, that had Devin look sharply at him before he turned and padded toward the coffee pot in the kitchen. Lionel entered the apartment and shut the door behind him. He looked around for evidence of what he expected to see. Yes, the sofa looked like it had done battle and lost. He could see through the door to the bedroom that there'd been a frantic skirmish in there too. Devin was a neatnic, definitely neater than this, when left to himself.

"So, you said you wanted to date other guys. How is that working for you?" He sat on the sofa and gave a good sniff. Yep, smelled like sweat, musk, and lust. He smiled a little smile.

Devin came out of the kitchen carrying two cups of coffee. Looking around at him, Lionel saw the two wine glasses on the dining table—and the liquid spill. He smiled into his cup as he lifted it to his mouth.

He also saw that Devin grimaced as he moved and wasn't walking straight. Andre had told him about Marcus Black and how he dated—that he was hung like a horse and had a powerhouse thrust. Lionel almost felt sorry for Devin, but not really. The little prick had dumped him. Well, the little prick had found out how rough it could get out in the dating world.

"I'm doing just fine," Devin said, giving Lionel a level stare. He'd worked it out in the middle of the night. Marcus' connection to Andre. Andre's connection to Lionel. Lionel's pettiness—which was a big reason Devin left him—leaving him for that and because Lionel was a vanilla fucker. No excitement or testing with Lionel. Never had been. Never the feel of a breathtaking date. They might as well have been . . . married.

"In fact I had a date last night with a big black football player one and a half times my size and with a cock twice the size of yours. We had a great date and then he came home with me and fucked the stuffing out of me. I've been up for hours writing black bruiser on white twink fuck stories for an anthology for my publisher. I think he's going to love them."

"You're shitting me," Lionel said, setting his coffee cup down on the coffee table lest he spill it in his consternation. "You got banged hard by a black bull last night, and you aren't curled up in a fetal ball this morning?"

"Nope. Marcus is coming back to scout the Nighthawks' game next Saturday. We have a date to do it all over again. He agreed to stay the night this time and do me on the hour. He fucked me just the way I've been aching to be fucked. He really knows how to date a man."

It had been worth it—his little speech—to see the expression on Lionel's face. The most rewarding part was that it all was true. Marcus had called him on his cell from the Solstice fifteen minutes after he'd left, asking Devin for a follow-up date, and Devin had been quick as he could be to say yes

# Rain Check

Parker saw him walk into the hardware store again and work his way around the outer aisle. Parker was helping a customer pick out paint and wondered if the good-looking man would work his way over to Parker's station, being attracted to Parker, or if this was the hardware store he had always come to and Parker just hadn't noticed him before his visit the other day. Parker regretted that the stimulating exchange had gone south the last time Gabe had been in the store.

Gabe. That's right, Parker thought. The man had told him his name was Gabriel, but that he preferred being called Gabe. He was all the things that Parker found arousingly attractive in a man, and a couple of things Parker found scarily attractive too. He was older. Parker was twenty-five, but he'd always gone with an older man. He liked to be daddied. The man wasn't exactly old, though. Maybe in his thirties. And he was good looking and built strong. He'd shown Parker a nice, easy smile when they'd talked before and the man had had an easy way of moving in to show interest in Parker—if, indeed, that was what he'd done. Under the circumstances Parker was a bit confused and more than a bit afraid.

The scary attractions were that Gabriel—if that's what his name really was—was black and he had a colored right sleeve tattoo that peeked out below the sleeve line of the polo shirt he had been wearing. A black sex partner and one with extensive tattooing were both worlds beyond anywhere Parker had ever gone.

There weren't that many black people who came to this small beach town—and practically none of them lived in this area—and tattoos. The combination spelled danger and taboo in Parker's mind. He kept more to a group of friends who enjoyed girlie talk and more talk than action, although all had experienced sex with men—or claimed they had. His experience and the experiences his friends talked about were usually with middle-aged businessmen coming into Gaucho on the sly for just a bit of sucking or, at the most, a quick fuck in the backseats of their cars in the dimly lit parking area. Something vanilla that Parker and his friends would feed on for weeks as they sat at a table together at Gaucho and shared coquettish stares with men bellied up to the bar.

The most flamboyant Parker got was that he occasionally had a "gone wild" Saturday night and danced on one of the poles at Gaucho for free drinks. He had a nice body, he knew, a dancer's body, and a face that was more pretty than handsome, And he was a favorite dancer for the Saturday night crowd at Gaucho. He usually had to be pretty pissed to dance the pole, though, as he wasn't the exhibitionist that some of his friends were. Truth be told, however, he was more in demand than any of his friends were.

Despite his shyness toward any man sniffing around him with any sense of danger or roughness to him, Parker had flirted with Gabe when he'd come into the store three days previously. Like today, Gabe had moved around the store, ostensibly looking at a variety of goods, but every time Parker thought to look in his direction, the black man would be looking at him—and smiling. And

Parker was smiling back. He couldn't help himself. The man just looked too attractive and arousing.

When Gabe finally came up to him that first time, it was to use a variation on a line that so many men on the make with Parker in the store used. But when Gabe said it, all sorts of bells and whistles of interest went off in Parker's mind. And not only in his mind; his body was telling him he was interested in this man too.

Parker had opened. "Can I help you? Were you interested in paint?" Parker worked mainly in the paint department and that's where he was standing at this moment.

"I already have an eight-inch screw driver, so I guess it's paint I'm looking for today, at least at the moment."

"Well, screw drivers are interesting, but what I can help you with is paint," Parker had answered. He'd added a little smile to convey that he understood the code Gabe was using and wasn't turning away from it.

"I really do need paint," Gabe had said. "I've just bought a small vacation house here at the beach and it's sadly in need of a coat or two of paint. So maybe you can help me with that for starters. My name's Gabe—short for Gabriel, by the way."

"For starters?" Parker asked. "And, umm, my name is Parker." He lifted his thumb to draw attention to the store name badge he was wearing. The guy had already made a point of looking at his name, so there was nothing untoward in giving it to him.

"Yes. Me being new here in the area maybe you could help with where the best place to go for this or that is. You look like you might know. But, the paint. I'm not sure what colors I need—what would fit in with the beach community here? Do you guys ever leave the store to help a customer choose something like the right paint? I think I need someone in the know here to actually look at the house."

"Yeah, we make house calls . . . sometimes," Parker said, thinking that the guy moved kind of fast, if he wasn't misinterpreting the conversation. It was obvious by the way the guy had been eyeballing him that he was interested. But, although Parker had almost involuntarily responded because the man was such a hunk, he was black and he had those tattoos. This wasn't Parker's style at all. And maybe moving fast was a cocky black thing that was something beyond the pace he could keep up with. Parker didn't want to be sending any false signals here that got him in too deep.

"But obviously not today—not now," he answered. "It's raining like there's no tomorrow out there now."

"I see," Gabe said, turning and looking out of the plate glass windows at the front of the store as if he just now was noticing the rain outside. "So, maybe a rain check on that."

"Yeah, that would be wise," Parker answered.

"I was going to ask where there was a good place to pick up a beer in this town too. Rainy days are good for supporting the local taverns."

"We have all kinds of beer joints and bars here," Parker said. "It sort of depends on the kind of place you'd be comfortable in."

"I've heard of a place called Gaucho. That sounds like a comfortable place. I'm looking for a guys' place."

Parker snapped his eyes around to look into Gabe's face. And he saw that Gabe was looking pointedly at him. More signaling, and pretty clear signaling, Parker thought. Gaucho was a gay bar—the one where he sometimes danced the pole on Saturday nights. He looked Gabe over again, still finding him attractive and arousing, even though he knew he shouldn't. He was still trying to formulate what to say next, knowing he should send out the signal that he went with a different crowd. But he couldn't say he wasn't interested and be telling the truth. Gabe saved him the decision of what to say.

"I've already been in there—at Gaucho—on Saturday night. Liked what I saw. Wondered if that's the only bar of that kind around."

So, he knew. He knew before he even walked up to Parker. Parker had danced the pole at Gaucho on Saturday night. And the place had been packed and filled with cigarette smoke. This Gabe could have been in there while Parker was dancing the pole, and Parker could have missed seeing him while Gabe could hardly have missed seeing Parker dancing the pole.

"What time do you get off work?" Gabe asked. "You could take a look at my house and I could stand you a beer at Gaucho for your trouble."

But before Parker could answer—before he decided what he wanted to answer and reconciled that with what he knew he should answer—two things happened. First a woman drifted in who wanted a can of paint mixed to the color of her choice and was a bit pushy about being served right away, and, second, the family arrived. As Parker turned to the paint-seeking woman to tell her he'd be with her in a moment, out of the corner of his eye he caught Gabe turn and step back as a young black woman and two of what obviously were her—and Gabe's, as well—young kids showed up. The woman was closing an umbrella and the boy and girl were brushing rainwater off the slickers they were wearing. All three of them were gushing at Gabe about what they'd found in the variety store next door.

When Gabe had a moment to turn back to Parker to get an answer on when the work day was over for him—and evidently then to move into reiterating the offer of a drink at Gaucho—Parker had let the circumstance make the decision for him and had moved off with the woman customer toward the paint-mixing machine.

And here it was, three days later, and the man was moving around the store, ever closer to him, waiting for Parker to be finished mixing paint for another man. This time there was no evidence of Gabe's family.

When Gabe got to him, he politely stood to the side, paint cards in his hand, while Parker finished up with an older man who was looking askance at the hulking black Gabe with something of a mix of slight fear and disapproval in his face. This was an affluent beach town in the American south, where blacks had been confined to the service industries for generations and lived and shopped elsewhere. It only was in recent years that there were blacks affluent enough to be building summer homes here as well—and needing hardware stores such as this.

And admittedly, with his overpowering musculature and that tattoo design peeking out below the right sleeve of Gabe's polo shirt and also up on his neck on that side, Gabe could be seen to be somewhat intimidating.

"Yes, sir, may I help you?" Parker said as he finished with the older man and turned to Gabe.

"So, we're going to start from the beginning again?" Gabe asked, an easy smile on his face and amusement in his voice. "If so, I'll note that I already have an eight-inch—"

"Do you want those colors mixed up? Interior or exterior?" Parker broke in, indicating their conversation could be overheard by nodding his head toward the older man who was shuffling off toward the cash registers none to swiftly.

When he was gone, Gabe said, "Sorry. I don't really know if these are the colors I want. Something for the outside walls and something for the shutters and trim—something that the community here will not

102

criticize a black man for when painting his house. I thought you had agreed to come look at the house when it wasn't raining and advise me. It hasn't rained for two days. I gave you my phone number. I thought we were going to arrange for you to look at the house."

It was Parker's turn to say he was sorry.

"What is it? I thought we were doing well. The way you looked at me, I thought I had a chance. I know you dance at Gaucho, and I thought that meant you were gay. Not so?"

"Yes, I'm gay," Parker said.

"And again, the way you looked at me, I thought you were interested. Is it because I'm black?"

That was part of it, and because he was built football-player big and because of that tattooing. Just a whole different world. But Parker couldn't say that, because all of that was just as much why he'd given Gabe the interested looks he had—and why his body had reacted—and still was reacting—to the man as it was.

But there had been a more immediate reason. "I don't mess with married men—especially ones with young children. Sorry, that's just it."

"I'm not married. I don't have . . . oh, you saw Raisa and her kids the other day. Raisa's my sister. The kids couldn't wait to see the beach house I'd bought until after I'd gotten it all fixed up. They were just down for the day. They live up in Charleston. I'm not married. I'm not attached. I top men. And I fancy you. You dance a pole in the most sexy way and I saw you go into a back room at the bar with a man, so I thought . . . hell, if you let men fuck you, I'd like to be one of those men. Is that clear enough for you?"

"Yes," Parker said, casting his eyes down, automatically taking a subservient position to Gabe's dominance. And trembling in the bowing to the dominance.

"I'm sorry. Am I scaring you?"

"Yes, a little."

"But it excites you a little too, doesn't it?"

"Yes."

"Well, I don't want to leave the wrong impression. I don't bite. I won't hurt you. I don't fuck rough—unless it's something you want." As if to prove this point, Gabe took a step back.

Parker looked up into his face. "If you'll give me your address, we can arrange a time for me to come by and advise you on colors."

"And perhaps you'll come inside?"

"Perhaps."

"I checked with the manager on when this shift is over. I can wait the twenty minutes and we could go over together. I could drive you back to your car after we're done."

"Doesn't look like that will work today," Parker said, looking beyond Gabe toward the plate glass windows at the front of the store. "Looks like the rain has swept in again and is settling in for a while. I'll want to look at the house in the sunshine. And, well, I already have plans for after work today. Sorry."

"So, is this another no? A final no? I can live with that if so. Just tell me."

"No, it's not a no. It has to be another rain check, I guess. Give me your address. I'm off tomorrow. I can be there at 1:00 p.m. Sorry, I'm a late sleeper."

Gabe came in close then and put a hand on Parker's arm. It was the right hand and the movement caused his shirt sleeve to ride up higher, showing more of the swirling tattoo there in vibrant colors. Parker shuddered.

"If you let me, I can be very good to you," Gabe whispered. "I'll give it to you any way you like."

Parker shuddered again, his mind aswirl with the blackness of the man, his musky, heady scent when up close, the intriguing and primeval feeling that tattoo of his gave Parker, the easy way in which he talked about fucking a man, about fucking Parker—and, not least, that reference to an eight-inch screw driver. Parker had a feeling that wasn't an exaggeration.

\* \* \* \*

It was only 12:30, but Parker had found the beach house faster than he thought, and he didn't think Gabe would be upset if he arrived early. The house was in a more upscale section of the seaside than he thought it would be and was right on the ocean. Very expensive real estate. It wasn't a large cottage, but it was in a nice setting and looked like it had been kept up well. The siding was faded-white wooden shingles, and, to Parker's color sense, he thought a colonial blue paint with reddish-purple trim would fit into the neighborhood perfectly.

He was to regret that he'd arrived early, though, because when he got to within sight of the cottage, a young man was emerging from the doorway. He was pulling his T-shirt on and his long, black hair had obviously just come from the shower. Gabe stood inside the doorway, just in low-slung shorts—showing magnificent musculature and a tattoo in a riot of color covering his right shoulder and pectoral—and a coffee cup in his hand.

Parker didn't like the idea of being just part of a revolving stream of young men in Gabe's bed, so he turned around and walked back to the main road and to his Subaru Baja and drove off.

That evening, at Gaucho, Parker's gaggle of friends gave him a rough time about what he almost had done.

"That black hulk?" Jeremy asked. "How could you even think of going with him, honey? Why he would have reamed you a new one. He plays for a much more dangerous team than you do. How big did you say he was again?"

"He alluded to eight inches," Parker said, staring down into his beer glass. Everyone at the table was skimpily dressed. At least he had an excuse. He was going on the pole in a few minutes.

One of the guys moaned theatrically and fanned his heavily made-up face with a napkin.

Jeremy grimaced and shuddered. But it too was theatrically done, and one of the other friends of Parker, the redhead, Sean, picked up on that immediately. "You just wish for an eight incher, sweetheart," he barked at Jeremy. The bark was concluded with a cougher's hack.

"I know who you mean," their Hispanic friend, Ramon, spoke up. "I think he's the guy who runs a salvage yard over in Johnsonville. Names Hal something. Smith, I think. And the guy with the long black hair you saw might be Gwen—in her man phase. I hear that salvage yard black man put Gwen in the hospital he was so big cocked and rough."

"Gabe. He said his name was Gabe," Parker said.

"Man ain't gonna give you his real name if he's gonna split you and put you in the hospital, is he now?" Ramon retorted with a snort. "Of course you'd probably be grinning on the gurney when they rolled you into the ER."

"You people aren't helping," Parker said in an exasperated voice.

"We're helping in keeping your insides from being all cut up, sugar," Sean said. "I think you can thank that guy with the long black hair from you goin' into that cottage and to your funeral. And you can thank us for bringing you back to your right mind."

"Still, handsome you say, and muscular and black and with an eight incher," Jeremy said dreamily. "And a tattoo covering his bulging tit? Oh my, oh my."

"It's time for me to go on. Thanks for your usual nothing," Parker said, as he rose from the table and moved toward the stage where there were two poles and a DJ's booth.

"Don't mention it. Glad to help, sweetie," Ramon called after him.

Half way through his set, Parker saw Gabe—half sitting and half perched on a stool at the bar. He was wearing tight jeans, and the way he was sitting projected the bulge out at his crotch. Parker gave a shudder—but one with curiosity and arousal mixed in with the fear—at seeing the bulge. He could well understand the eight-inch claim. It didn't just bulge. There was something snaking far down the man's left pant leg. He was wearing a button-down shirt that wasn't buttoned more than two places up, and his perfectly sculpted muscular torso was visible. The tattoo on the right shoulder extending out to cover his bulging right pectoral was on full display.

All during Parker's dance set, he fought with himself. He'd go straight to Gabe after getting off the pole. He take Gabe into one of the back rooms and let the black hunk do whatever he wanted with him. No he wouldn't. He'd heed his friends' advice. His zany friends. When had they ever given him good advice before? Even the suggestion of eight inches scared him. But it thrilled him too. And if they were thick inches. Ow, ow, ow. But Oolala, too. If he just didn't look like he would give it so rough. The size of him and that tattoo. What kind of man gets a tattoo like that? What else could he be advertising but that he would give it rough?

A man in control, that's who. A man who knows what he wants and takes it.

The set came to an end, and Parker had made his decision. But now when he looked up, Gabe wasn't alone. There was a blond preppy college type guy talking to Gabe, their faces very close together. As Parker climbed down from the stage, still able to move naturally in more than one direction—back to the table of his friends or toward the bar where Gabe was perched—he saw Gabe rise off his stool and follow the preppy blond out of the entrance to Gaucho.

Pretending that the decision he'd made had been a different one, Parker turned toward the table of his friends, where he sat and started tuning into the conversation as he walked, pissed off that the topic really hadn't changed.

"Well, all the black men who've done me had at least eight inches. And they were rough."

"Honey, the last black man who did you probably was just homeless with a year's accumulation of soot and he was using a garden hose on you."

When Parker left the bar, sure enough, it was raining again. Lately he'd felt like it was continually raining on his life. He wondered where he could get a rain check just for getting the loving he was aching for. Loving without all the ache that went with it.

\* \* \* \*

Parker decided that he needed to be professional about the color advice for Gabe's beach house. And he *had* found some colors to suggest. The man was a customer of the hardware store and *had* asked for help. The beach out by Gabe's place also looked inviting and he was off this Sunday. So, he decided to knock off two opportunities with one ride up to Gabe's upscale neighborhood. He wrote a note to go with the colonial blue and purplish-red color cards he'd pulled, put them in an envelope with Gabe's name on it, pulled on a Speedo and a T-shirt, grabbed a towel and his car keys, and headed up the coastal road. He'd just slip the envelope in Gabe's mail slot. The man probably wouldn't even be home.

When he got to Gabe's house, having walked across the dunes from the side of the road, where he'd left the Baja, he approached as if he was going to rob the place, slipped the envelope through the mail slot, and padded off for the beach. If he regretted that Gabe hadn't caught him in the act, he didn't admit as much to himself.

He was lying on the towel on the sand, taking in the rays, when Gabe rose up like a glorious Poseidon out of the ocean just a few yards up the beach. There was no avoiding seeing each other. Parker shrank toward the side of his towel as Gabe walked over to him.

The man's body was magnificent, just as Parker knew it would be. He'd seen most of it exposed before, but the Speedo Gabe was wearing was a chocolate brown, which gave the impression that he was naked. In any event, the Speedo was so tight that the material did nothing to disguise the long, thick curve of his cock. Maybe more than eight inches. In his nakedness, the multicolored tattoo covering his right shoulder and bulging pectoral stood out wild and primordial as never before. His thighs, which Parker was seeing for the first time, were those of a soccer player or football halfback.

Parker's body ached for him. The bulge at Gabe's crotch hadn't been noticeable from a distance, but as he moved closer to Parker, it became the focal point of the man. Parker could hardly breathe when Gabe reached him and crouched down on his haunches beside him.

"You came here for me?" he asked.

"I wanted to deliver my advice for the house colors—you're a store customer. I wanted to do my job.

And while I was here, well, the beach here is better than it is down where I usually go."

"So, what about the colors?"

"I put color cards in an envelope and put it through your mail slot. I could tell you what—"

"I don't give a shit about color advice. I don't plan to paint the house. I think that weathered white with weathered gray trim suits the place perfectly."

"You aren't painting the . . . ? So all that was—"

"Just a plan to get you out here so I could fuck you, yes. And you're here, so I guess you want to be fucked. You didn't show the other day, though. We made an appointment and you didn't show. Does me fucking you have you that scared?"

"You know it does," Parker answered in a small voice. "I did come out, though. I was early. A dude was leaving your house. You'd just fucked him obviously. I didn't want to be just another guy you were fucking that day."

"You wouldn't be just another guy. I've been concentrating on fucking you, not anyone else this week. There's no need for you to be scared. I'll treat you right. And you must have seen the guy who's replastering the kitchen leave. He got himself all grotty, so I let him shower and change before he left. Yes, he wanted me to fuck him. That's why, I'm sure, he angled to get in my shower. But he's not my style. You're my style."

"I'm not a blond college preppy type. Last night, the guy you left with—"

". . . had seen me arrive in my Corvette. He was interested in the car. I took him out to show the car to him. When I returned, you were in the midst of that giggly klatch. I like that you're a bit girly, but I'm not going to wade into a passel of cats like that to bring you out. I came for you last night, but I need you to meet me half way. I need for you to let me know you want me to fuck

110

you. If you aren't here because you want me to fuck you, just say so."

Parker sat up and cupped the back of Gabe's neck and drew his face in for a long, lingering kiss.

"Is this enough of a signal?" he asked in a ragged voice.

"I can tell you want it," Gabe whispered, "But I also know you are holding back—that you're scared." He took one of Parker's hands in his and guided it under the waistband of the brown Speedo. Parker shuddered at the feel of the mammoth hard cock. "Don't be afraid of it," Gabe murmured. "When I put it in, you'll be open enough for it. Don't be scared of it. It's going to make love to you in ways you've never experienced before."

Parker shuddered, and he involuntarily was trembling, but he forced himself to pull the cock out of the Speedo, lowering the waistline to below Gabe's heavy balls. Leaning over more and holding and separating the balls in his hand, Parker opened his mouth over the bulb of the cock and began to suck it.

Yes, he wanted the cock inside him.

After several minutes, Gabe gently pushed him back, took his hand, pulled him up from the towel, and said in a low, hoarse voice, "Let's go into the house and shower first. We're getting sand into everything. I want to do this right."

Parker was showering when Gabe entered the shower, all massive muscle and an erection sticking out a mile. Parker moaned as Gabe turned him to the shower tiles, under the cascading water, palmed Parker's belly and moved his legs to spread and pull them away from the wall, with Parker's buttocks jutting out from the wall, and knelt behind him. Parker's forearms were raised to anchor himself against the slick wall, and he pressed his cheek into the tiles, moaning as Gabe's tongue went to his asshole and Gabe's hand pulled Parker's cock and balls through his legs.

Gabe worked Parker's ass for a good half an hour to open him up, alternating between tonguing his hole and stroking his cock with his hand and giving Parker's cock and balls the benefit of his sucking mouth. Parker was begging for it when he heard the snap of the condom being rolled in place. He had come long before that and knew that he was coming again soon.

Even with all that preparation, Gabe didn't just slide in. But he took his time and gave Parker all the attention he needed in kisses and stroking with Gabe's hand as he slowly worked the cock inside Parker's channel.

Parker was panting and Gabe too was breathing heavy when Gabe whispered in Parker's ear, "That's it, baby. I'm all inside you now. I knew you could do it. Now I'm going to take you to heaven."

Gabe didn't go further for a few minutes though, holding there, fully inside Parker, his cock throbbing, teasing Parker's channel muscles to shimmer and open more to him, as Parker whimpered in response to the full possession. More than eight inches he again thought. He turned his face to Gabe's and they sank into a deep, tongue-sucking kiss.

Parker writhed and cried out in ecstasy, groaning his pain-pleasure and letting Gabe know he was hitting all the spots as Gabe proceeded to pump him to heaven. Long, deep, relentless strokes with varied intensity and rhythm that kept Parker off guard and murmuring, "Yes, like that, just like that. God, you're huge. Fuck. Fuck. Fuck me."

Later, spent from his third ejaculation, Parker was sitting in Gabe's lap in the middle of Gabe's bed next to a large window overlooking the never-ending lapping of the surf onto the beach. Gabe's legs were stretched out behind Parker, and Parker's torso was cantilevered back, supported by Gabe's strong hands on his waist. Parker's legs were wrapped around the small of Gabe's back, holding the black bull's cock inside Parker to the root. Parker's head was thrown back, his eyes focused on the ceiling of the bedroom, his tongue lolling out of his mouth, his arms dangling at his side. Gabe was gently moving his hips, having taken up the rhythm of the sound of the waves rolling up on the shore, pulling slightly out during the sucking sound of the waves pulling back off the beach, and then pushing in again with the return of the waves.

Parker's softening cock was nestled in gobs of his white cum dotting Gabe's flat belly. Parker marveled at the gentle, yet total ways in which Gabe had taken him. Not the wild man at all, but a masterful, inventive lover. He was moaning but he also was purring.

"Hush," Gabe whispered, giving a low laugh. "Do you hear that?"

"What?" Parker murmured.

"Do you hear the rain on the roof? It's raining again."

"Who gives a fuck if it's raining? We're here together. There's no need for a rain check now," Parker answered. "In fact, it means I can't leave. I might melt in the rain. I have to stay here and let you do whatever you want with me. When we've recovered enough I want you to show me another one of your special positions."

"I'll show you now, baby. I'm still hard for you." Gabe was moving them off the bed, standing beside the bed, with Parker's groaning and moaning body draped, head toward the floor, down Gabe's torso. He started to pull Parker's channel on and off his cock, and Parker, his balls aching from the draining of cum, began to feel his own cock coming back to life again.

# BLUE DRAGON

"No, sweetie, I don't want to hear about Key West again. That's *your* little impossible dream. I'm getting my dream right here, thank you very much."

"I'm telling you it's neither a dream nor impossible, Jewel," I said, as I mixed two cappuccinos for a pair of matrons incongruously dressed to the nines over by the front window. You only needed to look out of the window and up and down the street to realize that there wasn't anything in Clarksburg, Ohio, to dress to the nines for. Nearly half the storefront windows on the three-block Main Street were soaped over. The dusty little burg too far away from both Springfield and I-70 to attract any real business was dying. So was I—dying from boredom from being stuck here.

Dying from the boring sex. What good was it to come out as gay in middle America when the gay sex scene where I was was so boring?

"Soon as I've got enough money scraped together," I continued, "I'm going to blow this joint. Key West was a real eye-opener. That was what real living was like—not like you and I face in this town."

I took a long look at Jewel. That wasn't his real name, of course. He had been Jerry most of the lifetime we'd known each other, growing up in this hick town, hanging together as the only two from the town who would admit to having the "affliction" the townspeople didn't want to give an honest word to—even though I could name a few leading lights around here who were equally afflicted.

Jewel, the other guy who worked behind the counter with me as a coffee maker—in a more sophisticated town we'd be called baristas—was more "out there" than I was. We both were wearing tight slim jeans and cut-off T-shirts that showed our sculpted abs and pert belly buttons as a lifestyle statement. But Jewel was pushing it. He wasn't into a sex change or anything, but he swished around like a junior high school cheerleader; grew his auburn hair long, down to his shoulders; and used heavy makeup on his face.

I said nothing, as his "coming out" became more pronounced. He was my best—just about my only—friend, and I wouldn't have even this job in the Coffee Palace, the only shop with pretentions on the dying three-block main drag in Clarksburg, if it hadn't been for him. As it was, we were key to the ambiance of the place. Most of the square-cut, "upright" citizens of the area surrounding the village drank their coffee in one of two diners. We were here for the eclectic crowd. The wealthier matrons who wanted to pretend Clarksburg wasn't still in the Middle Ages and students from the colleges in nearby Springfield—Wittenberg and the community college—who wanted to brush against gaydom but didn't want that known where they went to college.

I had the job because Phil, the owner, did guys and preferred them cross dressed. His choices in Clarksburg were down to Jewel, and Jewel didn't agree to work either for or under Phil unless I was given a job too. Happily, Phil, middle-aged, dumpy, and rarely in the mood, wasn't attracted to me. I wouldn't put on a bustier and garter belt for him in private. I would, though, occasionally meet up with one of the supposedly upright citizens of the area for a quickie in the back of their car.

Despite the drought here, I did need occasional reminders that I wanted to be fucked by another man.

I had thought that was something—an occasional furtive suck or fuck—until I'd gone to the Florida keys for a week and gotten into one long fuck fest with men to be drooled over. Now, there was nothing more I wanted to do than to get out of this town to some place freer and more interesting in the way I'd experienced in Key West.

The topic had come up today because of the cut-off T-shirt I'd worn to work. Jewel and I both were wearing them, but whereas his had the saucy word "Anytime" across the front, I, steeped in misery from a "nothing happening" life, had chosen one saying "Anywhere Else" on it. Phil had scowled at me when he'd seen it and might have sent me home to change if the early morning rush hadn't been so heavy.

Jewel had asked, "Where else, for instance?" and of course I had answered "Key West." He knew I would. It was him picking at this scab, not me.

Twenty minutes later, almost precisely at 2:30 in the afternoon, the daily phenomenon set it. The customers had deserted the coffee shop, not to return until 4:00 p.m., when once again they would be there in force, each in her or his own section of the room— matrons in at least pairs in the windows; artsy college students, mostly males and most of these nervously looking around, in the center of the room; and in the afternoon hours, the last hour and a half we were open, occasionally a middle-aged man from the area skulking in the shadowy corners. Men who watched the other two groups: the women, to ensure their wives hadn't shown up, and the center to speculate on picking a likely young man off.

This was what kept the Coffee Palace open—this last hour and a half of business—when nervous young male college students came in to hook up with a middle-aged local who would as likely shoot you dead for even hinting they were interested in young men. But I knew who they were. Men like the senior Realtor and owner of Slocum Reality down the block, Jim Slocum, that leading citizen and head of household for a bouncy blonde wife, three tow-headed teenagers, two dogs, and a cat.

College students from nearby Springfield weren't the only ones who sometimes left the Coffee Palace at 5:30 with these upstanding town fathers. Sometimes, when I was desperate for attention, it was me.

No one I'd ever hooked up with from Clarksburg was anything like that week I'd gloried through in Key West the previous summer, though. A quickie blow job on the sly or a lap fuck in the backseat of a car or one bent over the hood of a car in a deserted, shadowed park lot. That was it here. Everything on the sly and quick and furtive. Vanilla at its blandest.

What that left me with was wanting some of what I'd experienced in Key West—not knowing anything about any of that before; not experiencing any of it since. Wanting to get out of this nowhere town. To somewhere more exciting. Could I live full time in Key West? It scared me to think of doing that, though, a small-town hick like me. I had the looks, I thought. But the style? No way.

And I was frightened to even think of getting the sex that had turned me on the most.

At the both mysterious and predictable café clearing at 2:30, I walked to the front window and looked out. Nada. People didn't just clear out of the Coffee Palace. They'd cleared out of the center of the dying village. I went out onto the sidewalk and looked up and down the road. A few cars were parked at the curb. There had to be people around somewhere. Just not anywhere I could see.

I lifted my head and arms and gave a howl. Nada. No one came to the windows of the few stores open to see what was happening over at the Coffee Palace. No one came out onto the street.

I went back inside and behind the counter. Jewel wasn't here, of course. This was his "quality" time with Phil. I don't know what they did at home at night, but they certainly did it here, in the kitchen during the mystical hour and a half downtime in the afternoon. I guess it gave them a little thrill to do it here, where there was a chance a customer might walk in and want more than coffee and somehow would get as far as the door into the kitchen and see what was happening back there. Any sandwiches or anything like that were made by Phil, who wasn't just the shop owner, he also was its cook, accountant, and floor scrubber.

I had to be a little jealous of them—of Jewel and Phil—I thought. They at least had a little danger and "something-other-than-vanilla" in their lives. It almost made me want to put on a dress and join them. Almost; except. Except that someone had to man the counter just in case. And the big except—Phil was an ugly pig. A one-time muscle man who had gone soft and to fat and who had lost three too many fist fights. All of the men I'd met and hooked up with in Key West were gods, not Phils. To pander to Phil's fetishes would definitely be going in the wrong direction.

Jewel just didn't know. He hadn't experienced anything better. Better that he not, I thought. Key West had ruined me for real life in the Midwest.

With a sigh, followed by another "just to be sure" look beyond the front window to the deserted street, I pulled my stash of *Drummer* magazines—the gay male BDSM mag from the seventies through the nineties—out

118

of my personal drawer under the counter and started scanning through a well-thumbed *Drummer* issue.

Some of this, yes, in Key West. But only the mildest elements of it. Still, even the thought of what little of it there was was stirring me. I felt myself harden as I thumbed through the magazines and looked at the photos and illustrations and read the captions.

My long sigh segued into a rumbling sound from beyond the café window, a sound that grew louder until, there, appearing on the street just outside the window, as if he were one of the models from *Drummer*, was a black-clad figure on a muscled-up Harley-Davidson. I looked down at the magazine and blinked my eyes and looked back up, through the window. It was like the man was walking off the page of *Drummer* as he swung his black-booted leg over the saddle of the cycle, lifted the monster machine on a kick stand, and turned and looked at me through the window of the café.

He couldn't actually see me from the outside, of course, but it seemed like he could more than see me—that he could read my whole pathetic life with his eyes boring into me.

I gave a little gasp and a shudder, already fantasizing him inside me, as he strode to the door, opened it, and walked in. It was 2:45 in the afternoon. No one came into the coffee shop between 2:30 and 4:00. I knew I was in a dream. But it also seemed all so real. I knew my hard on was real.

He stood inside the door, looking around, his eyes taking me in, undressing me, and then moving on, around the room, seeing it all—all the dreary hick townness of it. His eyes came back to me, and a little smile formed on his mouth.

He looked dangerous. Swarthy, Italian, sensual, and pouty—a little cruel even. A shiver went up my spine. And he exhibited as being in total control of everything around him. Dominant. He certainly was in instant control of my emotions.

He was dressed completely in black, which went with his dark complexion and the black curly hair on his head, a lock of which hung down on his forehead. He took a couple of steps toward the counter, and I gasped as he came more into focus.

Still all in biker's black, tight black leather pants, polished black boots, a black leather jacket hanging wide open. It was the shirt, though, that had me gasping—and more what it caged. The shirt was a black mesh athletic muscle shirt, and inside that, on his bronzed skin, was a caged animal. A full chest tattoo, mostly in a dark blue, with black outline and a few highlights in orange and red. Some sort of lizard was caged under his black-mesh T. The head was in the hollow of his left shoulder, a flicking red tongue reaching up and lapping around the man's neck. An appendage reached up to his right shoulder, claws digging in there. The body of the lizard—or dragon, I guess, as I looked more closely at it—slanted down from his left to his right side, disappearing into his pants—making me, yes, want to see him pantless to be able to see where it went from there. Where was the tail? Was there a tail? The dragon's right front appendage wrapped around the man's chest on the left, reaching who knew where?

This couldn't be real. This had to be a hallucination—stepping out of the pages of the *Drummer* magazine I'd been thumbing through.

But then he became all too real. "You open? Can a guy get a sandwich and a beer here?" he said, his voice baritone low, as he strode forward and perched on a stool on the other side of the counter from me.

* * * *

"We can do the sandwich, but we don't serve beer here. Sorry. Here's a menu of what we can do."

I handed over the menu, captivated by his eyes. I had thought they were black, but they weren't. They were a dark blue—dark as the blue of the caged tattoo on his chest I was having trouble not speaking to.

"Not old enough to serve beer?"

"No, that's not it," I answered, defensive and a little breathless. "I'm twenty. We don't have a liquor license of any sort. This is a coffee house. There's a beer joint—a roadhouse—out west of town on the cross street two blocks down. But they don't open until 8:00."

I don't know if I would have told him about the roadhouse if I didn't know it was closed. "There's a minimart across the street and at the end of the block where you can buy an iced six pack, but you couldn't drink it in here." Had I said too much? Was I going to lose him?

"You don't look twenty," he said. "I'll have a burger with fries and, I guess, coffee. A big one."

"Anything special coffee?" I asked, pointing up to the menu board on the back wall. I knew I didn't look twenty. Didn't hardly look eighteen. Most of the men I encountered liked that. But I knew, I guess, why I established age right away. As for him, he could be anything from his late twenties into his early thirties. He was solid, not too tall or too short. He wouldn't have to adjust his height when he bent me over.

Now why did I think of that?

And he had a weathered look about him. Probably went from riding the cycle across the country. He had to have come from somewhere else far away. He was much too exotic for southwest Ohio.

"None of that shit, thanks. Uh, sorry. Just make it black—and strong," he said.

"I'll put your burger order in and then come back to make up the coffee."

I must have sounded like a dummy. He had me tongue-tied. I backed off to the swinging door to the kitchen, not taking my eyes off the guy. Still half believing I was hallucinating from something I'd seen in *Drummer*.

"Hey Phil," I said, as I came through the door just enough to be in the kitchen rather than the café. "Customer out here wants a burger and fries. Medium?" I asked, looking back at the counter. My heart racing to find he was still sitting there.

"Moo, moo rare," he answered.

I sent the word on. I was having trouble keeping a straight face. Here there was this rough-trade-looking dude bellied up to the counter and giving me a hard on, and there in the kitchen I'd caught Phil pushing Jewel, face to wall, up against the tiles next to Phil's office door. Jewel's jeans were off, and he'd been wearing black mesh stockings underneath held up with a garter belt. His feet were in red heels. Phil was fucking him from the backside.

Here was me, suspended between two worlds. Not getting anything from either one—or at least not yet. It would have been comical if it didn't have me wound up so tightly.

"It's the down hour," Phil growled, without extracting himself from Jewel's ass.

What? He thought I was playing a joke? Rattling their cage for kicks?

"Nonetheless there's a customer out here wanting a burger, and we have the 'Open' sign turned on. Want to check it out yourself? An out-of-towner."

I could safely say that. There weren't so many folks living here that I didn't know them all at least on sight.

Phil then did pull out, zip himself up, and turn and walk toward me, giving me a hard look all the time. "This better not . . ." But he didn't get any further, as he could see through the door to the counter now and verify for himself that there was customer. "Oh, for the love of . . . ," he started to say, but then, after taking a hard look at the customer, he turned and headed for the stove.

I thought he was going to say something like no one was sitting at the counter. I would have believed that and it would have halfway verified what I already suspected. This was just too delicious to be real. But I guess that him going for the burger patties told me he could see the mysterious stranger too.

I went back to the counter, just on the other side of the exotic hunk, and, with hands trembling, started to make his coffee. Before the smell of the brewing coffee took over, I could smell him—a musky aftershave, but also the heady scent of man sweat. He'd been on a cycle on the road for who knew how long under the sun. And he was wearing black leather. My mind flipped back to Key West. It didn't help me get control of my trembling hands.

There was a lot of sun and worked-up man sweat in Key West too. And release. A lot of glorious release in Key West.

"You aren't from around here, are you?" I asked. I had to do something to cut the thick silence and my mind flipping off into all sorts of fantasies. Also, the look Phil had given the guy had startled me—sort of like he recognized him. It made me think I should recognize him too. I didn't. I'm sure I would have remembered him if I'd ever seen him before—and subsequently dreamed about him. A lot.

"Just passing through," he answered.

That surprised me and I let him know that it did. "Passing through? This isn't really a passing through town. The town you would have come from would have been Nowhere and the next one you'd reach would be Nowhereelse."

"I can appreciate that. A lot of nothing around here, it appears. I have a bit of business here, though. You don't like being here much, do you?"

"Oh, does it show that much?" I asked. God, I wasn't showing him a bad attitude, was I? It was circumstances just like this that kept me from becoming flouncy, like Jewel. I didn't want to be all girlie and whiny for a macho guy like this.

"It's on your shirt. The 'Anywhere Else' statement sort of gives you away."

I laughed. He smiled. It was going to be OK. "Yeah, the shirt says it all, I guess."

"It also says nice abs and belly button," he said, pointing to what the cut-off T revealed. "Bet you're sculpted nice up top too."

Was he flirting with me? Oh, god, was he putting the make on me? I already was as hard as I thought I was going to get. Yes, I worked my body. But it wasn't anything like his.

"That earring—in your right ear," he went on to say. "Is that a statement in the traditional sense?"

"This earring?" I asked, lifting my thumb and forefinger to the diamond stud in my right ear. There wasn't a matching one in the left. "Traditional sense?"

"Yeah, as in the old signal of an earring in the right ear meaning you take cock. You are gay, aren't you? So, do you take cock? Do you want to take cock?"

"Yes, I'm gay," I said. But, blushing, I turned away. The coffee was screaming that it was ready. And just at the right moment. Or wrong moment. Or whatever. I was beginning to hyperventilate. This had to be a dream. It was all moving too fast—and maybe too far too. Was what I thought I wanted being tested? Is this you, God, testing me?

I turned, still blushing, not able to look into his eyes, and set his coffee mug down on the counter in front of him. My eyes were on the turbulent liquid almost sloshing out of the cup because of my trembling hand. He reached for the hand and held it, maybe to calm me. But it wasn't working that way.

"I asked if you took cock. I've had a long, dusty ride today. I need to get laid pretty bad. I'm tense. I need to give cock, and I don't need a runaround about who will take it from me."

The bell from the kitchen rang. "Your burger must be ready," I said. And fled into the kitchen, where, indeed, the burger and fries were ready. Phil was already pushing Jewel's cheek back to the wall when I came out of the kitchen.

The guy was sitting there when I returned, plate of burger and fries in hand, bottle of catsup under arm. He sat there calmly, completely nonplused, like he hadn't just dropped a "let's fuck" bomb on me, a bit of a smile on his face, and drinking his coffee.

I set the burger down in front of him.

"Yes, I take cock," I blurted out and then found some counter cleaning that cried out to be done and meant I didn't have to look at him.

"They call me Angel," he said, his voice muffled a bit by the bite he'd taken of the burger.

I'll just bet they do, I thought.

"You have a name?" he asked.

"Yes, I'm Casey," I said, turning now, leaning on the back counter, my arms crossed over my chest, letting him take me all in, if that's what he wanted to do. The shock was wearing off me, being replaced with lust and want. The man screamed of Key West—of release. Of good times. "And, yes, I take cock, I just said." I hadn't thought when I'd said it the first time. But since it had been said, I didn't want it to be forgotten.

"And you *want* to take cock? Mine, for instance?"

"Yes, sure, why not?"

"You're not sure?"

"Yes, I'll take your cock." And then when he just sat there looking at me like I hadn't said enough, I said, "Yes, I want your cock. Yes, I want you to fuck me."

"How much?" he asked, relaxing and smiling.

"Excuse me? I'm not going to pay you to fuck me."

"No, how much do you want me to pay you for your ass? And then how much for more than that?"

I couldn't help but sound wounded by that. I turned away again.

"Sorry. I didn't mean to offend, just to have the understanding between us quite clear. Have you ever been given a ride on a Harley, Casey?"

"No, never," I answered, turning back to face him again. Not interested in a little misunderstanding that I was a whore getting in the way of what I suddenly wanted. That I suddenly wanted to be a whore for him.

"So, you've never been ridden on a Harley either?"

"Excuse me?"

"Ridden on a Harley, Casey. Fucked on a Harley. Strapped down on a Harley with your butt in the air, a cock working your ass. You want to get out of this town, Casey? You tired of the same old, same old? I can take you to places, do shit to you that you'll remember forever. I'll make you part of that Harley out there and fuck your lights out. What do you say?"

What I wanted to say was how did he get into my mind? How did he know what I wanted—know that that, indeed, was what I wanted from him? But it was all moving so fast, so far. "You move pretty fast. Pretty sure of yourself, aren't you?" is what I said. I moved down the counter from him and worked at taking the coffee basket out of the cappuccino machine and tossing the grounds out.

"I know what I want when I see it," he answered, his voice still calm, matter-of-fact. We could be talking about what he wanted for desert here—the apple pie or the chocolate cake. "And I told you I wanted it too bad to play around getting it. I want to fuck you, and I think you want to be fucked. Fucked in a special way. I think you want to have Clarksburg fucked out of you. I think you're wearing that T-shirt on purpose."

"Sorry, I got work to do," I said, scrubbing needlessly at the counter with a rag. "But it's something to think about." I could just as well have said "bingo."

"Yes, it's something to think about," he said. "Think about the message you have scrawled across that nice chest of yours. For a couple of hours I can take you not just anywhere else, but over the moon." He went back to biting on his burger. It was three quarters gone. I had one fourth of a burger to decide one way or the other. Just how brave was I? Did I believe all the shit I had been saying to Jewel about what I wanted?

"And, yeah, sure, I'm cocky about what I have to give. I have a cock that I could put in your ass and scrub the back of your teeth with."

I grabbed a wet rag, came around the end of the counter, and started scrubbing tables down, getting ready for the 4:00 p.m. crowd. It already was pushing 3:30.

I was leaning over a table when I first became aware of his hot breath on my neck. Next I knew he had slapped the stack of *Drummer* magazines—the gay male BDSM magazines—down on top of the table I was swabbing. He obviously had gone behind the counter and found them laying there. He came in close behind me, pushing my body forward so that I had to stretch out my arms and dig my knuckles into the table top for support. I was looking out on the deserted street through the front window. How long would it be deserted, though? A shudder went through my body, at least partially, I had to admit, from the thrill of the danger of possible discovery.

"Is this what you want?" He hissed, his finger stabbing at the covers of *Drummer.*

"Yes . . . I think so," I stammered.

"You think so. I can give you this. I can give you lots of this."

He had his hands on my hips. But they slid around to the front from there and he was working my belt buckle, and then my zipper. And then I felt my jeans and briefs shimmy off my hips and down to my knees. I was huffing and puffing, hyperventilating.

"Nice," he muttered, in reaction to moving a hand around to my lower belly, finding me in full erection, and fisting my cock. "I can do everything you see in those magazines. I will give you a great ride."

"Oh shit, oh fuck," I whined as he began to stroke my cock. And then a more forceful "Oh fuck!" as his fingers went to the rim of my asshole and inside. He began to finger fuck me.

I looked wildly out on the street. A car pulled up across the street and a couple got out of it and went into the furniture store. I was just that far from being seen being sexually assaulted. And there were Phil and Jewel in the back, from whence they could emerge at any moment. It was scary. It was exhilarating. It was so Key West. So much not Clarksburg.

Feeling me tighten, ready to blow, his hand moved down to the base of my cock, where he could get a grip on my balls too. He rolled the balls in his hand and then squeezed hard. Totally turned on, I ejaculated quickly, spouting my cream out on the cover of a *Drummer* magazine.

He laughed, moving his hands around to cover my pecs under the cut-off T-shirt and nuzzling his face in the hollow of my neck. He bit me there and I gave a little yelp. He laughed again. "You're a sweet little piece. I'll do you six ways from Sunday. I'll do you in *Drummer* style. What time do you get off?"

Both relief and disappointment flooded in from different corners. He wasn't going to do me right here—at least not any more than he'd already done me. "5:45, I croaked."

"I'll be here. Waiting for you out on the Harley. And just so you know, I bareback. I don't do rubbers. But I keep clean."

Both my arms and my knees gave out as he let loose of me, turned, and strode out the door. I was almost totally spread out on the table top, my bare belly rubbing my own cum into the cover of the *Drummer* magazine, as I watched him mount the Harley and drive off down the street.

The image of him mounting the Harley segued into the image of him mounting my ass, and I moaned.

No way I was going to do this, though. He was a sadist. He'd latched right into the *Drummer* world. Too chicken despite all I had said. Come 5:35, I'd be out the door in the back, into my Honda Civic, and taking back roads home.

This threatened to be way, way beyond Key West.

But it wasn't a question of whether or not I wanted to have sex with him. I'd already had sex with him.

* * * *

So, this was what he'd meant about being made one with the Harley. The motorcycle was secured on strong stands, and I, naked, was belly down on the saddle, my arms raised and spread, tied off with leather strips on the handlebars. My ankles were pulled back on either side and tied off on the hubs of the back wheels. One of the saddlebags was under my lower belly, raising my ass toward the sky. Standing on the stirrups over my back, crouched over me, his hands on the handles of the Harley, a naked Angel was fucking my ass hard, deep, and fast.

I'd be screaming my head off except for two things. One, I had a ball gag in my mouth. Two, we were out in the country—who knew where?—behind what appeared to be an abandoned farmhouse well off a country road. Who was out here to hear me scream? I was completely at this man's mercy. If anything, that made me go harder.

I couldn't say my screams wouldn't be cries of passion. God, the man had a talented cock on him. Other than the threat of it—or possibly because of the threat of it—the fuck was glorious, and I was loving every exotic, pain-pleasure stroke of it.

Angel hadn't been sitting out front, on his Harley, waiting from me at 5:45. He had been sitting on his Harley beside my Civic, in the back alley at 5:35—waiting for me.

I didn't argue. It was karma. Fate, I decided. I swung my leg over the saddle, behind him, encircled his waist with my arms, and held on for dear life as he took me for a ride all through town and out into the countryside in several directions, not arriving at the abandoned farm until after 6:30. He seemed to know where he was going—and I knew the general area we were in, to the east of town. We'd crossed I-70—and took a sharp turn into the farm's drive at a good clip, sending up gravel, and scaring the shit out of me—not for the first time during the ride.

Not for the last time that night.

I was exhausted when we arrived, in a grove of trees at the back of the dark and obviously abandoned Cape Cod-style farmhouse. And I think that exhausted—and cowed—was how he wanted me. We stood off at the side of the Harley, our bodies rocking against each other, as Angel pulled his jacket and mesh shirt off his body and then my T over my head. We kissed deeply as he worked both belt buckles and sent my jeans and briefs and his leather pants to the ground.

He was sucking on my tongue and rubbing our dicks together—his quite a bit longer than mine—when he broke away and whispered, "Tell me you're over eighteen again."

"I'm twenty. Want to see my driver's license?"

"Tell me again you want me to fuck you."

"I want you to fuck me."

"Tell me you want me to do things to you. Things you've seen in *Drummer*."

"What things?"

"Whatever I want. You don't tell me that, I'll take off and leave you here unfucked."

"Do what you want with me. Do what they show in *Drummer*. Just don't hurt me bad." It was reluctantly given, with a whine. But he'd taken me too far for me not to want completion.

Fucking me, bound, on the Harley, was what he wanted to do with me. At least for the second round. For round one, he had me kneeling in front of him, sucking his cock. I'd given blow jobs before—lots of times—but, as with everything with Angel, this was something else. Not only did he have a thick Prince Albert ring through the glans, but there also were little gold balls running up the underside of his cock. I'd experienced a PA in Key West, but never those gold balls.

As over-the-top arousing as the subsequent belly-down position on the Harley was, I went up to cloud thirteen when Angel turned me onto my back on the Harley and retied me—my wrists to the handlebars again, but now my ankles bound together around his waist—and fucked me head on. What was special about this position was that I he held his torso away from my chest and I could watch the blue dragon on his chest move as his

131

chest and belly muscles undulated in the effort of the vigorous, deep fuck. He also, somehow, got deeper inside me in this position. Deeper than I could remember anyone else having gone. And vigorous enough to pull multiple ejaculations out of me.

As he hit the zenith—and after I'd shot my load up his belly—he leaned his face down into mine, our foreheads touching, our eyes locked, as I felt him tense, hold, jerk, and give me his cum deep inside me. I'd never been barebacked before, and I didn't know if I'd ever risk doing it again—or escape the consequences of having let him do it this time—but I'd never forget having done it, the total taking of it. Condom sex would never feel as complete again.

He pulled the ball gag over my head, tossed it to the side, and went immediately into a deep kiss—sticking his tongue down my throat and making me gag, before sucking on my tongue, holding my tongue between his teeth—applying pressure with his teeth. I began writhing under him, sure he was going to bite my tongue off, but just when I thought he was going to do it, he released the tongue, laughed, and whispered, "I never want you to become complacent with me. I always want fear to be part of your pleasure. But now all pleasure."

I wondered what he meant, but only for a moment—until I realized that he was hard inside me again and was beginning to pump. Slowly this time, and this time I felt both the PA and the gold beads working my channel walls. Slowly, caressing them. He reached for my wrists, one after the other, freeing them, and reached back for the tie around my ankles, letting them separate, my heels to glide down and press into his buttocks. We embraced closely, rocking against each other, rocking with the rhythm of the slow pumping of his cock.

When I felt him tense again, ready to explode, he suddenly pushed up from me, and with his first release of cum slapped me hard against one check. Then he backhanded me on the down sweep at a second spouting. My head snapped back and forth in surprise and I cried out.

"Never want you not to know it can hurt," he muttered.

Then he moved up my body, suspending his torso out over the front of the Harley, with his hands gripping on the handlebars, bearing his weight, while he presented his cock to my mouth for cleaning.

I'd thought we were done. We were both off the motorcycle and picking up our clothes.

"No, don't put your jeans on. Let's go in the house."

"In the house? The place is deserted. No one lives here."

"I do, at least for now," he said, with a laugh.

We were in the kitchen, me sitting, still naked, and with my ankles bound to the back legs of the chair on either side and a dog collar around my neck, chained to the top slat of the chair back. Angel, naked, with me watching how the dragon played on his torso, moved around the kitchen like he really did live there. The electricity, if there ever had been any, was turned off, so, as it was getting dark, the candle light took over. There were candles everywhere. I was afraid he'd burn the place down. And, yes, it frightened me. I was bound to this chair. I could muscle it to the back door, but could I do it fast enough if the fire started in here?

"Aren't the candles dangerous?" I asked.

"Scared?"

"Yes."

"Good. It keeps you on edge. More sensitive to everything I do to you." He stepped over to beside the chair and wagged his cock at me. "Suck it."

I took his cock in my mouth, and he reached down and crushed my balls in a fist. My eyes were watering; I was writhing and moaning. I pushed on his belly and thigh with my hands, but he was too strong for me. He didn't budge.

"Don't you dare bite the cock," he demanded. He released my balls and started pumping my cock with his hand. But he was just teasing me. He released me, pulled his cock out of my mouth, and moved back to the stove. It was a wood stove, so he could fry the steaks he had in a skillet.

"I can burn the place down, if I want, you know. It's mine."

"What? For as long as you are squatting here?"

"No. It's why I'm in Clarksburg. Signing the final papers that dump this place. It really is mine—for a couple of more days. Shall we fuck on the floor in the living room with the house burning around us?"

"Maybe not a good idea," I said.

"But it would be memorable, wouldn't it? Give you a memory of Clarksburg worth having."

"I guess so." I didn't even want to think whether he was serious about that. By now, I would have believed it. The man was a fiend. But he also was an angel. I was lost to him. Even his torture made me go instantly hard and come fast and big.

After we ate. Fried steak, hunks of bread, and beer to wash it down—I don't know when I'd had as big an appetite as this—he pushed my chair away from the table, knelt down in front of me, leaned over, took my balls in his mouth, and started to suck on them. At first gently, with me moaning and holding his head between my hands and then ever harder, with me writhing and whimpering and begging him to stop and trying, unsuccessfully, to push him away. He did pull away from me, but only to again tie my hands behind the back of the chair, and then he was back sucking my balls hard, with me crying and begging him to stop.

But I was hard. Not only that, but I came for him again. Never before had I come as often and prodigiously—not even during that week in Key West. It told me something about what I wanted. I couldn't hide that this turned me on—and turned me up—as well. He moved his mouth to cover my cock and gave me head. But at the point of my next ejaculation, he was fisting and crushing my balls again. I gave him my cum in thrashing agony-pleasure, and even I noticed that I was so aroused that I just kept spouting.

He left me there, torso sagging in the chair, whimpering and fully exhausted, as he moved out of the room, taking two of the biggest candles with him. He came back several times, leaving with more candles.

"You'll spend the night, of course," he said when he came in for the last two candles. It didn't sound like a question.

"I hadn't thought I would. I hadn't really—"

"I like you. I like you a lot. I want you to sleep with me tonight. I think we're both lonely."

What could I say? For starters he had me tied up, I had no transportation out of here other than his Harley, he was strong enough to manhandle me as he wanted, and my curiosity was always my downfall. For closers, I didn't want this fantasy to end—even the pain part of it. Maybe especially the pain part of it. This was my Key West dream—over the top of my Key West dream. Right here in Clarksburg. When I woke up from this fantasy, I didn't want the wonder and disappointment of having cut anything off short of what he wanted to do to me. Even if I could stop it.

I'd been thumbing through the *Drummer* magazines for years. I had melted at the thought of the experiences depicted in them. I'd never come this close to testing that out.

I'd had no idea two men could do what we did in his bedroom, a room with just a double-bed cot with a thin mattress.

I knew what doggy style was, but I was surprised when he said we were playing horsey, and he brought out a bridle tailored for such play, put it on me, and rode my ass around the room, with me moving on my hands and knees on the bare, worn wooden floor. I'd seen this done in *Drummer*. So this was what that was like.

Later, my wrists tied together and my legs bent around his waist, the ankles bound together, I was upended on my shoulders, my back rising against the side of the cot, and he was standing over me, facing the cot, and jack-hammering his cock down into my hole, while reaching back and milking my cock.

There was more, but it was the last act, deep into the night, that had me crying, jerking at the restraints, and, eventually blacking out. I was spread-eagled on the bed, my wrists and ankles tied off at the four corners, the ball gag back in my mouth. I was finding that the candles had another purpose than lighting the room. He was holding them, one by one, over my writhing body, tipping them, and letting the molten wax drip on my body—on my thighs and belly, my chest and arms. My calves and feet. Even on my dick and balls, although he was careful not to let the wax hit my bulb.

After doing my front, he turned me on my back and did it there too. I watched him, then, standing beside the bed, gathering molten wax, letting it cool a bit in his hand, and then slathering it on his cock. He came up on the bed, put an arm around my belly, lifting me up to my knees, mounted me with the still-warm wax slathered over his cock, and fucked me hard. Sometime after that, I blacked out, more from the rush of too much adrenaline and the exhaustion of the evening and night than from any real damage from the wax.

When I woke up in the morning, he was gone. And the restraints were gone as well. But I was covered in wax, so I knew it hadn't all been a fantasy. I padded out to the kitchen, found a case knife, and peeled as much of the wax off me as I could reach. There was no way I was going to try the grungy shower in this house, and cold water—there surely being no hot water available—wouldn't help.

I dressed and went outside. No Angel and no Harley. I'd been used, abused, and thrown aside. There was nothing that the *Drummer* magazine layouts had on me. This was more than Key West had been. It had been frightening, and it had been painful. And it had been glorious. I never had been taken that totally before. I was scared and ashamed and walking on the clouds.

I walked up the driveway and out onto the road. Not too far down the road, a Cadillac sedan came up behind me and honked its horn. Jim Slocum agreed to give me a ride to Main Street in Clarksburg and refrained from asking questions after it was obvious I wasn't going to answer them. All I had to do for him was to lean over from the passenger seat in a remote parking area of the William Rogers Clark Park on the way into town and give him a vanilla blow job.

Usually he paid for it; this time the taxi ride covered the bill. Harkening back to having been insulted when Angel asked me for a price, I decided I was a too-tier provider. The Angels of the world didn't pay; the Jim Slocums did.

"Your car was here when we opened up this morning," Jewel said, when I entered the back door of the Coffee Palace and hobbled in. The ass hurt, yes, but the balls ached, having been totally drained of cum—not to mention crushed.

"I didn't go home last night. I went somewhere else."

"That dangerous-looking hunk who was sitting on his Harley out there when we closed?"

"Yep," I answered, noncommittally as I started up the coffee machines. I saw no reason to keep secrets from Jewel. I never had—other than not telling him I wasn't thrilled he had so obviously gone "girl."

"What's that all over your arms?"

"Wax," I said. "Candle wax."

Jewel whistled. "Did we perhaps have a Key West night?"

"More than that," I answered, not looking around.

"So, you met Angelo Fonti." The voice was Phil's. He was standing in the door to the kitchen, a big grin on his face.

"Who?"

"Angelo Fonti. The guy who was in here in the quiet hour yesterday. The burger and fries."

"You know him?"

"I knew the family. They had a farm out east of town. Wops. A strange crew. There were stories about happenings out there—and about this kid, Angelo. Suddenly just packed up and left. Nothing's happening out there now. Just as well they left. Didn't fit in here."

I almost laughed at the "nothing happening out there" comment. If Phil only knew. He probably thought his fetishes were what was happening. He didn't have a clue. But Angel was telling the truth then. He was here to sign papers on the sale of that farm. It was his farm. He wasn't squatting. But it also meant he was just passing through.

Well, he had used me and thrown me aside. That was that. I wouldn't give it much thought.

"You're covered with goop," Phil said, not curious enough to pursue the question of what goop and why.

138

"Go home and clean up. I don't want the customers to see you that way. And change that damn shirt. The statement of 'Anywhere Else' doesn't cut it with the customers here either. Most of our customers are stuck in Clarksburg, just like we are, and will continue to be stuck in Clarksburg."

I went home and stood under a hot shower until I could get the wax—all that I could reach—melted off my body. And it certainly wasn't true that I didn't give Angel another thought. He was all I thought about the whole day.

Thus, at 5:45, I wasn't driving home. I was driving out to the old Fonti farm. I'd kept mental notes of where it was from here while Jim Slocum was driving me into town.

The Harley was there, in the backyard of the run-down house, when I pulled in. But so was an old farm truck. It looked like one that Jim Slocum drove into town occasionally. But surely it couldn't be Slocum's—unless, of course, they were doing a walkthrough of the house. It stood to reason that Slocum was the Realtor on the sale.

I knew I should turn the Civic around and drive out of there, but I'd come all this way. I don't even know why I'd come here. Angel had cast me aside after using me hard. What else could I hope for but more pain and sadism? Yeah, I guess that's what I was hoping for, truth be told. More releases. Coming until my balls ached. A little fear with my sex.

I walked around the house, as quietly as possible. I'd just peek in the windows and assure myself that Jim Slocum was there in connection with the sale of the farm. I couldn't see him and Angel together for any other purpose.

There was a Slocum there, all right, but it wasn't Jim. It was Jim's eighteen-year-old Wittenberg University son, Jason. And it depended on your definitions on whether it was a social or a business call.

They were in the living room—Angel and Jason. Both naked. Jason was suspended from the ceiling on a chain with wrist restraints. Jason could barely stand on his tippy toes and move a limited distance each way from center to try, unsuccessfully, to escape the flicking of the multistrand leather whip on his torso and legs. He was in full erection, so I decided he didn't need to have the cavalry called in. Angel was in erection too, and my eyes immediately went to enjoying the undulation of the blue dragon tattoo on his chest as he swung the whip and connected with a snap and a jerk of Jason's body. I could hear Jason's muffled responses, but I couldn't hear whether he was begging Angel to stop or egging him on, because he was wearing a ball gag—no doubt the same one with my teeth marks in it from the previous night.

I stayed around long enough to see Angel dispense with the whip, run his hands over Jason's body, to crush Jason's balls with his fist in that way I remembered so well—making Jason's eyes water just as mine had done—and to watch him fuck Jason. Jason was flexible. I think he was on the Wittenberg gymnastic team. He managed to hold his legs straight out to the side, toes pointed, as Angel held his thighs up with his hands and fucked up into him from the rear. I watched through the point at which Jason, young and virile, shot his load in a high arc across the room. And I watched until I was sure that Angel, with a jerk and a little victory cry, had bathed Jason's insides.

Knowing Angel, even though it had only been for a day, I continued watching, as he rode Jason to the floor and continued fucking him, doggy style, until he'd come again, and then rolled Jason over, straddled his chest, and made Jason clean his cock with his mouth.

Then I turned, returned to the Civic, and drove off.

Fuck him, I thought. He wanted me so bad that he left me in the house by myself and has already moved on to a younger model.

Still, I wasn't happy.

\* \* \* \*

"You left the other day."

My head snapped up. It was 3:00 p.m. the next day. Dead time at the Coffee Palace. I had been flipping through copies of *Drummer*, looking for the depiction of the wax sex. I knew I'd seen it somewhere in these pages before. I thought that looking at it now would give it extra meaning—an extra little jolt to my cock—for me.

The question gave me that jolt, though. I looked up and into Angel's dark blue eyes. The blue dragon wasn't just caged today, it was behind doors. The tight T-shirt Angel was wearing was a solid black.

"You left *me*, don't you mean?" I responded, trying, probably unsuccessfully, to keep the whine out of my voice. "I woke up and you were gone."

"There wasn't any breakfast in the house. I came back with enough breakfast sandwiches to choke a horse and had to eat them myself. If I become a fatty, it's your fault." He was just laughing it off. There was a worse part to this.

"You could have left a note or something."

It hit me then. He hadn't left me. God, he hadn't walked out on me. My spirits were soaring—at least until the memory of Jason's visit to the farm roared in.

"Not much in the way of paper or pen in the house," Angel answered.

"I came back last evening. Jason Slocum was there."

141

"I know that you knew that. I saw you watching us from outside. You couldn't have been too disgusted. You stayed through the first show. You could have come inside and I would have done you both in some special way. Maybe bound you together hanging from the hook, his cock inside you, and flogged you both together."

I knew it shouldn't have, but that made me tremble in arousal. I'm sure he wasn't lying.

"Just the first show? How many shows——?"

"There were only three. Jason doesn't have your stamina. He also didn't hold my interest as long as you did. He doesn't bring out the creative juices in me like you do."

"Is that some sort of compliment?" The suspended flogging and fuck seemed quite creative enough to me. I sure would have liked to have Angel do that to me.

"Yes, it is. Doesn't it sound like a compliment? I want to fuck you again. I want to take you beyond where we went."

I could feel my chest tighten, my air becoming constricted. I wondered if Angel could hear me panting. I was hard hard again. Yes, dammit, I wanted it.

"But you went right to Jason. You didn't come to find out why I'd walked away."

"For most of the day I'd thought that's what you did—walked away. And I had to give you that right. Seeing you coming back, I then knew it hadn't been too much. You wouldn't have come back if you didn't want more of it. You wanted more of it, didn't you, Casey?"

"Yes," I answered in a small voice—although not immediately. I was still struggling with myself on my own wants. But, shit, I wanted Angel to go on and on.

"You want more if it, don't you? You want it now. You want it harder. You want it more cruel. You want to show me stuff in *Drummer* and have me do it to you, don't you?"

142

"Yes. But if you're going to run right to the next—"

"I'll fuck anyone I want, anytime I want. Got that?" Angel growled. "If you accept that, most of the time it will be you. Can you live with that?"

"What are you saying?"

"I'm leaving town. Are you going with me?"

"Just up and leave? Just like that?"

"Yes, just like that. What is it you want, Casey? Clarksburg or excitement? Excitement and fear and not knowing what comes next? Pain and unbounded ecstasy? Do you want to live or do you want to die along with Clarksburg? You can always come back to Clarksburg; you can't always move ahead into new sexual testing."

"Well, when you put it like that."

The shot came out of nowhere, his fist connecting with my chin. I went down to the floor behind the counter in shock and total surprise. Then he was behind the counter, dragging me up by my hair, unzipping his leather pants, forcing his cock between my lips, making me suck him off.

"This is what you want, baby, isn't it? The excitement of never knowing what it will be when. This goes with the territory."

I couldn't argue with him. It was exactly what I wanted.

He gave into my only request before we left the Clarksburg area, me just leaving the Coffee Palace with him, thrown over his shoulder and dumped on the Harley, leaving my whole world behind, not even saying good-bye to Phil and Jewel, who were having their own party in the kitchen.

He took me back to the farmhouse, suspended me from the ceiling, flogged me, and gave me the same fucking I'd watched him give Jason Slocum the day before.

143

"I was thinking of your body the whole time I was doing Jason Slocum," he whispered in my ear as he was releasing my wrists.

I soared up to heaven on the comment.

"Did I give you what you want, Daddy?" I asked.

"You will always give me what I want. We will keep at it until you do. Now I have a little surprise for you before we go. Casey, I want you to meet Neal. He's going to be riding with us. That's after he and I ride you together, of course."

Angel laughed, as I turned to see that a hulking black man, swathed in black leather, had entered the room.

I immediately began to pant and Angel embraced me close so I wouldn't entertain any idea of bolting.

All I can reveal beyond the obvious about the surprise was that it was glorious and far, far more than Key West, where, before the week was out, I'd been doubled more than once. But nothing like Angel and Neal did it, right there, right then.

# SIMPATICO

The nurse signaled and moved into the corridor. When the door to the hall was shut and Rich was assured there was someone on the lookout, he rose from the deep, vinyl-upholstered chair where he had been keeping vigil while reading a Gore Vidal novel and moved over to the hospital bed.

He looked down at his older partner of the past six years, Miles Trent, and reminisced a few moments on how good their life had been. And it reminded him how well Miles had taken care of him up until his recent series of strokes that had left him entirely incapacitated in some ways but fully functional in others. Life could be so cruel. It had been good to them for over half a decade, but now this.

He supposed it could be worse. Miles might have resented having different appendages that wouldn't work.

Miles was fully awake, his eyes following Rich around the hospital room, his oxygen mask burbling merrily in the rhythm that Rich had come to be able to interpret over the past couple of weeks as wakefulness rather than repose—excitement even. Miles knew what was coming next. They did this two or three times a day when Rich could manage it—when he was able to arrange enough private time.

Rich moved around to the side of the bed facing the window wall, drawing a round-seat metal stool with him, which he rolled in line with Miles' thighs and sat on. Reaching under the sheet, he gently rolled Miles' pelvis toward him. Miles had a hospital gown on under the sheet, but it was fully open in front, the ties having come undone. He was in full erection, as Rich knew he would be.

Miles made a muffled sound through his oxygen mask that Rich had learned was encouragement rather than anger. Miles hadn't been able to speak for weeks. He probably never would be able to speak again. His whole left side was paralyzed, and, ironically, he was left-handed. All attempts to get him to communicate through writing, using his right hand, had gone for naught other than unintelligible scrawl. And now he had grown so weak that it was an effort for him even to raise the right hand. At fifty, entirely too young to be dying, Miles nevertheless was dying.

It was, perhaps, a curse that it was happening in stages. Rich wondered if he would fight it—or if he'd welcome the emptiness if he'd gotten in this condition. Thus far Miles was fighting it—fighting it as if there was something he had to do before checking out.

He'd always been so alive. He had had no trouble keeping up with Rich, who was barely twenty-six now. He had had no trouble, in fact, in dominating Rich and keeping him satisfied, even though Rich had a condition of needing attention frequently—several times a day to keep him from some form of withdrawal symptoms. If anyone had suffered more in that way over the past few weeks, it was Rich rather than Miles. But Rich had made sure Miles, at least, was regularly satisfied, just as he proceeded to do now.

He encircled the base of Miles' cock with his fingers, cupping the older man's ball sac in the palm of his

146

hand, licked up one side of the erect phallus and down the other, and then opened his mouth over the bulb and started to suck. Miles' oxygen mask was gurgling merrily. There was nothing wrong with Miles' mind, and there had been no damage to the connection between his cock and the pleasure zones in his mind.

There also was nothing wrong with his ability to create and expel cum.

Miles was enjoying the blow job as much as he did earlier in the morning or last month or last year or when he originally picked Rich up in a bar on the Norfolk waterfront. Rich had been a Navy sailor just mustered out and celebrating that, but with little idea where to go from there. Miles had moved in on him, taken him back to his Hampton home, and fucked him three times during the night. As it happened, he had quickly discovered Rich's special needs—he needed to be dominated, and he needed to be fucked three or four times a day to be humming along at cruising speed. He'd had no trouble getting that in the Navy—sometimes from more than one sailor at a time. Miles had been able to satisfy both needs. Right up to his first of several strokes in the past three weeks.

Somehow Miles managed to move his pelvis, toward Rich and then away—then back—enough to be participating in the blow job. He was gently fucking Rich's mouth, and he managed to bring his right hand down and lay it on Rich's cheek to express his gratitude at his younger lover's loyalty and sustained attention to the need his strokes had not yet taken from him.

Miles managed an ejaculation, his oxygen mask merrily bubbling away. Rich swallowed the cum, cleaned the cock with his tongue, and kissed the palm of the hand that had been cupping his cheek. Then, almost reluctantly, knowing there should be more but also knowing there wouldn't be, he rose, pulled the sheet back from Miles' chest, kissed him on the nipples, and kissed up to the older man's cheek. It had been more than a week since Miles had been able to tolerate a kiss on the lips. He would be gasping for air and turning blue if they tried that now.

Rich sat back down on the stool, took Miles' right hand between his hands and looked into Miles' face, conveying all the love that he was able to put into an expression, but also fighting not to let Miles see his tears. It was a special day. Valentine's Day. At one point the doctors had said Miles wouldn't be here to mark the day. But he had proved them wrong. He was hanging on for some unknown reason. Although he'd never voice it, Rich wished Miles would just give up—for his own sake.

For the first week in hospital—not the initial few days, but the week following that—Rich had managed, with the nurses' help as a lookout, to climb onto the bed, hold his body over Miles' body, and fuck himself on Miles' cock, to the satisfaction of them both. They had done this three or four times through the day and night just as they would do at home. But eventually the private-duty nurse had said this was too much for Miles, and Rich had had to scale back to giving Miles regular blow jobs.

This met Miles' need, but not Rich's.

"Happy Valentine's Day, lover," Rich murmured, impressing upon the older man that he had made it to February 14th. "Or, should I say," he whispered after a moment, "Happy Valentine's Day, Daddy?" It occurred to him that this was the day the adoption papers went into effect.

He wasn't just Miles' younger live-in lover anymore—the personal assistant to the prolific pop-song music composer, which was the fig leaf thrown out to the public. He legally was Miles' son now.

"And thank you for that, Daddy," Rich murmured. A change in the bubbling of the oxygen mask assured Rich that Miles had heard and understood the conveying

148

of the thanks. It had been something Miles had put into train many months ago, when the doctors first told him what likely was coming in his failing health. He'd gone as far in the process as he could without Rich knowing, because, his lawyer had told Rich, Miles was afraid Rich would leave him when he learned of his failing health. But at some point an adoptee needs to know and accede to the process.

To Rich's credit, he hadn't hesitated in hanging in there with Miles. As Miles' strength had lessened, he'd had to force Rich to go out to the bars again in those months of Thanksgiving into January to be serviced when Miles was having a bad day. Rich had an equally bad day on any day he wasn't fucked at least once. But even when Rich went out, he always returned to cuddle with Miles and give him a blow or hand job.

He had always thought of Miles as his daddy—but not literally until today. Miles had taken care of everything for him since picking him up in the Norfolk bar. Of course, Rich had taken on a full share of household chores and had functioned fully as a personal assistant. The world at large had no opportunity to question whether he was doing that job. And he'd always put Miles first and lived in his shadow.

What was he going to do now, without Miles? Could he live anywhere but in a man's shadow? What was he going to do without a man who took care of his need several times a day?

Could he—should he—even reveal that over the past four years, many of Miles' most popular song tunes actually were written by Rich? No, he couldn't—he wouldn't—do that to Miles' reputation—his legacy— especially not now when Miles had arranged for him to inherit everything the songs had provided. Luckily, there was no immediate family to challenge the move.

So, was what he'd just done incest now, he wondered, with a jolt that brought him off the stool and moving around the bed to go to the door and let the nurse know the deed was done—again—for at least the next several hours. If it was, he didn't really give a shit, he decided. Let others worry and ruffle their feathers about that, if they wished.

Opening the door, Rich signaled to the nurse, Dave, a strapping, big-boned, ruddy-cheeked, redhead.

"He's done. Now me," Rich said.

Dave grinned, unbuttoning his white hospital tunic as he followed Rich into the hospital room's bathroom and shut the door behind them. They couldn't lock it, but as Dave was Miles' daytime full-duty nurse, it was unlikely they'd be discovered or disturbed.

Naked, Rich stood, angled into the wall over the toilet, his arms spread and the heels of his hands pressed into the tiled wall behind the toilet. His feet were spread. They had the routine down on this, having done it once or twice a day since the schedule had been established of giving, first, Miles, and then, Rich, release. Dave was being richly compensated for this—beyond enjoying fucking Rich.

Dave went down on his haunches behind Rich, pulled the not-much-older man's cock and balls back through his spread thighs, and gave them and Rich's hole slobbery attention until Rich was moaning, writhing slightly, and open to Dave's oversized cock.

Hearing the familiar snap of the condom setting in place, Rich steeled himself and held his breath for the always-challenging entry of the nurse's cock inside him. Then, fully saddled, Dave grabbed Rich's hips initially to start the pumping and swinging of Rich's buttocks back to meet the thrusts of the cock. Moaning, Rich arched back and nestled the back of his head into the hollow of the bigger man's shoulder until, the rhythm of the fuck established and quickening, the two men turned their faces to the other and went into a deep kiss.

Knowing that Rich's condition prevented him from taking care of himself—requiring the partner to bring his cock to ejaculation—Dave reached around Rich's waist with one hand, grasped Rich's cock, and jerked him off. When Rich ejaculated, the cum arced neatly into the open toilet. The two had become experts at this.

Dave pumped for a couple of more moments before tensing, jerking, and releasing with a shared sigh.

The arrangement wasn't optimum, but it was minimally satisfactory. And it was, Rich knew, better than he was facing once Miles had died. Dave had come with the package Miles had prearranged, and Miles, not Rich, had initiated the way for Rich to obtain release.

What was he to do then, when Miles was gone? Sure, he would have sufficient income and a place to stay that he owned, but what did he know of maintaining any of that? His parents had taken care of him, then the Navy had taken care of him, and, since then, Miles had taken care of him. He and Miles had been so simpatico, each with his own function. Rich had never really had to deal with life itself.

He needed someone to take care of him—and not just sexually. But sexually was most important, of course.

\* \* \* \*

"Rich, I have someone out here I want you to meet." It was spoken softly and brought Rich awake smoothly from the doze he'd gone into in the arm chair near Miles' bed. He somewhat reluctantly came out of the comfort of the doze, though, as he'd been so jittery that it had taken some time and effort to reach a state of calm.

Rich looked over to ensure that Miles was still breathing before he turned his head to Dave, the nurse, at the door.

Dave wasn't alone. Next to him stood a distinguished-looking man in a doctor's coat. He looked to be in his fifties, European, extremely good looking, and trim, but with a broad chest and narrow waist. He looked like elegance and money. His hair was of auburn shade, with graying at the temples; his eyes were hazel. His smile was easy, friendly. If he was here to give Rich bad news about Miles, Rich was glad it was someone like him to deliver it.

"Dr. Charbeneau," Dave said simply and then withdrew. The doctor reached a hand out. Long, sensuous fingers. Curly auburn hair on the knuckles. Rich melted to pelted men. Miles had considerable body hair as far as Rich could ascertain. Wondering to what extent that was true was arousing to Rich—especially as he was in need of attention.

"Are you here to tell me something about Mr. Trent's condition?" Rich asked.

"No, not really," Charbeneau said a smile. "I came to talk with you about *your* condition."

"My condition?"

"Yes. How all of this is affecting you. How well you are coping. The private duty nurse suggested that we should talk."

"Dave brought you in to talk to me about me?"

"Concerns about you brought me. It goes beyond that, but Dave reported that it's time."

"I'm not sure I understand."

"Perhaps we could go for a coffee and we could discuss it."

"I'm not really all that wild about the hospital cafeteria coffee."

"Neither am I. So, my suggestion is that we go to my apartment. It's an easy walk from here. I assure you that my coffee is good. And we'll have complete privacy."

"OK, I guess so. I could use the exercise."

"I agree. Dave says that, other than going home to sleep at night, you haven't been out of this room for more than an hour or so since Mr. Trent was brought here. He says that you haven't been getting enough exercise."

Well, Dave has been exercising me, Rich thought, with an ironical little smile. But he did welcome this chance to stretch and be away. There was no guilt in it. Doctor's orders.

The apartment, indeed, was just a couple of blocks away, in a swanky high rise building. And the apartment itself was large and expensively furnished, big floor-to-ceiling windows providing vistas out over the city. Of course, he was a doctor. He probably could afford it, and being this close to the hospital was a distinct convenience.

"You don't really want coffee, do you?" Charbeneau said, when he'd directed Rich to a long, deep sofa set beside a floor-to-ceiling plate glass window overlooking the city. He'd taken off his doctor's jacket and hung it around the back of a Chippendale side chair. Going even further, he'd unbuttoned his sports shirt and pulled it open, revealing a tanned, muscular, and hirsute torso.

Rich felt himself going hard. The man's torso was pelted, just as Rich had fantasized.

It had been nearly eight hours since Dave had fucked him in the hospital room bathroom, and, by what had been his normal schedule, he was overdue. To top this off, the doctor was a hunk. Older, the way Rich liked men, but in great shape—and with curly auburn hair swirling around his pecs and cascading down into his trousers. Rich wouldn't have been surprised if he found the man groomed his chest hair for best effect. Of course

153

Rich immediately wondered about the man's pubic hair. Trimmed? Shaved?

Dr. Charbeneau was standing next to the island between the living area and the kitchen, leaning into the counter casually, supported on an elbow. To a Rich in sexual need, he looked great.

"You find you don't have coffee to offer?" Rich responded. "That's OK. I could have anything you—"

"No. I meant you're not really in the condition to have coffee, are you? You're all keyed up and jittery. You almost bounced on your way over here. Couldn't walk a straight line. And you are slurring your words a bit. Coffee wouldn't help with that. Just the opposite."

"Yes, well, it's—"

"I know, it's your condition. Nothing to be ashamed of. It's a medical condition."

"You know about—?"

"Yes, I know about your need—your medical need—and that you need help with that. Dave is helping you with that in the hospital, but it's not enough, is it? You're jittery because you need to be fucked."

"I don't know what to say."

"You don't have to say much of anything. I'm here to help. Look up at me. Am I someone who could help you with your condition? Would you let me put my dick inside you and give you release?"

Rich had been looking anywhere but at the doctor, embarrassed that they were even discussing this, but unable to deny that he was keyed up or what was causing this. Now, when he did look up, he gasped. Charbeneau had dropped his trousers and kicked them to the side and was standing there just in the open sports shirt. His body was beautiful. His cock, in half erection, was thick and long.

"Oh shit, oh fuck," Rich muttered, feeling himself shuddering and going full hard.

"Your condition is that you need to be fucked several times a day," Charbeneau said, in a low voice. "And you can't take care of your need on your own. How many times have you been fucked today?"

"Once," Rich responded, the utterance coming out like a croak. God, the man's body was something to behold. And he was going harder. Longer, thicker.

"Once obviously isn't enough. Dave tries, but he says you aren't getting all that you need. Interestingly enough, my condition is the flip side of yours."

"The flip side of my condition?" Rich's condition was causing him to be slow on the uptake.

"Yes," Charbeneau answered, giving Rich a glittering smile, not at all embarrassed that he was standing before Rich nearly naked. "I have to have a man's ass a couple of times a day. I've been wanting to have yours ever since I saw you moving about the hospital. We both need frequent release. But whereas your need is for a man to possess you to bring release, I need to top a man to get there. Yin and yang. We're simpatico that way, wouldn't you say? You needing to get it and me needing to have it—frequently. Isn't that what you and Mr. Trent had before his strokes? Does that give you any ideas here?"

"But I'm—"

"You wouldn't be betraying Miles Trent, you know. You and he were simpatico in this way. You and I could be. Miles knew that—about the potential for you and me. Miles and I used to hunt together . . . before he became besotted with you and settled down. Do you find me repugnant or therapeutic? This is all according to the plan, you know."

"Hunt?" Rich asked.

"Yes. We used to hunt young men together to fuck."

Rich was draped over the side of the sofa, facing the window out onto the city, his belly on the sofa's arm, his arms and head dangling down toward the thick carpet, his knees buried in the cushions of the sofa, as, mounted on his pelvis and grasping his hips in long, sensuous fingers, Charbeneau's thick, long cock worked its way deep inside Rich's channel.

Embarrassed to be thinking it, nonetheless Rich panted heavily at the thickness and length of the man, reveling in how much more possessing it was than Miles' had ever been or than Dave, the nurse's, was. Throwing a hairy, muscled arm around Rich's neck, the older man drew the younger man's back up to his chest, drawing Rich's head into the hollow of his shoulder. Rich arched his back, luxuriating in the feel of the soft hair on his shoulder blades, buried the heels of his hands into the arm of the sofa, and gasped at the hard, deep possession. He cried out as the cock slid out to bulb at rim and then dove deep. Out and in. Again and again. Rich writhed in ecstasy as Charbeneau pump, pump, pumped him to a mutual cry of victory. Two needs being gloriously met.

Simpatico.

* * * *

"What did you mean when you said this was all according to plan?" Rich asked of the ceiling in Charbeneau's bedroom. "You said you knew Miles before he had his strokes—before I met him."

He couldn't ask it directly of Charbeneau, because the hirsute hunk was underneath him, his arms wrapped under Rich's armpits, trapping the younger man's arms above his head, his legs laced between and around Rich's, his cock still hard, but beginning to soften, inside Rich's channel. They'd just had their second fuck. Charbeneau had called out the number after ejaculation—as if he planned to keep count all night—as if he were keeping the medical treatment veneer on the couplings.

Two hours after the first fucking on the sofa, they had done it again on Charbeneau's bed. Charbeneau promised that they'd do it every two hours until Rich lost the jitters—unless Charbeneau's own condition dictated that they do it even more. Rich had moaned in ecstasy at this last statement.

"We'll get on a regular schedule after tonight," Charbeneau had said. "And there will still be the nurse at the hospital. I know you want to spend most of your time at Trent's bedside. I'm just a fifteen-minute walk away from the hospital; we can fuck regularly. But for tonight, we're going to scratch both of our itches until they bleed."

Returning to the rest period after the second fuck, Charbeneau answered Rich's question about a plan. "You only learned of Miles Trent's deteriorating health about Thanksgiving time, didn't you?"

"Yes, but what do you know about that? And you didn't answer me about knowing Miles. You said you have known Miles Trent for some time."

"Yes, I know Miles. Miles and I have been friends for decades. We were close—intimately so. We used to cruise together, procure for each other. He knew of my need. I knew he had to have a lot of it too. We'd find prospects together, or one of us would cruise and bring young men to the other. We'd sometimes fuck them together. Does that disgust you?"

"No," Rich responded in a small voice.

Charbeneau continued. "We'll return to that. Our collaboration changed when you came into Miles' life. I didn't begrudge him his happiness, though. You made him very happy, you know. He wanted to be sure you knew that. Especially today. Now that I think back on those days, I think I liked the sharing more than Miles did. How do you feel about that, Rich? Do you like to have two men sharing you—have men shared you before?"

"Yes." Rich responded in a small, shaky voice, and answer going to both of the questions. In the Navy. It was common in the Navy in the close sleeping quarters when they were out to sea and the sailors were bored. Bored and randy. Rich had had just the slim, somewhat androgynous prettiness that attracted randy sailors. He'd learned to take all sorts of things—and, eventually, to enjoy doing so—in the Navy.

"Not just being together, but totally sharing you? Both inside your channel at the same—"

"Yes." Rich hadn't misunderstood what Charbeneau was asking.

"Did Miles share you with other men?"

"No."

"Have you missed that a bit?"

"Yes." And then because Rich didn't want to get into anything that lessened the quality of his life with Miles, even though he'd given up some acts from his previous sex life in the Navy that he'd enjoyed, he changed the topic. "You aren't really a doctor at the hospital, are you?"

"No, certainly not. I haven't done a lick of work in my life. And I don't intend to. I just intend to fuck around—several times a day. I'm filthy rich; don't need to work. In my condition, that's a blessing. It frees my time—makes me perpetually available. Just like you have been with Miles; what you could be with me."

"And arranged by Miles. Just like Dave was arranged?"

"Yes. Arranged beforehand. Just like me. Just like me being here, inside you. I've known about you for years. Wanted to fuck you for years. Knew from our separate conditions that we were simpatico that way. But you were with Miles."

"And now, with Miles dying, you are—"

"I'm not taking advantage of Miles' condition. I am doing what Miles arranged for me to do. He knew he was dying a long time before he let you know he was. He made all of these arrangements beforehand. He knew what you needed. And that you needed someone to take care of you, control you, dominate you. Fuck you regularly. I can do that—as long as you open your channel to me three or four times a day—just like your arrangement with Miles. It's what you need."

"But today. Why today? Miles is still here, alive."

"And I'll let you go back to Miles. We'll work into this gradually. I'm not cutting Miles out. He wasn't sure he'd still be here today. He's fought to still be here today."

"Because of the adoption papers going through today?"

"Yes, but even that was arranged for today. He didn't want me to declare before today, because he wanted you to have options. You can turn the arrangement down. You'll have all the money you need to live on your own, if that's what you want."

Rich shuddered at the mere thought of living alone, having to take care of himself.

"I sense you don't want that," Charbeneau whispered.

"No, I don't want that. I've never had to take care of myself. I want a daddy."

"You'll accept me in that role?"

"Yes. Oh, yes."

"You want to live with me, leaving the decisions to me, me fucking you three and four times a day?"

"Yes. But why today, especially?"

"It's Valentine's Day. Miles is sentimental that way. He wanted you to know the depth of his love. He recorded a message to you—in case he wasn't around to

159

tell you himself, which, in great part, he isn't. Do you want to listen—?"

"Yes, but later." Rich was panting and trembling.

"But now you feel that I've gone hard again, don't you? You want me to fuck you again, don't you?"

"Yes."

Without pulling out, being capable of that because of his great length, Charbeneau gently rolled Rich over on his stomach, rolling with him, so that Rich was on his belly, arms and legs splayed, and Charbeneau was mounted on his ass, the heels of his hands buried in Rich's shoulder blades. As Rich started to moan, Charbeneau mined his ass in long, slow strokes.

The session was interrupted by a buzzing. The front door.

Charbeneau, as if he was expecting this, reached over to the nightstand and clicked a remote control. It must have opened the front door, because Rich heard the sound of someone moving across the apartment toward the bedroom door.

"Here you are, Dave," Charbeneau said. And then to Rich: "You now know that Miles and I used to enjoy fucking young men together. You've acknowledged having done it before—missing it. Dave and I are going to work you over together now. Real sharing. Both of us inside your channel at the same time. Stretching you to the limit. Double loving."

Rich moaned deeply. But it was a happy moan. Happy, Happy, Happy Valentine's Day, he thought.

# NOAH FLIP FLOP

I rolled back over and surveyed the body stretched out beside me. He was lying on his back, panting slightly, his legs still spread and knees bent. The pillow not yet out from underneath the small of his back. He gave me a wan smile, wrapped a hand around my neck, and drew me in for a kiss, barely giving me time to take the joint from my mouth that I had turned to take a drag from. We shared the smoke from the reefer in the kiss.

Such a cute little trick. I'd picked him up—or, rather, let him pick me up, since we were in his flat off Oxford Road now—at Sydney's Midnight Shift Club in the heart of the Australian city's extensive gay district. I'd gone to try out the bar there, only to find it was being renovated. I was waved upstairs to the club, where it was too early for their 4:00 p.m. opening, but where a bartender was checking over the inventory and was all "no problems" about pouring me a drink. The cute trick was perched on a stool at the other end of the bar. The bartender went to carry in some more liquor to even out his stock and the trick fluttered his eyelashes at me and asked if I might be interested in more than a drink.

I was, actually.

I could have taken him back to where I was staying—the City Crown Motel nearby, quite obviously a gay-friendly establishment—but in my air hops west across the South Pacific, where I had stopped in Fiji, Vanuatu, and New Caledonia, en route to Sydney to pick up a plane back to the States, I'd made a policy of going to the guy's room or a hotel room other than mine so I had the option of leaving when I wanted.

I was still reveling in the mere week's-old discovery that I was versatile. For two years I'd been in training as a bottom—in progressively more taxing fetish situations. I hadn't realized that I could enjoy going both ways until I was ridden on a tramp steamer en route to Pago Pago. I'd been exercising that knowledge back across the South Seas.

He was small—less than five and a half feet tall, I estimated—and with a willowy, dancer's body. In fact, I'd ascertained that he was a dancer—a pole dancer at the Midnight Shift. A strawberry blond. A classic "David" physique down to the pert cock and small, but distinctly separate balls. I had enjoyed rolling them about, distending them, and inhaling them into my mouth and sucking them in both cheeks. He had enjoyed that too. Just as he had tried the same with me and couldn't get them both in his mouth—and most certainly had gagging problems in deep-throating what I was packing. He'd been game, though. And experienced.

Slightly effeminate, as had been the others I'd practiced topping on my way back to civilization. And, although it was subtle, he used makeup to enhance his eyes and eyelashes and to produce unnaturally cherry-red lips. He'd also rouged his nubs, but I had sucked the makeup off them. And done his nails, in a lavender, very much like the sweet little thing I'd gone with in Western Samoa.

I don't really think the attraction was the type of men I was picking up to fuck. This was more of a transition, I believed—and hoped—and being sure if I

162

could do the same with a more manly man. I certainly hoped I would be able to do so. As nice as I'd found pieces like this one to be for topping, there still was something missing in my sex life. But then there had been something missing in my life as a bottom too. Not arousal or lust, certainly—but something else.

I wondered if the makeup went with the slinky dresses I saw hanging around the small, one-room flat, or the high heels kicked into the closet. I'd never knowingly gone with a transvestite before . . . not that that mattered here because I knew this was a one-afternoon stand and he hadn't come on to me in that way.

I took another drag from the joint and shared it with him in a kiss, while my other hand glided down his smooth, boyish chest, the fingers dragging across the silver ring in his navel and his closely trimmed pubes as he shuddered when I grasped his cock and slow stroked him.

"Fuck me again," he murmured as we came out of the kiss.

"Liked that, did you?" I asked, still struggling over whether I could do this top thing convincingly.

"Loved it, stud. You're so big."

"Perhaps because you are so small."

"No, honey, I know hung and hard when I feel it. And you're still hard, and I want to feel it again."

"We could go for some supper and then come back."

"Can't sorry. Gotta go to work. You'll come and watch me dance?"

"Maybe. And afterward?"

"Fuck me again now. There may be no later. Can't come back here later. I have a roommate."

"A woman?" asked, gesturing to dresses hanging about.

"No, sweetie. Those are mine."

The flat was small—I could see it all from here. There was just this one double bed. "So you mean a boyfriend, not just a roommate?"

"He thinks so, and a big bruiser he is. That bartender who served you a drink at the Midnight Shift. Not as big where it counts as you are, though, honey. Com'on, mate, do me again. You do it so well."

What could I do? The pot was helping to keep me hard and aroused. I rolled back over on top of him, slid inside, and began to pump. He threw his arms around my neck, running fingers into the hair on the back of my head, arched his back, began to push down into every stroke, and cried out, "Oh, yes. Give it to me. Deep, hard. Oh, you stud! Ball me! Ball me hard!"

Later, after I'd left him and was walking down toward Circular Quay at the Rocks, one of the places where all Sydney mingled, to catch some dinner, I luxuriated in the thought that I'd obviously satisfied him as a top. That didn't mean I'd lost interest in bottoming as well, and maybe before I left Sydney on the flight out to Los Angeles the day after the next, I'd be able to get a little of that too.

I laughed at the realization that I'd neither asked the sweet little piece for his name nor given him mine. It had been the same way at all of the overnight bars on the hops by plane from Western Samoa to here. I wondered if sharing names was part of the "not quite" I felt in satisfaction in my sex life.

I don't know what had drawn me to Circular Quay and the view of the Sydney Opera house out on a small peninsula beyond, other than that I wanted to be in the middle of a lively crowd without direct interaction. I wasn't looking for a hookup. I'd had that today already. Tomorrow I planned some last-minute browsing in the area around Oxford Road, and the day after that I'd be on a plane for the States, my junior year summer exploration from Princeton over and ready to start my senior year in a month's time. And quite a summer it had been, traveling the South Pacific on tramp steamers supplying all of the small archipelagos across the sea. And quite an experience in sexual awakenings, just as I had hoped it would be.

I also don't know what drew me first to the busker leaning up against a closed ferry ticket window wall—his music or the clothes he was wearing. Or maybe it was the natural sensuality of the man. But, since I wasn't looking for sex, I'll pick the clothes he was wearing—and wearing quite well, I might add.

I had to laugh. Early in my summer adventure, I'd been seduced by a Frenchman—Etienne—who had coaxed me to take a tramp steamer with him from Nouméa, in the New Caldonia archipelago, to Suva, in Fiji. He had robbed and deserted me in Fiji. But he had taken not only my cash and credit cards but also my favorite fringed deer-skin cowboy vest and my cowboy boots. As melting as Etienne had been as a lover, missing those articles of clothing was what I remembered about him the most.

The busker was wearing them. Not my own vest and boots, of course. There were differences. But the similarities were close enough to arrest my attention and for me to make the connection. He was wearing a cowboy hat too, but as I hadn't lost one, I didn't focus on that. So, I stopped to admire the clothes, worn on top of tight, worn jeans, and a tight T-shirt, both tight because of his pronounced musculature. His face was easy to look at too. He was hirsute, but not grossly so. He maybe was in his late twenties, six or seven years older than I was. His faced showed both the cares and joys of a longer life than his body revealed him to be. Both the care and joy came through his rich baritone voice too.

He looked like the authentic rendering of an Australian cowboy, if Australia had them, and, with the

165

country's vast outback, I realized they must have them. That, I guess, was what they called stockmen or jackaroos.

His songs were accompanied by a scruffy guitar with a sweet tone that matched his voice perfectly. I remained, loitering on the fringe of those passing by, for four songs. None of the tunes were familiar to me. All of them were good enough that I probably should have heard them before, though.

I eventually was embarrassed that I was hanging around so long when others were swirling around us, just passing by. All happy and boisterous. During the fourth song, I felt the isolation—not just of me, but of the busker too. But it wasn't an isolation of the two of us together, although I would have to say I found him arousing—not arousing in the sense of the new-found topping activity I was experiencing, but more in the older, more known sense of him on top of me, possessing me fully with his cock. I knew it would be a plump, long one. My trained eyes could see that in the basket of his worn, tight jeans.

The feeling of isolation in a bustling world—even from each other—saddened me. It didn't help that the song was a sad one too. I came closer to him. He looked up and smiled at me, a smile that went beyond the friendly. He interrupted the song long enough to give me the traditional "Gd-day, mate" greeting, revealing that he had noticed me stop and listen to him when all the rest had passed him by—even the ones who had dropped money in his open guitar case in passing.

I had only come closer to add my contribution to the case—a large sum since I was coming to the end of my visit and had Australian notes to burn. I mumbled something to him, he tipped his hat and started to say something, but I turned and walked away.

The music started again in my wake. He took up in the sad song where he had left off. I got the sense, though, that he was singing just to me now. There was a clutch in his voice. My instincts fought among themselves. Should I turn and return to him? Suggest a break and a coffee somewhere—and maybe a little fuck in the shadows? Or should I cut and run? Should I acknowledging that my "down under" across the Southern Pacific adventure ended the next day and just let it go?

I went directly back to the City Crown Motel, took a cold shower, and laid on the bed. I would forget him—but maybe tomorrow. In the meantime, I'd masturbate myself to sleep thinking of his body—wearing my cowboy vest and boots.

One of my dream scenarios was being out in the old, wild West in the States. Riding up into the Rockies on horseback with a hunky, horse-hung cowboy, and being fucked all night over a saddle and under the stars. It wasn't really a Brokeback Mountain dream—that movie had fallen far short of the sex action I wanted in my dreams. Having sex with a man was neither a frustration nor a guilty complex for me.

Tonight, it wasn't an American cowboy I dreamed of. It was an Australian jackaroo—I really liked that term for a hung man taking me. And it wasn't just any jackaroo. It was the busker from Circular Quay. My very own jackaroo, wearing only the fringed vest and cowboy boots I'd loved so well. He could wear his hat too, for all I cared.

* * * *

"Gd-day again there, mate."

The voice sounded familiar and when I looked around I confirmed I was facing the good-natured grin of the busker from the previous evening at the Circular Quay—the jackaroo of my dreams.

167

"Oh, hi," I said. "You're the singer from last night." He was even more than that, which was immediately electrifying me. We were both in a gay bookstore, the Bookshop Darlinghurst. The busker who had turned me on the previous evening was standing here in a gay book store—with a book in his hand. It had to be a gay book; it was a gay bookstore. So, he was probably gay. Extremely good information to know.

Everyone I'd told I'd be in Sydney had told me that I must visit the Bookshop Darlinghurst. It was my last day in Australia, and I had found, by walking around the Oxford Street area, that the bookstore was near my motel. So, here I was—and suddenly very glad I'd decided to visit here.

"Ah, an American accent. You an American then, mate? Just visiting Sydney?"

"Yes, American. And yes again, just visiting. I'm leaving for the States tomorrow."

"So, we'll have to work fast here." A grin of a smile.

I felt a chill go up my spine. I didn't know how to respond to that to not come off as easy as I was feeling in his presence. I wasn't about to say or do anything that would put him off me. He was really lighting my fire. So I didn't answer at all.

He pointed to the book I had in my hand. I'd barely opened it before he'd interrupted with his "Gd-day, mate," but it had made quite an impression on me—such a shock. A book this daring out on the table in a bookstore. I didn't know any bookstore in the States that wouldn't have it confined to a backroom, and, even then, probably locked in a cabinet and available only to customers who knew what they were looking for. It made me think of the stories the Frenchmen, Christophe, was writing as I traveled across the South Pacific with him.

Stories meant for a small, highly jaded and well-heeled clientele.

I'd only had a moment to glance at some of the photographs—but what I'd seen was way beyond just provocative. More sensual even than photos of men fucking. More imagination and arousal food than that, which porn videos had taken the edge off of.

"I see you've found the Saxon book. Turn you on, does it?"

"I haven't had much time to look at it. What I've seen is shocking. It's—"

"The title pretty much reveals it, if you knew the photographer—Steven Saxon. The photos are all conquests of his. The title, *After Saxon*. You can see it. The fucker has the biggest dick I've ever seen. The photos are all taken after he's reamed them a new one."

"I got that," I said. "All of the poses."

"Showing their holes, making clear they'd been rebored larger than before they'd met Steve. So, does it turn you on?"

He had moved closer to me, an arm was around my back, the knuckle pressed into the table I was standing next to. He was significantly taller than I was, and it was like he was looking over my shoulder at the book, which I had open to facing pages showing two really good-looking guys, on their backs, obviously right after sex, their legs open, the men looking totally wasted, their assholes yawning open, their facile expressions leaving the impression of eyeballs swimming in rising cum.

"You call him by his first name and seem to confirm he's superhung. So, do you know him, this Saxon photographer?"

"Sure. We live in the same building. Artsy types live there. It's nearby. He's a visual artist. My gig is music. I compose."

"I thought maybe so," I said. "The songs I heard last night. Catchy, but I've never heard them before. Your own?"

"Yes. I sell them for others to record. But I try them out at Circular Quay to see how they do in public. Not so well last night. You were one of the few who stayed for any time—you were there for four songs. Left the biggest tip of the night. Wouldn't have forgotten you."

"Because of the tip? And you knew how many songs I'd stayed for?"

"I latched onto you the minute you showed up. Hoped you'd linger, and you did. You were the dream of my evening."

I blushed and looked back at the photos in the book. Should I tell him that he was the dream—the wet dream—of my night too? Was it my imagination, or was he leaning in closer to me?

"You interested in getting what these blokes got? I could introduce you to Steve. I'm sure he'd be interested in doing you and taking photos. You could be a model; could actually be a model, for all I know. Don't ask for an introduction unless you want to be lured into doing his will, though. He's a very persuasive man."

I shuddered, and I'm sure he was close enough into me to feel it. "I think he'd kill me."

"Never been doubled before? Never fisted?"

I didn't answer, so he assumed I had. And he was right.

"Not much different than that."

"You saying that from experience?" I asked.

"Page fourteen," he said, reaching over and turning the pages for me. "Did I tell you that Saxon was a very persuasive man?"

"Shit. That's you." I felt the deflation immediately. He was a bottom. He was gorgeous in the photo. Hung, still in erection in the photo; well muscled; melting hair

170

patterns on his body. Even with that wide-open hole. The expression on his face reflected that he gotten exactly what he wanted—and then some. No pay-for-gay expression there. I nearly laughed, though. All he was wearing in the photo was a fringed vest, cowboy boots, and a cowboy hat.

I was gaining experience as a top, but I hadn't reacted to him as a bottom. He was much too masculine and dominant looking. I'd only thought of getting something else from him. "So, you're a bottom." I doubt I was able to keep the disappointment out of my voice.

"Mate, if you'd go with me, I'd be anything you want. I do both. How about you?"

"Yes."

"Yes what?"

"I've done both."

"Going to buy that book? Want that introduction to Steve Saxon?"

"There's no way I could get this book through U.S. Customs. How about we go for a drink instead?" I said.

"Sure. We could go to a bar. There are several nearby. Some of them even open."

"You said you live nearby. You have anything to drink there?"

"Yes."

"And you have a bed?"

"So, you want to fuck me or do you want me to fuck you?"

"Yes."

\* \* \* \*

It took us a while to get to the bed. We stopped and began stripping just inside the door of what was a very nice, well-appointed flat. The artwork seemed to be mainly Steve Saxon photos of sexy young men, but not like what he focused on in *After Saxon*.

He placed his hands on my shoulders and, taking the signal, I sank to my knees in front of him. He'd already pushed his shorts down to his ankles, and I took his cock in my mouth and gave suck. He appreciated that I could deep throat, even though he was built large. He wasn't cut and moaned deeply as I edged his foreskin with my teeth, pushed it back with my lips, and pressure sucked his bulb.

I had a slight indecision who would be doing the taking first, but he was anxious to get past the first fuck and pushed me down on the carpet near the door on all fours, mounted my hips, and pistoned me hard and deep. He took me in long thrusts, and as we both neared ejaculation, he laced his arms through mine in a full Nelson, pulling my shoulder blades up to his hairy chest, and latched onto one of my earlobes with his teeth as he thrust hard up into me again and again. I shot my wad off in a high arc across his living room floor and collapsed on the carpet as he withdrew, jerked the condom off his cock, and spread his load on the small of my back.

The second topping went to him as well, although we'd made to his bed. The first coupling being high heat, the second one was the one that made me never want to leave his bed. He made slow love to my body from my toes to my ears with his tongue and teeth, spending significant time at the halfway point, beyond which he refused to go until I'd ejaculated down his throat. Then he fucked me in a rocking motion, with us embracing as closely as we could, with me trapping his body to mine by locking my ankles behind the small of his back, our lips locked in a deep kiss until we came almost simultaneously.

And, although, with a muttered, "Now me, mate," he claimed his turn as a bottom, he remained dominant. I was trapped on my back under his greater weight and

172

strength, and he rode my cock like a cowboy—like a jackaroo—not only rising and falling on my hard staff but also moving forward and back and from side to side as he rubbed every inch of his passage on my throbbing staff, massaged my pecs with his hands, and worked my nubs with his fingers and thumbs.

It was dark outside his windows before we were both satiated and exhausted. In the time I'd been with him, I realized what I had been missing in the two years of sex, including both bottom and top, classic positions and fetish, rough and not. It was passion. As arousing, heated, and fulfilling as the fucks had been before this, none were as passionate as I had with this beautiful Aussie. And it was the first time I thought of another man in terms of being a lover. Even though he'd remained dominant throughout, there had never before been the equal giving and taking—the concern for the pleasure of the other— that there was with this man.

"I'm afraid we haven't been introduced properly," he whispered after he'd rolled over on his side, taking me with him, still embedded inside him, and he nuzzled his way into my embrace. "I'm Noah."

"And I'm Nathan," I said. I'd come all the way back west across the South Seas, fucking young men almost nightly, and yet I hadn't told any of them my name. I was sure it was significant of something that I'd so readily told Noah mine—and that I had given him my real name. I knew he had. I'd taken a good look at the nameplate on his flat mailbox as we came up to his flat.

"You say you are flying out tomorrow?" he asked.

"I lied," I said. "I can stay for nearly a month longer." My mind was racing on the need to get to a telephone to cancel my plane reservations for the next day.

"If you don't want to stay wherever you're staying—"

173

"Thank you, I'd like that," I answered. "One thing, though, Noah."

"What?"

"Can you tell me where you got the fringed vest and cowboy boots you were wearing last night?"

"You only want me for my clothes?" he asked.

"Absolutely," I said, as I rolled him onto his belly, rolled with him, stretched out on his back, and started showing him he didn't have to be dominant every time.

# THREE ON A DATE

I gingerly pulled Fraser's arm from across my chest and slowly moved my hips forward to pull my channel off his now-flaccid cock. There was nothing wrong with the length of him—that was his most notable feature for someone looking for sex from another man. He could remain deep inside me flaccid after a side-splitting fuck like we had just had. He was the only man I'd had who could reach deep inside me in a side split.

There wasn't much wrong with his looks and body, either, when his age and work life were taken into account. He was some twenty years older than I was and, being a department head at the Smithsonian Institution who lived for his work, he was soft except where it mattered most in sex. He wasn't fat; he, in fact, could go all day without food in the excitement of a new find or a developing exhibit for the American History Museum on the national mall, which, over the years, had led to him appearing gaunt.

He was tall, dressed elegantly, had once been quite handsome, and was both glib and witty. He had taken me under his wing when I'd first come to the Freer Gallery, across the mall from his museum but also in the Smithsonian system, right after completing a doctorate in art history and museum curating at Case Western Reserve in Cleveland, Ohio. We met at an orientation meeting for new Smithsonian employees. I was straight out of the Midwest. I wasn't naïve in terms of sex. I was actively gay but without hookups yet in D.C.

Fraser had given several orientation lectures for new Smithsonian employees in which he'd been witty and erudite and oh so welcoming. From the first lecture, he seemed to be looking at me as he spoke. We were introduced to each other and spoke sporadically and shallowly in the revolve of a cocktail party at the American History Museum Stars and Stripes café after museum hours. In one of our brief conversation groups, the question arose of whether any of us had tried out a new restaurant in Georgetown. Everyone in the group had, except me. Fraser said I must go—and that I must go that night after the cocktail party. And he would take me there. He said he wanted to know more about the program at Case Western Reserve anyway.

He was sparkling at the restaurant. We had another cocktail while waiting for our food and wine with dinner and port afterward. The conversation was easy and he an expert interviewer. I have no idea when I told him I was gay, but I did. Or when I told him I was unattached and at loose ends so far in D.C. Or when he first put his hand on my thigh under the table. Or when I told him that, yes, I found him attractive.

But I let him drive me home to my small apartment near Dupont Circle, come up to my bedroom, and wow me with how long it took him to uncoil his cock from his trousers and with how far he could put it up my channel. I'd never gone with an older man before, but in the dark, there was just him holding me close from behind, and that long cock of his. He took me quickly and efficiently with little foreplay or postcoidal cuddling. And then he got dressed and went home to his wife.

The next day he took me to lunch, again to a high-end restaurant in Georgetown. He apologized for the previous evening, saying we'd both had too much to drink and that he'd found me overpoweringly attractive. He said his wife, who was a Smithsonian archeologist, was frequently in the field and that they had a marriage of convenience—one that they were both happy in. But, he admitted, he had needs and sometimes acted on them—especially when she was gone. She, in fact, had left that morning for a dig in Egypt.

I sympathized with him, and after lunch, before we returned to work, he fucked me deep with that thin but long cock of his in the missionary position on my bed in my conveniently nearby apartment. He took me quickly and efficiently once again. The previous night had been in the doggy position leaning over my bed. Today was missionary. He had one other position—the side split—and he religiously worked his way through that pattern—doggy, missionary, side split—on Tuesday and Thursday noontime breaks in my apartment. Little foreplay, quick and efficient taking, and not much cuddling afterward—except, when his wife was out of town, he'd sleep in my bed on Sunday nights—one fuck following the pattern and then spooned sleeping in the bed—and give me a lift to the Smithsonian complex on Monday morning.

He had a parking space in a museum garage. I didn't. I took the subway. The Monday morning ride seemed worth the night before. The best part was sleeping with a long cock up inside me.

This was a Sunday night. He'd taken me to dinner—he was quite generous with that perk—come home with me, fucked me once on my bed—in a side split—and gone to sleep with my back burrowed in close to his spare frame, his cock going flaccid inside me.

As long as he was plowing me with that long cock, the coupling was fine. It was so scheduled and vanilla,

177

though, that I was getting restless. I'd been in Washington, D.C., for five months and no one else had fucked me—no one younger than forty or muscular or spontaneous in his approach and carry through, or playful or even cruel.

I had fantasies of rough and cruel.

I had grown restless. I had done research. Research was what I was trained to do. I'd found a specialized subscription gay male dating site on the Internet. And I had paid for a subscription on Saturday, yesterday.

After extricating myself from Fraser, I padded out to the small room that had been rented to me as a second bedroom but that was little bigger than a closet. I used it as a home office. I turned on the computer and opened the homepage of the specialized dating service I'd found. It was specialized because it set up dates of single men with male couples. Threesome dating. The service made no bones about the purpose of the date being sex, and it's profile descriptions emphasized that.

I'd shot my load in an introductory perusal of the site Saturday night just in reading the profiles.

I'd never gone with two men before in a threesome. I hadn't done much of anything kinky before. There were a hell of a lot of sexual arrangements I hadn't tried before. And as time passed with Fraser, being denied anything that wasn't scheduled, vanilla, and over before I had had time to become deeply aroused, I began to feel more and more left out of the excitement of life. Fraser didn't seem to care if I had an ejaculation or not, as long as he did. So, increasingly, it wasn't happening for me every time.

The Web site made no bones about the goal being just dinner and a good-night kiss. The questioning for the profile was detailed and intrusive, although it was formatted mostly in a series of images of this and that, asking me to click on a scale of how much I was interested in this and that. The questions delved deep into fantasies and were constructed so that I was pulling much more out of my concept of desires than I'd even dared give thought to before.

The primary fantasy it brought out of me was being with two men at once. That was enough of a surface desire that I had sought out the dating service in the first place. I didn't know that would attract me when I started to look for something different than I was getting, but I knew it was something that attracted me as soon as I uncovered the Web site.

The questionnaire also was detailed in personal attributes, including both clothed and unclothed photos. I didn't have any trouble responding to that—either technically because I had shared nude photos with men when I was in Cleveland or in the need to hide anything. I had every reason to be proud of my physique, appearance, and equipment. Whereas most of the Smithsonian curators either took long, fattening lunches or ate at their desks while they worked, on Monday, Wednesday, and Friday I grabbed a quick salad at the museum café and then went to my nearby club and swam laps. On Saturday I worked out. I had kept myself in shape—great shape— while most who worked in my field sank into a mound of work-obsessed, unexercised Jell-O. And everyone told me that I reminded them of that "young movie heartthrob whatshisname," so I felt confident on the looks side of things.

The deal was that singles and couples signaled their interest to the Web site on the basis of the profiles made up from the questionnaires. If matches were found, dates were set up through the Web site, and the couple paid for the hookup.

There weren't that many couples profiled on the Web site that hit all of my buttons. Many of them were older-younger pairs. There were a few, though, that had my cock bobbing, and that evening, while Fraser snored lightly in my bedroom, I pushed the "interested" button on four couples.

I closed down the computer and went back to bed. Fraser had turned over on his back. His flaccid cock curled along his thigh almost down to one of his knees. His legs were spread enough that I could sink between them. I had the strongest urge to do so and to give him a sensuous blow job he'd long remember.

But Fraser had made clear the first time that we fucked that he wasn't interested in such intimacy.

* * * *

The couple I was paired with were named Nash and Grant. Nash's profile was what attracted me first. Working as a horse breeder at a stables in the northern Virginia hunt country near Middleburg jumped right out at me. Beyond that I'd read biographies of the Kennedys. They'd kept a home in Middleburg so that Jackie could ride. I'd remembered that. I'd asked Fraser to drive me out there someday to see what the area was like, but he hadn't done so yet.

Of course both men were hunks—or I wouldn't have clicked on them. Nash claimed to be twenty-eight, two years older than I was. Grant listed at thirty-one. Nash was the muscle man. Blond; smooth-shaved all over, with a close-trimmed blond bush; cut (talking both body and cock here); rugged, chiseled features; just a couple of inches taller than I was; solidly built; an open, sunny smile. Big hands. Big dick. Not abnormally long, but really thick—what some term a Coke can cock. He wasn't erect in the photo, leading to the speculation on how he'd lengthen when aroused. Hefty balls, nestled close in under the cock.

His photos gave off the aura of aggressive stance, power, and straightforward honesty. I could see him working in the horse ring, shirtless, his muscular torso covered in a sheen of clean, musky-scented sweat.

Grant was quite a contrast to Nash. He was listed as an accountant and tennis club pro in Reston, an upscale enclave township south of Washington, in Virginia, which had originally been built as a high-end self-contained city set down in the countryside. Since then, Reston had been swallowed up by suburban sprawl, but it fought hard to maintain its separate identity.

Where Nash was blond and built powerful and close to the ground, Grant was dark, tall and slim. He did have good muscular definition, but where Nash was sunny openness, Grant was sulky and sensuous, with a secretive aura. His hair was jet black and curly—and it covered much of his body—in arousing ways for anyone who liked hirsute men. And I did. If I had to characterize him in one word, it would be foxy. And I'd do so tapping various aspect of that word. He looked to be highly intelligent—and the degrees he listed supported that—but he gave off the aspect of having secrets and being much smarter than anyone else in the room—both thinking he was and actually being right about that.

His hair appeared to be designed. Nash was clean shaven; Grant maintained what seemed to be a perpetual five-o'clock shadow. His chest hair swirled in a perfect pattern around nipples that protruded out noticeably, and the hair descended to his sculpted jet-black pubes in a thin line down his sternum and flat belly. His thighs and calves were heavily matted, as were his forearms, the knuckles on his hands, and the joints on his toes.

He cultivated the foxy and sensual look, facing the camera with a sneery smile, seeming to have pointed ears, and unabashedly exhibitionist, leaning back on some sort of credenza, his pelvis jutting out and sporting a full, upturned erection, the cock long, the ball sac hanging low between spread legs. A gay sex site shot.

Nash was listed as a top; Grant as versatile. I, of course, had listed as a bottom. That had been what was at the base of the matchup. There were other obvious matchups. My profile had said I was seeking adventure, variety, and testing—none of which I had explicitly stated. That must have been extracted from my choices of voting the scale on images the questionnaire presented. Their profiles indicated they were looking for—me. Most notably, I saw, because all three of us were listed as being willing to fuck on the first date and all three showed interest in double penetration. I certainly hadn't directly said I was. I'd have to think about that over the course of the date. Yes, of course I had fantasized about it—apparently in the questionnaire phase.

And all three had expressed an interest in big cocks, sports events, movie house sex, and barebacking. How the questionnaire had arrived at these for me mystified me. Disturbingly, I had apparently gone wild in filling the questionnaire out, no doubt from frustration with Fraser, showing interest in being controlled, bondage, and even flogging—acts I don't remember ever even thinking of before—but I must have if the questionnaire had pulled the desires out of me. And black bulls, exhibitionism, and gang bangs.

There seemed to be no end to the fetishes I'd allowed the computer to think I was interested in. And I suppose I'd always been curious and the frustration with Fraser had brought out the wanton in me. I couldn't deny that it gave me a hard on to read the list—and to contemplate the possibility that any of that would happen on a day of dating. There certainly would be no time to do it all. And, just as the questionnaires had brought out exaggeration from me, I'm sure it brought it out of these other two also. I had been permitted to review the list. My hand did hover over the edit button. But I was just so frustrated with the vanilla of Jasper and the lack of other opportunities beyond this dating service. I let the profile stand.

They came for me—by car—at a restaurant on M Street in Georgetown, just over Key Bridge from Roslyn, on the Virginia shore of the Potomac. Nash was driving a new red Mustang. Grant was in the backseat. They were controlling the date. For a day they were going to be controlling me. I couldn't have driven anyway. I didn't have a car in Washington.

Grant ushered me into the backseat with him, and Nash drove up Wisconsin Avenue, turned left onto P Street, pulled over to the curb, and let the car idle, as Grant turned and put an arm around my shoulders, pulling me close in beside him, and laid a hand on my package.

It was clear now and throughout the day that Grant was the leader and Nash the follower—and I the boy toy.

"So far so good," he said, "you're the same honey in the photos. But before we go any further, we need to establish what you'll do. If you don't stand behind the profile we bid on, we should know that now. You can get back out of the car here. We can get our money back for a date that doesn't get off the ground."

He was squeezing my package and I must have given him a pained, shocked look. I'd had no idea it would start this soon.

"You claimed interest in a whole lot of kinky stuff on your profile. You going to stand behind that? This isn't your normal date. Nash and I have paid a pretty penny for this. We will do a lot of what you showed interest in. We'll use you all day. We'll abuse you part of the day. If you don't want to deliver on your profile, it's good-bye here."

I was scared but I was exhilarated too. This was the jolt I had been seeking when I paid my $200 to register at the dating service. I didn't consciously know I wanted to experience these things listed in my profile.

But I did. Even if it was the only one time.

"I'll stay in the car."

"Have you done all that shit listed in your profile?"

"Just some of it," I answered. "The questionnaire pulling those out were about desires—what I want to try."

"You'll do it all?"

"I'll stay in the car."

"Strip your jeans and briefs off," Grant commanded. "Before Nash starts to drive, strip down."

"Excuse me?"

"Gotta know if you're shitting us or if you're serious. Strip your jeans and briefs off. We're starting out at a horse show outside Middleburg. The date starts now. I'm going to do you back here while Nash drives us out there. Don't want that, get out of the car."

"I'm not wearing briefs," I answered as I started undoing my belt buckle.

That set him back. He gave me a surprised look. In the front seat, Nash laughed and pulled the car away from the curb, heading back down Wisconsin to M Street and then over Key Bridge into Virginia.

Grant was kissing me hard on the lips and jacking my cock with a fist before we hit the Virginia shore.

* * * *

After the forty-five-minute drive into the Virginia countryside during which Grant jacked me, I gave him a blow job, and I rode his cock, facing him, my knees pressed into the fold where seat back met seat cushion on either side of his hips, several hours of the remaining day, with a single exception, were downright staid—just what anyone would expect on a first date.

184

Except that my date was with two randy men, not one or with a woman.

"You had expressed an interest in sporting events, and Nash breeds and trains horses, so we thought you'd enjoy seeing a horse show and auction." He'd seen the little smile I'd given when he'd said that as we got out of the backseat of the Mustang. Nash had popped out of the front seat and was striding toward a big horse barn with a riding ring behind it. Cars were parked haphazardly in the field Nash had parked in and people already were lining the rails of the riding ring. Beyond them I could see horses in the ring and handlers guiding them around.

"I see you reacted to Nash, horses, and breeding. Is that what attracted you to our profile on the dating service Web site? You clicked on interest in us first. We would have clicked on you—your photo and all of those kinks you were interested in—if you hadn't shown interest in us first. Your attention was arrested by riding and breeding and how Nash was hung?"

"I was attracted by how both of you are hung," I said. I surprised myself when I said that. I was determined to "get into" this date, even though it already was well outside my experience zone.

He laughed and drew me to him and gave me a sloppy kiss on the lips. I looked quickly around to see if we'd been observed, but all of the attention seemed to be concentrated on what was going on in the riding ring.

"Never fear as far as Nash is concerned," he said. "Before the night is done, he will ride you and breed you. We won you in an auction, and we're going to wear you out."

A shudder went up my spine—but one of anticipation and exhilaration.

By the time we got to the riding ring, Nash was already inside, leading a magnificent brute of a pure-white stallion around the ring. As they walked, the stallion must

185

have seen a mare he wanted, because suddenly a thick pink tube of a cock started expanding between his hindquarters to become the definition of "horse-hung" cock. There were murmurs and snickers in the crowd, as Nash fought—and won—a struggle by the horse to get away from him and pursue its interests.

Two men, an older one and a much younger, were at the rail beside Grant and me. They were standing close, the older—obviously wealthy one—had a hand lightly pressed to the younger one's back. They were close enough to me that I could hear them converse.

"A magnificent beast," the younger one said, gesturing to where Nash was leading the stallion. "I'd love to ride that one."

"The stallion or the man?" the older one asked.

"They are both stallions, James," the younger one said, with a light laugh. "I was speaking of the horse. I've already been ridden by the man. A magnificent beast as well. Thickest cock I've ever taken. And he could ride all night."

The older man gave the younger one a sour look, turned away from him, and took a step away.

"Give over, James," the younger man said. "It was just a joke. Come back."

"Just a joke that Chuck Hastings has fucked you?"

"No, that part isn't a joke," the young man said. "Not a joke at all. Couldn't walk straight for two days."

The older man snorted and continued walking away.

So, his name wasn't really Nash, I thought. I guess I should have assumed that. I wasn't Ty either. I was Travis.

I turned back to watching Nash, if that's what he wanted to be called, in the ring. It was true that he was a magnificent beast. And to think that sometime in the next

186

few hours he'd be fucking me. It caused me to go half hard and to tremble at the thought.

It didn't happen in the next few hours, though. After the auction, Nash went back to the car and brought a duffle bag from the trunk.

"There's someplace for us to change in the stable," he said, as he led us into a cavernous barn and on to a series of workrooms in a wing off the room with the horse stalls. The last in line was a well appointed office and tack room.

"Change?" I asked.

"Yes," Grant answered. "We going to play dress-up for the next stops."

The next stops.

We were all nearly naked and ready to put on the smart dinner clothes they were providing, knowing my sizes precisely—tailored trousers, light cashmere turtle-neck sweaters, and camel-hair jackets—when Nash, who I couldn't help but noticing was hard, muttered, "Fuck it, my balls ache from waiting," and pushed me down on my knees in front of him. "Suck it."

"Here? Won't we be seen? Does the stable owner—?" It wasn't that I was unwilling. It just was all so open.

"I own the stable, and who the fuck cares if we're seen?"

"You said you were interested in exhibitionism." The voice came from behind me. Grant. They'd read my profile closely. Maybe too closely, I thought.

It almost unhinged my jaw to take Nash in my mouth. But take him I did. I even took him when, like the stallion earlier, his cock elongated significantly as I gagged, trying to deep throat it. He placed his hands on the back of my head and guided the face-fucking motion. Grant came in close behind me, rubbed his hard cock on my neck and cheeks from behind, and reached down and twisted my nipples with his fingers, while I writhed between them and, after several minutes, took Nash's cum in my throat.

\* \* \* \*

Dinner was nearby, still in the Northern Virginia hunt club region, but in Paris. Not Paris, France. Paris, Virginia. We ate a gourmet meal in a former plantation house, turned country restaurant, the Ashby Inn. The host and waiter seemed to know Grant and Nash well—either that, or they were expertly trained to treat all guests that way. As they treated me well too, it might have been the latter.

We lingered over the meal, wine, port, and coffee. The discussion was about all things other than sex. I could have been out for an evening with well-heeled and well-informed museum colleagues with both an interest in and expertise in all things art, history, and sports. I wondered if, at the end of dinner, this will have been it and I'd be driven back to the city. I'd given them both sex. But, then, Grant had said that Nash would ride and breed me, which hadn't happened yet. But it already was getting late, past ten.

Nash had pulled the car off onto a dirt road through a grove of trees before we'd left the horse stable property.

This is it, I thought. They were going to fuck the shit out of me here and leave me for dead.

"Another change of clothes," Grant said as he was climbing out of the Mustang and Nash was popping the trunk. "We're going clubbing."

This time I was given tight leather trousers with a laced crotch flap that would drop and could be pulled all the way back through my legs and relaced on the waistband behind, leaving both equipment and hole exposed and accessible. The two men had identical pants. And all three of us had mesh athlete T-shirts for on top. And black leather boots. We were triplets. But we wouldn't be triplets for long.

Nash drove the Mustang back toward Washington, D.C., getting off Route 66 at the Route 28 access to Dulles International Airport. The club was in a warehouse district abutting a runway fence of the airport and down an industrial-district road. Everything in the area looked deserted except for the parking lot of the club, which turned out to be a full-scale gay club.

We saddled up to a bar in a big room where music was blasting, a dance floor was jiving and being bombarded with a laser light display, and off to the side, under a lower ceiling and clouds of smoke, several pool tables were in use.

As I drank the beer Grant handed me and leaned back into Nash's lap, he on the stool and me between his legs, I scanned the room. Nash held me to him possessively with his palm pressing where my groin met the inner top of my left thigh. My attention focused on two black bulls playing pool at one of the tables. Clothing was optional in the room, and neither one of them wore any. Their tall, big-boned, muscular frames were magnificent, their half hards were horse hung—even larger if there was something larger on that scale.

Grant, who was sitting on a stool beside us, facing us, a hand on my basket, sensed I was getting excited about something from what he could feel in my crotch. He scanned the room too. "Who do you see, Ty? Who out there do you want? Ah, those two black bulls at the pool table?"

"Yes," I answered in a whisper. I'd never been fucked by a black man before, let alone by a black bull.

"Maybe later," Grant said, "but we're going to the movies now."

"We're leaving the club already?" I asked.

"You sound so disappointed. No, we're not leaving the club. They have an old-style porn movie house right here."

And indeed they did, all with the old theater seating in front of a stage backed by a movie screen. The curved rows of theater seats were set with more than the usual room for legs—or whatever. As we entered, a dancer was just leaving the stage, carrying his feather boa and G-string in his hand, the lights were going down lower, and a movie was coming up on the screen.

A male-on-male-on-male heavy porn movie, of course.

Grant and Nash were sitting on either side of me in a row about half way to the screen. As the movie got under way, Nash was pulling my mesh T over my head and Grant was working the leather trousers down off my legs. So much for us being triplets in our clothes. I wasn't dressed in anything for the rest of the evening at that club.

"Nash is gonna blow you and then fuck you hard now," Grant whispered in my earn. I just moaned my acquiescence and anticipation.

I could barely see what was going on on the movie screen for what was going on in the seating row we were in. There were men—couples mostly—scattered about the room in various stages of cock sucking and copulation. Grant and Nash wasted no time in catching up with them—with me. They had their hands and tongues all over me. Their heads bobbed around between my line of sight and the movie screen until Nash had moved his face down my belly and his mouth onto my cock. Grant was up on his knees in the seat next to me, his arms around my neck, pulling my head back by grabbing and pulling on the hair at the back of my head, his face over mine, taking my mouth with his in deep, tongue penetrating kisses.

Nash sank to the floor between my legs—showing why there was extra spaces between the rows. One after the other, he lifted my legs and hooked them on the seat arms. His hands were clutching my buttocks, rolling my rump up to Nash's searching tongue, which had found my asshole. When his mouth left my cock, Grant's hand replaced it and he slow-stroked me.

"You listed a movie house fantasy," Grant whispered to me when he'd come out of the kiss. He was still holding my head and torso arched back, my head over the seat back with one arm around my neck while he stroked my cock with the hand of the other arm.

I winced as Nash's tongue at my hole was replaced with one search finger, then a second, then a third.

"Open to him. You'll want to be as open to Nash as you can be," Grant whispered. "Remember the white stallion we say. Think of Nash as that white stallion, putting all of that up inside you. Breeding you."

I could see in my peripheral vision that other men were gathering around now, sensing a show to come.

Grant was right. I wanted to be open to Nash even wider than I was when he rose up into a crouch, placed the bulb of his thick, thick cock at my rim and started working his way inside me. I writhed and cried out at the impossibly thick, increasingly long invasion, but they held fast, Grant at my head, Nash holding my legs up and out from the arms of the seat. Other men moved in to help him—to pull my legs up almost to beside my ears, pulling my body up the seat back, drooping my head more over the back of the seat.

Men helped pin my arms down, as Grant scrambled over the back of the bank of seats, cupped my ears with hands on both side, and slid his cock into my mouth.

In to the hilt now, deep inside, still expanding, channel-splitting wide, Nash started to pound my ass in long, deep slides. And then faster and harder thrusts. Grant continued to face fuck me. All around men were groaning and egging Grant and Nash on—and expressing interest in joining them.

I strained at taking Nash. I soared to the heights at taking Nash. To the extent I could, I met his thrusts with counterthrusts and we settled into a mutually satisfying rhythm that led to an ejaculation from each of us.

Nash slurped out of me and fell back into the seat next to mine. He was still fully clothed except for the open flap at the crotch from which his still-throbbing, now-gigantic cock protruded. Grant came down in the seat on the other side of him.

I could see that Nash's cock—of such circumference and length that I still was amazed I had taken it—was dripping with cum. To show him I'd appreciated the taking, I slipped down on the floor between his spread knees and cleaned his cock with my mouth.

"Thanks," he said, with a laugh, "but you're missing the movie."

I returned to my seat, but now I saw that Grant had his cock out and was holding it in his hand. I still didn't see the rest of the movie, because, with a hand on the back of my neck, Grant was forcing me to bend over the arm of the seat and slide my lips down his cock.

So, this is what a three-man date is like, I thought. Double the attention. As soon as one is finished, the other one wants attention. I could see how such a date would be highly taxing.

Grant left the theater before Nash and I did. It wasn't long before I found out why.

When Nash told me it was time for us to go and we exited the theater, he led me further into the club complex rather than back to the main bar room. We went down a corridor with doors to rooms on either side spaced at intervals to indicate same-sized rooms of about eighteen feet in width. The sounds I heard coming from inside the doors of some of these rooms left little doubt that these were rooms for private sex sessions.

The room Nash ushered me into was obviously that. The walls, ceiling, and floor were all a dull black. Prominent in the room were two blue vinyl cube platforms I knew to be called the Liberator—cubes with wedge shapes in the form that aided the angle of penetration during sex. Many such devices had restraints attached to them. These two did. The one in the center of the room was of an elaborate configuration. The one off to the side was simpler in surface structure.

These weren't the only prominent furnishings in the room. Grant, of course, was there. But so were the black bulls I had admired playing pool in the main room. That's where Grant had gone—to enlist the aid of the black bulls. I sensed that I might begin to hyperventilate, so I concentrated on light-pant breathing.

"Lay down on the center cube, Ty," Grant said.

"What?"

"We're all going to fuck you. Your fantasy of black bulls and gang bangs—of bondage and double penetration—with the help of these big bruisers, we're going to fulfill several of your fantasies."

Double penetration. By black bulls. Oh shit.

"Or do you want the date to be over?" he asked. It was a challenge. At several junctures like that, I was offered an out. I would never know if they were serious with the offer, as I never took it. If this was going to be my one "do it all" day, I would suspend all fear and take it.

"Which way do you want me to lie on the cube?" I asked.

He showed me. I was on my back, my head toward the lower incline of a wedge shape and resting on a head rest attached at one end. My wrists went into restraints on

193

the sides of the wedge. The other end of the cube flared out, with side pieces that, when my legs were strapped to them, were raised, spread wide, and bent below my knees, stretching, raising, and bending my legs. I felt like I was going to give birth—except I knew something very big was going to be going in rather than coming out. The edge of the wedge at that end inclined sharply so that my butt resting on it was rolled up.

Meanwhile, Grant was lowering his belly on the cube to the side, his arms and legs being strapped into restraints on the sides of the cube, his butt end at the top of a steeper incline at the back of his cube, which was lower in the middle. His torso was raised a bit on an incline in the other direction. He had been stripped naked. The black bulls already were naked, just as they were at the pool table, but now they were in full erection, licking their lips, moving around the room on the balls of their feet like gliding panthers, waiting for the action to begin, ready to pounce at a signal of release.

After Nash handed around bottles of lube and strings of Magnum packets, the fun began. Nash stripped, saddled up behind Grant, covered Grant's body with his, worked his cock inside Grant, and began to fuck him. I turned my head toward them and tried to concentrate on what they were doing rather than that there was a black bull between my legs working my hole with his lubed fingers and, as I writhed, huffed and puffed, and yielded an occasion expletive and scream, continually urged me to open to him.

"You wanna be more open for this, bitch," he muttered.

When I could feel the knuckles of his hand pressing at my rim, with the four fingers inside me, he seemed satisfied. I struggled against the restraints, arched my back, and cried out to the ceiling, as he worked his cock inside me. Thank god my first black bull was the lesser hung of the two—not that it made much difference.

When he was in and starting to pump, the other black bull came around to my head and dropped the headrest, causing my head to arch back. He grabbed my ears, forced, his cock inside my mouth, managing to get deep because of the angle of my head, and slow pumped my throat. I had to loosen my jaw to take him.

When he pulled out, I understood that relief wasn't in order, because he was smiling and rolling a Magnum onto his cock. He moved out of sight, I felt the other black bull pulling out of me, and the second took over fucking me. The first black bull went over to the other cube and relieved Nash. Nash came over to me and took up the face fuck station at my head. Reaching over my torso, he encased my cock in a hand and started jacking me off.

I came for him fairly quickly, being right on the top edge of arousal at what was happening.

After a good fifteen minutes of pumping inside me, the biggest black bull jerked and filled the bulb of his condom. He pulled out of me and went over to the other cube, where black bull one was still stroking inside Grant's ass. He grabbed Grant by the hair, lifted his head, and pushed his cock inside Grant's mouth. Grant deep-throated him for a few minutes and then pulled his mouth back and was sucking hard on the bulb. Both black bulls unloaded at nearly the same time.

Meanwhile Nash had freed me from the restraints and lowered the leg pieces, but he came up on the surface of the cube, pushed his knees under my buttocks, entered my now-gaping hole with his thick cock—which I could now take easily after the reaming by the black bulls—embraced me close, possessed my lips with his, and pistoned my channel hard. He wasn't wearing a condom, and I knew when he had creamed me deep inside.

"Whooee, love barebacking you, Ty," he murmured. "Glad you requested it."

I didn't remember requesting it. But it was glorious. I just hoped . . .

He left me and I lay there, exhausted and watching the other cube as the black bulls finished with Grant. When they had done so, they freed him, he hobbled off the cube, and the bigger of the two turned and said, "We're ready for him."

Ready for me?

Grant and Nash both moved me over to the other cube and the smaller black laid on it on his back, his cock hard again and jutting up to the ceiling.

"Ride the cock," Grant commanded, and I dutifully crawled over his waist, facing him, and, with Grant's help, lowered my channel on his cock.

I didn't have time for more than a dozen rises and falls on the cock, when he was enveloping me in his arms and pulling my chest down to his, which rolled my buttocks up . . . and which gave the other black bull the right angle to saddle up behind me and start working his cock into my channel on top of his buddies. He was the one who stroked me, while I went from weeping and crying out for mercy to whimpering and groaning to near semiconsciousness.

Afterward I lay there, sprawled on the cube, moaning and whimpering, while the four of them chatted, reviewed what they'd done, and said their good-byes.

The two black bulls left the room, and I moaned in reviewing what had been done to me in this room, both shocked and exhilarated by it. I'd done it. I'd taken two cocks at once. If I never did so again . . .

But then I realized that Grant and Nash were approaching me with big grins. Grant lay on his back at the end of the cube, his feet on the floor, me on top of him, facing away, my channel sheathing his cock. The palms of Grants hands were clutching my pecs. Nash approached from in front of me, reaching down and grabbing my ankles, wishboning my legs, pushing his pelvis between my thighs, screwing that thick, thick, thick cock inside me on top of Grants. And beginning to pump. As he pumped, he reached between us, fisted my cock, and began to stroke it in the rhythm of the fuck.

"Want you to remember DPing real good," Grant muttered.

* * * *

"Good for you. You passed the tests."

"Tests? What tests?" I asked Grant, turning my face to him. The three of us were sitting on the Liberator cube he'd been fucked on—that I'd been double fucked on. The incline wedges at either end of the cube had been lowered so that the surface was flat. We had showered in a bathroom connected to this room and put our party clothes back on—the leather pants and boots and the mesh T-shirts.

"You apparently are game for just about anything," he said. "You didn't flinch, even from the DP."

"I was curious," I answered. "And I've been frustrated with vanilla. It doesn't mean that I do this every day."

"You wouldn't be willing to do it again?" Grant asked, taking a sharp look at me.

"I didn't say never again," I answered, defensively.

"But has the date lived up to your expectations?"

"In spades, yes," I answered. "Are we driving back to D.C. now?"

"We could do that . . . unless you wanted to earn $400 for some more of the same and something even more tonight."

"You don't have to pay me, you know," I said. "The paperwork I signed said the date could go to dawn."

"We wouldn't be paying you. There's another club. They'll pay if you'll go on stage—let men use you in the act. It would be similar acts to the sex acts we've done. But on stage, with a select clientele watching."

"Ah, the exhibition part."

"That part and others. Something you haven't done yet. Perhaps even something you've never thought of doing. Not life threatening, of course. If this is a one-time shot for you to experience it all, as you've told us was your interest in this date, you haven't experienced it all yet."

"$400 did you say?" That would cover my subscription to the dating site, my end of the bid on Grant and Nash, and another couple of bids if I decided to do this again before the subscription ran out. But what were the chances I'd do it again? It had been far more taxing and degrading than I had imagined it would be. I thought back to the sexual rut I'd been in before, how much pleasure and spilling of seed I had experienced already in acts I'd never considered doing before. "Just to dawn?" I asked.

"Just to dawn. The other club's about a thirty-minute drive from here. You'd be driven home."

The other club was a bit more than a thirty-minute drive, back to the Beltway around Washington, to the Maryland side, and then in toward D.C. again, from the north, on Wisconsin Avenue. Several blocks in from the Beltway, the Mustang turned right into what seemed to be an alley in a residential community of large mansions and then turned left into an underground garage. The garage was cavernous. As we'd entered, I looked at what was above it: extensive grounds, now cloaked in darkness, and an imposing Tudor-style mansion. The garage seemed to take up all of the ground under the entire property. The garage wasn't filled, by any means, but there were quite a few expensive cars parked there, most gathered around an elevator shaft.

When the elevator stopped rising and the doors opened, I realized, with a shock, that Grant didn't remind me of a fox after all. Grant was a form of satyr. The realization hit me because we were greeted in a marble foyer—floor, walls, and ceiling, all deeply veined ochre marble—by a pair of satyrs.

They were more like satyrs than Grant was, but he was close. All that he lacked were the small horns they had peeking out of their hair at the temples, goatees, horse tails, and the semblance of cloven feet. Grant shared with them the sensual, sneery smile, the pointed ears, the curved-up perpetual hard on, and the body hair, most notably the hairy legs, natural in Grant's case, a form of chaps in the case of the welcoming satyrs. The chaps were held up by a waistband which also provided the base for their horse tails. Their cloven feet were largely an illusion. They were wearing wedge heels, with the wedge being made out of clear acrylic. This forced them to walk on their toes in shoes fashioned like hooves.

"This is Ty, who has agreed to perform tonight. Please take him to Xavier." This was spoken by Grant.

Standing next to him, Nash put a hand on my arm and slid it down to take my hand. There was a calling card palmed in his hand, which I palmed, slid into a pocket of my leather pants, and later found to have a telephone number written on it. Our eyes met, and he said, "Good-bye, Ty. I really enjoyed you."

The two stepped back in the elevator, the doors closed, and they were out of my life for that evening.

"Please come with me, Mr. Ty," one of the satyr's said. He minced off toward a door on a side wall of the foyer, rather than the double doors that were directly across from the elevator, and I followed him.

I was taken to a dressing room. There were several dressing tables at one end of the room, with strong lights shining in bulbs all around the edge of a mirror covering nearly the entire wall. Clothes racks were spread around at haphazard angles with costumes on some of them—mostly satyr gear and hangers with skimpy shorts and vests in forest colors. Some of the racks had a variety of street clothes hanging from them, no doubt the clothes of the performers. In the middle of the space was a brown-leather divan. Like the cubes in the other club, there were restraints attached along the sides of the divan and there was a wedge at the end facing the dressing tables and mirror walls that rose to near the bottom edge of the divan. In the space before the end of the divan were circular depressions. It didn't need much imagination to know that knees went in there.

"Xavier will be with you shortly," the satyr said. As he withdrew from the room, he added, "Strip all of our clothes off, please. Receive Xavier naked, standing up, full frontal to the door. You are being judged." I could hear the sound of an audience cheering and clapping somewhere in the not-too-far distance, as he exited and closed the door behind him.

"Shortly" was almost immediately. The satyr who entered nearly filled the room by his presence. This was an impossibly tall—surely almost seven feet tall—big-boned, and muscular satyr. Thus far all of the satyrs I'd seen had been small or regular-sized men and more willowy of figure than muscular. This one stood out as a symbol of power and strength, and, from the size of his erect, upturned cock, imposing equipment. Xavier.

"You look good. Let us see how well you will perform," he said, as he strode to me and manipulated me, despite my shocked and ineffectual attempt at struggling or at least slowing down the inevitable. He pushed me down onto the divan, bound my wrists to the sides and my ankles as well. My buttocks was rising toward the end of the divan.

There was no ceremony or preliminary, and I soon was too busy crying out and grunting and groaning to try to reason with him. He came up on the divan, his knees going into the circular depressions, his hands pressing down on the hollows where my arms met my trunk, and his cock thrust inside my ass, lifting me up off the surface of the divan as far as the restraints would allow, and with a cry to the ceiling, he began pumping me immediately in long, strong strokes. I could feel on my knees and see in the mirror that his long horse's tail was swishing back and forth to the rhythm of his stroking.

He took me swiftly, brutally, never decreasing the pistoning of his stroke, occasionally lowered his face to mine for a brutal kiss on the mouth and then down to chew my nipples, as I strained against the restraints and moaned. But after that first shocked scream of the mammoth cock striking deep inside me, I steeled myself against begging for mercy or letting him hear me cry out.

He stroked me off expertly and quickly with a fist while he fucked me and muttered, "Good, a strong arc," when I came for him.

He barebacked me, and when he came, with a jerk and a lurch and a little cry of his own, his tail went wild in its swishing. He blasted me six times—a rear back, a thrust inside, a blast of cum, a frantic swish of the tail, a rear back, a thrust inside, a blast of cum, a frantic swish if the tail, and repeat, and repeat, and repeat, and again. By the fourth blast, I had collapsed, and just lay there, murmuring, "Oh, God yes. Give it to me," begging "Again. Again," with each creaming.

I didn't pretend that I didn't love what he'd done to me.

Immediately after the last blast, he gave me a big grin, rose off my body, slapped me on the belly, muttered,

"Excellent," and went to the door. He turned to me and said, "You are one of the rare ones who takes it stoically. Bawling and cursing is entertaining, but our audiences like to see our forest boys react differently. Still, one tip: Be entertaining and it will go better for you. Giving into it gradually out there will create an illusion the audience will love."

He turned away from me and opened the door. "He will do fine," he said to whoever was on the other side. "Clean him up, dress him, and bring him to the stage."

The dressing room was a flurry of the smaller-sized satyrs then—releasing me from the restraints; helping me off the divan, with no apparent concern that Xavier's cum was flowing down my thighs when I stood; and taking me to a bathroom with a communal shower, instructing me to clean myself out well—and quickly. I was needed on stage.

It seemed that all of the staff members of the club were outfitted as satyrs. I half expected to be dressed that way too. But I wasn't. I was outfitted with not much of a costume at all—soft brown suede ankle boots with pointed toes; a Lederhosen-style pair of shorts in a flimsy material that I could see had breakaway seams and that I assumed—rightly, it transpired—wouldn't be on me for very long; a skimpy brown leather vest that didn't meet across my chest and was held in place with laces; brown leather bicep bands; a thin strap around my waist that sent a leather strip down each crease of my groin and attached to a harness at the base of my cock, holding the cock out, pressing tight enough to keep me hard, and squeezing my balls into a tight ball; and a Robin Hood-style forester cap.

This obviously was what Xavier had meant by forest boys, I thought.

Then I was led to the darkened wings of what looked to be a lit-up stage. Beyond the flying buttress curtains I could see brown columns toward the back of the stage. These were decorated as trees, with dense green foliage in the branches. Also in the branches, though, I could see figures. Not satyrs but man monkeys. Tails and monkey masks and not much else on. They were moving through the branches acrobatically and in slow motion to the sound of jungle music.

But nearer to that, positioned at the edge of the stage, stood Xavier. He turned, and one of the satyrs handed me over to him with the comment, "As you have tested, the substitute for the third performer, Xavier."

Xavier held a hand out to me and said, "Come."

I couldn't help but notice that he had a flogger whip in his other hand, with many long, thin leather strands.

I let him take my hand and lead me out onto the stage of a small auditorium. The artificial grove of trees with the man monkeys swinging in the branches lined the back of the stage. At the front of the stage, a platform jutted out into the audience area, which was a semicircle of raised rows of banquettes behind small, circular-top tables. Most of the seating was occupied. I couldn't make out much in the audience because of the dim light there and the blinding light turned toward the stage, but it gave the impression of a teeming mass of men, in various stages of attention to what was going on on the stage, stages of dress, and stages of cock sucking and copulation. Satyr waiters moved among the levels with trays of drinks. The bar appeared to be at the back of the auditorium, at the top-most level.

The projecting platform was a square. Set in the middle of it, though, was a circular revolving stage. In the middle of this was a flat, leather-covered Roman-style divan, probably a later model than the one in the dressing room. This was unoccupied—for the moment.

Satyrs were roaming over the stage—big men, although not as big as Xavier. By quick count I located six of them. When picking them out I also for the first time saw the two acrylic X frames set at either side of back stage at the edges next to the wings. Like the center, projecting stage, each of these was set on a revolving circle.

Hanging from these frames, by wrist and ankle restraints on the four arm extensions, the cross of the X being at the level of the shoulder blades, were two young men. Both were dressed just as I was, except that their shorts had already been pulled away. Each was being fucked in the ass by a satyr standing behind them and flogged on the chest and thighs by another satyr when they revolved around to full frontal.

Now that I knew they were there, I could separate the sounds they were making from the other sounds around me. The one on the right side of the stage was writhing to the extent his bonds permitted and was crying out and bawling like a baby. The one on the left side of the stage just hung forward on his X frame, head lowered toward the ground and whimpering.

Xavier led me out to the footlights of the platform projecting into the auditorium, where two tall, muscular satyrs were waiting for me between the footlights and the revolving inset. With a sneery smile at me, Xavier handed me over to the two satyrs. To a cheer from the portion of the audience that was paying attention, they whipped my shorts off, exposing my half hard cock, which the two, coming close to either side of me alternated working with a hand with kneading my buttocks and opening my hole with lubricated fingers. Both were sheathed with condoms—there was a profusion of both condom packets and used condoms littering the floor of the stage.

Remembering Xavier's advice, I struggled ineffectually with them, refused to turn as they wanted until they'd slapped my thighs, butt, and cock, and generally acted as if I wasn't there by my own free will.

There, after a period of preparing me—working my cock and ass, taking turns in kissing me and pushing me down on my knees to suck their cocks, before pulling me up for more work on my hole, they lifted me off the floor, sandwiched me between them, and fucked me together, one entering me from the front and the other from the rear as I writhed between them, my legs hooked on the hips of the satyr facing me.

I wasn't being stoic about this. I was screaming my bloody head off. A good part of that was ecstasy. The black bulls—even Grant and Nash—had been bigger inside me. The audience was noisy too, voicing its approval and egging the satyrs on.

When they were done, they guided me onto the revolving stage and then to the divan, where I was laid on my back and my wrists and ankles were bound by long leather leads to the sides of the couch. The two satyrs left me then, trading off with the pair of satyrs assaulting the young man on the X frame to the right of the couch.

Those two new satyrs came to the divan. One worked his way under my back, lifted my hips, and set my channel down on his up-curved cock. The other satyr moved in between my spread legs, thrust his cock inside me above that of the first satyr, and the approving audience was entertained with yet another form of double fuck.

I took this with a little less histrionics than the first double fuck. Some of that was put on. I kept thinking of Xavier's "Be entertaining" tip. As long as they thought they were taxing me to my edge of endurance maybe they wouldn't be prompted to come up with something more painful. And if I reacted with a bit less strain with each taking, maybe the audience would appreciate that. I was that much interested in the exhibitionist aspect of this experience now that I was wholly into it.

When the third set of satyrs came to me from the other X frame, I was unbound, Turned face down, my channel skewered on the cock of a satyr now lying on his back under me on the divan, rerestrained, and sixth satyr came in behind me, thrust his cock inside me above that of his comrade, and pumped me to an ejaculation.

This time, I moved my hips with them, throwing my head back and screaming "Yes. Fuck me. Fuck me! Drill that hole," joining in the spirit of the fuck. The audience went wild at seeing me become actively involved in the act.

After the three exhibitions of a double penetration fuck for a appreciative audience, I was half comatose; blubbering, but not necessarily in a bad way; and had come with each separate taking. Each time the satyrs had managed to turn me toward the audience so that it could see me spout, which was met with a cheer each time.

The three "taker" performers were rotated, with me, first, on the X frame to the right of the stage, and then to the left, as each of the other two young men were taken—a second time, I surmised—through the succession of double fucks. Throughout the performance, Xavier walked around the stage, swishing his flogger, and punishing any performer, forest "boy," satyr, man monkey who was within distance of the flick of his whip.

While the third forest "boy" was being taken on the divan, the four satyrs fucking and flogging the other forest "boy" and me withdrew and the men monkeys came down from the trees and tormented us, pinching our nipples; slapping our cocks; squeezing, distending, and crushing our balls; fingering our asses; and fucking us from behind.

I was the finale. The satyrs carried the forest "boys" off the stage and to the showers. The men monkeys swept off as well, leaving just Xavier and me on the divan, under a single strong spotlight, where he fucked me interminably in a variety of exotic positions that had the audience on its feet and clapping.

When I was dressed again in the party clothes I'd worn to the club, I was led, walking very gingerly to an office, where Xavier, now in a silk robe sat behind a desk.

"Please sit," he said, as I was led in. With some effort I lowered myself in a chair facing his desk.

"You did very well tonight . . . Ty, is it? The procurers selected and prepared you well."

The procurers. So, Grant and Nash weren't just a pair of randy and kinky men looking for a third on the dating service. They had set out to procure a performer for the show here at this club from the beginning. I tried to build up a resentment, but I couldn't. This had been the fulfillment of a fantasy. I was in pain now, but I had been aroused beyond my wildest dreams and couldn't separate the pain from the pleasure. I didn't want to separate the pain from the pleasure. I would relive this for some time to come. I might even seek it out again.

He was handing over five hundred-dollar bills. I'd only been promised four hundred, but I wasn't about to quibble over an overpayment. I don't know if I would have carried through with this added offer if Grant had told me all that it entailed.

"This show goes on every Saturday night," he said. "You did well enough to be a permanent performer—for as long as you like."

"I don't know . . . I don't think—"

"We pay $1,500 a night," he said.

$1,500, I thought. So those fuckers maybe kept $900 for themselves for tonight. But then there had been expenses in getting me here—and in finding me on the dating service.

"Just sign this contract, and I'll have someone drive you home. You live near Dupont Circle, don't you?

And a car will pick you up there at 1:30 a.m. next Saturday."

When I entered my apartment, I went straight to my computer and brought up the dating service Web page. I was denied access to Grant and Nash's page. I wasn't surprised. I knew that capability came with membership. I knew they didn't have to recruit me a second time. But I had wondered if they might want to take me out on a date separate from the satyr club deal sometime. I can't believe that all we had done together was just a job to them.

The satyr club experience had been the icing on the cake—all of those acts I said I was curious about and I hadn't mentioned being fucked by satyrs. It was quite some experience, though.

And the date before that with Grant and Nash had been something too. But now I couldn't . . . but, yes, I could. I could contact Nash, at least. He had slipped me his telephone number. Maybe one of these days . . .

\* \* \* \*

Sunday night was missionary position night with Fraser. The obligatory fuck went as always, although I yearned for more than just the long cock deep inside me—especially now that I'd experienced so much more.

We stretched out on the bed, me cuddled into his front, his arm over me, his cock flaccid inside me, as always. And as always, after I heard his breath setting a regular pattern, I lifted his arm off me, slipped out from underneath him, and went into the kitchen for a cup of coffee.

When I returned, he had turned on his back, and as before, I had the urge to come down between his spread legs and take his cock into my mouth. "Fuck it," I said. Tonight would be a little bit different. There was no reason not to try to break this out of its routine. Fraser was quite attractive and sexy enough—especially in the semidark—and he had that impossibly long cock. He was worth the effort.

I came down between his thighs, slid my mouth down the length of his cock as I glided my hands up to this nipples, and started to suck. He responded to me. Moaning even before he came awake. Reaching down and guiding my head as I gave him deep head. Groaning and moving his hips in the rhythm of the fuck.

I rose up his body, saddled myself on his cock, and rode him as he grew thicker, longer, harder inside me and started to buck back. He was groaning and telling me how good it was, luxuriating in the exotic—for him—fuck until he couldn't take any more. With a roar, he pushed me off him, ran an arm under my stomach, lifted me up, pushed his knees under my buttocks, and snaked his cock back up into me, while, being supported by his arm encircling my waist, I cantilevered backward, arms dangling at my sides and head thrown back, concentrating all of my sensations on the cock thrusting again and again up into my passage and his hand fisting and stroking my cock. Seeking, working toward, a found mutual ejaculation.

Afterward, embracing me from behind, he declared what a surprisingly good fuck that was and how aroused he was by the variety of it. Could we fuck like that more often?

I assured him that we certainly could, myself fully satisfied with him for the first time and looking forward to progress in that direction.

He leaned his lips to my ear and whispered, "We've never done it before, but what I really would like now—"

"Yes you can fuck me again," I answered, turning my face away from him so that he couldn't see my wide grin.

# SARGE

"I think he's signaling to you, sugar."

I'd stopped to talk to the two guys who regularly positioned themselves at the corner of 4th Street Northwest in Albuquerque and the alley in which I temporarily resided in a cardboard carton. I hadn't been there long following a relocation from Las Vegas and, although I'd found some work as a gofer on a high-rise construction project downtown, I didn't have near enough funds yet to rent a room—or even to have three squares a day.

"What? Who?" I asked, swiveling my head toward the street. A dark sedan had pulled over to the curb, but I didn't see anything unusual in that. That's what they did to pick up one of the guys staked out on this corner—the guys I'd stopped to talk to after a long, dusty day walking the beams of a barebones high-rise structure.

Oh.

"The one in the car, sweetie. He's lookin' at you, I'm sure. Good looker hisself too—for his age."

"Go on, honey," the other rent-boy said. "You can have this one. He wants you. Time you got out of that carton back in the alley. Lee and I here have rooms. You want one of those—and, believe me, it can get cold here in the winter, no matter what folks say about the sunny southwest—you need to expand your profit takin'."

"I don't know. I don't—"

"Don't tell me you never sucked a cock before," the first rent-boy said with exaggerated shock. "Pretty boy like you. You gotta have them linin' up."

As a matter of fact I had sucked a cock before—and had fallen into a rut of it here in Albuquerque. The job situation was very tight when I got here. Being picked up here, on 4th Street, while I was walking and minding my own business, by one of the construction foremen on the high rise project had been what had gotten me the minimal job I had. And I made more out of the occasional blow job and quick fuck I had to give him in nooks and crannies of the construction site than I got paid for chasing around on errands on the site.

"Ask for fifty and don't settle for less than twenty," rent-boy number two was advising. "If he wants more, nothin' less than a hundred. Not just for you. We have standards to keep up on this corner."

"And don't expect us to let you cut in on the business," said number one. "You just look like you haven't had a meal for a while."

At the side of the car, I leaned down and looked into the open passenger window. It was obvious what he was there for. He already had his cock out, his hand was wrapped around it, and it was hard—a long, thick hard. He was a military type. Not young, but hunky. Tall, solid, broad-chested, well-muscled. The gray buzz cut showed his age; so did the craggy, yet still handsome face. He was wearing gym shorts, the waistband pulled down to under his meaty balls, and a pristine white T-shirt on top.

I made him speak first.

"You available?"

"Maybe, for a price," I answered. "Fifty dollars. Just a BJ, though."

He gestured to the top of the dashboard, where a ten and twenty were already laid out, side by side. "I know the going rates," he said. "Get in."

I opened the door and slid into the passenger seat. The interior of the car was neat as a pin. He looked clean too. I felt like a pig pen, having just come from the construction site and not having had anyplace to clean up for a couple of days. The water was off at the site for work on the lines. I usually cleaned up there, my foreman finding an opportunity for me in the construction trailer.

I reached over for his cock, one of the biggest I'd ever seen, but he pushed my hand away. "Not here. Too risky. Won't go far, though. I'll bring you right back."

We didn't, in fact, go far—just around the corner and up a block was a closed-down gas station, the pumps having been jerked out being a good sign it wasn't open for business. There still were some clunker cars on the lot, though, and the john pulled his sedan between two of these. We couldn't be seen from the street. Someone would have to walk in almost to the tail end of the car to know it was occupied.

The john obviously had done this before.

He turned and looked at me and seemed to do a double take as if only now seeing me clearly. I felt self-conscious. I wasn't at my best with a streak of dirt on my face and wearing my baggy shorts, plaid shirt open to a dingy white T underneath, and scruffy, worn construction boots. For a second I thought he was going to tell me to get out of his nice, clean car. But his eyes went dull and I saw him relax back into his seat. He'd had his hand on his cock, but he took it off and lowered his arms to his side.

I took all that arranging of himself as a signal, and, leaning over, I took the cock in one of my hands, opened my mouth over the bulb, ran my tongue around that, and put sucking pressure on it. He stiffened and then relaxed again and let out a long groan. I ran my lips down the side

212

of the dick, seeing how far I initially could get. I knew he'd want me to try to deep-throat it. It was a big one, though.

After just three rises and falls on the cock, however, he grasped my head and pushed it off his cock, the motion causing me to sit back up in the passenger seat and lean away from him against the passenger door.

"What? It isn't what—?"

"Not here, like this. You smell. Sorry, but I can't get past that. When was the last time you showered? When was the last time you ate anything? You're a great-looking guy, but I can't do this with someone in your condition."

"Uh, sorry," I said. "I didn't plan on this. Was just coming home from work. The guys on the corner said you wanted me, not them."

"I did. I did want you. I do. You looked so . . . and even more when you got in the car. But not like this. Coming home? You have a job? You live somewhere near where I picked you up?"

"Yeah, I got a job. Not much of one, though."

"Don't tell me. You're homeless. That's why you're in this condition."

"That, and, as I said, I was comin' home from a job. I work on that high rise they're building on Central, near the I-25 interchange. I wasn't plannin' on this."

"And you live—?"

"In the alley where you picked me up."

"And that's why you and your clothes are in the condition they're in? You don't have much of a place to get them washed?"

"Yeah, I guess."

"And the last time you had a good meal?"

"There was a bologna sandwich from a lunch wagon at noon."

"And for breakfast?"

"There was a bologna sandwich from a lunch wagon at noon."

"We can't do this here, like this."

"OK, I'll just get out. But I was willin', so at least the ten." I reached out toward the dashboard.

"You can take it all. Get your clothes cleaned at a Laundromat and get a good meal."

"And then you'll come back for me?" I asked. He was a hunk and a half even though he must have been in his late forties, at least. He was a lot better than the construction foreman. Nice big cock too. I'd already had thoughts of what more he could do with me with that cock than just a blow job.

"You'd go with me then?" he asked.

"Yeah, sure. You're hunky."

"You indicated you didn't regularly do this."

"I know what men do with men with their cocks," I said. "Just because I'm not in the business doesn't mean I'm not interested."

"So, what would you charge for all day?"

What was it the guys at the corner had said? The part about not undercharging so as not to undermine their business? Otherwise, I might go with the man for free. He was a hunk and a half, I liked them older, and this thing in the car business was making me horny. But the guys on the corner told me to keep up their standards.

"Another hundred dollars, on top of the thirty, which I use to clean up."

"Tell you what," he said, as he took out a wallet. "I'll make it a hundred and fifty total, paid up to dawn tomorrow, and we'll go back to the alley and get your other clothes, if you have any. You can come to my apartment—I live in an apartment house over on Lomas. I'll feed you and clean all of your clothes tonight and have you back here in the morning. How does that sound?"

"I have to be at work on Central by eight."

"I can get you there. No problem."

The two rent-boys weren't at the corner of 4th and my alley when we drove back, so there were no explanations that I had to give while I gathered up my stuff. There wasn't much more than a small pile of clothes, so I took it all. Better with me tonight than left here and stolen during the night. That's when this alley came to life—at night.

He marched me right to his apartment house in an older, brick-fronted six-story building with maybe two two-bedroom units on each floor. His was the only basement unit, across from a communal laundry room and storage cubicles. He had his own washer and dryer, though. The apartment was adequately furnished, obviously a bachelor's pad, but, like his car, spic and span.

"Straight to the shower," he said. "Toss out all of your clothes, and I'll toss in a pair of briefs you can wear while the clothes are washing."

The briefs were a couple of sizes too big for me, so they hung low on my waist. It's not that he was fat. Far from it. He was a fit as they came. He was just that much bigger than I was. I padded out to the combination living room, dining room, and kitchen area when I had stood under the shower for what seemed to be a half hour, luxuriating in the steam and musk-scented liquid soap and the shampoo I found there. This was heaven. I hadn't been dirty and smelly by choice.

My thoughts went back to Las Vegas and why I'd left. I'd been raised in comfort there. Falling under the control of a bouncer at a casino right out of high school, though, had changed my life—made me need to move out of town and beyond his reach. He wasn't just rough; he had a temper and liked to punch to make his points.

I saddled up on one of the stools on the living room side of a kitchen island while I was still rubbing my wet hair with a towel. The man was working in the kitchen. Steaks were out on a platter for frying in a skillet he was heating up. I could see that there were baked potatoes in the microwave. My stomach gave a lurch. It had been some time since I'd had a steak dinner.

He turned and looked at me. For a moment I saw the same look of surprise and what seemed to be both sadness and yearning in his eyes before he went duller, more remote in expression. It wasn't just his eyes that were hard, I could see him getting harder under the flimsy material of his gym shorts too as he moved along the kitchen counter, cooking with fluid, efficient movements, washing cooking pans and utensils in soapy water in the sink as he moved. Spic and span man. That was him. I thought of the Mr. Clean commercials figure. That was this guy, except that this guy had hair, albeit a close buzz clip, and craggy facial features. Same hunky build, though.

He set out a cold beer in a bottle for me. Didn't even ask my age, although I was prepared to show him my driver's license, if he did, to prove I was old enough. He nursed another one himself, while moving around in his compact kitchen area. As he cooked, he took snatches of looks at me, each time that shocked and sad expression followed by a hardening and distancing.

We ate in silence. I more like inhaled the food. He got up and fried another steak, and I devoured that one as well.

"Sorry," I said afterward. "I'm a pig."

"I can see you were hungry. I'll fry up another one if you want."

"No, thanks. I'm not that much of a pig."

"You aren't a pig at all. You are a lovely young man. You are so much like . . . well, you are achingly good looking."

"Thanks," I answered. "You're a hunk and a half yourself."

This was it then, I thought. To the bedroom to earn that $150. But, no, that wasn't happening—yet.

"You look worn out too," he said. "Both my washer and dryer are really slow. You'll have nothing to wear all night."

Here it comes, I thought.

"Why don't you go on back to the bedroom I showed you, turn in, and get a good sleep? I'll set my alarm for six, and we'll get you to work on time in the morning."

"But the $150."

"You needed setting back on your feet again. Just something I felt I needed to do. Go on now. I have some paperwork to do. I'll keep the noise down. Can't say the same for the tenants in the apartment above us. Should have evicted them a long time ago."

\* \* \* \*

He was right about the people overhead. Probably a couple. Both a male and female voice, the female voice very shrill, turning breathy later. A vocal battle raged in their living area for two hours, during which I only got snatches of sleep on the double bed taking up most of the room of the man's second bedroom. Then, when they moved to their bedroom, bedroom calisthenics, with screeching bedsprings and a headboard rhythmically bouncing against the wall behind my head for another thirty or forty minutes. When there was silence, I went out like a light.

The man visited me in the darkest of night. I wasn't surprised that he would. I don't know how long he'd been cuddled in behind me, naked, his hard cock pressing up the small of my back, embracing me, with a hand encasing my cock, and kissing the back of my neck, before I was awake enough to know he was there. The

217

hand work was sporadic, hesitating, as if he was trying to make up his mind what he wanted to do.

I was still in a hazy zone when I felt him slipping the briefs I'd worn to bed—his briefs—off my legs.

When I was fully awake, I just sighed for him and pressed my body back into his, letting him know he could have me. He'd paid for me, he'd treated me real well, and, well, he was a hunk and a half with a big cock that I'd already wondered about taking. It's not that I was fast or easy. But it also wasn't as if I hadn't been fucked before. And I had taken his money for staying the night.

I had agreed to give him sex before I'd ever gotten into his car.

Once having been reassured that I'd take him, he started off slow and sensual. Kissing my neck and shoulders and, when I turned my face to him, kissing me tenderly on the lips. His hands glided all over my body, always pausing to give my cock strokes. I felt like I should give him attention, and I did reach back for his cock, but he moved it away from me, signaling that he wanted to work my body. And work it, he did, tenderly and gently, but with a sensuality that had me moaning and sighing and moving my hips. As he kissed and tongued and worked my body with one hand, he loosened the grip on my cock to provide a sleeve for me to fuck his fist. At some point, he'd slathered his hand with lube, and I stroked in the sheath his hand provided until, with a long sigh, I came.

He moved down my naked body, pressing his hands on my butt cheeks and pulling them apart. I felt his hot breath on my hole, blowing on it, and then his tongue pressing against the rim, breaching the rim, pushing into me deep. I raised my buttocks to him—presenting not only for what he was doing now, but for a good angle for the slide of the cock.

"Yes, yes," I murmured. I couldn't signal any better than this that he could fuck me.

Kneading my butt cheeks, keeping them pressed apart, the wetness of lube, the pressing of fingers. One . . . two . . . three.

"Open for me. Open for me, baby," I heard him murmur. "I'll be good to you. I don't want to hurt you."

To the extent I could open to that big cock of his, I did. "Yes, yes," I whispered with a sigh. My hips involuntary raised themselves further and went into a fucking motion. My cock was hard again, the bulb dragging back and forth on the sheet. He encased it again with a hand.

"Fuck me, fuck me. Give it to me now," I whined.

I heard the snap of the condom being rolled onto this cock and adjusted, and I moaned in want for him. "Yes, fuck me," I murmured again, more eloquent words escaping me in my need for it.

When he started sliding it into me, I was almost open enough to take him. Almost. He was patient, moving into me at a glacial pace. I kept chanting, "Give it to me. Bury it deep. Give it to me. Giveittome."

Fully mounted, he moved slowly inside me, giving me all of it, pulling back, slowly sliding in. He was stretched out above me, but not putting his full weight on me, an arm embracing my chest, his lips in the hollow of my neck, a hand slow stroking my cock.

Whispering in my ear, "You're so nice, so tight, so good." And he seemed to be whispering a name too. Not mine, though, one I couldn't quite hear. It hit me then that he didn't know my name—and I didn't know his. We hadn't exchanged names. How weird, I briefly thought. But this wasn't a time for thought. This was a time for pleasure and for building up to that next ejaculation.

"Faster, harder. Give it to me harder," I cried out, feeling my sap rising again, but wanting to blow in fury, not romance.

With a groan and a grunt, he pulled me up fully to my knees, grasped my waist with one strong hand, and buried the other one in the hair at the back of my head and arching me, painfully, back toward him. He was crouching over me, though, set in a stance of power, set to pound my ass, hard and deep, the power of his whole weight going into each thrust. Each thrust causing me to jerk and cry out.

"Shit! Fuck! Shitshitshit!" I screamed as he pounded me hard. Pounded, pounded, pounded.

I came again. He pulled out of me, jerked off the condom, and gave me three wads of cum over the small of my back. He immediately climbed down from the bed, muttering, "Sorry. I'm so sorry."

He was out of the room before I could say, "Don't be sorry. I asked for it. I wanted. I loved it." But I said it anyway.

\* \* \* \*

He couldn't look at me in the morning while he was fixing our breakfast—a full country breakfast of eggs, bacon, toast, even a couple of pancakes with butter and syrup. A pint of OJ; a gallon of coffee.

The most he would say was, "A construction worker needs a good start on the day."

Especially one who'd had the stuffing exhaustively fucked out of him the night before, I thought. I wanted to say that I wasn't a real construction worker, just a gofer for tools and construction material and guys' lunch boxes. But I could see that each time I said something, he winced. Like he preferred to pretend I wasn't even there. At least that I couldn't speak, couldn't call him out for losing control with me last night.

He drove me to the construction site in silence. Before I got out of the car, he said, "Your clothes will be ready by the time you finish work. Sorry I didn't get them folded before we left this morning."

Ironed and folded, I'll bet, I thought. "It's OK, there are buses back to where you live. I'll stop in for them."

"And I'll feed you dinner?" It was a question, not a statement. He wasn't claiming possession or anything.

"Yeah, sure, that would be great," I answered as I got out of the car. It could just be dinner and that was all. I'd take him again if he wanted me. I'd be happy to, without money. He already was giving me stuff. His cooking was great—and free. I'd be happy to lie under him again. It just didn't seem to be what he wanted. Last night had really shut him down. Guess I wasn't that great after all, I thought.

I couldn't figure out what I was supposed to do last night, what would have pleased him. I somehow did something wrong and made him angry during the fuck. I just didn't know what it was. But it was good for me both ways.

That day, although the construction foreman made suggestions of getting me alone, I fended them off. I had no idea why I did that. I did, though, stay hard most of the day thinking of the royal fucking I'd gotten the previous night.

When I got back to the apartment, the man was a bit more relaxed, more open.

"I went through your things. Most of your stuff is beyond its last leg. And those boots. They're about to fall apart. What say we go shopping after dinner."

"I can't afford new clothes," I said.

"My treat," he answered. "You need toiletries too. Toothpaste and brush, shaving stuff, soap, deodorant. The works. What you brought was well past its death date."

I started to say that I didn't take handouts like that, but I could see how anxious he was to do it. Then, in the only mention of the previous night, he said, "It's the least I can do. I was out of line. I shouldn't have . . . not like that . . ."

I wanted to tell him that I'd loved it, had begged for it, but I could see that he really didn't want to talk about it beyond what he said. So, instead, I just agreed to shop after dinner. He looked relieved. I chalked whatever he bought as payment for if he wanted to do me again when we got back from shopping.

I wanted him to do me again when we got back from shopping. Just like last night would be just fine with me.

He apparently didn't want to do me again, though. We got back from shopping very late. He bought me a lot of stuff—but it was practical stuff, not any sexy fuck wear like most daddies would buy their fuck boys when they took them clothes shopping. Or so I'd heard. Certainly not what the casino bouncer bought me in Las Vegas when he took me shopping.

Most of it was what I could wear to work. The new construction boots were great—and cost him a pretty penny. If he wanted to fuck me when we got home like he'd done the night before, he'd paid the fare. Although, I liked it enough that I couldn't see charging him.

"It's late. You might as well stay the night," he said when we got home.

"Yeah, I guess so," I said, almost licking my chops at the thought of another visitation in the dark of the night.

I stayed awake most of the night, waiting for him, watching the door to the corridor, with the light from the hallway showing in a large gap at the base of the door. He did come to the door. I snapped awake at seeing the shadow of his feet under the door and hearing the rub of his hand on the other side of the door. I even heard the long sigh and deep groan.

But he didn't come in.

At breakfast, we started off saying nothing about where I was going after work the next day. That question just sat there, heavy, in the air. He was more relaxed, though. Still, there was some sadness about him. We were becoming more comfortable with each other. And for the first time, he told me his name was Sarge and I told him I was Kevin.

"What brought you to Albuquerque, Kevin? You weren't raised in that cardboard carton in the alley, were you?"

"No. A good family. A normal family. Outside Las Vegas. A bad relationship, though. I decided to move on."

"Ah," he said. Before he could ask more, although I didn't get the impression that he'd worry that wound, I got in a question.

"Sarge?" I asked. "You were military with a nickname like Sarge?"

"Yes. Marines."

I would have guessed. He was that squared away and put together that well. "Served overseas?"

"Yes. both Iraq and Afghanistan."

"I don't see any stuff around that's military. Souvenirs and campaign medals and such."

"No, you don't."

I sensed he was closing down on me, so I changed the subject. "About this evening, after work—"

"I have tickets to a farm team baseball game . . . if you'd like to go."

"Yes, I'd like that," I said, keeping my smile to myself. We were getting comfortable with each other. Maybe he'd get over whatever barrier was being raised between us sex wise. "But the expense."

"I'm not a pauper, Kevin. I'm the super of this apartment building. But I also own it. You don't see me going to work, because I work right here. But I make good money off of this apartment house. Bought it as soon as I left the service. Needed to get away from that."

"Ah," I said. But even that maybe was too much.

He did sort of a double take, like maybe he'd said too much about leaving the Marines. I didn't pursue the point. We were getting along so well.

* * * *

There was a step back that evening when I came home from work—and then a few more disturbing withdrawals after that.

I'd gotten a ride back to Sarge's place on the back of a construction worker's motorcycle. Sarge must have heard the roar of the muffler, because he was up the stairs and on the sidewalk before I could get off the bike.

"Never do that. You should never do that," he cried out.

Shocked that he would react this way to me being with a construction worker—who was quite hunky and also totally hetero—took me back. It was the first sign of possessiveness. It both disturbed and impressed me.

"Let's discuss this inside," I said to Sarge. I turned to thank Dave for the ride home and to apologize for Sarge's outburst, and when I turned, Sarge was gone.

He was sitting in a chair in the living room, seething, wrapping his arms around his chest, and rocking back and forth.

"There's nothing between me and that guy, Sarge," I said when I came in. "It was just a ride home." Funny that I didn't trip even a little bit on calling Sarge's apartment "home."

"It's not the guy," Sarge said through set teeth. "It's the ride. Motorcycles are only good for killing people. Don't do that to me again . . . please. Don't show up here on a motorcycle again."

I could see that it really set him off, so I quickly said that, sure, I would stay off motorcycles. It was yet another sign I was getting that the man had issues, though. I didn't know how many such issues I could deal with in a fluid situation like this.

We went to the ball game and had a good time, but there remained something under the surface for both of us—whatever Sarge's demons were and me not sensing any solid ground here to stand on with him. I wished he'd just fuck me like he did the other night—claim me as his territory. I would have minded less him taking off on me being cuddled behind Dave—who was a real hunk—on a motorcycle than the inexplicable rage at riding a motorcycle. This was the West and I was twenty-two. Loads of twenty-two-year-old men rode motorcycles here.

When we got back from the game, nothing was said about me leaving and going back to the alley either. I didn't want to go—at least unless Sarge got stranger—so I didn't bring it up. And then he made his position on that obvious.

"If you need transportation, I'll get you a car," he said. And then he went to the refrigerator to pull out a beer, handed me one in passing, and planted himself in front of the TV, giving his full attention to a pro baseball game—as if we hadn't seen enough baseball that day.

And he came through on a car. When I came home the next day, he had an old, beat-up Civic coup waiting for me. "It's old, but it runs good," he said, as he handed me the keys. "It's gassed up. Let me know when it's running low and I'll gas it up again."

I knew I could take that as an indication that he wanted me to stay, but that was what happened the next day. By then I was in a tailspin over what happened the previous night, after the trip to the ball field, after I'd gone to bed, leaving a brooding Sarge glued to the TV set and swigging his third beer.

Sometime after eleven that night, while the couple over head were thumping their headboard against the wall, I heard Sarge's front door open and then close again. Shortly before midnight, I heard him return. But not just him. I heard voices, men's voices, both set low, as they passed in the hallway outside my door. The thumping overhead had stopped, but the thumping just behind my headboard, in Sarge's bedroom, started up. And the sounds of taking and receiving. The sounds of being taken hard and deep, the pistoned, rhythmic pounding of the headboard of Sarge's bed against the bedroom wall. Impassioned cries in Spanish.

Miserable and with the draining emotions of having been rejected, I pulled a pillow over my head and fought for sleep—for anything that would end my confusion, frustration, and dejection.

Nothing was said in the morning while Sarge fixed breakfast. I'd heard the front door open and close— twice—later in the night, so I knew whoever Sarge had brought home had been taken away again in the morning. And nothing was said when I returned from work that day, our attention taken up with the car he provided me.

It was so confusing. Sarge didn't want to fuck me, but he still wanted to keep me here. He didn't mention me leaving. He gave me a car to drive between his apartment and the construction site.

We went another day in an atmosphere of false normalcy. I bristled and analyzed everything he said, everything he did. I'm sure he was doing the same with me. Increasingly, the apartment, which seemed such a commodious space when I first arrived, began to constrict around me—around us. We were getting in each other's way as we moved about it, looking at each other when we did, each of us about to say something, but stifling ourselves.

The next night, the young man Sarge brought home after midnight and fucked—repeatedly during the night—was still there in the morning. When I went to the bathroom—the main one off the hallway rather than the small one off Sarge's bedroom—the young man was standing at the sink, naked. The room was misted up. He'd just come out of the shower. He was shaving—using my razor and shaving cream—the razor and shaving cream Sarge had bought for me the evening he'd taken me clothes shopping.

I simply took them out of his hands, glowered at him, and pointed toward the door. I'd meant the door exiting the apartment, but he turned the other way in the hall—back to Sarge's room, shook his pert little buttocks at me, and entered Sarge's room. While I performed my own morning hygiene ritual with shaky hands, Sarge was fucking the young man again in his bedroom, the headboard bumping rhythmically against the wall.

I dressed quickly, just glanced at the kitchen on my way out the door, and couldn't leave the apartment fast enough. There would be two for breakfast in that kitchen, as usual. But one of them wouldn't be me.

When I came home that evening, there was a note from Sarge that he was working on a plumbing issue in an apartment up on the fourth floor. Nothing written about the visitation of the young man.

I walked into Sarge's bedroom—the first time I'd ever been in there—to see if the guy perhaps was still there, or if there was evidence that he was moving in. I didn't find that, but what I did find were framed photographs on Sarge's nightstand. They all were of two men, a tall, muscular one, and a shorter, younger guy. The tall figure in the photos were Sarge. Sarge in his Marine uniform, Sarge in a tuxedo, Sarge in a Speedo at the beach. The younger man was appropriately dressed in each photo—each photo clearly showing an intimate relationship between the two. Each one had an effect of longing on me, of the two having something together that I wanted with Sarge too.

But those weren't the aspects of the photographs that gave me pause. What arrested my attention was that the other figure in the photographs were always the same young man—a young man who was the spitting image of me.

"The other man in the photograph is Andy, my lover," Sarge said softly. "The photo with the tuxedos was the day we took vows of commitment. There wasn't an option of marriage in those days." I looked up from where I was sitting on the edge of his bed, holding one of the photographs.

"You have a lover—one who looks like me?"

"Had a lover, yes. We were together for six years. He's dead. Died in a motorcycle accident."

"Ah," I said. There didn't seem to be any more to be said. This went a long way to explain his strangeness.

Having said that much, though, Sarge seemed to think there was more to be said. "We were in the Marines together. We found each other when we were serving in Afghanistan. We were discovered and sent home. Dishonorable discharge both, despite a chest full of combat medals each. They don't do that anymore in cases like ours, but they did it then, and there's no changing that. I do have medals. So did Andy. I can't and won't display them, though. We moved here. We were happy. We were committed. I kept my commitment; I'm sure Andy did as well. And then I bought Andy a motorcycle. You are so like him. Too, too much like him . . . I'm so conflicted."

"Shush," I whispered putting a finger up to his lips. His voice faltered and stopped, running out of gas. There were tears in his eyes.

"You don't have to say anymore," I whispered. "Just hold me, kiss me, fuck me." He already was embracing me in his arms. Then he was kissing me. All that remained was . . .

"I . . . I can't hold back. I can't control myself when I'm with you. I couldn't with Andy either."

"But he wanted it that way, didn't he?"

"Yes, I guess so," Sarge answered, his voice faltering.

"So do I. As hard, fast, and deep as you can. But the gentle, making love, start to it. Making love to my body until I'm begging for something more intense. And then giving that to me. Drilling me hard and deep. Putting me to the sword, taking no prisoners possession. Losing yourself in wanting me, as you did when you fucked me. That's one of only two things I have in common with Andy. That and the fact that we look alike. Otherwise I'm not Andy. I'm Kevin. We can start again, just the two of us. Not Sarge and Andy, but Sarge and Kevin. Just don't hold back from me. Give it all to me. You don't need to bring anyone else home to hold me up on some sort pedestal. Fuck me hard, punish me, make me totally yours."

"But I lose control. I did so the other night more with you than I did with Andy. I can't control my lust."

"I don't want you to control your lust with me. It shows me your passion. It shows me how deeply you want to do it with me. No one has shown me before how much they wanted me as you did the other night. That was the moment that I realized I loved you."

"That you loved me?" he asked, stunned. "That you could love me as I knew almost from the beginning that I loved you?"

229

I pulled out the drawer of his nightstand, assuming I'd find what I did there—lube and condoms.

He took me hard on the bed, harder even than that one night we had together. But, as requested, he romanced me to begin with, made sensual love to my body to where I was beside myself in wanting him inside me and begged him for the fuck. And then the headboard did a mean ratatatat against the wall as he fucked me doggy style again, crouching over my buttocks and holding me at the waist, using the leverage of his feet on the bed and the power shift of his pelvis to thrust hard and deep again and again and again and . . .

Begging no mercy; receiving no mercy. Both of us lost in want of each other. Him not being able to meld enough with me; me not being able to get him deep enough, thick enough, punishing enough inside me.

As the military recruitment commercials said: Nobody can do it like a Marine can do it.

Afterward, lying in each other's embrace, still panting from the exertion, I thanked him. The air still needed to be cleared, however.

"Those other young men, the last couple of days. Was it because I remind you so much of Andy, or have I displeased you somehow?"

"I've been a crazy man. Underneath it all, I suppose I was trying to drive you away. I couldn't send you away, so I needed you to want to leave. I'd had you once—in the form of Andy. I had him, but I ruined his military career through my own lusts, and in the end I killed him. I bought him a motorcycle and urged him to learn to ride it. I even told him the streets weren't slick enough from rain that morning for him not to ride his motorcycle."

"Shush on that," I whispered. "I think what you did give Andy was more than enough in life from his perspective. You can't go on blaming yourself."

230

"And sheer frustration from wanting you and thinking I had to stay away from you—while still not letting you go," Sarge continued. "Sexual frustration, needing sexual release. I think I wore those young men out."

"It wore me out just listening from the other side of the wall of you fucking them." I forced a laugh; he was too emotional to join me.

We were silent for a few moments. Then I spoke again. "I would like you to wear me out like you did those young men—to fuck me totally and often."

"I think I can do that."

"I know you can do that." A pause and then, "I like your bedroom better than mine. Can I move into your bed?"

"You know you can."

"Can I stay here . . . forever?"

"You'd really want to do that? I've got a good twenty-five years on you. You'll still be young and vigorous when I'm doddering."

"Did you plan for Andy to still be here when you were doddering?"

"Yes, of course. But I've grown wiser . . . and more realistic."

"Is there something you had with Andy you don't have with me?"

"Well, there is an aspect of intimacy, symbols of total commitment. Something understood when we took our commitment vows."

"Ah, you mean you barebacked him."

A pause and then the answer of, "Yes. For us it made all the difference. The commitment was total. The pleasure was total. The pledge of loyalty was there each time we fucked."

"Would you give up those other men for me?"

"In a flash. I only fucked them because of you."

231

"But you cruised before. You picked me up cruising."

"I was looking. And I found you. I didn't cruise when I was with Andy. I'd found him."

A long pause again, and then I rolled over on top of him. "I'm going to ride you now," I said, "But I'm off work tomorrow. I'd like you to take me somewhere."

"Oh, where? You have a car now. You can drive yourself anywhere you want to go."

"Yes, but I need you there too. I want you to take me to the free clinic—for both of us to be tested. And when we are both tested as safe, I want you to bring me home and fuck the stuffing out of me—bareback. I promise it will only be you from then on."

I was straddling him and riding his cock while I was making another silent vow to him: I also would never get on a motorcycle again.

# Unexpected Inheritance

Simon Clore, the senior partner of Clore & Son, where I worked as an accountant, passed by me frequently during the evening office party, lightly touching me intimately each time, leaving no doubt what he wanted from me. He had me in such a vice. Not only did my livelihood depend on keeping him satisfied with me, but also he was married to my second cousin, Betsy, who I thought a lot of and who was going through an ordeal with cancer. I didn't, for the world, want to burden her with any more grief than she already was coping with. Simon was using that to his advantage. As soon as he had learned that I was gay, he started taking advantage of me.

He finally came up beside me at the punch bowl. "I want you to stay after the party and help me . . . clean up, Paul."

Simon Clore wasn't the type who cleaned anything up, especially an office party, so the other office workers were surprised and extra grateful when he announced that he and I would take care of everything afterward. I knew what "everything" entailed. I, in fact, was horny tonight, but it wasn't from Simon's touches and hints of what was in the offing. During the party I kept looking over at the "son" part of the Clore & Son partnership. Young, hunky Hal was perpetually surrounded by adoring young women, and tonight was no exception. We played tennis together and each time I fantasized about him taking me in the locker room shower—I melted at the sight of him, hunky and hung, when we showered at the club after playing, but it was a "no go" with Hal. He obviously was a woman's man and had his hands full without thinking of me—at least not in the way I thought of him.

The post-party assignation was over in twenty-five minutes, and a good fifteen minutes of that was me working to get Simon's small cock up as he sat in his office chair and I knelt between his knees and worked on the old man's cock with my mouth. The fuck itself was only five slides—yes, I counted them, wondering if the old man ever would get up to ten—and a jerk and a spurt in a condom that barely was able to stay on his dick—as I bent over his desk and he poked me from behind.

He left me to finish the cleanup—he'd done practically nothing toward the end, of course—and then, when my car wouldn't start, he offered to drive me home to my apartment.

In front of the apartment, he asked, hopefully, "I'd like to come up. Betsy's in the hospital overnight again. They want to monitor something. That's why she wasn't at the party. I didn't want to cloud the employees' enjoyment, so I didn't say anything."

Of course, most of us already knew Betsy was in the hospital again. Hal had told one of the receptionists that their tryst that night had to be postponed because he was visiting his mother in the hospital. There was a pact not to talk to Simon about his wife's lingering death, so we all were keeping mum about her hospital stay as well.

"That would be lovely, Simon," I said. "But there's the problem of Demont."

"Ah, yes, Demont. Possibly you could come on to my house for the night, then."

I shook my head sadly—or at least tried to make it look sad. "Alas, there's still Demont. He's the jealous type, I'm sure you know. He expects me to be in bed under him every night."

"Yes, I see." Simon might be expected to be disappointed at having missed out on an entire night with me—which I could have guaranteed him would be no more than fifteen minutes of me working him up, six pokes from him, and him snoring off for the rest of the night—but his eyes were flashing with arousal and he was licking his lips. He often quizzed me about what Demont did with me, and I tried not to disappoint in my descriptions.

"So, I'll see you at the office Monday?"

"No, not until Thursday," I answered, already, thankfully, out of his car and leaning down and looking through the open passenger door. "I'm sure you remember that I'm taking most of the week off in vacation time. I'll be home working on your and Betsy's personal taxes for three days."

"Ah, yes." He answered. No "thank you for doing my taxes on your personal time," just an "ah, yes." But that was Simon. Just a taker. I smiled as he drove off—not at the memory of him screwing me, which he did in various forms, but at the taillights of his car moving away from me.

There was no Demont waiting for me upstairs. I had invented a jealous black bull roommate to aid in holding Simon off precisely for circumstances like this. There was no one waiting for me upstairs The legend of Demont had worked somewhat of an opposite effect to the one I was going after, though. Since I'd made the mistake of describing to Simon some of Demont's rough

235

sex and bondage positions, the descriptions had aroused him and made him more horny for me.

I went upstairs and, while coffee was brewing to take the buzz off me from whatever someone had spiked the punch with at the office party, I sifted through the mail I'd taken out of the box downstairs. Mostly "gimmee" letters and catalogs from stores I'd shopped online for Christmas gifts and that assumed I was going to give gifts weekly from then on. There was a letter from Professor Hollins, at my alma mater, who wrote longing letters to me almost monthly. He who had taken my virginity during a picnic near the river and who wanted to continue reliving that moment. And there was a bulkier, official-looking letter with British stamps on it.

I started to open the letter but then noticed that the coffee was ready. I really needed that coffee. The letter from Hollins also had put me in a "mood." He'd been a proficient lover with a long cock, and he'd been my first. I'd save the letter to read later, I thought, as I set it aside, on top of the letter from England, and rose to pour coffee.

The postmark on the bulkier letter had also made me think of Phil and Rigger, the gay couple I chatted with, who lived in England. I was in the mood to chat. I went to my computer and started to compose my daily chat to my fantasy pen pals.

*Sorry this chat is late. The Curtis & Caldwell office party ran overtime tonight and I came home late—and sore and exhausted. Steven Curtis came up behind me at the spiked punchbowl I'd made three too many visits to and, squeezing one of my butt cheeks hard, whispered that he and I had a separate party to go to in his office. I knew what he wanted, and the thrill of doing it just a closed, but not locked, door away from the office party in full swing was both a frightening and an arousing sensation. When we got there, he pulled the fleeced-lined handcuffs I've told you about from his desk drawer and in no time he had my wrists bound behind my back and me bent over his desk, fucking me furiously from behind, my belt looped around my throat and Curtis using the belt as reins, choking me as he pulled back hard on the reins with each thrust.*

*I heard the increased noise of the party beyond the private office as the door opened, and there was the hunky Hank Caldwell—you remember, the other, younger partner who fucked me on top of the Xerox machine? I watched him make a phone call for Dion to come up from the loading dock before he was grabbing my hair and forcing my mouth down on his cock on the other side of the desk from where Curtis was furiously fucking me in the ass. And when the black bull Dion came into the office, he relieved Curtis in drilling me. I nearly passed out from that monster cock of his plowing my ass.*

*It didn't stop there either. When I left the office, my car wouldn't start and Curtis volunteered to drop me off in his limo, which Dion was driving, on his way home. They doubled me in the parking garage of my apartment house, Curtis on his back on the hood of the car—the bonnet to you lot—with that long cock of his snaked up into me from the rear, while Dion pumped me from the front with that monster cock of his. I only wish it had been you two. I'm not sure I can hobble out of bed for work tomorrow. What do you say, should I bother to wear a thong pouch to the next office party? *smile* Gotta go and soak in the tub, both legs over the side to sooth my bruised ass channel. Kisses to and a deep-throated suck for you both. Todd.*

I'd been slipping my hand to my crotch during the chat and now, finished and the e-mail sent, I opened the chat they had sent me, full of descriptions of a threesome on a bale of hay in a barn, and I unzipped myself and stroked off to that.

I went back to the kitchen counter and refilled my coffee cup, remembered the letter from Professor Hollins, and, feeling mellow and a bit melancholy, reached for the letter. Pulling it away, my eye caught the bulkier letter from England. Curious, I slit it open. Several pages of very official looking legalese unfolded in my hand.

I sat down at the table and read over it several times. It had to be one of the most elaborate scam letters I'd ever read. Although, even though I was an experienced accountant, for the life of me I couldn't figure out how the scam worked. The papers claimed I had inherited a third interest in a pub south of Gloucester, England, called The Laughing Lion, as well as a third interest in an ancient house near the pub in the Forest of Dean.

Where the hell was Gloucester? I wondered. Or the Forest of Dean, for that matter. I didn't know anyone in England, or anyone anywhere else who would die and leave me anything.

It had to be a scam. But, for the life of me, I couldn't figure out what the scam was. It was both frustrating and intriguing, and I knew I had to check it out and figure it out or I wouldn't sleep well all weekend. I decided to call Aaron, my lawyer, in the morning and have him read the legalese and tell me what the scam was. It would mean calling him on Saturday morning, but I knew he worked Saturdays, and he didn't hesitate to call me on Saturdays to ask how I was coming on doing his taxes. This would be justifiable tit for tat.

I went to bed and masturbated myself to the drowsy state before sleep slipped in, dreaming of a big brute fucking me rough and standing against a wall, with an arm being painfully pulled high up my back. Seeking the height of all the sensations I could—pain as well as pleasure—and to be totally controlled and used by a man—or men.

\* \* \* \*

Waking with the morning light from the Gloucester hotel room window hitting me in the face through the gap that the curtains wouldn't cover, I felt groggy from the drink the previous evening and took a moment to remember where I was. I was laying stretched against him, my back cuddled into his chest. A mop of reddish-blond hair was tickling the hollow of my neck. A beefy arm, ruddy and covered in reddish down, was thrown over my torso. A similarly beefy leg was thrown over my thigh. His left leg stretched down mine, his foot barely reaching my ankle. The thickness of his cock pressed into the small of my back. Bulldog thickness. He was built like a bull dog—close to the ground; stocky, but muscular, not fat; young, younger than I was; the ruddy good looks and vitality of what they'd call a footballer over here; his cock not appreciably long flaccid, but unusual thick and lengthening significantly in arousal, the bulb an angry red; even his balls, pulled tight up to his groin, were beefy.

He was a powerful, muscular man—powerful in his thrusts. I'd been ridden hard the previous night. That I could remember. Nothing like I'd ever had in the States. It was good for me. Nothing had been meeting my fantasies in the States, certainly not the fantasies I'd spun with my English pen pals.

I gently lifted his arm off my torso and then pulled out from underneath his leg, hoping not to disturb his light snoring. But as I sat up on the side of the bed, he snorted and turned over onto his back. A hand came down and scratched his balls. He was half hard.

"Where you goin'?"

"To the bathroom. To take a piss and maybe a shower."

"In a minute," he said, a light growl in the depth of his throat. He'd used the same growl in telling what he wanted me to do the previous night. And I'd done it.

239

He raised his torso, cupped the back of my neck, and brought my face down to his crotch. I opened my mouth to him and gave him head for nearly a minute. Pulling off him then, I said, "I really do have to take a piss."

"OK, but the shower can wait."

When I returned from the bathroom, he was sitting on the other side of the bed, smoking a cigarette, rolling a condom on his cock, and slathering his sheathed cock with lube.

He fucked me with me on my back, legs spread and bent, hands gripping the rails of the headboard over my head, back arched, mouth hanging open in a big yawn, and his bulldog body between my legs. His torso was raised, his fists dug in the bedspread at each side of my chest, his buttocks moving forward and back with hard powerful thrusts.

Welcome to England. I'd been here less than twenty hours.

* * * *

Aaron called me back early Saturday afternoon. "I don't know what's going on either, Paul, but it's no scam. After I couldn't see anything wrong with the documents, I called the solicitors in Gloucester, England, listed on the letterhead—after I'd checked with a couple of firms in England I knew of and was told the Gloucester firm was legit. The inheritance is also legit, apparently. You don't know a Peter Townsend, a Brit, by that name?"

"No, never heard of him."

"Well, he's left you one third of a British pub on the Severn River and one third of an old house in the hills above a town called Newnham. Either one ring a bell?"

"Not a tinkle. I'm thoroughly confused."

240

"The solicitors are quite anxious to see you. They've schedule a meeting with you at their chambers in Gloucester for 3:00 p.m. Monday. Do you think you can make it, or should I try to schedule later?"

"I don't know. Where in England are Gloucester and the Severn River anyway?"

"I don't know, but the solicitors suggested you fly to Birmingham and rent a car from there. Are you curious enough to break away that soon?"

"You bet I am," I answered.

"In that case, you'd better find out where those places are quickly. Good luck, Paul, and keep me posted on what this is all about. I'm almost curious enough to go with you."

I had no trouble booking a flight from New York that night, although all I could get in the way of a seat was steerage. I'd also booked a subcompact Kia Rio at the Birmingham airport. They tried to get me to upscale in size, but I'm glad I refused. Driving right-hand drive on narrow lanes hemmed in by hedgerows was about as much fright in life as I could endure. The somewhat seedy three-star Station Hotel in Gloucester, just off the AA30 ring road, was the best I could do for booking on such short notice. In the eventuality, that was a good thing. The desk clerk didn't even bat an eye when I came in half drunk on Sunday night and took a man up to my room.

I'd arrived in Birmingham in late morning after an all-night endurance flight, and the drive south, after the hour of getting out of the airport and into a car, took more than two hours. The driving wasn't bad, though. I'd driven on the left both in England and Australia before and the roads were all highways. Working against that was being tired from only dozing during the night in the crowded plane.

I grabbed a bite to eat—I couldn't remember what it was ten minutes after I finished it: some sort of soggy sandwich wrapped in plastic, a piece of sandwich meat and a pimento spread, I think—after I'd check into the hotel and then went upstairs and tried to sleep. But, of course, I couldn't. I kept thinking of this pub I supposedly now owned a piece of.

Since I couldn't sleep, I decided to check the pub out before meeting with the solicitors the next day.

I had picked the hotel in Gloucester from the available choices because it was on the south side of the city. When I asked at the desk where the road along the west side of the Severn toward Cardiff, in Wales, was, the A48, I was pleased to find that it was easy to find from the hotel.

I'd been told the Laughing Lion Pub was on the bank of the river on A48 just before I reached the village of Newnham. I had no trouble finding it. I surveyed it as I got out of the car, which had been making rather disturbing noises for the last mile of the drive. The building rambled a bit and looked like it almost, but not quite, was in need of remodeling. Still, it looked inviting and there were a fair number of cars in the car park, so it also looked reasonably prosperous. As indicated on the map, it did, indeed, sit just above the river on a riprap-enforced embankment. The river was fairly broad at this point, but the maps told me it would broaden significantly before entering the Bristol Channel. I could see small container ships moving on the river toward or from Gloucester. And there was considerable car traffic on the A48, even for a Sunday. The pub was well located.

Still, I had already decided to sell out my third as soon as possible. It was still a mystery why I had inherited it.

I entered the pub, the main room of which was divided off in three zones. To the left as I entered at the side of the building, was a large room with continuous windows on three sides looking out on the river. This was

242

what first caught my attention, as it was where the light was the brightest. To my right, in a section with a step up and the ceiling lowered, was a long bar, swathed in shadow, with points of light above the bar and on the few tables in this area. Straight ahead, in a separate room, served by a wide entrance, was a smoky pool room. I could see three tables, two of them in use. The river room, as I thought of it, was occupied, but not to overflowing, with the patrons coming and going frequently.

No one was in the bar area except for the bartender taking up position behind the bar. He was young looking, a sportsmen type—something rugged like rugby or soccer, which they called football here. Sandy haired, ruddy complexion. A nose that had been broken more than once, the second time seemingly back toward where it originally was. It gave him a somewhat dangerous, thuggish look, but, in fact, added to the attraction of him. He smiled at me, as I entered, so I was drawn to the bar and perched on a stool. I noticed then, in the darkness, that a few of the tables in the bar were occupied too.

The barman came around the bar occasionally to serve the table, but then he always came back to me.

I ordered a Guinness Stout, if for no other reason than I assumed that was what one drank in a pub. And, famished, off schedule, and with less-than-fond memories of the soggy sandwich I'd last eaten, I asked him if they were serving food yet.

"It's a bit early, but I think I could have fish and chips served up for you."

"Thank you, that would be great," I answered. And when it came, indeed it *was* great. Far better than the fish and chips I could get served in New York, not that I ordered it very often.

"Sorry," I said, when it came and when I ordered another Guinness, the barman having been off to clean tables in the river room for several minutes, "I've just gotten off a plane from the States. I don't even know what time you'd be serving here."

"The evening food service won't come on for another hour. We close at 10:30 on Sunday nights, though, so last calls on everything would be at 10:00. I'd be out of here at 10:31." He laughed, and I laughed with him. He had a hearty laugh and a very nice smile. "American or Canadian, are you?" he asked.

"American. From New York."

"Sweet. You here for pleasure or business? In England, I mean. You'd be here in the pub for pleasure."

That sounded a bit strange, but I answered what I thought was being asked. "Business. I'm staying in Gloucester—at The Station Hotel. Tried to sleep and couldn't. Discovered I was hungry and thirsty and decided to take a short drive down the Severn. I wonder, is the owner of the pub in this evening?"

"Peter died recently. But I guess just having come from across the pond you wouldn't know that. Ralph. Ralph Barnes isn't in tonight. So, you've come because you've heard about the pub? Decided to do a little cruising, have you? Top or bottom? I could give you leads. Might even be interested myself. Might definitely be interested myself, depending."

"Cruising?"

"You're a poofter, aren't you?"

"A poofter?"

"An Oscar?"

That really threw me and I just looked at him, surprise written all over my face, I'm sure.

"Oscar Wilde," he explained, with a laugh. "Queer . . . gay . . . a fag. Look around, sweet thing. What do you see none of here?"

I looked around. It hit me almost immediately. "No women. I just see men."

244

"That's because this is a men-only pub. For hook ups and just to be comfortable among our own kind."

Our own kind. I turned to him, "So you are—?"

"A power top. Hoping that you might be a bottom."

"As it happens, I am," I answered.

He gave me a big grin—and took my almost-empty glass and filled it with stout again. "Well, then, hallelujah, have a drink on me. And then remember how nice I was to you if you stay till last call. And if you do stay until last call . . ." He didn't finish that sentence. He just gave me a wink and went off into the pool room to collect empty glasses.

So, I had inherited one third of a gay bar. Could this get any more weird?

I hung around, watching the operation of the pub, and occasionally talking with the barman, whose name was Sean, until last call. He was speaking so free and easy with me, flittering but not getting aggressive or making direct propositions that I didn't want to leave. The hotel room was pretty Spartan—and would be quite lonely.

He didn't stop me from pulling away from the bar and moving rather unsteadily toward the door other than to call out a "You sure you should be driving? Be careful. You could have company on the drive back, of course. Any number of lads in here. Or you could remember how nice I was to you and be nice back. Maybe on your back." He winked at me again and smiled, leaving me in doubt as to how much of it was just friendly banter. It was a real turn on, whatever it was.

I smiled in return, waved to him, and weaved my way out the door and to the Kia . . . which wouldn't crank over. I tried it several times.

Sean appeared at the door of the car. "Here, leave it. Get out and I'll see what I can do."

I exchanged places with him and he cranked at the ignition, not doing any better with it than I had. "Did you fill it with petrol before leaving Birmingham?" he turned his head to me and asked.

"No. Should I have?"

"They would have given you as little petrol as they could at the rental desk and it's a good drive from there to here. What your problem is is that you are out of petrol."

"Shit."

"No problem, though. I could drive you to your Gloucester hotel. It's not far. Less than twenty minutes."

"I have a meeting tomorrow," I said. "I'd have to figure out how to get back here with gas before that."

"I could drive you back in the morning. We could stop on the way back for petrol. Nothing open at this hour."

"Drive me back?"

"It would cost you, though," he said, with a grin. "Are you understanding what I'm suggesting?" He was gripping one of my knees with a strong hand.

He fucked me doggy style on the bed in my hotel room. He took charge as soon as we'd entered the room, using that low growl to tell me what I would do for him, and half drunk, more than half exhausted, and totally lost to the arousal of the situation, I gave him what he wanted.

Telling me to lose my shirt as soon as we entered the room, he stripped his off as well, pulling me into an embrace and a kiss. Taller than he was, I had to dip my face down for the kiss. As we kissed, he worked both of our belts open, pushed our trousers and briefs down to our knees, and worked our cocks together. We were both uncut and not yet fully hard, and I took my breath in as he docked the cocks, putting them together, bulb to bulb, pushing the foreskin of his over the foreskin of mine, and slowly stroked them together, making the piss slits kiss.

246

With a moan, I arched my back away from him and he worked my nipples with his teeth.

"Give me some head," he growled, and, as he sat down on the end of the bed, he forced me down between his spread thighs on my knees, and I sucked his cock hard, as he demanded.

Growling again, he moved me in position on the bed, on elbows and knees, cheek to bedspread, left arm stretched out over the bedspread, fist grasping at the bedding, and right hand stroking my cock, as he crouched over my hips, grabbed the sides of my chest and power fucked my ass.

When he was done, he just pushed me over on my side, and landed behind me. Totally exhausted and totally fucked, I zoned out into sleep immediately. I was only half conscious when he took me in a side-split again in the dark of the night, with me only aware enough to respond as he wished to whatever commands he was growling at me. Well, also being aware that I was loving what he was doing to me and spouted great globs of cum on the hotel sheets.

Imagine my surprise the next afternoon when, sitting across from the other two owners of the pub and the house in the solicitor's offices, I saw not only the unfamiliar face of a tall, almost gaunt dark-haired man several years older than I was, but also . . . Sean, who was introduced to me as Sean Anderson. The other man I'd already had a name for, Ralph Barnes.

That still didn't mean much to me and I was showing my confusion to the solicitors while trying not to look at the grinning Sean Anderson until Barnes asked the solicitor to step out of the office for a moment.

When he had, Barnes spoke, "You know me by another name, just as I know you by another name. I know you as Todd. You know me as Rigger. The man who died and left you his share of the pub and house you knew as Phil."

"Oh," I said. So much clearer now. My English pen pals. The men I'd fantasized with concerning sex—rough and kinky sex. And threesomes. And then it sank in. These were men I had fantasized with concerning what my secret desires were—things I'd never actually done, though.

"And Sean here," Barnes continued. "We never included him in our on-line chats, but he's been with Peter and me for a while. We enjoyed our threesomes with you so much that we brought him in to help us act on what we chatted about."

They'd actually done what we chatted about over the Internet. I felt myself beginning to hyperventilate, but Barnes called the solicitor back in before I could melt down and then we became busy discussing the terms of Peter's will and the implications of triple ownership.

"We can discuss that," the solicitor said when I noted that I wanted to sell my third immediately.

"You haven't seen the properties yet," Barnes said.

"He's seen the pub," Sean chipped in.

Barnes turned to me. "Yes, I've already visited the Laughing Lion," I said.

"But you haven't seen the house."

"No, he hasn't," Sean answered for me, with a smile on his face. "He's staying at The Station Hotel in Gloucester."

"Ah, so, you've already—" Barnes turned to a grinning Sean with this comment.

"Yes, I have, as a matter of fact," Sean answered, the grin plastered on his face. "I sussed him out within minutes of coming into the pub. An American just arrived, staying at a Gloucester hotel but just happening to come to our pub—and asking for the owner."

"And so, you didn't come home last night because—"

"Yes, he was very nice. Very nice indeed."

As they bantered back and forth, both the solicitor and I followed the exchange like the volleying of a yellow ball in a tennis match. The solicitor was just confused. I was getting red as a beet. Discussing like that right in front of me. And all of what we'd already laid out in months and months of dirty e-mail exchanges. What could they be thinking I was into sexually? Well, I knew what they were thinking, now didn't I? It was both frightening and arousing at the same time.

The e-mail chats, after all, had represented fantasies of what I really would like to do.

Barnes turned to me. "You can't possibly make a decision on what you want to do with the properties if you haven't seen them all. The house is large—there are Peter's rooms just sitting there unused. They are far better than that hotel you're staying in."

"The Station Hotel," Sean interjected. "The beds are lumpy; the box springs screech; the brass headboards thump against the wall." He was grinning from ear to ear.

"I got that," Barnes said. He turned back to me. "You must see the house before you decide what you want to do. We'll move you from the hotel right after this meeting."

It wasn't a request. If Sean had said it, I guess it would be with a little growl, and I would have given in immediately. Barnes didn't growl, but I still gave in immediately. It was, after all, a reasonable point. At least that's what I kept telling myself on why I'd agreed to the move.

\* \* \* \*

We were slouched there, three across, on a sofa in the sitting room on the second floor of the ancient main section of the Forest of Dean house. We still had our trousers on, but all three of us were shirtless. I was in the middle. We were watching a male-on-male porn DVD on a big screen TV opposite the sofa. Barnes said the elderly woman who had served us a dinner in the formal dining room next to this room was from the nearby village and would go home after serving, cleaning up after the dinner the next day. So, by the time we were finished with dessert and coffee, the three of us were alone in the house.

All three of us had our cocks out and were hand stroking them as we watched the DVD. Barnes was tall and slim and hirsute and dark to Sean's ruddy reddish-blondness, short and solid build, and near-smooth skin. And where Sean's cock was thick and short until hard, Ralph Barnes' was a snake—long and thin. Sean was uncut; Barnes cut.

Almost on signal, the two of them let loose of their own cocks; turned to me, each putting an arm around my neck, Barnes slapping my hand away from my cock, and each fisting it, Barnes' hand over Sean's. The two and began kissing me, from my face down to my nipples. The grip on my cock loosened, and, as they worked my head and torso with their lips, I stroked my cock up into the sheath they'd made with their hands until I had shot my load in an arc onto the coffee table our legs were stretched out on.

Here it comes, both of them together, I thought. Barnes hadn't bothered to ask me if I took cock—Sean had already made that obvious to him. And my fantasy chats would have given him the impression that I was easy and hot for it. But it wasn't both of them together and it didn't go to the lengths I thought it would. They just bent my torso over, first to the right to Sean and then to the left to Ralph, and I gave them both head to their ejaculations in my throat.

Nothing of the kinky nature we'd exchanged e-mails about. Well, at least not yet.

After they'd both ejaculated, Ralph switched off the TV and we all went downstairs, to the long kitchen in a "modern" wing, dating only to the eighteenth century, that ran off the back of the house. This obviously was where they did most of their living. Descending three steps from the hall running across the back of the ancient house and down into a stone-walled room, one first encountered a comfortable-looking sitting area facing a fireplace. Then a dining area, and only then the restaurant-sized kitchen, beyond which there was a laundry room.

We sat at the dining table, drank beer, and Barnes told me about the house and grounds. We had driven past the pub and into Newnham, three vehicles in tandem, mine in the middle, behind Barnes' and ahead of Sean's, before turning right, away from the river and, via a narrow, hedge-row lined road, up into the Forest of Dean.

The main section of the house went back to Norman days. It had been a manor house built in the twelfth century. Three stories, two rooms per floor. A stair hall along the back had been added a few centuries later and then the two-and-a-half story kitchen wing off the back in the eighteenth century. The history of the grounds was even older than the house, the foundations of the house having been set on the ruins of a Roman temple.

The house had been conveniently split up for the use of the three men. The first two stories and the kitchen floor were common rooms. The first floor of the old house made up a reception hall and an office. The living and formal dining rooms were on the second floor. Peter's rooms had been on the third floor. Ralph's apartment ran across the kitchen wing and had an entrance into the old house in the hall at the back. Sean lived in attic rooms about Ralph's apartment and could access the main house via a circular staircase in a narrow tower rising between the main house and the kitchen wing.

"Time to turn in," Ralph said after telling me of a very interesting history of the house over the centuries. All of what he said clawed at my determination to sell my interest in it and the pub and run right back to the safety of the States. I had loved the house at first sight. "I'll show you up to your rooms."

"I'm sure I can find them my—" I started to say, as I rose from the table.

"I'll show you to your rooms," Ralph said, his voice commanding.

And so it began.

He followed close behind me up the staircase. On the second floor, he grabbed me and spun me around, embracing me and giving me a hard kiss on the lips.

"You know why I'm coming upstairs with you, don't you?" he asked in a guttural voice.

"Yes, of course."

"I could fuck you right here on the staircase, you know. You included that in a chat once. You made it sound so sexy. Peter was very much taken with the scene you wrote for us. I fucked him just half way up this staircase after we'd read that chat, just like you described."

Yes, I'd remembered writing that. I was extra randy that night. No, I hadn't ever actually done it, but I was here, now, steeped in fantasies of my own devising. I saw no reason not to give in to them, if just for tonight.

"You can fuck me anywhere you want, any way you want," I heard myself saying. "you want me to go down on my belly here on the staircase? Or do you want me to sit on a stair tread and open my legs to you?"

"I want you to come upstairs," he said, with a hiss, grabbing one of my wrists, bending my arm painfully behind my back, and propelling me up the stairs to the third floor.

He pushed me up to the wall beside the door into what was to be my bedroom—my belly to the wall, my trousers and briefs hitting the floor, my chin cupped and pulled back to the hollow of his shoulder with one of his hands. His other hand palmed my belly, his hard cock snaking up into my ass channel, and working my channel, kissing every surface of the shimmering muscles of my passageway with the bulb of his cock, as I moaned and moved my buttocks in coordinated movement with the cock.

"Do you remember writing this in a chat?" he muttered.

Yes, I did. Writing it, not actually doing it. But at the time I had been aching for someone to rough fuck me that way. Here, now, I was aching for Ralph to rough fuck me that way. My answer to him was to push my buttocks back into his groin and to roll them up to give him deeper penetration, I arched my back and raised my arms, locking my fists behind his neck.

"Can you do it as well for me as the black bull in my chat did it for me?" I challenged. "If so, do your worst."

With a roar he gave me a cruel upward thrust of his dick that nearly lifted me off my feet and made me yelp in surprise and pain.

"Yes, yes, fuck me. Drill me. Harder, deeper," I murmured in a low, hoarse voice, moaning for him. He sucked in his breath, no doubt surprised at my total surrender to him—and then, spurred on by my tease, complied with the harder and deeper plea.

"Very nice, very nice indeed," he whispered after I'd come and had sunk to the floor when he released me. He hadn't come yet, and instead of leaving me there, he pulled me up from the floor and pushed me into the bedroom and onto Peter's huge four-poster bed.

I recognized the position he put me in. I'd e-mailed Ralph and Peter—as Rigger and Phil—about it quite recently, even though I hadn't done it then.

I certainly did it now.

My hands were handcuffed behind my back. I was on my spread knees on the bed, cheek to bedspread—at least until Ralph started pulling on the leather strap attached to the choke collar around my throat, pulling my torso up off the bedspread as, crouched over my hips, he fucked my passage in long, hard, fast thrusts, working up to his own ejaculation.

Sean had come into the room. He climbed onto the bed, knelt in front of me, grabbing my ears in his hands, forcing my face down to his cock, with Ralph easing the pull on the choke collar just enough to accommodate Sean's needs.

After Sean had creamed my tonsils—with Ralph still fucking away in my channel—he lowered his own face to my cock and blew me.

They stayed with me a few hours, holding me between them, working my body with their hands, lips, and teeth until I'd had another ejaculation. And then, arm in arm, they silently withdrew into the darkness.

It was almost exactly what I was going for in my fantasized e-mail to Phil and Rigger. I went to sleep both moaning and humming.

* * * *

Nothing was said about the previous night during breakfast. Perhaps that was because the housekeeper was there, puttering around in the kitchen beside the informal dining table while we ate. She had prepared a full country breakfast, though, apparently realizing we had worked up a good appetite. I doubted she didn't know what three men had been up to living here together—or what I had brought to the table here.

Ralph was working on a laptop to the side of his place setting as he ate.

"You need to come to the pub today to go over the books with us," he said, looking at me. "And to watch the operation more closely. It's a going business, but neither Sean nor I can afford to buy your third out. For obvious reasons we don't want to be looking for an investor here."

"We want you to stay," Sean said. "I would think that this is fairly obvious to you."

"And to take Peter's place in all ways?" I asked.

"Yes, of course," Ralph answered.

"What did Peter die of?" I asked.

"Not from what you might think," Ralph answered. "At no time do we go too far. We've done nothing you haven't done before. You've gone much further. It was an auto accident, if you must know. He was in glowing health. He was enjoying life immensely—and all that life brought to him."

What could I say? How could I tell them that I'd written my chats with them in fantasy terms? That I had assumed they were doing so too. But it seems they were not—and that they believed I'd done so much more. So much that I had fantasized doing. Like what had been done the previous night. No, I hadn't been hurt, really. I'd been taken to heaven. Aroused and satisfied as never before. My thoughts went back to what was waiting for me in the States—Simon pawing at me and fucking me ineffectually. Hal beyond my grasp.

Ralph turned the monitor and keyboard of the laptop to where it was facing me. "Here, I've called up the files on your e-mail chats to us."

"You saved the e-mails?" I asked, flabbergasted.

"Yes, of course. Tonight we are going to double you."

"Double me?"

"Yes, just like this last chat from you—two inside you at once. You obviously loved that. You wrote that it was your favorite way to be taken."

I started to hyperventilate. Fantasizing it was one thing. Doing it was another. But, of course I'd only written of it because I dreamed of doing it.

"I want you to go through the chats in which you've told us of your double penetration experiences. Pick one out. Peter always wanted to do that with you. He loved it when Sean came into the picture and we could do it for him."

"You two have done it?"

"Yes, of course. Many times. Peter couldn't get enough of it. We may have done it as many times as you have—it obviously is a favorite of yours too, considering how often you told us about doing it. Sean and I can't wait for it. You pick a favorite scenario out from what you've written about, or I will. You can show us which one you've picked when we get back from the pub tonight."

Oh shit.

* * * *

Sean was sitting on the end of the bed as I threw a thigh over his lap, facing him, and came down, with his help, on his lap. I first sat at the edge of his knees, as Sean brought the bulbs of our cocks together, rubbing the piss slits, each emitting precum together, and then pulling his foreskin over mine, docking the cocks, stroking them together until slowly, both cocks filled out, the foreskin pulling back of its own accord from the bulbs.

"Oh god, Sean," I whimpered. "Fuck me. fuck me now."

"Sit on it," he growled. I moved farther up his thighs, reached under my buttocks and held his cock erect, as I slowly descended my channel on his hard shaft. He already was cupping my head in his hands, bringing my face to his for kisses—then pulling my head back from his by grabbing the hair at the back of my hand, his lips and teeth going to my nipples. I groaned. Using the leverage of my calves and knees bent and running on either side of his hips, I began to rise and fall on his cock.

This didn't last long, though. He wrapped his arms around my chest, trapping my arms with them, and reclined back, bringing my chest down on his and rolling my buttocks in the air. I whimpered and struggled a bit, but ineffectually as strongly as he embraced me and trapped my arms. Ralph hadn't been in the bedroom when we started, but now I saw that he was, naked and erect, saddling up between Sean's thighs.

I tried to jerk away, without success, as I felt the head of his cock at my hole, above where Sean's cock was buried inside me. I panted hard and groaned deeply as he entered and entered and entered me above Sean's cock.

"What a slut," Ralph muttered. "You open right up to both of them."

Amazingly, he was right. It was a talent I never knew I had, but it was one that I sure as hell was glad I had now. Still, I was straining and grunting when Ralph began to pump.

"Relax," Sean counseled. "Go limp and you'll be able to take it."

I did to the degree I could manage, and Sean was right. He even was right when Sean began counterpumping to the rhythm Ralph had set.

"Just like you wanted," Ralph cried out. "I can tell you're lovin' it."

And, strangely enough, I was.

We lay stretched out against each other, me in the middle and the other two running their hands and lips over my body afterward.

"That was very nice," I had to concede to Ralph.

"That was Act One," Ralph whispered back.

Act One? What the hell?

"You've shown us what you like. Now for what I like," he murmured. I did notice that both of them were hard again.

Sean lay on his back, holding me, facing the ceiling, on his body, his dick inside me. Ralph came between our legs again, grabbed my ankles and wishboned my legs. He snaked his cock inside me again, above Sean's cock, and I was being doubled again.

I loved that position too. The first two times I'd ever been taken by two men together like that. Not that Ralph and Sean knew that—or ever would.

\* \* \* \*

On Wednesday I put in a call to Simon Clore in New York.

"You're what?" he nearly yelled down the line.

"I won't be in on Thursday. I won't be in ever. I quit. I'm moving to England. I own part of a pub here. I won't be back. You'll have to send someone to my apartment to retrieve your tax documents and do them yourself."

"But, why, Paul? We had it so good."

"You wouldn't know what good was, Simon. I had to fantasize good. Now I'm living that fantasy. Good-bye and give my best to Betsy."

I was sitting on Ralph's cock and Sean was teasing my legs open, preparing to join Ralph inside me when I closed the connection on a blustering Simon.

# SHANGHAI SILK

Chad, breathing easily and looking mighty fine for a man of thirty-seven, ended his run at his usual bench beside a tool house in the remote Myrtle Beach park tucked into a golf course almost within sight of the ocean enough for most not to realize it was a separate public park. As usual, he ran in just athletic shorts and running shoes. His auburn red hair was boyishly tussled and reddish down swirled around his firm pecs and down the line of his sternum and six pack and under the waistband of the shorts. The raised sitting area was sheltered on the side opposite the running path by a semicircle of azalea bushes. The tool shed and bench sat on the top of a rise, and anyone in that area had to stand from the bench to be seen from the path down the slope.

He looked at his watch and stood up from the bench, moving his hand to the crotch of his athletic sorts, following the long and distinct line of his nestled cock, starting to come alive at the thought of what lay ahead. The figure of a young blond, tanned man, also in jogging shorts, also shirtless, was already on the path below, jogging slowly in place. The young man was looking up the slope. When he saw Chad standing up there, he stopped jogging and moved his hand to his crotch as well.

He was short, small, well-formed but looking young—too young. But that was what Chad was expecting. He knew otherwise, or had been assured otherwise. He would check, of course. He motioned with his head and sat back down on the bench. The young man appeared over the rise of the slope and sat, hesitatingly, next to Chad. The two turned toward each other, looking each other over.

"Interested in a blow job?" the young man asked, his voice low, his eyes looking furtively around.

"Did someone send you?" Chad asked.

"Yes."

"Who?"

"Ted."

Chad nodded his head. The prearranged signals had been the right ones. Ted was his best recruiter, concentrating on students at Webster College suddenly in need of money and already gay curious. He moved an arm around the young man's back across the back of the bench. Placing three fingers of that hand lightly on the young man's right bicep proved enough to hold him in place. The young man was a bit skittish, repeatedly scanning the area for anything amiss.

"Where we gonna do it? Behind these bushes?"

"In a minute. Some checking first," Chad answered. He moved his free hand to glide along the young man's pecs, down his sternum and belly, testing the hardness and resilience of the skin as if he were shopping for a thoroughbred race horse, which, in some sense, he was. It would take a special kind of young man to take on what he had in the plans. Here again Ted was crucial. He selected them very carefully.

The hand moved underneath the waistbands of the young man's athletic shorts and jock strap. The young man flinched and automatically spread his thighs as Chad cupped his balls and placed a thumb on the base of the young man's cock. The young man started breathing heavier and his cock started to engorge, but he held steady.

"Ted tell you what this was about?"

"Yes."

"And you still want to sign on?"

"Yes."

"Name?"

Hesitation. "Jake."

"Real name or the one you want to use with us?"

"The, uh . . . professional name I've chosen, I guess."

Chad started slow-stroking Jake's cock.

"Done fellatio before?"

"Fellah what?" Jake was trembling at the attention being given his cock, working hard to pay attention to that and what Chad was saying at the same time.

"Blow jobs. Have you sucked guys off before."

"Once or twice. You know, around the dorm. And Ted."

"Just a few times, you sure? Ted told you how important it was to be fresh, didn't he?"

"Yes. Shit, if you continue doin' that, I'm gonna come."

"Yes, you are, you're going to come for me, Jake. Are you sure it's only a few times?"

"Yes."

"But it's what you want? For the benefits you'll receive? Ted explained all of that, right?"

"Yes. It's what I want."

"Been anally fucked?"

"No . . . never." Ted had been very explicit about that.

"You sure? We'll check, you know. There's a full-time doctor on staff. He'll know." Of course there was no sure way of checking for the anal virginity in a man,

261

especially if it had been a while in the past, but Jake didn't need to know that. He was just a college kid—from the nearby Webster University, where Chad got most of his fresh meat, thanks to Ted—for which Ted was richly rewarded. Young college guys, looking good and in great shape, coming to the Carolina coast for college because they were drawn to the surf and the beach resort culture. Randy and needing money, finding it more expensive to live the beach life here than they had anticipated. More often than not willing to be gay for pay to bail them out even if not fully gay.

"Yes, I'm sure."

"But willing to give it up on screen for pay?"

"Yes."

"Bound? Ted made that clear?"

A slight hesitation, maybe more in trying to hold his ejaculation response in check than because Ted hadn't made clear what he'd have to do. "Yes. God, I think I'm gonna come."

"Not yet, Jake. You have to learn to control it. If you come before I tell you, the deal's off. You brought the documents? Your driver's license? Copy of a college transcript verifying your age? Don't worry about the name. I'll only look at it for a matchup and then forget it. You'll be paid in cash under the table. No taxes. And the doctor's certificate? My own doctor will verify that before your first anal—which could be as early as today. We have a client hot to fuck a virgin. We bareback, you understand, don't you? Ted was clear about this. Medical checks frequently."

"Yes, yes, to it all. Oh shit, I wanna come. Please let me come. Here, here are the docs." He was fumbling in the pocket of his shorts and came up with the demanded documents.

"Lay them on the bench beside you. And then you can come."

"Right here, in the jock pouch?"

"Yes, in the jock pouch, Jake."

Jake arched his head back, gave a lurch and a moan, and slathered the inside of his jock pouch with cum.

"Very nice. Quite a load," Chad said after a moment of holding there, both savoring the moment. "Most clients like a big shooter."

He extracted his hand, wiped it on the leg of Jake's shorts, and reached over Jake's lap, picking up the documents and perusing them, while Jake reclined, collapsed on the bench and panting shallowly.

"All is in order so far, Jake," Chad said.

Jake swiveled his head around. "So, Ted said I'd be sucking you off before you took me to this club place."

"Not in the bushes, Jake. I have a key to this tool shed here."

It was larger than a shed and Jake did a double take when Chad unlocked and opened the door and guided the young may inside. It wasn't like any tool shed Jake had ever seen before. First, no garden tools. Second, the walls were draped in some sort of shiny red material. Third, there was just one straight chair sitting in the middle of the floor. And fourth, now that he had looked around, Jake saw that there were video cameras in every corner, in the upper corners focused down and in the bottom corners focused up—all directed at the chair. And there were studio lights around the top of the walls.

Ten minutes later, both men were naked, Chad sitting in the chair, Jake kneeling between Chad's thighs. Chad was making the last adjustments on Jake's bonds. He had already turned on the studio lighting and video cameras.

"What's the red scarf for?" Jake asked, the first question he'd asked since they'd entered the shed. "And what's with the material on the walls?" Until then he was in awe of what he'd found in the shed. Chad was looping the long, ropey scarf around the link of the fleece-lined handcuffs holding Jake's wrists together behind his back and moving it to connect, first, with the ankle binding on Jake's left ankle where it was bound to the extender bar spreading Jake's legs and then running it to the right ankle and back to the handcuff links, effectively immobilizing Jake on his knees in front of the seated Chad.

"Shanghai silk, Jake. The signature of the Henry Benson Enterprises. Red silk. Attention-getting lovely, smooth to the touch, delicate in appearance, but the strength of steel. That's what you'll have to be if you work for us, Jake. Beautiful to look at, delicate to the senses, but the steel of a man. Can you do that?"

"I think so, but your cock. It's so thick and long. You'll be—?"

"There will be men thicker and longer than I am, Jake. And they will be what they want to be with you. If you work for me, you'll take it."

"I know, but, I haven't . . . much yet . . . I haven't. Oh shi . . . uhmpf . . . mmmpf . . ."

"And you'll get bigger tips if you make it seem that you haven't done it much, just like this," Chad said, with a laugh, as, clutching Jake's ears, and thrusting his hips, he brutally face fucked Jake with his cock.

He pulled Jake's face off the cock just to hear him suck in air, gasp and gag, and begin to beg for mercy, and then he pulled the mouth onto the cock again, and pumped to a deep-throat, gagging ejaculation.

Jake fell off to the side after Chad was finished coming.

"A lot of it will be just like that, Jake," he muttered.

\* \* \* \*

Chad had just entered his office on the third floor of the Henry Bensen Enterprises building on the North Myrtle Beach oceanfront when a call came through from China.

Chad wasn't Henry Bensen. Henry, who had died the previous year, had been Chad's bondage daddy. He'd brought Chad to the States from China, shared the world of his enterprises with Chad, and had left it all to Chad. The enterprises were extensive, profitable, and humming along—and all were located in this building. The basement and first floor provided not only covered parking protected from searching eyes but also a flood zone for the hurricanes that occasionally raced up the Atlantic seacoast of the States—although only rarely affecting this South Carolina beach resort. Floor two was the legitimate book and magazine publishing house fronting the enterprises. The third floor housed the integral, yet also separate, pornographic publishing operations.

A buffer floor of storage rooms, archive vaults, and security areas occupied the fourth floor. Everyone going above this floor was closely checked. The Handcuff Club, a very private and exclusive men's club occupied the next two floors, the public entertainment rooms on the fifth floor and the very private rooms plus photography and movie studio rooms and an Internet Web site studio on the sixth floor. An extensive medical clinic, manned by medical technicians around the clock and supervised by a full-time doctor, plus a few small apartments for a select number of staffers made of the seventh floor. On the waterfront side of the eighth floor were located more staff apartments, with the road side taken up by a two-story elaborate dungeon set. Chad's private penthouse started on the waterfront side of the ninth floor and took up the entire tenth floor, which also included extensive roof-top terracing.

"Hello, Sung," Chad responded to the telephone call from Shanghai. "This must be important for you to call in the middle of your night."

"It's Bao Chuan. You likely assumed it would be. He has become insufferable and is endangering my operations here. You had mentioned being able and willing to do something about that."

"Give me a few days to get a crew together and I'll be over there. You probably know I will be quite happy to handle Bao Chuan for you."

"I know you have never . . . forgotten him, Chan," Sung Li answered, using Chad's Chinese name. "It should not be messy, though, or redound on the theater."

"It won't. I think I've come up with an elegant solution for all of us. Tell me, is Bao Chuan still living in my parents' house?"

"Yes, the cheeky bastard, he is. I appreciate this, little one. It will be good to see you again. I've ached for you. You know how much I love you."

"Do you?" Chad asked, his voice a little harder now.

"Please, don't be like that. I long to have you inside me again."

Chad softened. "I long to be there with you too. Until then."

When he disconnected, he left the office and took the elevator up to sixth floor. The session with Jake should be over now, he thought. The doctor had given the young blond a clean bill and had even supposed that he probably had not had anal sex before. Chad reached the Tientsin room just as the patron was coming out of the studio, wrapped in a red silk robe, smiling, and taking the mask off his face that many of the patrons chose to wear while filming. Most wanted private copies of the films; few wanted to be identified by facial recognition in them, though.

The man was middle aged, but in very good shape and well equipped. The Henry Bensen Enterprises had as stringent standards that clients had to meet as it had for the male prostitutes. This included frequent and immediate before sessions medical testing.

The Henry Bensen Enterprises were an exclusively barebacking operation. That's what brought in the high profits.

"Did the session go well for you?" Chad asked, careful not to say a name, although of course he knew who the U.S. congressman was.

"Yes, very well, thank you. Splendidly. A screamer. You know my tastes so well. I want to hear about the next virgin you have so that I can bid on the first fucking. This one went extremely well. He looks so young, and he was highly vocal in the taking. And tight. I have no doubt I was in there first. Well worth the money."

Which was $2,000 from the congressman, which he no doubt would pass on as a business expense somehow. Plus a DVD for Harry Bensen Enterprises.

Chad continued on into the studio. The three cameramen were moving around the periphery, turning off the studio lights and checking the video footage they had taken, not even looking at the moaning and panting young man spread-eagled on his belly and bound on the bed in the center of the room. Like all of the rooms, red silk—Shanghai silk—predominated and there was an Oriental motif to the furnishings. Even the leads binding Jake's extremities to the four corners of the bed were made of red Shanghai silk.

Chad walked over and sat down on the bed beside Jake's bound body. Jake's head was turned toward him, his face showing a glassy-eyed expression, his face and back were covered with a thin veneer of sweat. A red-balled mouth gag lay close to his face, the red rubber almost bitten through, a sure sign that Jake's endurance had been taxed, even though Chad knew the ball gag hadn't been in long. The congressman was built big and he liked to listen to the virgins scream.

"I'm sorry, I don't think I took it well," Jake murmured to Chad. "I couldn't take it quietly."

"On the contrary, I think you took it just the way the client wanted."

Chad gave Jake a reassuring smile and patted him on the rump that was raised by a red silk wedge under his belly, which had presented Jake's ass for a good penetration angle from a man kneeling between his spread thighs. He let his hand glide down between the ass cheeks and felt the congressman's cum dribbling out of Jake's ass.

"He fucked me twice," Jake whimpered.

Not necessarily permitted, but Chad wasn't going to quibble with one of his best clients. "Yes, there's enough cum in your ass for that," he said. "Client's privilege. Get used to it."

Chad moved a finger into the passageway and Jake moaned for him. Letting the hand dip further down, he ran it along Jake's cock that had been pulled between his legs and was stretched out on the bed between his thighs. Chad checked for and found the cum from Jake on sheets below where his bulb lay. He encased the cock and stroked it, listening for and hearing Jake moan.

"You came for him, so you had pleasure too." It was a statement, not a question.

"Yes, I guess."

Good, he thought—about the reengorging of Jake's cock and the evidence that he had come. It was important to Chad that the prostitute enjoy his work.

He looked over on the nightstand and saw the two hundred-dollar bills. Jake's tip from the congressman. The bill for the session had already been paid. It had been a hefty one, in keeping with involving the taking of a virgin ass.

"It *was* satisfactory for you, wasn't it?" he asked Jake after determining in his own mind that it had been.

"It hurt like hell . . . but, yes, it's what I wanted. Was it like this for you too, the first time. Or have you never . . . ?"

"Yes, Jake, there was a first time for me too. Not now. Now I only top. But there was a first time being taken for me too. It gets easier. In time it will be a snap for you." And it was much more like this than I'll admit to you, he went on to think.

On the proverbial bearskin rug in front of a roaring fire in an ornate fireplace in his parents' European-style mansion in the hills above the Shanghai Bund, where his father had managed an export house. He'd been summoned home from his university studies at Cambridge by the tragic boating accident on the Yangtze River that had taken both of his parents' lives, leaving him an only child. Not exactly an orphan as he was eighteen. But alone and unprotected in the world just the same. And on the other side of the world from his world—in China.

The family's Chinese lawyer, Bao Chuan, taking advantage of the grieving young man. Hogtying him on the rug in front of the fireplace. A red silk scarf—strong Shanghai silk—run behind Chad's neck, binding his wrists on either side of his neck and continuing down and binding his ankles, immobilizing his movement. A red silk pillow under the small of his back, presenting his virginal hole for Bao Chuan's cock, his mouth initially gagged with a red silk scarf, but later taken away so that Bao Chuan could hear his screams of taking.

Bao Chuan taking him swiftly the first time, once the laborious chore of getting inside him was accomplished. Barebacking him, filling his passage with cum. Then rising and sitting in a wing chair by the fireplace, drinking Chad's father's best brandy, while watching and leering at Chad, laying, still bound on his side, panting and crying, the gag back in place because Bao Chuan didn't want to hear what Chad had to say. Fucking Chad again there, more slowly, Chad moaning and, to his shame, beginning to enjoy the fuck, having fantasies of his fulfilled. And then a third time before he was released from the bindings by the fireplace.

Chad was bareback fucked through the night on his parents' bed, spread-eagled, tied off at the four corner posters with strong red Shanghai silk scarves. To his shame, Chad readily hardened and ejaculated for Bao Chuan again and again, and, by the morning, totally cowed and resigned to what couldn't be recovered, he was clinging to the man and begging for his cock again—and also for the guilt-ridding bondage. Bao Chuan held Chad as his sexual slave for four days and nights, teaching Chad everything he knew, in his refined experience in bondage sex, concerning how to please him and other men.

Such was Chad's total surrender to Bao Chuan that by the third day, Bao was letting the young man bind and bareback him too, with Bao teaching Chad the nuances of being an arousing, masterful taker.

On the fifth day, Chad was taken by Bao Chuan into the Shanghai red-light district and sold to Sung Li, head of a traditional Chinese drama troupe housed in a male prostitute brothel, where Chad learned not only to act the part of a mincing female character—all of the characters in a traditional Chinese drama being played by men—but also to service any theater patrons made randy by his performance. There seemed to be no end of Chinese patrons willing to pay high fees to either bareback or be barebacked by a young, handsome, hung European.

Chad lost his innocence—and all inhibitions—in a fortnight.

Within weeks, everything Chad's family had owned in Shanghai was in Bao Chuan's name. Chad eventually was sold to a visiting theater patron and barebacking bondage aficionado Henry Bensen and brought to the States, where Chad serviced Bensen, who enjoyed employing bareback bondage; was featured in Bensen's porn films; and, in the end inherited Bensen's empire. To Chad's knowledge, Cambridge had never checked on why Chad hadn't returned to his studies from Shanghai. His fees were paid up to the end of that school year.

Yes, Chad's first time had been somewhat like Jake's.

"If you are to continue here," he said to Jake, still stroking Jake's cock, which was hard as a rock now, "your education in how to please a man to the maximum even when bound like this will start right now, with me." As he said it, he brought out his wallet, took out three hundred-dollar bills, and laid them beside the congressmen's two bills on the nightstand. Jake had already been paid $500 up front for congressman's initiation session.

"Do you wish to continue, Jake?"

"Yes," Jake whispered.

Chad stripped off his clothes, draped them over a chair out of camera range, and signaled the cameramen to turn on the lights and the cameras. This done, he mounted Jake's ass and worked his cock, which had been erect since he'd entered the room and seen Jake naked and spread-eagled on the bed, into Jake's passage, as Jake huffed and puffed and moaned at accommodating a cock even larger than the congressman's. Chad reached down and grabbed a hank of hair on the back of Jake's head, arching the young man's back up to him as far as the bonds would allow. While starting to give instruction to Jake on how to react to such a taking, the older man began pumping the young's man's ass.

The spotlights spotlighted, the cameras rolled, Jake writhed as best he could within his restraints and cried out in pain-passion, and, taking long strokes that pulled his cock bulb out to the surface at the withdrawal and then sheathed the full length of the thick shaft on the down stroke, Chad pounded away at the young, shortly before virgin ass. Chad's thoughts as he stroked away first went to the mint of money these two vids would make in his bareback bondage niche of the gay male porn flick market and then to his plans for Bao Chuan in Shanghai.

Later that evening he called both Ted and Jake into his office.

"How would the two of you like to take a trip to China at my expense and be eighteen-year-olds for a few days."

"Neat," Ted said.

"Sweet," said Jake. "But fifteen-year-olds?"

"You both look the part. I'll have fake documents made up. You'll travel on real passports, of course. Do you both have passports?"

They both nodded a yes.

"What are we going to do in China?" Ted asked.

"You're going to fuck an asshole into his grave. But, for tonight, Ted, I want you to bring Sasha, the virgin Russian exchange student you sent to me, to my apartment. I'm in the mood for indulging myself tonight."

On the penthouse level, in the Sian bedroom, furnished with a dominating red lacquer four-poster bed, the blond, smooth-skinned gymnast, Sasha, was butt to the end of the bed, both legs and arms stretched straight out from his hips, wrists tied to ankles and to bed posts with silken restraints, red silk pillow stuffed under the small of his back, rolling up his hips, as Chad, hanging onto a bar dropped down from the frame of the poster bed on silken cords and his feet nestling Sasha's head between them, swung his body back and forth, back and forth, with his long, thick cock stroking inside Sasha's passage in a second fucking, using the cum from the first as lubricant. Sasha's head was thrown back, his mouth open in a passionate commentary on his second taking, having just lost his anal virginity in the same position, as, Chad not one to waste any opportunity, had the lights focused on the end of the bed and the cameras rolling.

"Oh, oh! You're splitting me. You're killing me," The Russian cried out, straining at the severe stretching of his restraints.

"But you're loving every stroke of it, aren't you?" Chad growled.

"Da, da. YES! Fuck meeeee!"

* * * *

Operation Screw Bao went smoothly. Sung Li informed the lawyer that two virginal Americans of the age Bao liked were available. He couldn't resist. They fucked on Chad's parents' bed that Bao had kept in the European-style mansion in the hills above Shanghai that Bao had stolen from Chad's parents.

Bao apparently didn't know of the secret compartments in Chad's parents' bedroom, with the cleverly disguised peep holes. Chad did. The compartments were big enough for Chad's cameramen and the peep holes were big enough for the camera lenses.

Bao fucked a trussed Jake on the bed as Ted sat beside them and stroked Jake's cock. Then the two Americans coaxed Bao Chuan to be bound spread-eagled on the bed, while Ted rode his cock and Bao Chuan sucked off Jake. At the bottom corners of the video that then was quickly made, shots of Ted's and Jake's fake passports, showing each to be eighteen, were displayed. The vid was uploaded to the Internet and copies were sent to the local authorities.

Having sex with a man that young was a capital offense in China. Bao Chuan was off the streets in a matter of hours after the vid was received at the local police station.

Sending the young men and the film crew directly back to South Carolina, Chad lingered on at Sung Li's Shanghai flat for a few days.

Sung Li made clear that he longed for Chad's attentions as in the old days, and, as they sat beside each other, their legs folded under them, clad only in silken robes, at a tea table in Sung Li's bed chamber, Chad ran his hands into the folds of Sung Li's robe and began making love to the old theater master's body with his hands. The man was still hard-bodied, if wiry, and he still could manage an erection to be proud of.

"The silken bindings," Sung Li murmured. "And then fuck me hard."

With Sung Li's wrists bound behind his back and with red Shanghai silk scarfing that extended to his ankles, pulling the ankles toward his wrists, Chad held the master in his arms, kissing his lips, while he stroked Sung Li's cock to an ejaculation. Then he pushed the old man over onto his chest, mounted his ass, and fucked the hell out of him.

Later, after Chad took Sung Li in longer, slower strokes on Sung Li's bed, with the master on his back and Chad stretched between his legs along the line of his body, Sung Li's wrists tied behind Chad's neck and his ankles tied behind Chad's calves, the two lay in an embrace, panting to calmness, waiting for their breathing to normalize and Chad's cock to go flaccid inside Sung's cum-drowned passage.

"I sense that you are somewhat distant from me still, Chan," Sung Li whispered. "That makes me sad. When I say I love you, it doesn't come easily or falsely. I do not waste that sentiment on those it doesn't apply to. What is still between us and between you and the world, little one?"

"I might as well say it," Chad answered. "When you bought me, I was property, and you then sold me.

You can't love property as you do a man. And I am still angry, I guess, that the world took no heed of me as if I didn't exist. I disappeared and no one came looking for me."

"I must put you at rest on those points, Chan," Sung Li murmured. "I bought you from Bao Chuan because of his reputation for riding his conquests to the death. As soon as I saw you, I wanted you to live. And I wanted you for mine. I never thought of myself as owning you. I always thought of you as possessing me. It was with great regret that I turned you over to Henry Bensen. But I knew it was for the best. Bao Chuan was starting to claim you as his. He wanted to take you back. I feared for your life. And I didn't sell you to Bensen. I begged him to take you to America—to safety. He was good to you, wasn't he? I kept an eye on your relationship with him. I would have taken you back, somehow, if you had indicated you didn't want what he gave you."

"I never knew," Chad said in a small voice.

"And, as for people not looking for you, I acknowledge my greed in that. I wanted you so badly for myself that I turned away all enquires on what had happened to you. They came from Cambridge, and the English consulate, and even the local authorities. We manufactured a death for you to stop them coming. Please forgive an old man for being so selfish and thinking only of his own need and love for you."

Chad sighed, long-festering hurts lifted off his mind, and dozed off.

* * * *

Chad stood from the bench by the shed in his special park and looked down the hillside. The young man looking up was small, well-formed, dark, curly hair. A face more pretty than handsome. A nice tentative smile. In

275

other words, perfect for Chad's needs. He had such a deficiency of this type in his stable of young prostitutes. Ted had done well in his recruitment efforts here. Chad gestured and the young man walked up the slope to him.

Sitting side by side on the bench, Chad had an arm around the back of the young man, three fingers gently touching a nicely formed bicep, keeping the young man in place. He ran his free hand over the young man's slightly hirsute chest, ruffling up the dark down surrounding the young man's taut nipples.

"Tell me that you are still a virgin to anal penetration. Ted told you that was an absolute requirement, didn't he?"

"Yes, he did. No I have never been fucked in the ass."

"But for a price . . ."

"For a price, I'll do it all. Ted has told me everything, I think. I can't imagine that anything would have been left out. . . . ulp . . . oh, shit."

"Relax for me," Chad murmured. His hand had gone under the waistband of the athletic shorts and jock strap and encased the young man's balls and cock. "Nice, very nice. Relax for me. Are you going to let me jack you off inside your jock pouch?"

"Yes, if that's what you want," the young man answered as he relaxed his stance on the bench.

"But is that what you want?"

"That would be nice as long as later a man relieves me of my virginity and we get on with some good fucking."

"Good. You're very nice. Just what I need. You're going to come for me and then fellate me, and, if that goes well, then we'll see about getting top dollar for your virginal ass. We provide bareback bondage with full medical support. I trust Ted told you that. And our signature is red Shanghai silk restraints. Red silk.

Attention-getting lovely, smooth to the touch, delicate in appearance, but the strength of steel. That's what you'll have to be if you work for us. Beautiful to look at, delicate to the senses, but the steel of a man."

The young Jewish man, Aaron, came for Chad with a sigh.

"May I give you a blow job now? I'm feeling so, so horny."

Chad was thinking that this one was so nice and business had been so profitable of late that he might indulge himself again and take the virginity of this one himself. He was a bit cocky. Chad would like to relieve him of the burden of his virginity and hear him screaming for mercy.

# CONFESSIONS

"A Round for everyone on me. It's a healthy boy. Touch and go, but both are doing fine."

The young man at the pub bar in Little Stoke, a pocket village northwest of Exeter, Devon, raised his glass of ale and everyone cheered him—or the declaration of the free refill. A few came over and pounded the not-much-more-than-a lad on the back, congratulating him on the good news.

All was mirth in the pub, not only because of the free round, nor for happiness for this newly minted father not more than eight months invested in the tight little smallholding farm area, having come up from the wilds of Cornwall. Much of the laughter was from the general knowing that Mary Finch's baby wasn't his, but Tim Kennel's, who was holding court at one of the large tables of rowdies near the big window onto the street and celebrating with the best of them for what he had avoided.

As quickly as they had converged on him to pat him with one hand and to hold out their mugs for the free refill, the roughly dressed and mannered men in the pub at the conclusion of a hard working day drifted away from the well-formed young man with tussled blond curls; a face more pretty than handsome, as finely and sensitively chiseled as it was; and with bedroom eyes and full, sensuous lips. Six months was not enough to make him one of theirs—not by a long shot. He would remain what he had arrived in Devon as—the second son of a small farm holder in the wilds of Cornwall, bought for an appearances-sake white wash job with the promise of a smallholding farmer's claim in the rolling hills between Little Stoke and Higher Stoke.

James Hardesty looked up, almost glassy eyed at the rapidity with which an empty circle opened up around him in a crowded, smoky room of boisterous laughter and glad handing. This immediate withdrawal of camaraderie came with the exception of the table almost in the shadows at the far wall, where, his eyes following Jamie's every movement, sat the lord of what passed for a manor in Little Stokes.

Catching Jamie's eye, Thomas Owencraft, the village's major landholder, gestured with his hand, and looking for a connection, any connection, Jamie walked over to the table and took the proffered chair next to Thomas.

"Let me congratulate you on fatherhood, James Hardesty," Thomas said, as Jamie sat down at the table. The young man glowed a bit at the local high landowner knowing his name. "Sit and let me stand you one. You be drinking Black Jack if my eyes didn't deceive me."

"Yes, thanks, but I haven't finished the one I have."

"Well, you will, I'm sure, by the time Old Peter hobbles over here with another, and this is no occasion to be dry," Thomas said, raising Jamie's glass and signaling to the barman for another like it. "I wouldn't be neighborly if I didn't stand a new father a drink. Your first, is it?"

"I did have an ale before this."

"No, lad, I mean the first child." Owencraft laughed companionably as if the young man had made a purposeful joke—and successfully so.

279

Jamie nodded his head in the affirmative, blushing at his mistake.

"Ah, and a son. Both a comfort and a blessing in the long run, but a vexing burden now and again between. I must confess that I regret Edith and I never having had a child."

"Thank you," was all Jamie could think of saying. Having come into the pub for the company in a time that should be a celebration—an instant family and a promise of his own small farm if he kept to that family. It was more than he could have expected back in Cornwall, where, on top of being a second son in a land-poor family certain discomforting conditions had been building up so he was pleased for what he thought of as an escape.

"Ah, the Black Jack has arrived," Thomas said, with a little laugh. "Drink up the one you have lad so that you can tuck into the other."

"I really shouldn't drink too many of these," Jamie said. "I must confess that I can get lightheaded from the hard ale and lose myself." Nonetheless, he downed the last of his second glass of Black Jack so that Old Peter could take the empty away and pulled the fresh glass toward him.

"Tonight doesn't count on that; tonight is for celebrating," Thomas responded. "It's only once that a man celebrates the birth of a first son."

Jamie frowned at this. How well he knew the greater celebration that was had for a first son over a second.

Owencraft reached over and patted Jamie on the back and then squeezed his shoulder. "Uh, sorry," he said, as Jamie flinched at the touch. "Didn't mean to press. Some can be really sensitive. Some suffer from pain, although you're much too young for the arthritis, or, as some say, some are sensitive to the turn-on zones." He gave Jamie a wink.

"Turn-on zones?"

"Yes, what they call erogenous zones in fancier terms. We all have them, they say." But then he backed off a bit. "A bit too easily into the cups, you confess? I must confess that I shouldn't even be here tonight. Edith thinks I'm at a town counsel planning meeting. But I need to stop in here now and again—just to survive Edith— and to have my smokes. Edith thinks I've given them up, but I confess that I haven't been able to, not completely. Yet another deadly sin to confess. But we all have our sins to confess, do we not, James? Thank god she's gone to London to shop for the weekend. Your Mary birthed at home, on your farm, did she?"

"No. There were complications. She's at Doctor Granger's infirmary—with the baby—for a few days."

"Is she now?" A pause and then, "I also have to confess that I don't like ale all that much. I'm a wine man, myself. But I can hardly order that in this pub, can I? I like to mix with the working man now and again, but it wouldn't do for the lord of the manor to take on airs in this kind of pub, now would it? That's what they call me around the village—the lord of the manor—and don't I know they don't always keep a straight face when they say it?"

Jamie hadn't thought about this pub being a working man's pub, but as he looked around, he could see that that was what it was. Well, he was a working man now himself—hardly making do. Still not being accepted as one of them here, though. "Ah, I see what you mean. I really should be comfortable here then, but . . ." here he paused, as Thomas had signaled Old Peter again and another Black Jack appeared at Jamie's elbow ". . . I don't fit in here as yet. These men are making do. I must confess that if it wasn't for Mary's father adding to our take, I couldn't even be raising up to the working man level around here. The farm is so small and there is so much I have to learn about making a living off the land."

"So, you might be interested in some extra work here and there, are you saying? Like maybe with some light jobs around the manor house now and again for a bit extra? For a bit of give and take?"

"Yes, that would be very good of you," Jamie answered, taking a deep swig of his forth mug of Black Jack.

"I could be quite good for you," Thomas said in a distant voice. "It's hard to make friends in an isolated, close-knit village such as we have here. Especially if you're a bit different. With my position in the village, I'll always be a bit different, I confess. Do you feel a bit different, James?"

"Yes, a bit, I too confess."

"Still a man needs friends, doesn't he, James? I could be a good friend to you. the different people should hold together, don't you think?" A hand went to Jamie's knee and squeezed gently. Jamie jerked and looked up into Thomas' eyes with a somewhat glassy gaze.

"Oh, sorry, Is that one of those zones for you? I confess I have one myself. On my inner thighs. Have you none to confess? We all do."

"Uh, a hand on my lower belly can do it," Jamie answered, somewhat reluctantly.

"Yes, that's the right of it that I heard."

Jamie's head lifted up. He gave Thomas a look that seemed to convey that something had been said that was both significant and surprising, but that, after more than three glasses of Black Jack ale, he couldn't quite put his finger on.

Thomas became more explicit. "I confess too, James, that I became curious about you when you moved here—just appeared. And I checked with some friends down in Cornwall. As I said, we different people need to stick together."

"Oh." Jamie couldn't think of much else to say. He still wasn't fully catching on.

"But look at you, sitting in front of an empty glass. What sort of friend lets that happen for another friend." He was signaling to Old Peter.

"No, really, I've had more than enough. But thanks."

Another full mug of Black Jack hit the table top, and Old Peter scooped up the empty. Jamie nervously reached for the full glass, which was only half full when it came away from his lips. His hand was shaking. He sensed that he was missing something in the conversation— something important. Thomas moved his hand up from where it had been gripping Jamie's knee to Jamie's waist, where he gently pulled Jamie's T-shirt from the waistband of the young man's jeans and laid his palm on Jamie's lower belly. With a whimper and a sigh, Jamie noticeably relaxed his body into his chair and let his arms go limp beside him.

"I have an even darker confession to make, James," Thomas whispered. "I'm what they call bisexual. I fuck men as easily as I fuck women. Don't you have an equally dark confession to make, as well?"

"A dark confession? I've sold my soul for a few measly acres of farmland and a rundown stone cottage and barn," Jamie murmured. "The baby isn't even mine. It wouldn't be."

"Yes, lad, I know. Yes, I know it wouldn't be yours."

"You're going to fuck me, aren't you?" Jamie asked, his voice calm, matter of fact, and resigned, finally having caught up to the conversation, although his words were slurred and the gaze he turned to Thomas unfocused.

"It's time to leave the pub," Thomas said as he stood up from the table. "But you're in no condition to drive. I'll drive you. It's time we got you into bed."

\* \* \* \*

What brought Jamie fully awake was the penetration of the cock in his passageway. He came too with a jolt, arched his head back, opened his mouth to emit a long groan, and scrabbled to dig his fingers into the biceps of the gaunt, but hard-bodied older man kneeling between his legs, his torso hunched over Jamie's prone body. The cock slid in entirely too easily. It wasn't the first time the man had been in him in recent hours, Jamie realized.

The room—his room; his bed; Mary slept in the other room, where the baby's crib had been set up—was bathed in full, natural light. The last he remembered it was dark. He'd been in a pub. Talking with Thomas Owencraft, the large landholder. It obviously was the morning after. How many times had the man fucked him during the night? For some reason Jamie wasn't surprised that he had. Why hadn't Mary caught them . . . oh, but that was right. Mary was in the doctor's infirmary. She'd had the baby. It had been a hard delivery. This . . . this was hard on his passageway. Hard. Pumping. The man was moving his cock in and out. Harder thrusts. Deeper. Jamie moaned and a mouth came down to cover his.

He should do something. Struggle or something. At least object. But the man was palming his lower belly. His other arm propped his torso up as he hovered over Jamie, Jamie's pelvis rolled up to the assault of the man's cock by a pillow under the small of Jamie's back, his legs spread and bent, feet on the surface of the sheets, moving his legs back and forth in synch with the rhythm of the pounding of the cock in his ass. His pelvis was moving with the thrusting cock. He wasn't resisting; he was responding to the fuck. It was giving him pleasure. He lived to have a man's cock inside him.

Again the thought that he should do something, react in some way to show that he didn't want this. But the hand on his belly, making him lay there docilely, taking the cock. Wanting it.

He wanted to be fucked. "Yes, yes, please. Yes, like that," he heard a disembodied voice murmuring. His voice.

Jamie sighed and ran his hands up Thomas' chest. Hard, wiry muscles. Taut nipples. A hand went down to one of the man's thin but hard-muscled, constricting and releasing, butt cheeks. The other hand went to Jamie's own erect cock, and he sighed again, Thomas' cock furiously pistoning his passageway now, and began to stroke himself.

"Yes, yes. YES! Fuckkk me!"

Thomas' muscles tightened, he grunted and groaned, his body jerked with a growled, "It's coming." He pulled out and stood up on the side of the bed, unrolled the condom, and tossed it onto the bed. It landed by Jamie's hip. He stood, hunched, beside Jamie's body and shuddering, stroking his cock hard, shot his load on Jamie's chest. Then he sat down on the edge of the bed and reached over for a packet of Benson & Hedges.

Jamie made like he was going to rise, muttering a "What—?" But Thomas stopped him, placing the hand not holding a lit cigarette on Jamie's lower belly, which caused the young man to lie back with a soft groan of surrender.

"No, stay there, on your back." Thomas muttered. "Finish yourself. I want to watch." He moved his hand to below Jamie's balls, inserted a finger in Jamie's ass, and searched for, found, and began rubbing Jamie's prostate gland. Jamie, panting heavily, stroked himself to an ejaculation, shooting off in a high arc up his belly.

"Nice, very nice," Thomas murmured.

"How long . . . how many times?" Jamie asked in a low, exhausted voice.

"All night. Three times," Thomas said, point to the three spent condoms scattered on the sheets beside Jamie's hip. "You were great. Really wanted it. A really good lay. We're going to be such friends."

Jamie groaned and threw his arm over his face, only now realizing he was suffering the effects of too many Black Jack ales the night before.

"Are you going to confess that you enjoyed it? That you needed and wanted it?" Thomas asked.

There was a slight pause, but the "Yes" came out in a strangled, unwilling voice.

"You going to let me fuck you anytime I want you?"

"Yes."

"Good. Go get cleaned up now. The sun's up too high for a farmer still to be abed. Shower and dress and I'll take you back to your truck at the pub."

Jamie shuddered. The truck was parked at the pub still. "Won't people—?"

"It's a small, gossipy village. No telling what people know and will say. I knew, didn't I? Fuck them."

Jamie threw an arm over his face again, trying to blot the world out. This was why he'd left Cornwall—it wasn't just because there was no position for him there. It was also because of the positions he allowed his body to be put in by other men. That he allowed them to put their cocks inside him. It was because he had wanted what men were doing to him. Just as now he wanted Owencraft to fuck him again—when he was fully aware of what was happening.

He needed to keep his mouth shut. This weakness of confessing would be the end to him. But it was built into him by his religion. Confess, do penance, be absolved, and the slate is clean. Rubbish. But it was what he had been told to believe, so he refused to lose faith that it would make everything good in the end.

"Please, could you . . . again?"

"Go take a shower," Thomas growled.

Jamie was in the shower stall, soaping himself up under the stream of water, when the stall door was opened and a naked Thomas slipped in behind him. Turning Jamie's trembling body to the facing the wall, Thomas came in close behind him. Jamie could feel the taller man's erection at the small of his back. One of Thomas' hands came around to palm Jamie's lower belly, his lips went to the hollow of Jamie's neck, and his other hand made a few swirls of soap suds on Jamie's back. With a sigh of surrender, Jamie raised his arms and locked the fingers of his hands behind Thomas' neck, arched his back, and jutted his buttocks back, presenting his hole for penetration as Thomas' crowned cock slid up into his passageway and began to move inside him.

\* \* \* \*

Thomas stopped on the path behind Jamie where the young man had stopped for a breath and reached around and palmed Jamie's lower belly underneath his athletic shirt. He pulled Jamie behind a tool shed in the deer park where the two were jogging and slammed Jamie's back against the rough shingles of the shed's siding. He grabbed a hank of hair on the back of Jamie's head and pulled the young man's head back, burying his face in the exposed throat, as his other hand pushed the shorts and jock straps of both of them down to their knees. With a groan, Jamie climbed Thomas' hip with one of his legs, reached down to grab Thomas' erect cock, and moved the bulb of it to his hole. He gave a little cry and jerked as Thomas thrust home.

Passing Mary Finch—she'd made no effort to take Jamie's last name—and the baby outside the village church, a few days later, Thomas raised his hat and, after dutifully admiring the baby, asked what brought Mary to the village.

"We're quilting prayer quilts in the church hall this afternoon. Quite a lot to do," she answered.

Racing to the farm in his Jaguar, Thomas found a shirtless Jaime pitchforking hay into the bed of his truck. With Jamie on his back on the tailgate of the truck, the ankles of his spread legs restrained in the leather loops at the top, back edge of the truck bed designed to hold the tailgate in place when it was up, and Jamie's jeans in a puddle on the ground, Thomas hunched over Jamie's body between his spread legs. One of Thomas' hands palmed Jamie's lower belly, making him completely docile for the fucking, Thomas pounded Jamie's ass to an ejaculation. Afterward he sat, next to Jamie spread body, smoking a cigarette, with two fingers pushed up Jamie's ass and rubbing the young man's prostate, as he watched Jamie stroke himself to his own completion.

Edith Owencraft on a weekend shopping spree in London and Mary Finch in Exeter for the weekend to show the baby off to her grandmother, Jamie lay on his belly, cross-ways on the double bed in one of the guest rooms at the manor house. His arms swung listlessly over the side of the bed, his eyes were latched on the two spent condoms already on the floor beside the bed, as Thomas held his hips tightly between his knees and rode his ass hard.

* * * *

288

"You look tired . . . and worried, James. Is there anything I can do to help you?"

They were shaking hands at the door to the church after the service. Jamie's eyes were on Mary, carrying the baby, as she moved out of earshot and toward the church's car park. He turned his face back to the Vicar. Vicar Michael was young for a vicar and robust. He was hardly what some would think of as a vicar—certainly not the people of Little Stokes. He'd only been in the position for a couple of years. It would be at least twenty years more before the villagers stopped referring to him as the "new vicar," and stopped pursing their lips when they said it, making it sound like he was only on temporary assignment and hadn't unpacked his bags yet. He wasn't sufficiently pious for them. He was more the rugby player type and could be seen at the pub, bending his elbow with a pipe and smoking, in the company of Thomas Owencraft. And he wasn't married, despite having been repeatedly invited for dinner at every home in the village and surrounding countryside housing an eligible woman under forty-five.

"I don't think there's anything I need help with, Vicar," Jamie said, aware that his hand was still in the vicar's and there was a bit of a backup of church leavers in the narthex. "We're doing well. It's just hard keeping up with a farm, no matter how small, when you are just starting out learning it all."

"Well, you know the power of confession and repentance," Vicar Michael said in that rich baritone voice of his—no one in the village was complaining about his sermons or his singing voice—as he gave Jamie a piercing look that made Jamie feel like the man could see right into his soul—and discern his dilemma. Yes, Jamie did see it as a dilemma.

"I think you need to come see me. Say this Tuesday, at three, in the rectory."

"I don't know. There really isn't . . ."

But an impatient Margaret Parsons was pressing him from in back for her turn to complain to Vicar Michael about the choice of altar flowers, so Jamie just nodded and moved on.

"Yes, I rather thought it was something like that," Vicar Michael said on Tuesday as they sat in his study. He had brought the tea in himself, saying that the housekeeper was in Exeter that day. "So, we're all alone, and whatever you have to unburden yourself of will only be known by us and God," he said as he poured the tea.

"It's just that it's what I left Cornwall for. And this seemed to be a good idea for settling down."

"It's not always best to deny one's nature, James, nor to run away from it."

"I don't know. That's not the advice I'd expected . . . what? Ohhh."

Jamie had stood and moved to the desk, to put his empty cup back on the tea tray. Vicar Michael had come up behind him, close. He'd pushed the tray to the side and moved a hand around Jamie's waist, to his belly, where he brushed the tail of Jamie's shirt up and laid a palm on Jamie's lower belly.

Jamie relaxed in the vicar's embrace. He might have sunk to the floor, if Michael had not been embracing him and holding him up.

"I know what you need. I can give you relief and a penance," Michael whispered breathily in Jamie's ear. "You are to kneel before me now, unzip my trousers, and suck my shaft. Can you do that? Do you want to do that, James? I have the hard body you need."

"Yes," Jamie whispered as he turned and sank to his knees in front of the beefy vicar.

He had known already. He had known when he was half way through confessing to the vicar, unburdening himself of his sin and of being captive to his base needs

290

and desires. There had been a fire in the vicar's eyes, a way he had of licking his lips while Jamie spoke, his failure to condemn or counsel against anything, the obvious hard cock Jamie could see fighting to be freed from the vicar's trousers. The hard cock that Jamie would be freeing and moving his lips over.

There also was the feeling that the vicar had already heard his story—that he knew the full extent of the sins Jamie would confess.

As soon as Jamie had realized the vicar's desire, he also realized that it was what he wanted—that he'd had his eye on the vicar ever since he had surrendered to Thomas Owencraft and realized that the desire and the surrender had started all over again—that he hadn't escaped it by fleeing Cornwall. And as he realized that he wanted the vicar's cock churning inside him, his confessional became more detailed, more sordid in the specifics he related.

He was gratified—and relieved—to see that it had an effect on the vicar. He even made the move to pull his shirttail out of his waistband himself, to move his hand underneath, and to palm his own belly as he talked. It wasn't the same as another man doing it, but it was something. He was breathing heavier as his confessional came close to an end. The vicar was panting lightly too. And he was hard, noticeably hard.

"Now, I want you to bend over the desk and look out the window and watch the world go by while I take you on a tour of heaven. Do you want to go to heaven with me, James?"

"Yes, fuck me, please."

Michael raised Jamie to his feet, turned him and pushed gently between his shoulder blades as Jamie leaned forward over the desk, planting his fists in the leather of the desktop.

"I don't think . . . should we really . . ." he stammered, as if he were having second thoughts, but any objection he had was dashed when the vicar palmed his lower belly as he unbuckled Jamie's belt with the other hand and pushed Jamie's trousers and briefs down to the floor. The hand then went up to cup Jamie's chin and pull the back of Jamie's curly blond head into the hollow of his shoulder.

Jamie winced, widened his stance, and voluntarily rolled his pelvis up to the cock as he felt its bulb push into his entrance and then he lowered his head, set his arms, and began to pant and groan as the vicar moved his hands to grip Jamie's hips to hold him steady as he mined the young man's ass.

He watched the village butcher pedal slowly by on his bicycle and then noticed that, within a minute, the butcher pedaled back across the window from the other direction, his face turned toward the vicarage.

Two days later, as Jamie, shirtless, was using a hand scythe to cut four-foot tall stalks of grain in one of his small fields, the one farthest away from the cottage and barn, the butcher pedaled up on his bicycle.

As he got off the bike and Jamie watched him do so, the butcher said, in a low, hoarse voice, "I hear you take cock—and that you take it nice and easy, with nary an objection, if you are handled right."

He fucked Jamie doggy style in the middle of the field in an area where their thrashing bodies had mashed down the stalks of grain and you would have to be almost upon them to see them. As soon as the butcher had palmed Jamie's lower belly, the young man had gone complete docile, had widened the stance of his legs and had pleaded in a small voice for the man to be good to him—and to hurry to be inside him and to do his business—and then be gone. The butcher was eight thick, pounding inches good to him, and as long as the butcher kept his hand on Jamie's belly, the young man knelt there on all fours, docile and rock steady, appearing almost resigned and disinterested, while taking the rough ass pounding like a covered bitch in heat.

Jamie on all fours, briefs and jeans pulled down to around his knees, the thickset, solidly built butcher covering him from above and breathing heavily, fully clothed except for his hard shaft jutting out of his fly. Pounding, pounding.

It didn't matter to Jamie what cock was churning inside him, what man was covering him. It was all good for Jamie. Just like the way it had become in Cornwall. Men hearing about him from other men. Standing in line for it. Sometimes six or seven men in succession. Small English villages were the same across the country. He'd been a fool to think he could escape—more a fool for not accepting that he wanted it.

Afterward, Jamie lay on his back in the trampled stalks of grain, his face slathered with the butcher's cum, the butcher crouched beside him, three fingers of one hand crammed up Jamie's passage and pulsating, the palm of the other hand on Jamie's belly, as Jamie looked up into the man's eyes and stroked himself to an ejaculation.

"I'll be back, and you'll take me when I do," the butcher growled after Jamie had arced his cum up onto his belly.

"Yes," Jamie answered, not fighting it, not resenting it even. Knowing that it was a simple truth. If he remained here on this farm between Little Stoke and Higher Stoke, the butcher would be back. And others would come to. Just like in Cornwall.

The butcher obviously had known that the way to control Jamie was with the palm of a hand on his lower belly. And there had been only one other man with the technique of working Jamie's prostate with his fingers while watching him finish himself.

The next Tuesday at three, with the vicar's housekeeper in Exeter again, Jamie was on his back, lying cross-wise on a double bed in a guest room in the vicarage. Vicar Michael was crouched between his spread thighs at one side of the bed, cocking his ass. Thomas Owencraft was hunched over Jamie on the other side of the bed, where Jamie's head was thrown back over the side and Thomas, a hand resting gently on Jamie's lower belly, was slow-pumping his cock deep down Jamie's throat.

Friday night, the two took Jamie to a private men's pub in the suburbs of Exeter, where the two older men sat next to each other, at a table, drinking beer and watching a succession of men crouch between Jamie's raised and spread legs, his back on the top of a pool table, gang bang fucking him. The vicar and the lord of the manor discussed a ranking of the men moving between Jamie's legs, as other men gripped his ankles on their side, stretching his legs up and out, waiting their turn.

The two graded them on how firm and bulbous their buttocks were and how nicely the muscles expanded and contracted as they thrust at Jamie's ass.

Jamie said nothing on the way back to Little Stoke. There didn't seem to be anything to say—not even when the two men decided to share him again when they got back to the vicarage before taking him home, telling Mary that the small farmers meeting they all had attended at the vicarage had run very late.

\* \* \* \*

Thomas Owencraft waved the vicar over to his table in the Little Stoke pub as the man of God entered the bar.

As Vicar Michael settled at the table, he said, "So you've heard?"

294

"Of course. Nothing moves faster in Little Stoke than gossip about other people. Left in the middle of the night, I've heard."

"So I've heard as well. Couldn't take the responsibility of raising a family, I guess. Especially one that wasn't his own," Michael said.

"Just as well," Thomas said, with a sigh. "I confess that I was beginning to tire of him anyway. No fight in that young man. So docile, submissive. Not much of a challenge."

"I confess that, as well. And confession is good for the soul—but perhaps not all that wise in a small village like Little Stoke, as our young friend found out." The vicar's statement was accompanied by a small laugh. "Still . . ."

"Yes, he was, wasn't he?"

"Very. So what are we going to do for . . . what are you looking at?" The vicar turned his head to follow Owencraft's gaze. "Ah, the small Pakistani at the bar? Dark, willowy, pretty."

"Didn't we see him in the club near Exeter?"

"I have picked up vibes about him in various confessionals. I believe he's a carpenter over in Higher Stokes. And yes, I believe he's easy. I would think he has quite a lot to confess, and who better to take his confession than . . ."

But Thomas was already gesturing to the young Pakistani man at the bar, who now saw him, smiled, and started working his way to the table of the village vicar and he local lord of the manor.

# RESTORATION

"Are we sure we want to sell the house? It's in a great location and it should be scarfed right up. There won't be second thoughts to be had about it. Sales in Mystic are booming."

Daren Peters was standing at a window at the back of the house, taking a break with a cup of coffee, while his older sister, Peggy, chattered on as she continued packing boxes to send back to California. She was getting all of the good stuff, but that was fine with Daren. Once he'd left Mystic, he hadn't come back—even during college. There'd always been an away tennis match to go to or prepare for. And he had no place to put the stuff now anyway. As of the previous weekend, he had no place at all. Walking out on Tony in a gigantic blowout—the blowouts having increased in intensity the last few months—and getting the phone call from Mystic almost before he'd hit the street had both contributed to very bad timing.

His mother's health had been declining for some time, so her death didn't come as a surprise. They'd kept in touch over the past fourteen years, but he hadn't been back to Mystic since he'd taken off for his first year at the University of Connecticut. His mother had visited him often at the university but never had insisted that he come home. On some level, Daren had always thought his mother knew why Daren wasn't coming home and was content with letting it be. She, of course, didn't know that what he'd done in Mystic could almost as easily be done in Storrs, home to U.Conn.

After he graduated and took a job she regularly visited him in New York City, as well, as had Peggy, from her California movie studio job—over 3,000 miles and a whole universe away. His father had died when Daren was a toddler, lost at sea in the Gulf of Aqaba, when the naval ship he captained had gone down in a freak missile firing. Daren had gone fatherless until he found a substitute on his own. There were some who would say that would help explain some things in his life.

"I think so, Peg," he answered, although his attention was split between his sister's chattering—a false cheerfulness, he knew, as they were mere hours back from the funeral and Peggy had been very close to their mother—and the spread next door, where a young man was getting tennis instruction from an older one on a tennis court behind the neighboring house. "There's no way you're going to be lured back to Connecticut from the West Coast, I know, and this place is too large for me." And too many memories too, he thought.

"You never seemed to be content here," Peggy said.

"No. Those were frustrating years."

"But, still. It all worked out for you. Well, once . . . you know?"

"Once I accepted that I was gay and settled down with that notion, you mean?"

"Well . . . yes, I guess."

Peggy had been a brick about that. Both she and their mother had. Of course, it had been easier for Peggy. She'd been four years gone when Daren had been coming of age and was struggling with his sexual identity. And she was in the movie business in L.A. She no doubt had seen it all and learned to accept it all.

His mother had accepted it in a more tentative and on-edge way, going from wondering out loud where she'd gone wrong—while accepting that it was so—to continually being oversensitive and indulgent about it. She'd never said a peep about it being Tony's apartment she visited in New York or that Tony and Daren slept in the same bed.

"How is Tony, by the way?" Peggy asked, snapping Daren's attention back into the room, Peggy sounding so much like his mother that, for a second, the death and funeral were both swept away. But his own form of grief rushed right back in.

"I'm sure Tony is fine," he answered. At some point Peggy would get the point—that there wasn't a Tony anymore. That once more Daren was on his own.

"Of course New York isn't that far away. And you can do your work right here. You could bring the paintings back here to restore them, couldn't you? There are so many rooms in this house that you wouldn't have any trouble setting up a studio. But then Tony's work traps him in the city, doesn't it?"

She was fishing. She finally was on the beam and was fishing for a finish.

"Yes, Tony's work keeps him in New York. And I don't think I ever could come back to this house."

His eyes were back on the tennis court of the house next door. The tennis lesson seemed to be coming to a halt. The two were at the side of the court, toweling off, both with their shirts off. Both in great condition, even the older man. The two were chatting amicably. Daren wondered if . . . but it wasn't his business to wonder.

"I see that Stan Waller still lives next door," he said.

"Does he? I didn't know. I wonder if he's still playing on the pro circuit," Peggy said absentmindedly. "Are you sure you don't want this crystal bowl? It came down through Dad's family, and you're the boy. You have the family name."

"No, it's fine. I don't want the bowl. And, no, Stan isn't playing pro tennis anymore. He must be over fifty. Well, no, not quite fifty, I guess. But tennis players don't play very far into their thirties. He's coaching now, I know. I see him occasionally on TV during coverage of the Opens. Sitting in the coach's box."

"Do you? I didn't realize you had kept up with him." Did her voice have a sad edge to it when she said that? Daren didn't have time to think about that, as she continued to talk. "I wonder if this table runner is worth shipping."

Daren looked around to where Peggy was holding up a crocheted piece of material. "I think Grandmother Karen made that."

"Ah, well, to California it goes then. Maybe dry cleaning will brighten it up. I was thinking of going down to the harbor for lunch. Maybe Mystic Pizza isn't overwhelmed with tourists today. Do you want to come?"

"I think not. I see that Stan has ended a tennis lesson. I think I'll go over and talk with him." And indeed, the session next door appeared to be ending with the tennis student walking down to the driveway and a Mustang convertible and Stan entering the back porch of his house.

"Do you really think that's wise?" Peggy asked, her voice a little tight. "It's been how long? Fifteen years?"

"Only eleven." He paused at that. He should have said 'only thirteen,' but Peggy hadn't caught the gaff. He quickly continued talking. "I'm not sure that anything in life is wise," Daren said. "Go ahead down to the waterfront for lunch. You need a long break from this.

Perhaps we can go back there for dinner tonight. I'll probably be leaving tomorrow."

But where would he go when he left? He couldn't go back to Tony's apartment in the city. And even his art restoration studio was attached to Tony's import house. Daren hadn't thought about tomorrow. He hadn't even thought of coming here to see if there was anything he wanted from the house. He certainly hadn't thought about spying on Stan Waller giving a tennis lesson next door. He hadn't thought about any future at all beyond his mother's funeral earlier that day.

He looked intensely at the roof of the screened porch next door to see whether Stan Waller would come out of his house again.

\* \* \* \*

"Can I come up?"

Stan swiveled his head around to take in Daren Peters standing at the bottom of the steps up to the screened porch on the back of Stan's house.

"Yes, of course, Daren, please do. I was hoping you would come over. I was sorry to hear about your mother. I didn't feel it right to come to the funeral, though."

"I understand," Daren said as he entered the porch. Stan Waller was sitting in a wicker chair. There was another one near it, with a side table between. Four cans of frosted beer sat on the table.

Stan gestured to the empty chair. "Take a load off. Care for a beer?"

"You were going to drink four beers?" Daren asked, as he settled into the wicker chair and took a beer. He was turned toward Stan when he did. Still shirtless, Stan didn't look to Daren like he was forty-nine years old.

In physique he wasn't much less well-muscled than he'd been fourteen years ago when Daren turned eighteen.

"I'd hoped you would come over and join me. I saw you in the window of your mother's house, watching the tennis lesson. It's why I sent Brian on his way. I was hoping you would come down."

"Otherwise?"

"I would have taken him into the house, yes. A lot has changed in the last twenty years, Daren. Not that."

"Is Ken still—?"

"Ken died two years ago. He never made it far up into the rankings, so I guess his death in an auto accident didn't make the headlines. His career was essentially over anyway."

"I'm sorry."

"So am I. It gave me some stability in my life. You know, I'm surprised I never saw your name in the rankings. You showed great promise. An intercollegiate champ from U.Conn."

"You kept track."

"Yes, of course I did. You were one of my boys."

"Just one of them? The high school boys mowing your lawn in exchange for tennis lessons."

"Yes, but you were the best. You always were my best boy."

"My interests drifted off into something else. You did that for me as well."

"Oh?"

"The artwork you collected in your world travels on the circuit. The Shunga prints. The collection of old masters in oils—and in the basement, your Roberts prints in that room you set up out of the Arabian Nights. You still have that room?"

"Yes, but I don't understand about—"

"The artworks. You helped turn my interests toward art. Not painting it, although it started off there.

Restoring it. It became a good profession for me. I work out of New York."

"Ah, I'm glad to have had a beneficial effect on you in some way."

"Your effect on me was beneficial in every way, Stan," Daren said, as he reached for his second beer and looked directly into Stan's eyes. "It wasn't always clear at the time, but it clarified my life for me. I have few regrets there."

"And are you living with someone now?"

"No, not as of five days ago."

"Ah. You are looking good, Daren. Really good. You can't be keeping in shape by restoring artworks."

"I'm still playing tennis, and spending time in the gym. But thanks, you're looking great too. You've hardly changed since back then, when I'd just turned eighteen."

"Yes, when you turned eighteen. Do you remember that corny line, 'Want to come up and see my etchings?'" Stan asked, as he crushed the empty of his second beer can in the strong grip of his big hand. "To think it led to a career for you."

"It led to a lot, and yes, I had been dying to see your etchings."

"You asked about the Arabian Nights room." This said in a low, hoarse voice. "Would you like to come in and see my Arabian Nights room again?"

"Yes, Stan, I would like that very much."

\* \* \* \*

They fucked with abandon on a stack of silk pillows in a windowless basement room with red gauze-covered walls to simulate a tent. They fucked like they'd been hungry for each other for years, which they had been. They fucked like they'd been "perfect fit" lovers for

302

years, which for three years—one right here and two in motel rooms near the U.Conn. campus—they had been.

Before he rolled Daren over on his belly, encircled his waist to bring him up on all fours, and furiously fucked him to completion like a dog, Stan held the younger, moaning man in a side split, embracing him from behind, an arm around Daren's neck, bowing the younger man's back, and turning Daren's face to his for a deep, possessive, prolonged kiss. The hand of his other arm was pulling Daren's left leg back over on top of his thighs, as Stan strained to get his cock inside Daren as deeply as he could, which was deeper than any other man had been.

They rocked against each other's bodies, murmuring whenever they came up for air about how long it had been, how good it still was, how much they had missed each other, how tragic it was they'd let the time go by. The two of them panting, breathing heavily, grunting and groaning at the straining to merge their bodies into one hungry, powerful fucking machine. Daren crying out in passion as Stan dug deeper, thrust harder, pistoned faster.

"I'm going to come!" Daren called out in a strangled voice. Stan rolled off to the side, gripping the back of Daren's neck with one hand and bringing the other down to push two fingers into Daren's ass to gyrate the tips of his fingers on Daren's prostate, as Daren stroked his cock and sent an arc of cum up his belly. Immediately, Stan turned and pulled Daren's back into his chest, grabbed Daren's left leg and raised it in the air, and rolled his pelvis into Daren's buttocks. Daren arched his back and gave a little cry, as Stan's cock slid home again and started to pump.

They collapsed in a heap as the end approached, with Stan rising up on his knees beside Daren's trembling, prone body, stripping the condom off, shooting off on

Daren's cheek, and Daren opening his mouth to the cock to clean it off. Just like the old days.

Stan reached down and cupped, distended, and rolled Daren's balls, as, arching his backing and grimacing in intense concentration, Daren stroked his own cock to another completion.

Collapsing beside him and pulling him into his embrace, Stan whispered, "As good as it ever was. You always were my best boy. You've lost none of your flexibility. Hole's not as tight, of course, but that's to be expected. Opens to me faster now."

"Nor has your sexual prowess diminished. And you still are my best man," Daren murmured. The heat and sexual acrobatics had brought the realization to Daren's mind that Tony hadn't been coming close to satisfying him in bed—and to the understanding as well that being satisfied in bed was important to him. They had drifted into being a vanilla married couple—although they'd never gotten around to marrying, thank God. Stan was more than satisfying in bed—and in a chair and on the floor and on top of a table. He always had been; he still was. The biggest, thickest, most vigorous cock Daren had ever taken. He had ached for it as an eighteen-year-old. He ached for it now. He ached to have it again.

As if tuned into Daren's thoughts, Stan asked, perhaps a bit nervously, "Neither one of us is young enough to go all night as we used to. Have you had enough?"

"Never enough."

"We can take a break, and then do you want to see my old masters again?"

"You'll never be old to me; you'll always be my master."

"I mean the paintings upstairs." Stan laughed.

304

"I knew what you meant. I wanted to make the other perfectly clear, though. And how can you say old? You're hard again."

"Why, yes I am. I'm so glad you noticed." He already had another condom packet in his hand and was splitting it open. "I'll stop, though, if you want me to."

In answer, Daren reached down to roll the condom onto Stan's cock.

Daren cried out in passion and surrender, as Stan, on his back, his knees raised, with Daren's chest resting against his thighs, pulled Daren's now wide-open passage down on the cock, embraced Daren's chest in his arms, pulling his shoulder blades back into Stan's pecs, lacing his legs through Daren's and raising and spreading them, and, showing that he still was an athlete, started to pump hard up into Daren's hole. Making Daren scream across the top of the clouds like he hadn't done for eleven years.

Restoring Daren's sense of need for it.

\* \* \* \*

"Tell me," Daren asked as he sat on a stool across a kitchen island from Stan, who was leaning on the counter, supported on spread arms, "the rumors have always been that you were secretly working for U.S. Intelligence as you traveled the pro tennis circuit. I think they're called NOCs—nonofficial cover, I think that's what the acronym means. Is it true?"

Both men were naked still. Both had half hards. Both knew this was just an interlude to more fucking. Once started, Stan never took his men just once. Stan had always been virile and vigorous. He liked fucking men multiple times in a session, to exhaustion. Daren had every reason to know that.

"I couldn't say. I could say that when I graduated from the Naval Academy and then did my Marines stint, I worked a year in naval intelligence before going with tennis. I think that's where the rumors started. I went on the pro tennis circuit too late."

"Not too late to have gathered all of these valuable paintings with your winnings," Daren said. He'd gone hard just in walking around the first floor of the house and looking at the oil paintings Stan had.

"Well, it helps to have two incomes," Stan said, with a wink.

"You're a complex man, Stan. And there is much more to you than most see."

"Correct. Most don't see my cock." Stan laughed.

"That's the truth. It's the biggest and best cock I've ever had."

"Thank you. I aim to serve."

"There's certainly nothing wrong with your aim— or your serve."

"I meant it when I said you were my best boy," Stan said, suddenly more serious. "You could be my boy again, you know. I want to be your daddy again."

"Hard to think in those terms when I'm thirty-two."

"You know," Stan countered, "that age isn't an issue in a daddy and sub relationship. You know what I mean when I say I want to be your daddy—what I'd do with you and what you'd do for me. I know you. You want to be my boy. Age isn't the issue—as long as I can get it up and use it."

"You really messed up my teen years," Daren said, sliding off the issue Stan raised, something that had been germinating in the back of his mind as well. "I wanted you since I was fifteen. There were three years of maximum frustration there. It made my life hell. But you made me wait until I was eighteen." Stan had been the father figure Daren hadn't had for a good five years as he came into his teens and then, from age eighteen, had been his daddy in an entirely different sense. More recently, Tony, of the same general age as Stan, had been employed as a substitute father figure in both of those senses. But Daren realized now that this relationship hadn't cut it.

"Did you make all of your boys wait, Stan?" he continued. It had been an agonizing period of confusion, guilt, and frustration for Daren.

"All of them, yes. I wouldn't get into the shit of fucking anyone underage. I didn't need to. I didn't see any guy's desirability in terms of being his age."

He paused and looked away, but then turned back and continued. "There were no others that I had to take cold showers to stay away from when they were fifteen, like I did you. I didn't want you because you were fifteen; I wanted you because you were you. I was as anxious and frustrated at holding off as you were. And you teased and tortured me, noting from your seventeenth birthday how many days there were before your eighteenth birthday."

"And then on the morning of my eighteenth birthday I came over for a tennis lesson . . ."

". . . and we never made it to the court. I asked you that corny question about seeing my etchings, brought you in here, and fucked the hell out of you."

"It was a nightmare at first—even though I ached for it and for some time."

"You screamed like a stuck pig, but you insisted you didn't want me to stop. You'd teased me into a fury. I lost control, I never was more sorry."

"But after that first time, I begged for it again and again, and you fucked me again and again—and then it was all I imagined it could be. Just like today, down in the basement."

"God, I've missed you, Daren."

"You pulled away from me after those two years at U.Conn."

"Motel rooms became so tawdry. And the press was nosing around. I could only admit to so much—for both our sakes. You were gaining a reputation in intercollegiate tennis. And you were too good for me. I didn't want you to be in my shadow and I would never have been happy in yours. Ken came along. He was content to let me stand in the light. I settled down. You know, after Ken came along, it was just him. Then one was enough. One could be enough again, Daren."

"Do you really think so? That student you were teaching this morning. Brian, did you say his name was? Not more than nineteen, and cute as a button."

"I would have brought him inside and fucked his lights out if I hadn't seen you in the window. I'll admit to that. He was willing. I'd done it before. He begged for it. But I don't need young men anymore, Daren. I need experienced men. Maybe one man. Maybe a thirty-two-year-old man. Maybe a man named Daren Peters. There's a building out back, by the tennis court. It could easily be made into a studio where you could do your restorations. We aren't far from New York. Or Boston. You could do business from here."

"Do you still have the collection of homoerotic Shunga art upstairs?" Daren asked. "The ancient sex art of Japan."

"Yes, of course."

"I think I'd like to go upstairs and see your Shunga art now."

Stan fucked him missionary at the foot of the king-sized master room bed, Daren's ankles on Stan's shoulders, Stan hunched over Daren's torso and alternating lip work with chewing on Daren's nipples and pounding, pounding Daren's ass.

Imitating one of the Shunga prints on the bedroom wall, Daren sat on the cock in Stan's lap, as Stan sat on the foot of the bed. Daren was facing Stan, with his feet planted on Stan's pecs and gripping Stan's forearms, as Stan grasped Daren's waist and pulled him on and off the cock. In keeping with yet another one of the prints, Daren's shoulder blade were on the carpet and his legs hooked on the standing cock master's hips, as Stan jack hammered down into Daren's passage.

Fingers inside Daren's passage almost up to the knuckles and leaning over a prone Daren and possessing Daren's mouth, a spent Stan used the digits to worry Daren's prostrate while the younger man stroked his cock to a final ejaculation.

Tony would never have dreamed these positions were possible, let alone do them with Daren.

\* \* \* \*

"Sorry I didn't make dinner on the waterfront. I hope you went anyway."

"I did," Peggy answered.

She had gotten far with her packing while Daren was gone.

"I was next door."

"I knew you would be," Peggy said. It was said with a sigh, but it didn't sound to Daren like an exasperated one. Peggy had always understood.

"I think I might be staying in Mystic after all, Peggy. But not in this house."

"Next door, with Stan?"

"Yes."

"I think I always knew you would if you stopped avoiding coming back here. It certainly took you a long time to realize you would, though. I'm happy for you. Make the most of it."

"I will. I already have."

"Yes, I can see that," she said. She was smiling. "Your shorts are turned the wrong way."

~

# About the Author

Habu is one of the pen names of a former supersonic spy jet pilot, intelligence agent, male model, movie actor, and diplomat. A wild youth in South East Asia was spent enjoying whatever sexual opportunities came his way, and much of his gay male writing is about recalling incidents from those days and inventing ones he'd perhaps have liked to experience. He now leads a very quiet and ordinary happily married family life.

An American, he is a published mainstream novelist and short story writer under another name and in another dimension of his life. He has written or cowritten (with Sabb) approaching 1,000 published short stories and over 100 published erotica e-books, primarily of gay fiction but also memoir, straight fiction and ménage fiction. His hand and creative writing can be seen in stories and books by habu, sr71plt, Dirk Hessian, Shabbu, and Stephen Kessel—among unrevealed others that might surprise readers. The fictionalized GM memoir *Flying High, Diving Deep* is loosely based on his life experiences. He can be found at the adults only gay male site www.BarbarianSpy.com, which he shares with Sabb and Dirk Hessian.

Our authors always like to receive feedback, and appreciate it when readers post reviews at distributors and other sites.

# *BarbarianSpy*
## FOR LITERARY HEAT

**Not all books listed below may currently be on release.**
\* indicates the book is available in paperback and e-book.

**BOOKS BY CHRIS CROSS**
**Multisexual Adult Romance**
Pulaski Square

**BOOKS BY ALEX LOCKHEED**
**Transgender Romance**
Meeting Jenna
**Transgender Other**
Being Sarah

**BOOKS BY DIRK HESSIAN**
**Xtreme Historical Erotica**
The King's Men
Shores of Tripoli
Prophecy of Noto
Pretender's Fate
**General Historical Erotic Romance**
To the Hessian Hills
Fire Down the Valley\*
Constantinople\*
The Beautiful Way\*
Blue and Gray
Colonel's Treasure
Beginning of Time
Labyrinth

# BOOKS BY HABU

## Gay Erotica

### Memoir Faction
Flying High, Diving Deep*

### Xtreme Erotica
Tramp Steaming*
Escape to Girne
Silas' Choice*
Last Call
Choke Hold
Apyko: The Greek Pimp
Visits of the Schlange
Second Coming: Emile La Cour Unleashed
Vortex: Sacrificed by Curiosity*
Dark Angel Sounding *(in e-book & included in Sounding:Ultimate Control Paperback)**
Sounding: Ultimate Control (*Print Only*)*
Sounding Five *(in e-book & included in Sounding:Ultimate Control paperback)**

### Romance
Rain Check
Built for Pleasure (Sci Fi)
Danny's Choice
Pull of the Groove
Sugar n Spice Christmas
Friday Nights with Lenny (Christmas Romance)
Snowy, Snowy Nights (Christmas Romance)
Tank n Bull
Sail to the Sun
War Letters
Ravens Roost
Caribbean Cruise Top to Bottom
Arena Stage
Trading Partners (Valentine's Day)
Four Coins
Lower Than the Heart (Valentine's Day)
Brambleton
Gotta Keep Trying

Finding Amnad
Platres Conclave
**Other Novels/Novellas**
Temptation's Clutches*
Descent into Chaos
Escape to Girne
Journey Through Abilene
Harmony and Dissonance
Stallion Station
Racing With the Devil (espionage suspense)
Cruising Gigolo (bisexual)
Prepared in Cape Verdi
Gilded Cage
House on Park*
Anything for Ambition
Dance of the Ravishers
Hard Knocks U*
My Neighbor's Spa*
Man's Man: Tales of a High Priced Gay Hooker*
Trip Money
The Indian Doctor
Sailorboy
Home to Fire Island
**Murder Mysteries**
Death on a Ping Pong Table
Clint Folsom Mysteries Compendium Volume 1*
Death to Blonds - Stolen Judgment (Clint Folsom
Mystery)*
Clint Folsom Mysteries Compendium Volume 2*
**Gay Erotica Anthologies**
Earth Cry*
Shunga
Habu's Christmas Balls
Eight in D*
DevilMENt
Silas' Choices*
Stallion Station (A Novella in Parts)
Eleven to the Dogs*

Fifty Seventy*
Spy Tails 001*
Spy Tails 002*
Doubled*
Doubled Again*
Tails in the Tropics*
Tails in the Med*
Tails in the West*
Rough Riders*
Grab Bag 1*
Grab Bag 2*
Grab Bag 3*
Grab Bag 4*
Grab Bag 5*
Grab Bag 6*
Grab Bag 7*
Beyond the Beaded Curtain*
Habu's Christmas Balls
The Sporting Life*
Fetish Galore!*
**Literary Gay Erotica**
Cairo Surrender*
The Handyman*
Homeward Bound
Journey to Mirage*
**Bi-Sexual/Menage Erotica**
**Bisexual/Menage/Multisexual Erotica**
Two Men, One Woman*
Every Which Way
Vanishing Laura
Summer of Denial
Death on a Ping Pong Table
Cruising Gigolo
13 Ways for Halloween
Luther*
The Indian Prince*
**MF Erotica**
Chocolate in Vanilla*

## BOOKS BY SABB
Driver Reliever
Hiring in Hollywood
The Legend of Holleystone Grange
Surprise Encounters*
She is He
Wrong Man
Loyal to his King
Barbarian Tales - Book One - Traveler's Tales*
Barbarian Tales - Book Two - Journeys Begin*
Barbarian Tales - Book Three - The Inheritance*
Barbarian Tales - Book Four - Road to Persepolis*

## BOOKS BY SHABBU
Velvet Interrogation
Finding Jason
Dirty Pool
Operation Black Jade
Cigars!*
Angel in the Barn
Gayly Complicated*
Despoiling David
The Tree of Idleness*
I Met a Man
Rough Road to Happiness

## BOOKS BY STEPHEN KESSEL
**Gay Romance**
The Forever Man
Two Chances

## BOOKS BY KIM BLACK
**Lesbian Romance**
Transfixed on Tammie (F/T lesbian)